Fate: Intertwined

By: Hailey Monette

Dedication

To Jamamma,

For showing me how adventures are about the journey and not the destination.

Chapter 1

She ran like her life depended on it, and it did. Her battered feet splashed into a puddle of mud, decorating her bare calves with caked-on grime. Rain cascaded and drenched her body, chills sounding through her as she ran as far as her aching feet would carry.

Do not look back.

She repeated the phrase to herself, a deaf chant to whatever gods may be still listening. That's if there were any that would even cast a shroud of divinity upon her. Gods and goddesses were such a funny thing to the girl. So many people devoted their lives to worshipping those who were deemed higher than them. For what? She couldn't answer that. Eight years prior, she might've had some incline, but not now. Not for what they had put her through.

Shouts echoed in the trees behind her, reminding her of the horrors that she endured a few months ago. Blood stained the memories of the once quaint town from which she fled. A town once full of music and art that was known across the Seven Realms, one her mother visited frequently. But that was in the past. The destroyed ruins of Kyrneth proved that much.

Her drenched pack was loose and repeatedly brushed her back as she pushed herself to run faster. In the trees ahead, she spotted an alcove, one that was probably big enough for her to squeeze into. Brushing the cobwebs as she went in, curling into herself, arms wrapped around the bones she called legs.

The strain in her breath began to mellow to a controlled pace as she let all her fear and nerves dance on the inside. To the outer world, she had become one with the nature she took refuge in, just as she was taught. Then she waited.

With the patience of a hunter stalking their prey, with keen senses to back her. Surrounded by trees, the slight hum of the birds above, she was at ease. A moment of stillness.

The stars above her eventually gave into the morning light, but still, the sky stayed littered with clouds. But the once pouring rain had turned into a soft sprinkle that still dripped onto her olive skin. To a usual person the dew would be cold against their skin, but temperature never really mattered to the girl.

The downpour had displaced any tracks she made, and the Bellheim forces that had caught them should be heading southward. For the moment, she was in the clear, allowed to breathe and allow her thoughts to travel.

Not again.

Not here.

It wouldn't be a repeat of last time. Her emerald eyes were still haunted by what she had endured by their hands already.

Her body and bones screamed as she uncurled and maneuvered out of the tree. The grass beneath her feet was soft and wet. Taking a minute to assess the surroundings, she cupped her hands around her mouth before blowing across her thumb and into her palm.

A signal. One, only a single other person knew.

I'm safe.

The noise echoed across the forest. To any prying ears, it served as something akin to a forest creature. Perhaps a songbird that laid in wake at Kyrneth, reminiscent of what was lost.

But not to him.

A breath of relief escaped her lips as she heard a familiar call echo back.

I'll find you.

Relief flooded through her. Knowing he had made it out.

She knew it well, the code they had created over the past eight years of running and scouting. If they were to ever lose one another, they could still manage to communicate without giving themselves away.

She addressed herself for any new wounds she may have acquired in the past few days. Besides the soreness and taut muscles, she seemed mostly intact. The soles of her feet had been torn up from the ruined buildings she scaled the previous day, but nothing she hadn't experienced before.

The worn leather of her pack was welcoming a familiar feeling. The only real possessions she had, her entire life seemingly packed away into the pack. She fished out some dried meat and snacked on it whilst pulling out a skirt and slipping it over her undergarments.

Bellheim's scouts were able to get closer than comfortable due to the rain numbing their footfalls. She wouldn't make that mistake again. A mistake she wouldn't be so careless to make again.

The garments were stained and dirty, but the fabric was a deep brown and hid the filth well.

After a few moments, she let out another signal, allowing him to follow her calls. Still, she continued dressing herself in a green tunic that was far too big for her. She shifted to tuck the tunic into the waist band of her skirt and covered the seam with a thick brown belt. The sleeves fell past her wrists, creating a bell-like shape. Two hunting daggers were on either side of her hips for ease of access. The quiver on the belt was mostly barren, as she had to lose most of the arrows to fit everything inside her pack.

Only three were usable.

"Missing something?" He made no noise as he approached, but she knew who it was for that very reason. Without looking over her shoulder, she could feel his emerald eyes raking over her. Assessing. "Must you be so smug about it, Key?"

"You flatter me, Kaleopei," A snort came from the trees, where he sat dangling her legs from the branch. A devilish grin set into his features as he dangled a bow from his foot, only an arm's reach away. Kaleopei swiped the bow from her companion and slipped it over her torso. "Why the sour face, sweet sister?"

"Keylan, you know the reason. Those Bellheim soldiers shouldn't have been there. They have followed the same schedule for the past four years. We should have had a week longer to linger around Kyrneth. But, no! They happened to stumble into the area while I had my pants down. Not metaphorically." Kaleopei ranted, arms moving to accentuate her frustration

He fell to the ground, boots hitting the wet mud, and his cloak moving behind showed the steel that was strapped to his back. He held himself well, walking over to Kaleopei as he scanned her.

"But you're not hurt, right? Pants or skirts can be salvaged. Limbs can not." Kaleopei liked that particular garment, one gifted to her by her mentor.

"I'm fine, Key, still here. Now down a pair of pants, my nice ones too, but still have all my limbs." As if to further her point, she grabbed his hand and offered a tired grin to the male, whose eyes were a mirror of her own. Deep emerald like the forest that surrounded them.

They were two souls scarred and battered, but they were here. In some sick twist of fate, they stood side by side, readying themselves for what was next. "Don't stray from me, sister, not again."

"I do not plan on it, and those damn Bellheim leeches are going to have to try a little harder to sink their teeth into me."

"Do leeches even have teeth? Or do they just kind of gnaw on you?" Count on Keylan to make light of the situation.

"Not the point. We have a task at hand. Bellheim moving out of turn may not be a bad thing." Currently, they were near the northern border of Bellheim but still in what remained of the Elven Realm.

"Where to next, then?" He grinned, pulling out a map of the Seven Realms, but their writing and marks scattered the worn parchment. Places they had scouted and documented over the years. He ticked something off with a piece of charcoal.

One scout route had been changed. they were unfortunate enough to be in the group's sight.

Kaleopei plucked a wild flower from the ground, admiring its vibrant colors. Hues of deep blue, all the way to a lilac purple. Spring was always her favorite season, contrary to Keylan's teasing.

"I think it's time we pay a visit home, brother."

Chapter 2

The emerald-eyed siblings moved in tandem. Keylan was the taller of the two, standing a head above his sister with broad shoulders and lean muscles hidden underneath a tan-colored cloak that was draped over his stature. A deer thrown over his shoulders, with practiced ease, they approached the guarded border of Bellheim.

Kaleopei took the lead, a practiced, kind smile set upon her features as she strode up to the gate. Her usual bound hair was let loose, cascading to frame her face and fall just below her breasts. Her bow was strung and poised behind her back as unthreateningly as possible. Knives hidden neatly away from the guards' sight.

The perfect picture of an inexperienced hunter.

"Won't you hurry! Uncle will be so pleased when we return." The sickly sweet tone of her voice made her cringe. The guards caught the two who approached the gate, watching them with careful eyes. The two suns burned brightly in the sky; it had just past noon and the guard swap happened a half hour before they made their arrival.

A man dressed in the deep reds of Bellheim took a step forward, a hand on the pommel of his sword. A warning, for the bloodshed to come if she didn't play her part well.

"What is your business in Bellheim?" Direct and straight to the point. Kaleopei's smile widened with each step she took. Her confidence grew as she drew closer.

"Returning home after a successful hunt, I killed my first deer on Elven soil. My brooding uncle insisted my brother escort me." She dared to take her eyes off the human guard, casting a look of annoyance on Keylan. "However, I killed it all on my lonesome. A clean shot to the head."

The story rolled off her tongue. Practiced. Calculated. And Rehearsed

As if to confirm, the guard looked over the deer. It wasn't a clean shot, not in the slightest. She had veered to the left when she took the shot, no doubt leaving the creature alive for minutes instead of the killing blow that could've been bestowed.

Kaleopei hoped she showed it mercy; the poor creature had a broken limb when they came across it. It would have been unable to survive by itself.

"You have a seal of permission, I assume?" His eyes glanced towards Keylan, probably assuming he was the eldest of the duo. "Indeed."

Keylan slipped a piece of parchment to the guard, who reviewed it and nodded. He gave a curt nod, and the other guards at the wall opened the iron gate.

It wasn't until they could no longer see the gates did they spared a glance at each other. Keylan elbowed his sister, who had her sights set ahead of them. Down the dirt and cobbled road, they were a few hours away from the nearest town.

"Ellis probably thinks we're dead and gone... You think she'll be willing to make some stew?" His words extorted a snort from the shorter of the two. "She's a wicked ol' witch, will likely try to skin us for making her worry."

That couldn't be farther from the truth.

The surrounding forest began to thin, and across the hilly terrain lied Alstead. A smaller village in Bellheim, a place that had been their safe haven.

Keylan tried to keep his shoulder-length hair from swaying too much in the wind, eventually just deciding to flick the hood of his cloak over his features.

He looked ahead at his sister, who hadn't needed to cover her head. For the scars she carried would only be found by those who looked too close. He knew she wouldn't allow anybody the proximity.

But to the world, they were mere hunters, returning with their bounty. Nothing more.

That's what they needed to remain.

***

Alstead was no different from when they had last departed. The same merchants decorated the main square, making their living selling trinkets and provisions. The only real traffic the town saw was those who left and entered through the northern border.

Which in recent times wasn't many.

Other than that, it was quiet. Since the Elves all fled the Elven Realm, not many people have sought passage to the north. For all that lies is the beasts and creatures who roam the forest and whatever Soldiers the King sent over.

An older woman sat outside in the slight breeze, weaving flowers that spring bore into shapes and wearables. Her hair was beginning to gray, but her hazel eyes held life. Her fingers halted their craft when she saw the two brown-haired siblings stride through the market, the taller of the two carrying a deer.

She damn near could have died right there from the amount of excitement that overcame her. But she still had so much life in her.

"Children, you've come home." She outstretched her arms as the girl ran into her. A fond smile was set upon her aging features. Their embrace was firm, neither wanting to break contact.

Kaleopei whispered, "I swore it, didn't I?"

Kaleopei had the day they left nine months ago. Her word was worth its weight in gold, but she rarely gave it out. She was not one to make promises she wouldn't see through.

"Not to break this heartwarming reunion, but this deer is beginning to make my shoulders ache." Keylan laughed, pushing past the two to march his way inside. The women laughed, something Keylan engraved into his mind. He took pride in seeing them happy, especially his sister.

"Key's famished kept whining the whole way here. He spoke a great deal about of missing your cooking." Ellis elbowed the girl's side and followed the male.

"He's a beast of a man, no wonder he's hungry. Come, let's get you two settled in."

Kaleopei laughed, slouching onto the side of the table as she watched the two in front of her begin dressing the deer. It was mundane, watching them skillfully work around each other in the kitchen.

"Fueling his ego won't bring upon anything good, Ellis. His head is already too big for him." But Kaleopei was ignored, yet she was content listening to them.

"My head is perfectly normal."

"Oh, stop your bickering. I surely didn't miss that. I think this venison would make a delightful stew. Kaleopei, would you mind fetching some vegetables from the garden?" Keylan held in his smirk, watching playfully as his sister rolled her eyes.

A silent conversation passed between Keylan and Ellis. They both watched from the open window as Kaleopei greeted the chickens and made her way towards the garden.

"How is she?"

A pin could drop in the silence that fell. Keylan's hands froze for a moment. His usually gleaming eyes became lidded as he thought back to the past few months.

"Still hasn't said anything to me about what happened. She's acted as if everything was normal since we left." The knife in his hand went back to prepping the food in front of him.

"I worry for her, Keylan."

He didn't say anything else. What else was there to say? He agreed with the older women, one who had cared for them as if they were her own for most of their lives.

***

The three sat around the table, a dim candle lit at the center. The suns had set and dusk was setting in around them.

"This is delicious, Ellis. I have missed your cooking." Keylan laughed, picking up the bowls in front of the women. Ellis smiled in contentment. She had missed the loud home and the sibling's companionship more than she had realized.

Kaleopei had her nose stuck into a book the minute she could. One gifted to her by Ellis herself, it was one she had read dozens of times.

It was considered banned literature as it pertained to fables relating to the Elven Forest. The King wouldn't have anything with Elven culture in his Realm. But what he didn't know couldn't hurt.

"Did you two learn anything on your travels?"

Keylan washed the dishes and came back to join the two. But it was the brunette girl who spoke first, "Nothing besides more questions."

Kaleopei placed the book into her lab, her fingers gripping the binding tightly. The whole situation was entirely frustrating for them, but Keylan was good at hiding it if not for him, but for the sake of his sister.

"It doesn't make a lick of sense. An entire realm's worth of people scattered in the span of four days after Bellheim sacked Eviera. What was left was pillaged and burned by Bellheim." She scoffed, anger flushing onto her features. Ellis reached a hand across the table. "Why would an entire population up and flee at the presence of the humans? It was like there was no trace of any retaliation. They just let it happen, and I'm still not entirely sure why."

"Take a breath, darling-" Ellis moved to intervene in her thoughts.

"Why should I? Key and I have been chasing ghosts, nothing to be found. Not a sliver of useful information besides what we already knew!" Kaleopei lashed out at her own words. Each was a constant reminder that they were utterly failing. "It feels like everything we've done has been in vain."

She didn't mean that. Keylan and her were still alive; that had to amount to something.

The candle's dim flame began to grow brighter.

Heat radiated from the center of the table while her anger surged.

Kaleopei didn't even flinch as the temperature turned scalding. The flame was erupting and shifting in hues of vibrant greens and oranges.

Keylan was standing in a second, placing a hand on her forehead. His hand grew increasingly colder against her heated skin. The male recognized the signs of Kaleopei's magic and immediately began to soothe her.

Emotion was her worst enemy. Always caused her magic to flare in unpredictable ways, but it had its benefits in life-or-death scenarios.

Ellis stared into her eyes, whispering words that were deaf to the raging girl. But slowly, from Keylan's cold and damp hands, did she begin to calm?

For a moment, Ellis swore her emerald eyes glowed.

That is important for another time. Kaleopei rolled her shoulders, pushing away from Keylan's touch. Her brother flinched from how easily she brushed him off, shoving his hands to his side.

As the girl excused herself from the table, the candle's hue shifted towards a color of jade before returning to an orange ember.

"It's nothing. I'm fine."

Kaleopei didn't turn back as she walked towards her room. Leaving Keylan and Ellis concerned and confused around the empty table.

***

"She's resting, fast asleep in her cot." Ellis exited the girl's room, eyeing Keylan sitting with his back to her. He faced the small fireplace, watching it with an empty face. "You're allowed to be frustrated, too. She isn't the only one who lost things."

He didn't speak, not for a long moment, just looked away from the flame that had him captivated. His sword lay abandoned next to him, the metal shining from the faint light of the fire.

"You think I'm not?"

"I think you hide it well, Keylan." He met her determined gaze.

"I haven't another choice, and I have to be strong for her. For if she loses hope, I fear it will destroy her. She already thinks the gods have abandoned us and only trusts in herself and me. If I don't stay put together, then she'll fall apart."

His gaze returned to the fire, the wild flame a deep orange that illuminated the older woman's face, highlighting her age. He had thought about it too, the gods, what their plan was. What all the pain and suffering has been for. But one thing remained true through it all was that he and Kaleopei were still together.

He felt the gods had intended it that way.

It was why he still believed in them.

It was all he could ever ask of them. Keeping her safe, however far she strays.

"I think she is stronger than you think. What do you hope for?" Ellis scanned the boy's features, barely an adult, and yet, his features showed years beyond what they should.

"I hope that we can live content once more." He said it quickly, as if he had thought about it for a long time. "And I pray for any sort of closure. I just want to know why."

Ellis moved to his side, placing a kiss on the top of his head. Gently, she moved his hair to the side. Her hand glided along the pointed tips of his ears.

His elven ears.

"It pains me to think about what she went through in that place. They had her for *months,* and yet she hasn't uttered a word about anything that happened to her. All I can do is assume the worst." His heart broke as he thought about how he had failed his sister so greatly.

"She doesn't blame you. She never would." It was the truth, and he knew it. But a part of him is ridden with guilt that it was his fault. "It should've been me in her place. She *saved* me, and yet it took me months to try to get her out. Yet, she did it, not me. I felt as if I was in a dream when I saw her. Kaleopei was so broken she didn't utter a word for a week. I still don't know how she got out. She refused to get anywhere even near Louth while we've been out."

"I know, child, I remember it well." She indeed remembered those days with clarity. When Keylan returned with a shell of the girl she had once been. Thin and littered with new scars. Neither of them really knew the full depths of those scars. Perhaps they never would.

"I stand for her, I will. Now and until I am no longer of this soil. I made an oath to Maizelin eight years ago, and I have no intention of letting down my sister. Either of them."

Their conversation drifted after Ellis spotted the sheer determination in his eyes. *These two, their souls, connected from the day they were born.*

It wasn't until Keylan had also retired for the night did Ellis allowed her thoughts about the twins to consume her. She sat in front of the fire, the same as the boy before her. Quietly, she began to mumble a prayer.

Not for herself, but the two that currently resided under her roof. The children she had hidden and saved eight years ago. Atop the mantle was a shield and sword that hadn't been wielded in almost a decade.

The shield served as a sign of remembrance for her late husband and a totem of protection. So, she prayed to him, and whatever gods truly did watch over them.

She prayed for a sign. Anything to keep their wavering hope alive. They needed a spark, any kind of ember that they could fan into something bigger.

Ellis didn't know why, but she knew those two were something else. Despite her praying, she knew they didn't need gods or luck.

All they needed was each other.

Chapter 3

Lords of high ranking left the large conference room, none wanting to endure another moment of the tense conversation that had just been discussed. The only ones who remained were those of royal blood.

"Take this as a lesson, Casimir: advisors are only a show of goodwill. Make them feel heard, but you do not have to believe their words. As King, you will make your own decisions, not be spineless and bend to the will of those who seek to sway you."

The blonde-haired prince didn't dare defy his father. He had seen men hung for less. He wasn't a child, and he understood more than the King gave him credit for. But back talking him seemed to be at the bottom of his bucket list, not wanting to be the victim of the man's cruelty.

"I shall not be swayed by those beneath me, Father."

Did he believe those words? He had no other choice than to be convincing. Born to play a part he hadn't wanted. He was stuck in a never-ending game of politics.

The King of Bellheim had always been bold and stern, and was renown across the Realms as a conqueror of the Elves. Casimir didn't dare to look his father in the eye, for he would see a man who looked far too similar to himself.

He never wanted to be this kind of King.

He had seen what war did to a country from a young age. Not only that, but he still remembers the number of soldiers the Elves had wiped out. The bloodshed on the opposite side was greater. Yet, the King never revealed why they marched on the Elven Realm eight years ago. Why he had nearly slaughtered an entire kingdom, it was like the man who he knew as his father broke out of thin air, then set a blaze of violence in his wake.

Casimir's blue eyes moved to his uncle across from him. He was a man who couldn't be read, his face never wavering any kind of emotion or intention, even for the young prince who prided himself in the ability to read others, for there was always a way to see the truth in the actions of others.

It was something he was naturally innate at, something his mother had taught him before the queen fell ill.

It was a powerful tool and weapon. One that can sway a decision or gain movement in a battle. The Queen of Bellheim had said those words to him on many occasions.

But when it came to his uncle and father, it was useless. Able to avoid his watchful gaze with ease.

"We'll be moving Northward, continuing on with the settling. The council can refuse it all they want, but I get to make the final decision." His father's icy eyes remained set towards the window, almost glaring at the sun that burned bright overhead. "I've already recalled the scouts I sent to Louth. A few of my selections will lead the first wave North. Then I will send out a Carver." Casimir didn't dare utter a word, but something was off. He couldn't say why; call it a gut feeling of his.

"When the second wave goes, I will go with them. Casimir, my kin, will be seated on the throne for the time I depart."

This was news to him. They hadn't discussed this in the slightest. Casimir sneaked a glance to his side, seeing the wide-eyed expression his Uncle bore.

"Darren, is this really such a wise idea? Prince Casimir is young, and perhaps more time should be given to oversee his studies?"

It was the wrong thing to say.

"You dare question my rule, brother?" His brows furrowed, anger bubbling to the surface of his stern exterior. Casimir could practically see the red aura coming from his Father. "No, Darren, I am simply stating the facts."

"Do bide your tongue around me, Casimir; leave us. But be assured you will be taking up duties when I leave in the upcoming moons. Assure you are ready."

With his crown held pointedly on his head, the blonde-haired prince rose. Taking a bow to the two others in the room before making a calculated, swift exit.

Only once the door was shut did Casimir toss his head back. Relaxing the tension his entire body seemed to be holding on to.

***

The blonde-haired male walked down the familiar hall as if each stone were carved into his memory. Every servant he passed nodded in his direction. He didn't command respect like his father.

Casimir wished for those around him to respect him of their own accord. Not from a place of fear or hatred.

He peered into the library, seeing its mostly barren state as usual. The King wasn't particularly fond of learning things of old; instead opted to obtain knowledge through his own lens and not what the King tried to push onto him.

But in the large room, it was a haven, walls of stories that could distract him from his routine of trying to get into his father's head. Wooden accents carved into the very shelves felt mesmerizing as he brushed his thumb over it.

"Good afternoon, Prince Casimir. To what do I owe the pleasure?" A woman with coal-black hair and pale skin poked her head around the corner. She was petit and carried herself well, as most nobles were expected to do. "Must you address me in such a courtly manner, Zara?"

Her lips pulled upwards into a smirk as she practically pranced over and wrapped her arms around Casimir. "It's good to see you too, Cas."

"How long are you staying for?" Casimir scanned the girls' features; not much had changed since they last saw each other a few months prior. However, her eyes seemed to be dimmer than before. "Until your dear ole' daddy decided he has had enough with us Northern folk."

"So, a couple of hours?" He was quick to quip back, occupying a table in the corner of the library. Zara sat across from him, kicking her legs up onto the table in a way that would make most deem her unladylike. But Cas knew better than to comment, as it was just the two of them, and she would absolutely chew him out. Only those with a death wish would ever cross the cunning Zaratella.

"I actually suspect I'll be sent out on a scouting party soon as an official Carver." The boredom on her face was intense, laced with some other distasteful feelings. Zara was usually an open book around him, quick to display all of her emotions on her sleeve. Something he often teased her about, but only on days when his will to live was low.

"You always have had talents in seeking the arcane, but is that really what you want?" The two had been friends since they were infants, as her father was Lord of Lispin in the northern part of Bellheim and was an active part of the Royal Court. Her eyes narrowed as she snapped her head in the direction of the Prince.

"It doesn't matter what I want; you, of all people, should understand that." Her onyx eyes were sharp, snapping to his gaze in a haze of knowing glance.

"I'm simply making conversation, Zara. No one wishes to be a carver." The two sat in silence, both staring at one another as if waiting to see who would break first.

"That's for certain, but I hadn't a choice. Choice isn't a luxury those born like us are given. Huh, Mister Prince?"

"I know," his voice softened and lowered as he leaned against the table. His blonde hair seemed to glow in the wake of the lanterns that lit up the library. Casimir secretly wished for an immortal life. Solely so he could read the entirety of this library, or some of the bigger ones across the seas.

On the other hand, living that long seemed tiring when having to indulge himself in constant politics. He'd prefer to keep to himself, but that wasn't what the Gods intended.

The girl picked at her nails, avoiding eye contact with the prince across from her. Zara wore a concerned look, her teeth biting her lower lip. "Cas... you would tell me if something was wrong, right? You trust me?"

"Of course, I trust you. You're my dearest friend, Zara." Her onyx eyes seemed to scan him over, watching every slight shift that Casimir made.

"Good. This carving training makes me feel like I've missed so much. I haven't had the liberty to talk so freely in months. It's like they want me to be a drone, follow tasks mindlessly."

"You let them boss you around in such a manner?"

The Prince's head seemed to cock at her more vulnerable words. Instead, Casimir tried to make light of the situation. The sharp features of her face cast towards a shelf of books.

"Just until they trust me enough for some room on my leash. Then they will understand exactly who they are messing with."

"Spoken like a true lady." Casimir laughed.

"Doesn't a lady look best in red?" Zara crossed her legs on top of the table, hitting Casimir's arm with the toe of her boot.

"My opinion matters not, and I'm sure you have your own ideas of what ladies look best in," Casimir noted the smirk that grew across her features, challenging his own playful glare.

"I can feel as though a change is coming. But haven't decided if it'll be bad or good. Excuse my treasonous talk, but I do wish it was something cataclysmic. Gods know we could all use a little change."

She stood up, brushing the dark red dress she wore of non-existent dust. Cas continued to watch, now studying her deliberate motions. "I will let you know of anything life changing, Zara."

"Don't be sly with me. We both know I would wipe the floor with that royal ass of yours." The conversation turned more tense as a moment of silence fell between them. "How's Isla?"

"My mother hasn't spoken to me in months; she's ill. The healers aren't giving her too much longer." Zara placed a comforting hand on top of his, feeling the ring that his mother had given to him, sending the same pity everyone else did. From Zara, he knew it was real and not just a show most people did. But she had no interest in sugarcoating her words. "You're strong, Cas. Please remember that."

"Father's putting me in charge; he'll be leaving in a few days." The coldness in her eyes seemed to harden as he changed the subject. "Do me a favor, Cas. Don't be a raging prick like your father. Do some good for a change, kay?"

He didn't even have a chance to respond before her black hair whipped over her shoulder, and she turned the corner, fleeing out of his view.

Casimir slouched back into the chair. Taking in the storm that came along with Zaratella Eldridge. One thing was certain: she was hiding something from him.

Zaratella knew something and didn't say it forthright. Part of him wasn't sure to be concerned or relieved by her action.

***

When the Crowned Prince was allowed a moment of silence— it didn't come until he retired for the night— did he allow himself to fully relax? His room was far too extravagant for his taste. The only upside was the balcony that overlooked the garden.

His own secret place of serenity, one where he could simply escape from reality, shoved upon him.

Truthfully, Casimir never wanted to rule, much rather spend his days exploring and documenting the other realms. But his father ruined that entirely. A scribe wasn't something those of Royal Blood did— his father constantly reminded him.

They had a slim chance of making any kind of alliance with the other realms after the King moved on to the Elven Realm. So, traveling was likely out of the equation for the future.

Casimir pulled out a box from his closet, pulling out an ornate pipe and Myth. His father would reprimand him for partaking in such things, but it was his only escape. So he packed the pipe, grabbed a book from his nightstand and went to the balcony.

Peaceful silence.

No servants tended this particular garden, as it was his mother's passion project before she fell ill. He remembered all the vibrant colors of the growth, and his mother loved to grow an assortment of fauna. He spun the dark ring on his finger, something that made him feel connected to her.

"Life is a treasure any living thing should get to experience." The words fell from his lips. Then he took a hit of the Myth, letting the herbal smoke fill his lungs before exhaling slowly. He stared at the overgrown yet decaying garden. It had been over eight years since the queen had even been to the garden square.

No longer were the vibrant reds of the roses. Or the vibrant purple of lavender. All that lay were weeds and some wild that were too stubborn to die. All the species fought for dominance of the space, resulting in a constant change in the garden. Even the plants had to fight for their survival in the dreadful confines of the palace.

He took another hit, settling down into the plush armchair he dragged from the interior.

Then he let reality sink in.

Reality sucked.

Zara was right, people like them don't get choices. Just pawns in some game they didn't even know the rules of.

But he would play. Play until he found a way out of the game.

Which would be 'never'.

Flipping through the pages of an old tale, his guilty pleasure would always be reading some kind of outlandish tale. Where evil was squandered, and heroes emerged victorious.

It's an escapism from reality, emerging as someone through a work of fiction.

So he read.

Took a hit.

Read.

Hit.

The cycle went on and on until the sun began to set.

Maybe if he took enough hits, the world wouldn't seem so infuriating. Perhaps he would have control of his life.

The only person he was fooling was himself.

He had received word that his only friend was sent out by his Father. Zara left mere hours after their encounter in the library.

So he was alone.

Alone again.

Always alone, the only company was the breeze that made the pages of the novel shift.

What fate had decided that he should be a crowned prince? In what world could he ever lead a realm? Some days, he could barely make himself get out of bed to attend to his courtly duties.

Then he'd leave, sticking his nose into a book, and get high off some Myth.

Wake up and do it again. An endless cycle of politics and indulging himself in the herb. A feeble attempt at making politics vanish, even for a few measly hours.

He kept hitting the pipe until the herb was nothing more than ash that he scattered into the wind.

These were the moments he felt alive, not the numb, soulless man his father had molded him to be.

With an exhalation of the remaining smoke, he sunk further into his book, living a different life entirely.

Chapter 4

"The King executed seven in the Capital for speculated use of magic," The courier kept talking, recounting the latest headlines from Bellheim. They were grim like before, that hadn't seemed to change much.

"I don't miss the death counts, that's for sure," Kaleopei grumbled as she strolled alongside her brother, hands crossed firmly against her chest. "He rules by fear, and we've known that, sister."

"Doesn't mean I like it." Keylan glanced over to see her glaring at the courier from across the market. Crows were circling in the air, drawn to the market because of the various meats and produce that were out on display, begging to be picked up by the scavengers.

The soft breeze of the fall weather caressed Kaleopei's cheek, seemingly guiding her head back towards the stalls. Biting the inside of my cheek to stifle the laugh, Keylan held a knowing smile.

"Maybe they should hang me?" He shrugged. Kaleopei smacked him in response. Her anger was shown in her emerald gaze.

"Don't even joke like that, Key."

His eyes flicked from his sister to the market, then back to Kaleopei. His smile had dropped, head twitching to the side as he hooked his arm through her own.

The air seemed to shift, the market quieting as the sound of metal could be heard coming towards the square.

Kaleopei didn't dare question Keylan, not now, for she could make out the footfalls of a decent-sized group coming towards the village and the goosebumps on his arms. There was just a party of men that returned from the border, and it was far too soon for another Bellheim scouting party.

Unless the previous group found something.

Kaleopei didn't allow herself to think what that meant for them. For any Elf still clinging on to their survival throughout this continent.

"Keep your eyes down. We split across the market. You make your way back to the house to check on Ellis. Grab your bow, stick to the shadows." His voice was low and lacked the usual playful tone he usually used. He wasn't wrong, and if this was a search and seized, the house was full of contraband and items that would get them all killed. They hang people for less here. Imagine what they would do to Ellis. The thought alone was enough for the both of them to focus.

"How many knives do you have?" It was silent around them as the locals began looking confused about the disturbance the soldiers were bringing. Kaleopei thought she could give him one of hers if Key had nothing.

"Two in my boots, one across my chest."

"Do you want me to grab your sword?" They skimmed through the dwindling crowd, light on their feet as they maneuvered to the sides of buildings, using the shadows as cover. "How many can you make out Kaleopei?"

Kaleopei's back was pressed firmly against the wall as she focused on the sounds that were coming towards them. "A female and seventeen men. Perhaps a noblewoman seeking guidance out of Bellheim? Her steps are awfully light, and it's unlikely she is armed."

"If you think you can carry the blade along with your bow, then yes." With a nod, she went to turn. His wrist caught hers. "Be discreet. Do not stray, Kaleopei."

"We both know I can run circles without being caught in this town." He gave a stern look as she brought her hands to his hair, making sure his ears were covered by the earth-toned locks. He pulled away first, continuing into the square like nothing was amiss. Head held high, along with that annoyingly charming lob-sided grin.

By the time Kaleopei made it back to Ellis' abode, she could see a party of Bellheim soldiers from the porch. Seventeen men, as predicted, were armed to the teeth, bearing the signals of the Human Realm. They were hauling large crates of supplies with them. Far too much for a simple scouting party to be trekking with. Towards the back of their formation was a human-looking woman, black hair seeming to dull in the rays of sun that the early morning had brought. But it wasn't her appearance or younger age that caused Kaleopei to double-take.

No, it was the crest that was pinned on her clothes.

She was a Carver. The sigil was pinned over her breast. It was small and intricate, easily overlooked as a broach if one was unfamiliar with those who weren't aware of the King's own virtues in magic. She was gorgeous, an intrigue most men would fall for instantly.

Kaleopei was only slightly better than the common men, she still understood that Carver's were the enemy.

Was this my fault? Did my outburst yesterday alert the nearby Carver? There wasn't usually any posted this far away from the capital unless someone had tipped them off.

"Child, what is going on?" She pushed Ellis inside, closing the door behind in a quiet calm. Without missing a beat, Kaleopei jumped around the room, closing all the shutters. "Carver."

The word alone was enough for Ellis to begin grabbing books from around the house, shoving them into the floor where she had hidden us years ago. Adding to the collection that was already carefully organized beneath the planks.

I had to tell Key.

The stairs creaked as Kaleopei rushed up them, pushing her way into the barren room she called hers. Before even reaching the open window, she was whistling.

Loud.

Louder than she had ever needed to be before.

He had to hear her. Had to understand the threat that was currently threatening their home.

Kaleopei's voice croaked as shoulders pulled her away from the window, slamming the shutters. "Do you have a death wish, child?"

"No, you don't understand, Ellis. I have to tell him." They don't know what they are capable of. Ellis doesn't understand the sheer severity of what Carvers can do to those with magic. "You're worried about him, but making yourself a target isn't going to help. Child, look at me."

Kaleopei broke her gaze away from the closed wooden shutters, locking her gaze with Elli's eyes. Something was off about them; they were hardened, and she saw right through my worry.

"Do what you need to do, but be smart about it." Kaleopei had to resist the urge to laugh, as Key had practically said the same thing to her less than an hour ago. Kaleopei plucked her bow off the dresser, slinging the quiver around her neck with practiced speed.

They forget who I am. But I have not. One day, Kaleopei would make them say her name. Say the name of every single person they slaughtered in the name of King Haven.

"Ellis, stay here. Get everything hidden, and don't come out, no matter what you hear."

She didn't respond, only comforted Kaleopei with a soft embrace. Pressing a kiss to her sweating forehead and muttering something below her breath. With her skilled hearing, the words didn't go unnoticed, Kaleopei simply chose not to respond to them.

Kaleopei dashed out the door, slipping a cloak over her shoulders before her feet hit the slated roof. The hood snapped below her chin, hiding Key's sword that was strapped up her covered back.

Then she was bolting, pushing herself out the small upstairs window and out onto the roof. The Carver was moving in tangent with her guard, practiced and rehearsed, yet there was nothing natural about it. They didn't seem to have a hasty pace and weren't all as focused as if they were looking for something or someone.

They could be passing through, but the only thing north of here was the borders. Kaleopei kept me flat against any surface she could, maneuvering around the rooftops of the town, staying out of their line of sight and using shadows to aid her.

"I wish to stay the night here. Find us an inn." The Carver had stopped, talking to the guard that was on her left, but never once made eye contact with him. "It's been a long while since I've gotten to visit Alstead."

The townspeople were keeping their distance, but still going about their day. The tension was evident, and their presence hadn't gone unnoticed. Kaleopei spotted Keylan's built frame down in the market. He was exchanging the hide of the deer. So she made her move. Dashing across roofing that felt like it was close to caving and allowed herself to find footholds, skillfully scaling her way down some buildings.

One foot and then another.

Kaleopei's feet hit the soil. The carver was now out of her sight, but I could make out Keylan's voice from around the corner. She put on a smile, let her hood fall down and joined his side once more.

"Oh! You're back, Kaleopei, how was your apprenticeship? Must have been nice getting away from Alstead." It was a familiar-looking male, and he was a leather tanner in the town.

"It was rather pleasant, Jovan. I learned a lot. This is one of my first catches since being back."

"It's a mighty size. Say, I'll give you eight silvers for it. A little rough around the edges when it was dressed." Finally, Kaleopei allowed me to really look at him and not at the group of soldiers that were still gathered in the courtyard with the female.

"Well, Key can't quite seem to get the carving right. There are probably better ones here in Alstead he could learn from."

"Indeed, come see me anytime, my boy. You and your sister are always welcome around here. It's good to see you around again, Kaleopei. Hope to do some more business soon." He had olive skin and brown eyes that matched his ordinary human features. Sandy hair covered some wrinkles on his older face. Humans always age awfully quickly.

"Yes, and I hate to end this so soon, but I do believe we had prior commitments tonight. Isn't that right, sweet sister?" A mass of an arm was placed around her shoulders, Keylan no doubt feeling the pommel of his sword beneath her cloak.

"Funnily enough, I was just coming to fetch you, brother. Ellis spoke of needing your aid in the garden."

"Eh, you two leaving so soon? I won't keep you folk. Tell Ellis to get out some more. It feels like I haven't seen her outside of her house in ages." He exchanged the coin with Keylan, sending the twins a friendly wave as Kaleopei turned on her heel. Sneaking a glance out towards the clearing, she could make out the girl visiting some vendors.

She was undoubtedly the youngest carver Kaleopei had seen bearing the official symbol. Most carvers are at least well into their adulthood. She looks as though she couldn't be older than seventeen, with long ivory locks that curled perfectly around her face.

Kaleopei watched closely as she exchanged silver with a young girl who was selling wildflowers. Placing a deep red one into the locks of deep ivory. She was stupidly beautiful looking.

"Keep staring like that, and you'll set fire to the poor girl. Carver or not, you look like you're ready to kill." Keylan pushed against her back. Without a word exchanged, Kaleopei could feel his impatience. With no more than a sigh she reached behind herself to unfasten the sword currently placed in an uncomfortable manner against her spine. It began to fall.

"Watch it; you could damage the sharpness. I work hard to keep up the image of Skipper." He caught the hilt, seemingly inches before it pierced the ground.

"Do you seriously intend on bickering right now? Nothing you could say would beat me in an argument. You named your sword Skipper."

His voice grew low, still bantering, but his eyes were on the soldiers and girl she had pointed out with her gaze. "At least Skipper has a name. Fighting with Skipper will always be an honor, unlike your nameless bow and poor hunting knives."

"Let's just get back to the house before Ellis decides to try to find us on her own." Kaleopei huffed out, fed up with her brother's nonsense. "My bow, for your information, likes being nameless. No one has lived to tell the tale of her blow. If someone does, then they can name her."

"So it's a her?" Kaleopei pushed out the thought of punching her twin. Deciding she had bigger things to worry about.

"Can we please just get back to Ellis?"

Kaleopei rolled her eyes at her brother's antics. Being the jokester came far too easily to the male. Though, if Kaleopei were being honest, his words were comforting. A normalcy when she felt like burning shit to the ground.

***

"Stop your bickering. It won't solve anything." The twins stood across the table, hands fisted on the table, as they both snapped their heads towards the grey-haired woman brewing tea. Kaleopei let out an audible groan, pushing away from the table.

It was abundantly clear that Ellis was standing with Keylan. Neither of them listened to her argument with good intentions, and both already made their choice.

"Don't let your temper loose, girl. Listen to your brother this time." Ellis didn't even look over her shoulder as she spoke, pouring the lavender-smelling tea into three cups. The elven girl shook with anger and frustration.

"We should be doing something, not hiding away! We are past these points, Key. I'm not afraid of them."

"I don't disagree with you, but we shouldn't be too abrupt when making these kinds of decisions. Beheading her in a small town will bring forth attention, and none of the kind we want right now." The brown-haired male slumped down into a chair, extending his hand as if making an offer.

"I'm so tired of not being able to do more. There aren't that many. They are staying at Allen's Inn. There are only so many rooms they can occupy. We could be in and out in a matter of minutes without leaving a trace."

Kaleopei's eyes were unwavering under the tension. She all but glared her intentions into the room, hoping Keylan saw how much this meant to her.

She knew firsthand what that carver could do. He did not. Kaleopei witnessed their cruelty and inhumane actions firsthand. Keylan had no clue of just how far the rumors ran. Images of that dark and cold cell ran through her mind in vivid flashes; everything down to the pit made her bones shake.

Kaleopei supposed it wasn't entirely his fault for not listening to her, for she still hadn't indulged what she had gone through. Unable to find the right words or time that would make Keylan realize why she was so intent on the matter.

"Is that the message we are trying to convey?" He was calm against the fire in her eyes. It'd always been that way, a dynamic that was natural between them. But it wasn't always that way, and it used to be quite the opposite before Kaleopei was caught.

The girl let out an overdramatic sigh, frustrated with everything she was trying to convey. "Listen, Key, I'm not being brash. The carver has a large protection team that was surrounding her, there has got to be a reason for that. Most carvers are accompanied by an escort or two, not an entire squadron." Kaleopei pushed her point. Her heated gaze, never faltering.

"Doesn't that go against your case, sweet sister? She's probably important." His tone remained the same, but even Ellis could see the intrigue behind the boy's eyes. Kaleopei tended to be the more cunning of the pair, and by Keylan's posture, she knew she had him hanging on by a thread. So, with a level voice, Kaleopei continued.

"Not likely, she's young. Most carvers are seasoned and conditioned. Even the way she spoke sounded strange. She's likely new, hence the added company.

They don't think she could protect herself, or they think she's untrustworthy. Either way, she's easy pickings for some information, no matter how little it be. We could be passing up on the lead we have been searching for."

"We're suggesting we interrogate her?" Keylan crossed his arms over his chest. Just like that, he had already withdrawn once more. All the hope she had placed in her words diminished, knowing nothing short of the truth would make him sway. That wasn't a conversation she was willing to have at the moment. No, that would have to be saved for another time.

"I'm suggesting we do something!" Kaleopei snarled, not backing down from her smug opponent. Her emotions began to take hold of her words. Gone was her rationale.

"We do nothing tonight." Keylan was firm, though the conviction he had was still partially building with each passing moment. "We take this time as a time for them to settle. So we stay put, understand?"

"Ellis, tell him he's being unbearable. We both know my plan is a good one-"

"What plan? All you've suggested is going in, causing a bloodbath of eighteen Bellheim citizens, not to mention *capital* citizens." He shot back quickly, and he was grave about this. Ellis was absorbed into their argument, but it was clear the older woman still sided with her twin.

"I hope those gods of yours give you insomnia."

A snort left his body as he turned on his heel, flipping Kaleopei off in the process. "Talk to me when you aren't acting like a child, Kaleopei. Then maybe we can sort this out properly."

Keylan didn't look back; simply walked away from the two women.

"Where did he learn to be such an overbearing brute of a brother?!" Kaleopei collapsed into a chair, pouring out her frustrations into the air of the kitchen.

"Perhaps when he went without your company for months? He was a wreck of a man, unsure of his purpose without you." Ellis sat down at the table, nursing a cup of tea, nodding for Kaleopei to do the same. With a roll of her eyes, she compiled.

"Oh, so now you decided to grace us with your voice?"

"Don't take that tone with me. You know as well as I do that it doesn't work on me. You two are grown of the same fire. Best to let you two fan each other while I try to extinguish one of you in the aftermath. Nothing I said would have even registered while you were fighting. He just wants you safe, child." Kaleopei scoffed, rolling those green orbs for what felt like the hundredth time today.

"I am capable of defending myself." That much Kaleopei knew Keylan understood. He had been at her side through all their daring, albeit reckless, encounters. Her skills with metal were undeniable, and her shots were precise and accurate. Kaleopei made a formidable opponent, regardless of what she had at her disposal.

"He knows it, but he still worries. You two, all the family you have left. He would rather not be alone."

"You think I want that?" Kaleopei's tone rose as she slumped further into her seat. Pale, calloused hands ran down her face in an attempt to calm herself down.

"I think you're frustrated and hurt. You seek vengeance for what you've lost. Haste will make you vulnerable, and that will cost your life."

"Staying complacent in this realm will cost us our lives. He's just being stubborn."

"You both are nearly identical in that matter," Ellis let out a laugh, "You must understand the irony of your situation. It's rather often your stubbornness is usually the bane of his existence."

"At least I'm stubborn with a reason." Her arms were flush across her chest, her foot tapping restlessly against the wooden floor.

"Your safety isn't a reason?"

"Not when I am willing to put it on the line, no. He should respect that. It's my choice. It's not like he can control me." Ellis sipped on her tea, little clues to what she was currently thinking.

"Gods, I don't think anyone can control you, child. Perhaps you should have voiced that to him. He's still a boy, Kaleopei. To him, it seemed that you were eager to jump forthright into danger without so much as a plan to back yourself." Ellis reached across the table, taking Kaleopei's hand. "You two have always bickered, but never had it been because of a lack of communication. Is that something you are aware of?"

"No."

"Don't lie to me." Ellis had a knowing quirked brow.

"I mean, things have been a little different. I just don't know how to mend it." Kaleopei hated that Ellis was right. She was able to see straight through the dance she and Keylan had been playing for the past few months.

"You're far from dumb, and the answer is far from hidden. Perhaps a conversation might be able to settle this bout of misunderstanding?"

"I know."

"Then it seems I'm not the person you should be conversing with right now."

"Whatever." Her emerald eyes rolled to the side, pushing herself from the table. What Ellis said made far too much sense; therefore, it would still be a while before she allowed herself to confront Keylan.

"I love you, Kaleopei."

"Mhmm, give me a scolding, then try to make it better with a few words?" Kaleopei's voice was playful, watching Ellis mirror the expression.

"You two are my children, and I will always remind you of your worth to me and yourself. I love you."

"I love you too," Kaleopei grumbled in return. Catching sight of Ellis' pleased features as she headed for her room.

Chapter 5

In the moonlight of Alstead, most were asleep. Those who weren't usually graced the tavern. The warm glow that it emitted was inviting to those who stopped here during travel. Having access to the Northern border didn't gain them many visitors, especially in later years. But there was still enough to make a night presence.

"I'll show him what staying put means." Kaleopei was dressed in a green dress, the sleeves long but only covered her forearms, which left her shoulders exposed.

The fabric flowed to the ground in delicate bundles. She secured a brown corset around her midsection, pushing what little chest she had upwards with each tug of the strings.

Kaleopei twirled in front of the little mirror, checking herself. She was always a firecracker, and her beauty represented that extremely well. But in this instance, she was looking to see if any of the daggers she had hidden were visible when the dress hugged certain parts of her body tightly.

They weren't.

Not a single one. Kaleopei took a moment to admire her work, smiling as she brushed the hair out of her face.

"He's an elven asshole." The green in her eyes stood out against the coal she used to line her eyes. The feline shape she drew, heightening her sharp features.

Then, the swipe of blood-red pigment on her lips brought the whole look together. "I'll get intel and look hot as hell. Keylan won't know what to think."

Humble wasn't one of her strengths. Kaleopei knew what she excelled at.

She would reconcile with her brother in the morning. Perhaps even heading Ellis' words to an extent.

But right now, she was feeling rather petty.

Then she was out her window, creeping along the roof. Her face grimaced as she made careful steps around Keylan's room. Silently flipping off his window as she made her descent off the house. Something she did with practiced ease, having snuck out far too many times during her childhood. Once the balls of her feet hit the ground, she did what she did best.

Adopted a different personality for the evening, and she played the part.

She pushed her breasts up and smacked her lips together before she walked through the saloon-style doors. Lights clear from the road, alluding to the bustling commotion going on inside.

The music was loud, voices mixing through the prime hour of Elva's Tavern. A few males turned their gaze to her, and she resisted the urge to throw up at their predatory smiles.

Men. It's not exactly Kaleopei's forte.

"Kaleopei! I wasn't aware you were back!" Across the room, a slender woman with sleek blonde hair flagged her down. She was wearing intricate makeup, along with a simple red dress that hugged her like a second set of skin. Elva preferred the attention to be directed at her face.

"I returned a few days ago, Elva." The blonde woman pulled her into a quick embrace.

"Well, aren't we lucky? You have to grace us with a number. I'm sure that Landon would love to play for you again. He's been practicing nonstop." She was practically being shoved towards the platform they called a stage by the middle-aged women. Elva unknowingly played right into the facade she had going on.

"I guess a song or two couldn't hurt." Kaleopei's laugh was light and subtle, the epitome of ladylike. Not the usual full belly and snorting she did around Keylan. The raised height of the stage did offer a better vantage point of the room.

"That's the spirit. I'll let Landon know." Most of the regulars were easily recognizable, with their bellies full of mead and not enough food. Not to mention, they reek of alcohol and musk, only describable as masculine. A distasteful scent.

Others watched, some curious as to who she was, but she kept up the act. Flashing smiles to those in her vicinity and even throwing in a couple of winks here and there until she spotted her target. Clad in a lavender dress that should be classified as nightwear, hair pulled tightly on top of her head. A few pieces were left out, framing her rounded features.

Kaleopei turned her gaze away, hoping her slight stare didn't get noticed by the girl.

"Ladies and gentlemen," Elva was clinking spoons together, standing on top of the bar. He was nowhere in sight as the bartender held the eager woman steady. "Do I have a surprise for you tonight? Our muse has arrived. Please refrain from drink-throwing and let your ears feast upon her voice! It's one of a kind, I tell you, the best in the realm! And she's from these very streets of Alstead!"

"Elva, you are far too kind." Kaleopei eased herself into talking above the crowd, whose hollering had settled in the passing moments. Allowing her voice to carry throughout the room. "Alstead will always be my home. This realm, Bellheim, I would give my life to. But I think my voice would service those who fight in the building tonight."

Lies.

She unleashed her voice upon them. Soft and gentle, she sang the song of Bellheim. Beneath her voice, anger swelled as people drunkenly sang along, no care as they drank themselves away. Laboring away for a King who didn't appreciate anything they did. Out here, this close to the border, they were nothing more than cattle to him.

Landon played as perfectly as she remembered, a fine man he would turn out to be. He had grown almost a foot since she last saw the boy. Still a child with a dream of playing in a concert hall. Judging by the way his fingers graced the pianoforte, he would make it.

Kaleopei put on a show. She usually loved being the center of attention. Yearned for the praise of her voice when she was younger. Would sing for her parents and siblings any chance she could get, oftentimes with elaborate clothes. But in this setting, it made her skin crawl with disgust. Scanning the audience, left to right. Until she fell upon the bored face of the carver, she was lazily stirring the drink she had been nursing. No smile like the others, not even nodding along to the music that had no doubt been engraved in her head. Just pure, utter boredom on that pretty face of hers.

Kaleopei wasn't sure whether to be angry or flattered by the lack of attention...

A few stanzas later, Kaleopei was bowing, taking the praise that was thrown her way with a practiced smile. Accepting each with forced gratitude.

"You are such a wonderful crowd," Not. Silently, she wondered what would be different if she sang in Elven. Perhaps one of the old scripts, where the lyrics are intricate and meaningful, those songs were beautiful. There was real emotion behind them, not just some technique of crowd control.

Elva extended her hand out to the brown-haired girl, aiding her off the stage. Soft melodies still enchanted the bar, Landon's hands not stilling as he continued on the pianoforte. A wide smile was etched onto this dark face, the whites of his teeth on display with each note he played. The emotion brightened on his face as he was engulfed in the music.

Kaleopei couldn't remember the last time she was so carefree when singing.

"Thank was wonderful, dearest." More praise. "Care to sing another?"

"Maybe shortly; I'd like to get a drink." Elva nodded and left her alone, presumably to mix something up behind the bar. Kaleopei continued on, now allowing herself to mingle with some of the patrons. Making sure to ignore those who were whistling or throwing empty compliments at her.

Even if a man dared approach her, the blades strapped tightly to her body gave her confidence. She'd cut off their favorite parts without a second thought.

The crowd was loud, almost too loud for her ears. With a calculated glare, Kaleopei spotted the messy bun of the carver and wordlessly grabbed a seat next to her. Flagging Elva down to this end of the bar as she did so.

Being so close to the carver set Kaleopei on high alert and allowed for closer inspection. Anything less than using ethereal would be a crime to describe the bored women. She had rosy lips, a striking contrast against her pale complexion, exuding a subtle allure, their hue reminiscent of freshly spilled blood—a testament to the potency of her presence.

Right. This girl was dangerous. Kaleopei knew that with utmost certainty.

"You have a nice voice." While resisting the urge to double-take, Kaleopei brushed the lower part of her dress out, sitting on the stool. Suddenly, she was over-aware of every move her body made.

"That's very kind of you. Mother said it was my greatest talent, but between us, I'd say she overestimated me." The bout of confidence came out of nowhere. Each word made Kaleopei recoil with a cringe. "Say, I don't recognize you. I've lived here my whole life and am quite used to the locals."

"I'm from the Capital, just staying the night." There was nothing but a monotone behind her voice, as though she wasn't really interested in this conversation. It wasn't until Elva set a glass of wine in front of her did the girl even faced Kaleopei.

"I bet they have all kinds of music there, I do wish to visit someday." If she wasn't going to talk, Kaleopei would have to be the one to lead the dance she was trying to initiate. Perhaps a notion to ignite some allure?

"It's all the same, passionless and government-mandated." The girl laughed. Kaleopei shifted her body in accord with the laughter, pushing her chest out and lazily longing on her palm.

When the carver looked back, there was a slight blush appearing on her face. She had pale skin that could be mistaken for moonlight and eyes that rivaled the color of her hair. Finally, a look that wasn't boredom.

Keylan will surely have my head in the morning.

But the night was still far too young to think about the morning.

"Sorry, where's my manners? I'm Zaratella, but please call me Zara, and you are?" The identified girl raised her glass in question. There was a quiet confidence in the way Zaratella presented herself, making her all the more intriguing.

"Kaleopei, and it's a pleasure to meet you. Trust me, if I had it my way, I'd be writing my own music." Only when the King gets rid of the dumb rules regarding literature and music. Meaning never.

"Now, that sounds like something I ought to hear one day. Invite me to a show?"

They fell into a playful conversation, small talking back and forth. Elva refilled their glasses again and again. Time was only a concept as she conversed with the girl, carefully prying any information she could from those delicious-looking lips.

"Tell me why a pretty girl like you is armed to the teeth?" Kaleopei felt the air grow cold between them, a slight unease as she licked her lips. Zaratella had noticed the blades concealed beneath her garments.

What else did she notice?

Nothing. She noticed nothing, and Kaleopei had to convince herself. If she had sensed what brewed beneath her skin, she wouldn't be so complacent in conversation.

Unless the carver was toying with her?

Keep calm, answer and distract. With a sudden smirk, she tapped the end of a blade on her thing. It was a quiet tap, but Zaratella heard the clink of her nails against the metal.

"Men are pigs, had an altercation in the past I would rather not repeat. Since then, my family has caused a commotion if I were to leave unarmed." A smirk played over Zara's features, licking her lips as she leaned in closer. "Smart on their part. So you're well versed with them?"

"I could wipe the floor with any of these drunken brutes." Kaleopei quipped back, not backing away from the pale-skinned girl. A tint of red now washed over Zaratella's face from alcohol or something more. But neither pushed away from the other.

Each moment they sat in silence was one of competition between them. A game of dominance to see who'd back down first.

It wouldn't be Kaleopei. Her pride couldn't handle that today.

"That'd be a sight, Kaleopei," Zaratella pronounced each and every syllable of her name with a click of her tongue. "Next time the King holds a competition, should I expect to see you there?"

Kaleopei resisted the urge to shutter. It was a test she barely passed.

"The capital is a ways away, and I don't know if I could. Besides, the King is too misogynistic to let a female compete." The smirk fell away from Zara's face.

"Don't I know it?"

"Are you close with His Majesty?" Judging by her age, she could be close in age to the Crowned Prince. Kaleopei knew that most carvers were from the capital, so it wouldn't be an outlandish possibility.

He should be around 19 now. She could have grown up around him.

"Oh god's no, between you and me, he's a right prick." She laughed, looking at those who surrounded them. No doubt, making sure none of her escorts heard the comments. "My father is close with the King. So I was around the castle a good deal when I was younger."

"Any news on the Queen?" The fake concern that dripped from Kaleopei's rose-tinted lips was rehearsed. Zara downed a shot of what Kaleopei assumed was some potent shit after seeing the face she made.

"No idea, apparently, she doesn't leave her quarters."

"May the gods bless her highness." Kaleopei softly smiled, nursing the cup of lavender mead Elva kept refilling. Elva's special brew and one of Kaleopei's most loved forms of booze.

A brief look at the scattering patrons and the music slowing meant it was close to closing.

How long had we been talking for?

It didn't feel that long.

"I have to depart early in the morning, but I should be retuning through here in a couple of moons. Perhaps we could see each other again?" Zara was the one to initiate the goodbye. The ends of her lips curled up.

Even though she was supposed to be gathering intel, Kaleopei felt a small pool of warmth growing in her stomach. Excited about the chance to see the mysterious carver again.

"I'll be here. I'm always here."

"Good," Zara stood up swiftly, pecking a quick kiss on her cheek.

Kaleopei thought she was going to pass out from the heat that rose to her cheeks. The girl's lips were too soft for their own good, utterly kissable. Kaleopei wondered how long it would take to make them raw.

Too close. I've got to get her away. Her mind raced as she thought of all this could entail. *Keylan might actually kill me.*

The way that Zaratella giggled was enough of a goodbye. Being kind, Kaleopei nodded and turned on her heel, taking in a deep breath as soon as she was sure Zara could no longer see her face. Taking a moment to regain her composure.

In and out. Nothing bad happened.

So she made her way home, not caring to be discreet at the early hour. People could think about what they wanted about her endeavors. It hadn't stopped her before. Reputation was only the construct of other's opinions, and Kaleopei could care as to what they thought.

"Hey, wait!" She froze, every muscle tensing as she subconsciously tapped her thigh for the dagger. Kaleopei placed a smile on her face, turning to see Zara running towards her. Bundled up in her hands were a few wildflowers that grew along the road. Zara pushed the flowers into her hand. "Um, take these. I mean, they're for you. You're absolutely breathtaking, Kaleopei."

Kaleopei just stood there, unsure of what to say to the other. But it wasn't long before Zara smiled once more and took off down the road. Not leaving enough time for Kaleopei to formulate a response.

Carefully, she glanced over the rushed bouquet. Seeing the piece of parchment that was wrapped around the stems, she unrolled it. Glancing at the human language written.

Without wasting another moment, Kaleopei dropped the flowers and began sprinting towards the house.

Fuck. Fuck. Fuck.

****

Kaleopei burst through Keylan's door, not even caring to knock, and just hoped he was decent. "Time to get up!"

Her brother practically jumped to his feet, looking over the attire Kaleopei was currently clad in. Keylan's eyes were wide as he seemed to look over every last detail of her. He has had practice reading her, and his eyes practically screamed in concern at her expression.

"What did you do, Kaleopei?" The room was quaint and minimal. Easy to pack everything and move if needed. It's how they lived, never knowing when they would need to relocate.

"A couple of things, actually, been a night."

"Are you going to elaborate on them?" He was throwing a shirt over his torso, moving throughout the room, suiting up. What would she do without him?

Right. She had to tell him what actually happened.

"So I went to Elva's, hoping to do a little scouting of potential threats. Saw the Carver stuck around for a bit. Ended up flirting with the enemy. Then she gave me this, and I kind of, maybe, panicked and came straight here." Keylan's distaste was evident on his face. His forehead creased as Kaleopei handed him the parchment.

He seemed to be taking it all in. "Gods, Kaleopei, you're lucky I love that brain of yours. This one wasn't your finest."

"Don't even start with the lecture, and I am far more than my mind. We only have so much time before sunrise. We have to kill her." It was an extreme, Kaleopei would admit, but it would be necessary if the note meant what she thought it implied.

"Slow your killing tendencies for a second. All it says is 'I know,' that could mean many things." Regardless of his words, he still strapped Skipper to his back. All Kaleopei could do was scoff.

"It could be bad things, Key. It could mean literally anything. Who knows what freaky sensing abilities she has."

"So we're now going to assassinate the girl you spent a better part of the night flirting with? Not to mention, after I spoke about taking the night to understand more?" She didn't even humor him with a response; she simply flipped him off and went to grab her bow.

By the time she emerged from her own room, Keylan was fastening his cloak around his broad shoulders. He held hers in his other hand. "Not to belittle your capabilities, but are you really going to kill her in that dress?"

"For your information, I will be. She called me pretty. I want that to remain, even if I have to pierce an arrow through her throat. I don't want her to die thinking I looked better in green than black." She snatched the brown cloak from his hand, the other hand on her hip as she strode out the door.

"Whatever happened to my innocent sister?"

"Parents and sister got murdered, while the rest of my people disappeared. Changes a person, usually not for the better."

"That will never be funny."

"Did I forget to mention I was held prisoner for months?"

"Still not funny."

"Neither are your quips, Key."

"Touché."

The banter was a welcome change. It let them both disassociate from what they were about to do. Killing wasn't something the duo did lightly, only in extreme and dire circumstances. But with their identities on the line, Kaleopei thinks it's important. With the life they lived, both have overcome their fear of taking life. Having to come to terms with it for their survival.

Once the silence fell between them, her mind shifted.

Her breath was ragged as she held a piece of dark crystal in her hand. She held it like a weapon to any of the humans who came towards her. Kaleopei used it as such.

Their screams were loud as she couldn't grant them a swift death. Not after what they'd done. Not after what she'd seen in the pit.

But still, they screamed as if they were innocent. As if they didn't see how fucked up the things they were doing were.

So she slashed and hacked, using the deep purple rock as a weapon. She was getting out of here. She had to.

"Kaleopei, we're here." Keylan snapped her out of her own head. A few blocks away from them was the only inn in town that could accompany all eighteen of them.

"We are still going through with this?" His voice was low, only for her to hear. She took in a deep breath, ready to respond. But that was when the stench hit her. The acidic metal smell invaded her nostrils in an unpleasant flood.

The smell wasn't foreign by any means.

Her feet moved before she uttered another word to Keylan. They got closer, and he scowled, emitting the smallest growl as he came to the same realization she had.

They worked in unison as Kaleopei boosted Keylan up the wall to get to the second story. He reached down and pulled her up.

The smell made her want to hurl up the leftover stew she consumed earlier. Scents of blood filled her nostrils as they grew closer to the source. The stretch flooded her nose, staining it with the metallic smell.

But she didn't.

Instead, she shallowed out her breathing, Keylan doing the same. Taking another breath, she listened closely, trying to trace any movement with her ears. Kaleopei led the way, her brother never more than a pace behind.

She gave a slight nod to a door. It wasn't movement she heard, more like a drip. A subtle, consistent sound that lingered from whatever lay beyond the door. Keylan grabbed the door, pushing it inwards.

Kaleopei was swift to position herself inside, twin blades lodged between her palms and ready to fly or strike. Whatever suited the situation better.

Once her emerald eyes adjusted to the darkness, Kaleopei sized up the room. Four figures lay in their respective beds, but she could make out the blood stains beneath them. Her emerald eyes narrowed in on the drops of blood that hit the floorboards in a taunting, consistent pattern.

One after another, the drops hit the floor.

They were already dead, no heartbeats.

Another drop hit the floor.

Unmoving,

Another drop hit the floor.

Who could pull something like this off?

Another drop hit the floor.

A warm hand grabbed her shoulder, pulling her away from the dead soldiers. She was then back into the warm candlelit hallway of the inn. The cream-colored walls seemed closer this time, the world closing in around her. Keylan shut the door carefully, dulling the noise to the best of his ability. With the door shut, Kaleopei gained her ability to think straight once more.

Holy shit.

She had suggested doing the very same earlier, but to see the deed already done left far more questions in the air. Questions with answers she wasn't sure she wanted.

They both locked eyes with each other as if they were thinking the same thing. The question on the tip of her tongue.

What the hell happened here?

Chapter 6

Keylan stared at his sister, trying to make sense of all that he knew. Which admittedly did seem like much since Kaleopei had returned. *She was only gone a few hours at most. How much trouble can she get herself into?*

The answer was apparently endless; she was a magnet for trouble in every aspect. Kaleopei was the embodiment of chaos. He was in for a world of hurt, but he would endure it for her.

The scent of blood stained the entirety of the inn, and for some reason, it was getting to Kaleopei. Both had seen their fair share of fights and the scenes they remain in their wake. Violence wasn't something either had ever shied away from. This time wasn't even that gruesome. Keylan didn't even make out any large wounds.

For some unknown reason, Kaleopei was starting to work herself into a panic. He didn't dwell on the scene from before, instead choosing to focus on the quickened breaths Kaleopei was currently working through.

"Are you alright?" What was he saying? Of course, she wasn't. Her face was deathly pale, her hands shaking as she held on tightly to the twin hunting knives encased in her palms. Metal glinting in the dim candlelight, her knuckles white from the force.

Emerald's eyes snapped up, meeting his own set of orbs. Emerald meeting emerald. His heart ached, seeing her eyes so distant and haunted. Kaleopei curled in on herself but kept moving down the hall. Only tugging the cloak closer to her face.

"Fine. Let's keep going."

Keylan nodded, unsure of what else he was supposed to do. Usually, he'd make an effort to see that Kaleopei was calm enough to continue, but with the unknown threat looming in the space, that wasn't an option. In tangent, they continued, moving as one.

The sight of the men was indeed startling, especially with how unprepared they were. Someone else had to be nearby. Those bodies were far too fresh for his liking. Kaleopei halted her movement, holding up a single finger. Silently, she was communicating with him, an unspoken code only the two of them understood. There was one person behind that door.

Parts of him were envious of her heightened senses, but the headaches she often got from them made him glad. Nevertheless, the amount of pride he harbored for her knew no bounds, and her sharp mind was only one check on his list.

Once again, Keylan reached for the door handle, allowing Kaleopei a second to prepare herself. Then he swung the door open, allowing Kaleopei to make the first move. She would adjust more quickly, a flaw he was able to admit.

A loud crash resounded from inside, "Don't you know it's rude to enter without knocking? A little warning would have been nice."

The voice was feminine, light, and not at all what he was expecting. Kaleopei branded her hunting knives, both intricately ornate with flowers made of metal, but she hadn't thrown them. She had hesitated. Not very many things make his sister hesitate. Kaleopei understood the importance of seconds in a fight.

He moved to see inside the dimly lit inn room. Looking over Kaleopei's shoulder, brows raising at the sight before him.

A girl no older than eighteen was sitting on the desk with her legs crossed over one another, a large basin of water to her side. Upon a further look, it was clear the water was tainted with a crimson hue, as were her pointed nails. That wasn't even mentioning the retch of blood this room reeked of, and she was the center of it. The girl had long black hair. Almost pooling to the desk when she slouched. Parts of the dress she wore had dark spots, undoubtedly from blood splatter.

A singular thing made him go rigid. None of that blood was hers. At least, that's what he suspected. There wasn't a single wound he could see.

"Y'know, I did wonder how long it would take before you came looking for me." She was talking directly to Kaleopei, ignoring him. Her lip stain smeared to one side as she ran the back of her hand across that pale face, messing it up even further.

Keylan stepped in front of his sister, shielding her from the women. Keylan didn't remove his glare from the girl, "You're the Carver."

"Indeed, and she's the songbird from the bar. It appears you've brought a friend along for this show. Though it's far less pleasant compared to your show."

He couldn't believe she ignored him entirely, her eyes only sizing up Kaleopei like a predator would prey. It was intimidating seeing the woman observe so intently, much like Kaleopei does.

"I'm not playing this guessing game with you. Why'd you assassinate your guard?" Kaleopei stood with confidence, no sign of the vulnerable girl he had seen in the hall. The one who had witnessed the site of those maimed guards, no here stood a girl intimidating her opponent by using those calculated words. Only the slight tremble of her hands remained, easily mistaken as anger.

Keylan simply looked between the two of them. Trying to ascertain the tone of this encounter. It was clear he was currently stuck between the two highly trained and deadly women, who both looked ready to start a fight.

Do I step in? This is the female Kaleopei was flirting with?

He kept his thoughts as they were, not acting on any whim with the unknown in front of him. Perhaps he trusted Kaleopei too much, but he wouldn't stop now. Keylan is in far too deep.

The girl uncrossed her legs, leaning back slightly, so her shoulders hit the wall.

"Easy, I would rather not be a pawn in the King's game. So I took matters into my own hands." She laid it raw, just admitted guilt. "I will have a say in what I do with my life from here on out."

Be smart, Kaleopei. She could be toying with us.

Keylan was internally pleading to his sister, unsure of what this assailant was planning behind those iron eyes. Her face gave nothing as to what was going on in her head.

"Why here? Why now, Zaratella." So that was the Carver's name. She brushed her hair over her shoulder, each strand of black silk hair becoming bathed in crimson that was only visible when the dim light hit it just right. "You gave me hope, gorgeous. I recognized you almost the moment I saw you. No one knew your name, but they said you had eyes of green and were a pretty young thing."

"Kaleopei, what's the move?" Keylan shot at his sister. Unsure of what the tension in the room was currently. Knowing that Kaleopei was recognized, was unsettling, like a clock had just been set for them.

"Stand down, Key. We hear her out, then we decide." He nodded along, allowing her to call the shots. Kaleopei had more intel when dealing with this currently, but he still had little idea as to what was currently happening. The only intel he had was what he was observing. It seemed Kaleopei's reputation preceded her to the point where she was being recognized.

"I'm not going to sugarcoat this. They were sending me to Louth. Things have been... well, tense is the most accurate word since your stunt, but the King is moving forward with the process. I was to become an overseer of sorts, learning how to document Louth's research. Being a Carver does have the upside of classified information, and I recognized you almost instantly in that tavern. My placement was to not ensure Bellheim didn't have any more incidents like yours." Keylan's ears perked at the mention of Louth. That's where Kaleopei was when they had been separated. The place that seemed to break her entirely, leaving shards that Kaleopei was still slowly putting back together.

"News of this will spread faster than you think. The King will hear of this come nightfall. Alstead isn't a big town. People talk." Kaleopei pushed for more information. He was comfortable, just absorbing more and more as she prodded. Watching for any shift in the women's demeanor.

"Indeed he will. I will be the one communicating it."

Was her motive to be framing Kaleopei? But that still left the question of her agenda.

Keylan pondered, racking his brain as he watched her body language. The subtle way she moved her hands as talking. As though the blood on her fingertips weren't there.

Her iron eyes seemed to glint a dark shade of red. Her lids were hooded when she looked between the two of them. Heat began to emanate from beside him, Kaleopei's' face an unreadable amount of calm.

"I will bury this dagger between your throat if you're considering framing us. In the morning, the only thing that will be left is your lifeless bodies, all dead remaining here. No trace of who or what caused it." Kaleopei pulled the weapon closer to her chest. A warning. She was terrifying when wielding threats. Keylan knew it would land true.

Zaratella laughed.

"God's no, I have no interest in that. I think we would be more beneficial as allies in this." The girl must have lost it. That must be the reason for her words. "Can't imagine you two are pleased by what has been occurring."

She killed her guard and then lost her mind. That's the conclusion he came to terms with. Killing seventeen of her own supposed guards, then asking for trust and becoming allies.

"What do you know of Louth?" It appeared his sister was more intrigued by the deal than he was. The mere words made him bite his tongue, wanting to better understand what Kaleopei went through.

"Everything, darling." Keylan shifted, watching as Kaleopei stiffened. "Every painstaking detail of inhumane acts the King decreed. But as to why? Well, that's the million-silver question, isn't it?"

Chapter 7

Kaleopei had been silently sizing Zara up from the moment Keylan opened the door. There was nothing hostile about her as she spoke or the odd way she was cleaning herself of blood. Each word seemed to be a complete and utter truth. In a way, she almost seemed remorseful through her playful tone.

Keylan hadn't uttered a word since she had shut him down. Understanding that, Kaleopei was clearly intent on seeking what the carver had to say. Instead, he simply observed them intently.

"Let's say we entertain this idea of a mutual agreement. What exactly would we get out of it?" She knew how to sway this. This was a gamble. They could play right into a trap if Kaleopei wasn't careful with her words. Careful with how much trust she was willing to give as the price of this deal.

"Satisfaction of shutting Louth down? Vengeance for those who were lost." Kaleopei let her gaze fall. The sheer mention of Louth put her on edge. That place was hell. She didn't ever intend on stepping foot near it again. But that could be changed, given she was plotting to bring about its end. "Many things can come from this, and most are what you decide to do with it."

A chance for the pit to seized. No one else would have to endure it.

The mere idea of being able to take vengeance was insisting. Kaleopei was no different from a moth being drawn to a flame, and this fire was intense. Undoubtedly, she would be burned in the process.

Kaleopei had never been one to shy away from heat.

"I'll write to the king saying a creature got to my guard in the Elven realm. There was no documentation of us staying here. I paid some hefty silver to make sure of such. His majesty, as you called him, isn't one to check his sources when it comes to carvers. Especially me, I've been nothing but an obedient servant to him. My word is as good as gold to him. He'd never suspect one of his own to bluntly lie to him, so long as we are swift, we shouldn't expect an issue from their deaths."

She could be lying. I had no real way to know. In truth, I knew nothing about this abnormally gorgeous Carver. Was this worth putting Keylan in danger for?

Zaratella was an enigma. A force that Kaleopei hadn't encountered before, but she so desperately wanted to believe the sweet words she had sung. That was dangerous in its own right.

"For the record, I harbor no ill will towards the Elves. I hate most people equally, but I do deeply apologize for what the humans have done." It was soft-spoken, like Zara was unsure of if she should have even said it. Fearing it might have been the wrong thing to say. "I fear for what my alleged King will do to the other Realms if Louth is a success. Nobody else should have to suffer from his hands."

The two women looked at each other and truly saw each other. For a split second, Kaleopei could see the sadness in the other's eyes. But also the spark of will that quickly overcame it. She had a warrior's heart. Kaleopei could recognize that.

Still, she took her time to ponder all the words in her head, picking them carefully. Not wanting anything that spills from her lips to be used against them.

"If we do this, it will be done together, no deceits from here forth. Equally sharing the burden of what is to come. If you do, I will pierce you with my blade before you can even draw your own." Kaleopei spared a glance at her brother, seeing her flame reflected in his eyes. Zara's lips twitched, swaggering her way towards Kaleopei in an alluring blur.

A pale hand, still tinted crimson, was presented in front of her. Kaleopei noted that none of it appeared to be hers, all a mix of those she had slain. It appeared that she was completely unscathed from the matter.

"Then you both have yourself a deal."

Kaleopei didn't extend her hand, not satisfied with a handshake. This had to be real, concrete. There was only one way to ensure that Zaratella held up her end of the bargain.

"No, we honor it in Elven tradition. A blood rite." This wasn't something Kaleopei would budge on. A pact made on her own terms, with no human influence, and protected by magic.

"Okay, what do I do?" Zaratella blinked. No hint of mockery, just pure, utter curiosity. Zara was trusting her here. They both had to trust the other. The only person she fully trusts is Keylan. Letting another in would be difficult. Kaleopei could only trust her if she was willing to stride into the unknown.

Keylan took her hunting knives and, in slew, handed a dagger to her awaiting hands. Kaleopei took it, extending her left palm. Zara did the same, mirroring her motion.

With a steady hand, Kaleopei drew the dagger from thumb to pinky across her palm. Metal glided smoothly, creating a laceration in its wake.

The stench of her own blood invaded the room. She forgot about Keylan, who shifted to stand awkwardly by the window, his dismay clear on his face. In Elf tradition, this was usually a sacred ritual, only performed by those close to one another, and usually not done in front of others. Kaleopei didn't allow herself to think about the intimacy of their actions. The current trials of her life swayed Kaleopei's view. It was a fail-safe. To know for certain if Zaratella would ever jeopardize them.

And if it fails?

Well, then another body would be added to the inn.

Kaleopei's sole focus was on Zaratella as she handed the dagger to her, a show of trust. With a slight nod, the black-haired human did the same. Upon the initial cut, Kaleopei swore the blood ran black before beads of crimson pooled in Zara's palm. Zaratella's face did not waiver, convincing her it must have been a trick of the light.

Kaleopei clasped her hand on top of Zara's. Blood smeared into both of their palms. It was warm, but somehow not unpleasant.

"Repeat after me," Kaleopei closed her eyes, a testament to the trust she was willing to expend. Her magic danced inside her body, filling the room with warmth, that flame wanting to bounce across their intertwined palms. *"Valara. Sanktum."*

The Elven spilled out of her mouth, a familiar feeling of warmth and magic. A pact, like she had done with her brother many years ago.

"Valara. Sanktum."

Kaleopei felt the magic in her palm shifting and merging into the blood that dripped onto the floorboards. Familiar yet foreign to how she and Keylan had done it before.

She got sucked deep into her own spiriting magic, and for a brief second, she wondered what Zara would be feeling. Humans didn't have an innate reserve of magic; instead, any magic came from enchanted conduits with small reservoirs that they were able to call upon.

Kaleopei let herself spiral deeper into the depths of her magic, let her flame flicker ever so slightly against the carver's hand.

It wasn't until she opened her eyes did she saw the girl's face contorted into one of agony. Veins popped on her forearm as she fought to remain still. Kaleopei was aware of the heat her magic could give off and knew the dangers and degrees of burns it could cause. Still, the girl craned her neck, only showing the discomfort on her face.

Keylan saw her uneasy and quickly pulled Zaratella back, even he found it challenging to waive her heat when exposed to the brunt of it.

"Shit, you're scalding Kaleopei." Her eyes widened, pulling her hand close to her chest, seeing the bubbling blood on her palm, boiling with raw magic. Keylan let his attention move from Zara to Kaleopei, locking gazes. "You're fine. You're in control. Don't let the flame out without your permission."

Her eyes once again closed.

Suddenly, feeling the magic that was currently trying to escape became overwhelming.

Kaleopei had to sink deep into the dark pit that contained her magic. A seemingly bottomless pit that reached for ages, contesting her in every way. Refusing to be controlled.

When did she start breathing so hard?

Kaleopei searched for any kind of flicker. It took what seemed like hours until she saw the spark. Finding her flame, she shoved it down. Forcing it to yield to her, not allowing it to get the best of her.

You are in control.

You do not waiver.

You are in control.

Her emerald eyes gazed upon the white scar that lay in the wake of the dagger's sharp blade.

Kaleopei remembered where she was, the pact she had just made. Zaratella and Kaleopei were intertwined through an ancient rite. Until one breaks the arrangement or dies, a commitment.

Then she saw the burns welting into the palm of the Carver over the thin white line that mirrored hers. Her brother was no longer at her side, instead crouching before the girl, who was in a state of disbelief.

Keylan's hand was encased in water. It was glowing, the faintest color of blue mixed with a twinge of green. Zaratella watched intensely as his magic passed over her palm.

The immediate relief was present on Zara's face, taking in every second of Keylan's cool touch. Ridding her of the pain *she* had caused.

"Gods, that feels nice. Don't you two compliment each other? Hot and cold, very cliché." Kaleopei noted the light tone she took, not agitated in the slightest. Even the pain didn't take her suave demeanor. "Let me guess you two are siblings?"

"Twins, actually," Keylan answered as words seemed to burn before they could reach her throat. Fitting for the damage she had caused. "My name is Keylan. Seems you and my sister have become relatively acquainted."

"That's a word for it. We don't have to do the same blood thing, right? Because I might need a minute before I go again." Keylan removed his hands, the welts nothing more than little blisters that would go away in a day or so.

"No, a deal with her is good enough for me."

"Well, it seems we've founded an alliance. My name is Zaratella Eldridge." She pushed herself off her knees, wiping her hands on the lavender slip she wore. Coating it with more stains and grime, a testament to her previous activities. "Our first order of business will be discarding the bodies. Come along, Elven Twins!"

Kaleopei's eyes collided with her brother's. Zara striding towards the door allowed them little time to discuss what just happened in such a short amount of time.

What had I just gotten us into?

Chapter 8

A loud bang echoed throughout Casimir's chamber. Stilling him from the little slumber he was able to get. The Prince took a minute to realize the noise was coming from someone at his door, banging on the wood. Around him was the novel he had been reading last night and the slight stench of Myth.

Another three knocks sounded out. Utterly interrupting the only sleep he had gotten in what felt like days. The bags under his eyes only argued his state further.

The boy groaned, yawning as he pulled himself out of bed. Slipping on a tunic over his bare chest, an attempt to decent himself. A brief glimpse in the mirror showed his reddened blue eyes and the deep bags that were prominent underneath them.

Then another bang, this time substantially louder thanks to his proximity to the door. Maybe it was that the person grew tired of his slow pace. Either way, Casimir wasn't sure he particularly cared, given that the sun still hadn't risen.

Who was so persistent at an ungodly hour?

Grunting, Casimir swung the door open, resisting the urge to rub his eyes as he did so. The light from the hall partially blinded him, blocking him from seeing who pushed their way into his room. Casimir blinked a few times, turning to face whoever decided it was an intelligent idea to wake him.

There, dressed in pristine court wear, was his Uncle. His arms crossed in front of him, striding into the Prince's room. No greeting was exchanged between the two. The man held four books in his arms, placing the stack onto Casimir's exceedingly messy desk.

Quickly, the Prince shut the door, sensing his Uncle was in no pleasant mood. That made two of them. Casimir noted the furrowed brows, and he was unsure of what exchange was about to take place at such an early hour.

"Good morning to you too, Uncle Kelvin." Casimir snorted, taking the moment to give Kelvin a once-over. His appearance seemed worse for wear, his hair greying at the roots and unkept, he had sleepless eyes that resembled Casimir's and his attire was the only neat thing about him.

"I don't have the time, I'm to meet with Darren soon. Keep these close; memorize them if you have to. Then keep them hidden." His voice was stern, something Casimir hadn't heard from his Uncle very often. Something was very wrong. "No one must learn of their existence. Understand?"

"Why must I-"

"Because I asked you to. This isn't up for discussion. I can no longer hold onto them. It is your time." Then Kelvin was out the door. Not once had he ever taken that tone with Casimir. His prior conversation with Zara seemed to ring in his head.

Why must everyone be so cryptic? Would it kill a person to be straightforward with him? He's a prince, not some mind reader who could tell what every person he encountered intentions were. Kelvin made an authoritative statement, combined with his appearance, set the Prince into a slight frenzy. Not able to discern what was going on with his Uncle. It was entirely out of character, and Casimir wasn't high enough to dwell on it.

The door slammed in his Uncle's wake, sending Casimir to groan at the world. Kelvin was clearly agitated, something putting him on edge apparently that made it his problem.

Curiously, Casimir walked over to the desk. Seeing the books atop his many loose papers and open books.

The new additions were all worn with age, definitely not written in this century. Intricate woven symbols were etched into each of the covers, but not in any language he could recall.

Casimir bent the spine, looking into the script that was similar to the one on the cover. All around the text were scribbles in a unique language filled with runes and scripts unfamiliar to him. But he could vaguely make out the penmanship and the ink that accompanied it. Orange ink. Casimir knew only one person who was pompous enough to use it. It belonged to Kelvin but wasn't written in common. Casimir flipped between pages, none of it legible to him.

For fuck's sake, what was he supposed to do with these?

He let out a low sigh, placing them back onto the desk. The script could be ancient for all he knew. A translation might not even be in their library. Even if such a guide were viable to them, the books had hundreds of pages each. It'd take him hours of endless grueling over them to even translate the book's contents, not to mention Kelvin's notes.

The time that Casimir had other uses for, like reading books or getting high. Perhaps he'd even indulge in some knitting while smoking a pipe packed full of Myth, of course.

Casimir ran his hands through his ash-blonde hair. He needed air, needed a second to not be suffocated by the room he was in. Casimir walked onto the balcony. The suns were beginning to rise, and he'd be expected for breakfast soon. That he had to dress himself properly to assure his father he was fit to rule one day.

That was a rule he didn't care for. Having to be presentable all day was a burden he wasn't fond of; it was an entirely unrealistic expectation. Was he expected not to sleep next?

Though he supposed he had already followed that rule.

Casimir hated the thought of servants having to come to his aid daily, so he dismissed them entirely. Surely, he could dress and bathe himself.

Not having any doting staff also allowed more time for him to be alone. His father had chewed him out when word reached his ears, but the scolding was worth the peace. Privacy was a luxury, one he didn't have often. No servants would tend to him while in his chamber was what he had once ordered. The only order he had ever willingly given to those who worked inside the castle.

But his mind was nothing but peaceful today. No. Not at all. Instead, it was flooded with thoughts. So many thoughts that spiraled as he recounted Kelvin's actions.

Why were the books so important to Kelvin? And who was he supposed to hide them from? Why even give them to me? They'd probably be better off in the library. It's not like anybody actually visits that place.

But he unfortunately respected his Uncle. Far more than he respected his father. Meaning the books would remain in his room, like Kelvin had oddly wanted. Perhaps he'd get around to reading them sometime soon.

For his Uncle to cause a fuss, he assumed something inside of them had to be significant. What it may contain, he couldn't fathom at this hour. Stomach growling as he began to prepare himself for the day to come.

Pray it to be an uneventful one so he could hide out in his room earlier than predicted, hopefully with a pipe placed snugly between his lips.

***

Casimir nodded to every single person he passed, paying his respect to the servants. But he strode down the hall, dressed in his usual attire.

He made his way to the dining area, the large table flushed with divine-smelling dishes.

He glanced around the room. It was entirely void of people. Not a single person was sat in their usual spot.

I'm not early in the slightest.

"Excuse me, Prince Casimir?" Behind him was a servant bowing her head to him. The voice was meek and fragile.

"You may speak as you wish." He quirked a brow, confused as to what was happening.

"Oh, um, of course. The King said breakfast was canceled today. Some court dealings took priority."

"Thank you," He paused, looking expectedly at the girl.

"My name is Cadence, Your Highness."

"Well, thank you for informing me, Cadence. Please make sure the food gets delivered to the servants' wing. I'd hate for all of it to go to waste." Her brown eyes widened as she struggled to spit out words. "But this was prepared for the Court."

"Nonsense, it'd be a shame for it to spoil. Enjoy it, Cadence."

Casimir left. If a court was being held, why the hell wasn't he informed? Kelvin had mentioned nothing of it this morning. Kelvin had been dressed well, like he would if going to court. Should that have been suspicion enough?

Once again, Casimir walked the halls of the castle, each wing holding memories from his childhood. Each hall, void of any kind of art, looked exactly the same. He was sure he could wander endlessly in the halls, all the same.

Then he approached the council room, and for a minute, he debated knocking. The voices were muffled, but he could hear them. Something was definitely going on.

Dusting his shoulders and leaving no room for him to change his decision. Casimir pushed the door open. Striding right into the ongoing session.

All eyes went to him. The conversation turned silent as he looked for Kelvin. Who was sat with wide brows, and his blue eyes seemed to pierce Casimir's skull.

Casimir held his head high, not willing to be looked down upon. Part of him was enraged he was left out. Skipping voluntarily was one thing, but to not even be told was entirely different.

"Sorry, I'm late. A mishap with communication." He walked to his empty chair and took a seat. He dared a look at his father. His face was red, lines forming along his brow.

Then he moved his gaze to Kelvin once more. This time, he looked defeated. What has been discussed thus far?

"It's decided then, Casimir will wed the Princess of Acadar. I have arranged for her to come here in the coming days. As heir to the throne, you will be on your utmost behavior while Princess Melody is here."

Wait. Come again?

"Your majesty, don't you think you're being brash? There is still much for Casimir to learn before he takes a consort." Kelvin was the only one willing to stand up for him. But Casimir knew it would cause no such sway. His Father had made his decision far before holding this meeting.

His fate, we decided.

And his father made it without him.

Planned on making it without him.

"We have no allies. Securing a relationship with the Realm of Mer is of importance. There will be no further discussion of this, this is final. Kelvin, meet me in my office."

His father stormed out, not even looking at Casimir. They had no allies because the other Realms wanted nothing to do with them after Bellheim invaded the Elven Realm.

This was far too sudden of a topic. He must have been planning this for weeks. Or could it be something had changed? Silently, he fiddled with the ring on his finger. Paying little attention to how his ears and neck turned red.

How soon would I be wed? What is he thinking?

Others followed suit in exiting, the air becoming tense. Zara's father was in the room, sending a sympathetic smile towards him.

The Lord of Lispin had always wanted Zara to get Casimir's hand. Though Zara's interests are undoubtedly elsewhere, she'd never tell her father that. At least not until she set into her title as a Lady.

Prying eyes from the court felt like vultures sizing up their prey. Snide remarks and subtle taunts made their way to his ears. He didn't dare allow himself to appear emotional. Everything seemed to be too much, so he simply pushed it down. Channels whatever he feels into a pit in his stomach.

Casimir knew he shouldn't have been shocked. He was nineteen and would be approaching his day of birth soon. Human lifespans were far less than most others.

He was numb, unsure of how he was supposed to feel.

I need to get more Myth.

The shock had undoubtedly been a part of the King's plan. Casimir had interrupted without a reason. That warrants repercussions from his father. With luck, the issue would be brushed under the rug when his father returned.

Luck was never on Casimir's side. It constantly avoids him like some kind of plague. It was similar to his mother's garden, the luckless flower never getting the chance to taste the sun as they were buried by the lucky who overtook them.

He would forever be a wilted flower, hoping for his chance to see the sun.

Chapter 9

If you were to ask Keylan a day ago where he saw himself in the next coming days, the answer wouldn't be digging a hole for seventeen dead soldiers. He'd probably say something like researching Bellheim by the comfort of Ellis' fire place.

But no, here he was. Dropping corpse after corpse into the hole his sister was still digging.

Not to mention that there was currently a carver conversing with Ellis inside. Keylan wasn't certain what got him to this point in life, but he could only assume the Gods had something in store for him.

"What happened in Louth, Kaleopei?" It wasn't the time to ask, and he knew that. But he couldn't help himself. It was the first time it had been just him and her since she made the blood promise with Zaratella.

Her face dropped, movements stilling.

"A lot of things happened." This was a start. More than she had ever uttered before. "The whole thing is fucked, Keylan." "You won't tell me?"

Hurt. Keylan was crushed that she wouldn't share her pain.

"It's not that I do want to," She paused. Realizing that she had stopped shoveling. Her body trembled, shaking as she thought more. "I just *can't*. I want to, but every time I think of it, I just get so frustrated."

"What did they do to you, sister?" Kaleopei dropped the shovel and turned on her heel. Moved herself towards the house. She was running away from him. Avoiding the conversation.

"Kaleopei, wait. I didn't mean," She was already inside. His plea fell upon deaf ears.

Keylan finished what he was doing. Covering the hole they dug with dirt. Until the soldiers were no longer visible.

Ellis had almost had a heart attack when we returned in the early hours of the morning. In tow was Zara, still splattered with crimson. Ellis was a saint, a gift from the gods themselves, as she offered her garden as the burial site. Saying it would act as a fertilizer for her future crops.

Zara was currently with the older lady, getting cleaned up after hauling all the men from the inn to here. He didn't wish to know what Ellis was saying to her. That woman had the potential to be scarier than any beast he'd ever encounter if someone provoked her.

He hated that he was left out and not able to provide any help to his sister. Keylan wanted to, wanted to be involved in the downfall of the place that had destroyed Kaleopei.

But he simply was left in the dark.

As he placed the shovels back into the small shed, he saw Ellis. She was motioning for him to come over, a sad smile decorating her aging features. "Child, come eat something."

"I'm not a boy anymore, Ellis." He smiled at her, noting how tired she looked.

"You will always be a boy to me, no matter how gray your hair turns." He recoiled in fake hurt. Running his dirty hands through his hair.

"I haven't a single gray strand."

"Kept working and stressing yourself, and you will."

***

It wasn't until a few hours later, when he was relaxing in his room, did Keylan saw his sister again. Kaleopei knocked at the door, soft and unlike her.

He knew she had offered Zara her bed for the night. One night of rest before the three of them would begin planning. Besides, he was used to her being close. Secretly, he missed the days they'd spent sleeping in the same room. She was only ever an arm's length away from him. Keylan was constantly assured of her safety.

Kaleopei's hair was still damp but pulled back into a braid, her eyes painfully tired.

Neither of them said a word. Silently, she sat on the edge of his bed, laying her head in his lap. Keylan was quick to cradle her head.

Her skin was frozen to the touch. How long had she sat in the tub?

He reached for a wool blanket, tucking it around her shoulders tightly.

She looked like a tired and frightened child. Not something he was used to seeing from his explosive and determined sister.

"They kept me locked up in the beginning." Her voice was so soft. So unsure. Nothing like the prideful and courageous sister he knew so well. "Starved me, kept me weak."

Anger would do no good in this situation. So he let his rage simmer beneath his skin, not letting it show as he toyed with the end of her braid.

Keylan would listen to her story. Hold her as she spoke and do his part to lessen the burden she carried.

"I didn't speak a word for a month to any of them, barely even touched the food a soldier would shove through the bars. I fought like hell, trying to strangle them in the beginning. But they would bring a Carver to subdue me..." Her voice trailed off; he couldn't see her eyes. Keylan imagined they were void of the usual fire in that sea of green. "Then they brought me to the pit. Tossed me in with two other Elfs. They looked at me with hope in their eyes, Key. They wanted me to do something. *Anything* to try and save them."

The air was still, as though even the spring breeze wanted to hear the story his sister was sharing, as the gods themselves listened.

"They had no fight left in them. Louth broke them far before they lost their lives."

Kaleopei was trembling. Shaking in his arms. All he could do was pull her closer, running his hands over her forehead as she shook.

"I never learned their names. The pit claimed them. It was dark, so dark. The only light was from this crystal that covered the top of the pit. I think the Carvers used it as a conduit. It was strong, powerful... it terrified me. It just felt so wrong." She turned to her back, wet eyes looking up at him. Even now, fear was etched into her face. Each word she spoke was a reminder of what she had endured.

"They sucked every last bit of magic out of those two. Indescribable pain coursed through me as they tried harvesting my flame. But I held on. Held on so fucking hard. I wouldn't let them take it."

Silent tears cascaded down her cheeks, staining his trousers. Keylan didn't care. He just kept her in his arms. Nothing, for this moment, could get to her. She was safe.

"You are the strongest person I know. You're not there anymore. *You* survived."

It was so much worse than he could imagine. The horrors she endured without him.

"I snapped Key. I was so sick of everything they were doing. The second time I went to the pit, they cut my ears, trying to break my spirits. One after another, I watched others turn into husks. Those in the pit *couldn't* do anything. Except watch as more and more were slaughtered."

Keylan let her sob into him. Kaleopei desperately needed this. Needed an outlet that wasn't just bottling it all up. So he became her rock, grounding her.

"Then I lost control in the pit. All that magic I built up over the months, I just released it. I was able to push through the lead cuffs. The crystal shattered. I used the shards to kill every single soldier and carver I saw. Until I made it out." Guilt. Pure, unending guilt was what she felt.

"You did what you had to. *You* got yourself out of that place. They deserved any amount of pain you dealt to them. The world is not kind, Kaleopei. You knew it was the only choice."

He could never judge her, not for doing what she had to do to survive. He understood why she was so hellbent on figuring out Bellheim's motive. Zara offered that.

At that moment, he felt for his twin. His other half. The half that didn't stray from him.

He would make sure it stayed that way.

Keylan would fight against any odds to ensure Kaleopei got to feel happy once more.

At that moment, he understood her, would burden any pain he could to make her life easier. But he knew it wasn't that simple. She would always bear this pain.

"I love you, Keylan. I feel like I don't say it enough." Pain ached in his chest. Pride and admiration was something he had always felt towards his older sister. Nothing would ever change that. Even the gods themselves couldn't make him turn away from his sister.

"And I love you, Kaleopei. Do not stray from me."

"Not in this life."

Keylan doesn't know how long they sat in each other's silence. The comfort of being close was enough to settle all the rage he felt.

Silently, he kissed her forehead, "Or the next."

Chapter 10

Casimir rushed to get dressed. Lacing buttons and tying his royal sash tightly from shoulder to hip. The red was a profound contrast from the deep blue of his tunic.

It had only been a day.

Not even a full cycle of the sun.

That was all the time he had before meeting Princess Melody.

The very night it was announced, he received word that she would be here at dawn.

Instead of sleeping, he indulged himself in top-shelf myth. And got high.

So very high.

Which left him with semi-bloodshot eyes and an itch for sleep. Nonetheless, he got ready. Barely recognizing as Kelvin came into the room, bearing a concerned face.

"Casimir."

"I don't have pants on." Casimir tripped over himself, pulling the trousers up swiftly.

"That is the least of my worries right now. I need to tell you something."

"Can it wait until I'm clothed?"

"I don't have that kind of time." Casimir laced his pants, then turned around, seeing the lifeless face of his Uncle. An indescribable feeling of dread began to build.

"What's happened?"

"I tried, Cas. You have to know I tried."

"What do you mean? About the marriage, it was bound to come eventually. It's not your fault. In actuality, I believe it to be mine. I was angry and made a brash decision." He took in the sight before him. Gone was the confident nobleman. It looked like he hadn't taken care of himself in weeks. But Casimir had seen him yesterday. He didn't look this bad.

"No! Not about that." His demeanor shook something within Casimir. "You have to know I tried."

"Tried what Kelvin? You're not making sense." Kelvin trembled, tears welling up in the corner of his ocean eyes.

"Everything, I tried everything. Nothing worked." The spacious seemed suffocating as he watched his Uncle work himself into hysterics. The usual large windows were so impossibly close, the balcony so far. Casimir didn't know what to say. "I couldn't do anything with him watching me like a hawk since the last time."

"I don't understand!" This was not how he pictured his morning going.

"You have to understand, Casimir. You're the only one left who can fix this. You *have* to fix this."

"Fix what?" There was a loud bang at the door. Kelvin was the first to move, taking the books from his desk. "What is going on?"

He shoved them behind the plush silk pillows on his bed.

"Keep 'em' safe, Cas. Find them."

Another burst came from the door. Then, guards were flooding the room.

"Kelvin Haven, you are under arrest with the charges of treason."

Casimir stood still, unsure of what was happening. But his voice found its way out, "I demand you to seize this arrest."

"You don't have the clearance," Only one other person had higher authority than him. "The King himself ordered the arrest."

His Father suspects Kelvin of treason. What did Kelvin do?

Casimir's head raced. Time seemed to move slowly. They shackled his Uncle, who didn't even resist. Dragged him out of his room. Casimir watched.

He couldn't do anything.

What could he do?

His Father was no doubt already in the throne room, awaiting the arrival of the Princess.

The last guard bowed his head, "Sorry to disturb you, your highness."

Then, even he ducked out of the room.

Silence.

Not the usual peaceful he had come to enjoy.

No. This was deafening.

Stillness. Deafness.

Casimir wanted to scream, pull the skin off his bones.

Anything that would make him feel something.

He was already striking a match before he could make another choice.

He'd be late.

He didn't care.

Casimir took a deep breath, letting the smoke fill his being. Filled him with something apart from grief.

Anything was better than nothing.

The smoke flooded out his nostrils.

Again. Again. And Again.

Until his mind stopped racing.

Until he could think straight.

Until he wasn't a crowned prince.

Until he was a nobody.

Zara was right; We don't get choices.

He placed the pipe onto the desk next to the crown that sat atop an assortment of novels.

He'd give up everything to be a character in a book. They had it so easy.

He looked in the mirror. Casimir was a wreck. He decided he didn't care.

Shaking his head to try to tame the short locks on his head, then placed the crown atop his head. The gold was heavy on his shoulders.

Casimir breathed out once more.

Then made his way to the throne room.

There wasn't a single lax bone in his body. Casimir was entirely tense. Swaggering into the throne room, many officials gathered for the arrival of the Mer Princess of Acadar.

A brief look to the throne to see his Father, who eyed him up and down. But his right-hand side was empty, where Kelvin was supposed to be.

But nobody stood as the King's aid.

A reminder that what happened in his room was real.

The room was as grand as he remembered. Large pillars made of quartz lined the interior, decorated with the red colors of Bellheim.

Tall, stained-glass windows, each housing the red sun. Telling the story of his, it rises and sets, bestowing luck and fortune onto the Human Realm. It was intricate and beautifully made. That was the King he wanted to be. Wanted people to look to him for hope and not fear.

He omitted the part when the second sun rose and bestowed a drought upon the humans. Continuously forgetting the legend that they had to turn to eating their family for survival. No. That was left out entirely. Like the King simply wished to forget history.

The throne itself was placed on a pedestal of white carved stone, held above where the visitors would enter, symbolizing his power over them.

Wordlessly, Casimir twirled the ring on his finger, taking his throne a step below his Father.

"Glad for you to join us, son."

"I wanted to look my best," That was the only exchange between the two. Nothing else was said on either side. Casimir was grateful for the silence, unsure of what his mouth would filter. He prayed to the Suns, both suns, the King didn't see his eyes with too much detail. Not able to identify the blood shot side effects from inhaling Myth.

They didn't wait long before the large oak doors were opened. Revealing a small entourage, clad in a sea foam green. They bore tridents and had glamorous jewelry, most of which were pearls and sea glass.

Casimir had only ever heard stories about the people who hailed from the Mer Realm. Many races thrived and co-inhabited the land, unlike the single-raced Kingdom of humans.

In the center, surrounded by guards who carried in heights, was a woman. She stood rather tall, humanoid, with deep brown skin. Her hair, locks of white, with a teal tinge at their ends.

The room fell silent, no one daring to speak.

Slowly, they approached, moving through the space with unspoken confidence. It may have been the Myth, but they looked magical. The woman was radiant, transcendent even.

They reached the pedestal. She had mesmerizing sea foam eyes. She gazed up, but she held herself confidently. Not letting the height difference sway her swagger. Casimir would dare say it made her brow quirk in a challenge.

As if speaking out of turn, all eyes were on her. Her voice was like a song.

"You have a lovely Kingdom, Your Highness. My travels went well, with no note-worthy issues. I look forward to our partnership." As if to further her point, she dipped her chin the slightest bit, but her eyes never left the dais. Another silent challenge against the throne.

"I thought it was agreed upon to only have two guards?"

"My Father did convey that to me, but I have quite the attachment to my handmaiden. So she will be keeping my company along with two of my men. The rest will proceed to the Seas at the earliest convenience. I thought it was unwise to travel here with only two soldiers. What if we were to come across one of the human beasts that lurk on this continent."

"*My continent.*" He corrected the girl, "This miscommunication will not happen again, it will be overlooked this one. But don't go making a habit of undermining my authority. Do we have an understanding?"

Posed like a question, but the diction said otherwise. It was a threat. The two engaged in a silent battle of dominance, and for once, Casimir wasn't sure his father was entirely winning.

"Of course, I never had any ill will. Simply a precautionary measure to ensure my safety whilst traveling. My family would be beside themselves if something were to happen to me before I was wed."

Casimir hadn't uttered a word, the exchange between the two a battle of words. The Princess did not shy away from the onslaught that was his Father. She spits his icy words right back, only with composure and a sweet tone. One look at the King's face showed he wasn't pleased.

"Very good then. The Crown Prince will be your guide should you have any questions."

Briefly, the Princess looked at him, putting a face to the name.

"I appreciate the accommodations."

"We will discuss ceremony details when I return from my excursion. Until then, you will familiarize yourself with my Kingdom and Prince Casimir. Your belongings are being delivered to your room for the time being."

"I thank you for the welcome," Only the tiniest dip of her head signified the gratitude. Then she was moving, following the escorts that the King had lying in wait.

Casimir went to stand.

"Sit down, Boy. This discussion isn't done."

From the opposite entrance to the one the Princess left through was a commotion.

Bound and shackled, tied together by the manacles. There were six of them, all prisoners of some sort, being hurled into the throne room. They neared the center of the room, still lined up like cattle. His Father barked orders into the room.

Silently, Casimir gathered what was happening as they brought out a platform.

Ropes were slung over the rafters, one for each of the prisoners.

In the center of them all was the blue-eyed advisor. His Uncle is condemned to death by his own brother.

Casimir was going to throw up.

He should throw a fit cause of some kind of scene. Anything to give Kelvin a chance. Should ask what crimes they have committed and see if the punishment is just.

Casimir didn't do any of those things.

He sat upon his throne, no better than the man who sat behind him.

One by one, the captives were brought onto the platform. They all looked so lifeless. Two of them had pointed Ears. They probably didn't even do anything; they simply got caught existing.

The elf with blonde hair, braided into a crown, pointed his face upwards. Locking eyes with both the King and Casimir.

"Your injustice will be repaid tenfold. You're running on a clock, the time nea-"

The guards removed the platforms, their words dying in their throats.

Casimir wasn't sure how long he sat there. He couldn't bring himself to look away, let alone move. The threats dripped from the elf's mouth, not even reregistering as he just stared at the corpses swaying gently.

He was as lifeless as the bodies that hung in front of him.

"That's how we deal with insubordination. Should have let that Sea Princess see what her fate will be if she continues to be untamed."

Casimir wanted to be angry, wanted to feel *something*.

"Try not to disappoint me in my absence, son. Tame her."

Chapter 11

"I sent word via raven last night. With any luck, the King should have received the letter this morning." The teenagers all stood around Ellis' dining table. A map of the Realms held down by various trinkets. Each of them refreshed after a unique previous day. "Which means we only about six days until the King reaches Louth and realizes that I never even made it there."

They had been at this since dawn. Going back and forth for the best plan of action. Kaleopei pointed at the map, forging a path.

"We ditch Alstead, loosely follow the Stillwater and make our way to the capital away from any kind of road." Keylan nodded, agreeing with her. Zaratella didn't seem so keen on the initial idea, pushing back.

"That's a death wish waiting to happen. There are no wards off the roads. We'd be a constant moving target for any beast looking for a snack." The twins shared a smile. Kaleopei looked across the table, locking eyes with the iron-eyed girl.

"That won't be a problem. There isn't a single beast in the human realm we haven't killed. From mud crawlers to vilken, we've dealt with it all."

It was unspoken in the surrounding air, but there was a lack of trust. Zara wouldn't trust the twins to have her back continually. Kaleopei was able to decipher that much.

"My sister speaks true. We were practically an extermination unit a few years back when they were refurbishing the irrigation system from Stillwater to Alstead. You'll be in safe hands." The onyx-eyed girl looked between them, uncertainty spread across her face. Kaleopei preferred the confident Zaratella. "Besides, the worst we'll see this time of year is far more tame than a vilken. Kaleopei just likes to brag about her talents."

"I thought Elves were supposed to be connected with nature or whatever?" Zara was still skeptical, yet made conversation.

Kaleopei peered at Ellis, who snorted from the counter, the fresh smell of herbal tea wafting through the kitchen.

"An unspoken connection is true. But if provoked, we have every right to protect ourselves or the creatures that can't." Keylan explained, while Kaleopei still bore daggers into the back of Ellis' head. Why would she be laughing if not to provoke the green-eyed girl?

"That makes sense. I've heard tales of the beasts that live in the northern part of the Elven Realm. My father used vilken as a way to make me do chores when I was young, but some of those northern beasts terrified me."

Zara wasn't wrong, the creatures here were much more tame. Kaleopei smiled fondly, remembering all the times her Father would show her how to brandish a sword in case a stalker decided to attack. And his shocked face when Maizelin waltzed into the foyer with the head of one.

That had been an event.

"I can't believe I'm agreeing to this." Zaratella laughed at herself. So they continued planning the route, which Kaleopei would lead.

"What even is our plan when we reach the Capital, neither I nor Kaleopei have even set foot there. We'd be flying blind." Keylan voiced what the twins had been conscious about.

"The plan is to find information regarding what the King is truly trying to achieve in Louth. I know on good authority that he's storing power in those purple crystals, but beyond that, it's sensitive intel." The girl's voice remained level, carefully picking her words as she thought about the dilemma they faced. "I was trusted with a lot, but that seemed to be above my pay."

"So we break into the Royal castle, steal some things and then leave?" That was one way to dumb it down. But Kaleopei said it anyway, noticing her brother stifling a snort.

"Yes and no, getting in will be the easy part. I have many contacts in Bellheim. But the King's office is where we will run into the most trouble. It's locked in its own wing. Only select people are even granted access. We'll have to play our cards extremely well."

Kaleopei nodded along to her words, absorbing as much as she could.

"I can draw a map if you can remember the castle well?" Zara nodded to her question. "Good, then I think we have a good basis to leave."

Ellis had prepared a large sack, full to the brim, with whatever she thought was necessary for the trip. Kaleopei embraced her tightly, a goodbye. Not forever, but for a while.

The other two didn't say a word as Ellis pulled Kaleopei closer to her chest.

Ellis smelt of lavender, the scent, deep and rich. Kaleopei breathed it in. Committing the floral scent to memory. For a moment, she recalled all the memories that they had shared in this house. Kaleopei would give anything to have grown into a mundane life, but that had never been in the cards for her.

"Stay out of trouble, Children." When they finally pulled apart, Ellis was the first to wipe her eyes.

"Kaleopei will have a hard time honoring that."

"Watch your mouth, Key." Kaleopei swatted at the male. Keylan feigned hurt, moving away.

"Zara, watch over my children. And for God's sake, come and visit sooner than later."

Keylan slung the pack of assorted things over his back, along with Skipper and another pack.

How he managed not to topple over would remain a mystery to Kaleopei. He embraced Ellis once more, then headed for the door.

"They'll be back, I promise Ellis." Kaleopei grabbed the older woman's hand once the other two had left through the door.

"Is that your word?"

She wasn't naive. Ellis had undoubtedly caught the wording.

"Always."

"Then come back to me."

***

"So, is that woman like your mother?" Zaratella broke the silence when they departed. Unsure of what should be said between the trio.

"Ellis?" Keylan held up the rear, and Kaleopei the point. She took them south, towards the Stillwater, to create some distance from the road.

"Yes, She seems rather sweet."

"She may as well be. Took us in when we were nine. Her husband was an elf." Kaleopei remained silent, having not said anything since leaving Alstead. Choosing to focus on the path ahead instead of conversation.

"That's kind of her." An understatement entirely.

"She means the world to us. Risked everything for us." Keylan's words let a faint smile raise to Kaleopei's face.

"Where were you two born?" Kaleopei dared to raise a brow at Keylan. He dismissed the glare. A subtle look that conveyed a small amount of relief to his sister.

"Eviera. Though I can't say I remember too much about it."

"I heard it was beautiful and that the landscape was beautiful."

"It *is* beautiful." Those were the only words Kaleopei had said.

"How'd you become a Carver?" Keylan was quick to change the subject. Not wanting to raise tension any more than need be.

"Wasn't my choice." Kaleopei listened carefully, "I was only eleven when I found a conduit crystal in my Father's study. Long story short, I was good at it. So, my training began young. I was officially inducted a year and a half ago by the King himself."

"Yet you'd go against him?"

"In a heartbeat." There was no hesitation in her voice, "I learned a lot, being forced to grow up like I did. Something sinister is happening, and I would turn on him in a heartbeat to learn what. He's hurt people I care about. I'd say that warrants some vengeance."

"Comforting." Was Key's response. Snorting as they crossed a small stream.

Kaleopei let their chatter fade out, focusing on the surrounding sounds. Taking deep breaths of the fresh air.

They were surrounded by a forest, tall oaks providing protection from the spring sun and breeze. Soon, the leaves would start dying. Then the cold would come.

This, right here, was her comfort. Being encased in the warmth of the flora.

She allowed herself a moment to take it all in. Allow herself to dissociate from the reality that was coming closer.

She had a chance to stop others from getting hurt. Kaleopei would jump at the chance to make sure no more harm came to her people. Then, perhaps one day, those in hiding would return.

But that was hope for a dreamer, tales she told herself to fend off those nightmares. She, in fact, was a realist. Keylan might still believe in the gods for a shroud of good luck, but she believed in herself. Sometimes, even the brute she called her twin. In no lifetime would she ever put his safety in hands that weren't her own.

Her emerald eyes stilled on movement in front of them. Her ears picked up on the rustle of a bush far before her sight did.

It was still a bit in front of them, not huge. The suns were beginning to set. It was probably a vulture that had swooped in on some prey.

Still, she kept her guard heavy. Not enough to alert Keylan, who was still deep in conversation with Zaratella. At least they were getting along.

Kaleopei glanced into the tree line, keeping her eyes peeled for anything lurking beyond.

That's when she saw the red eyes glaring at them.

She looked back. They were gone. At this point, she stopped moving.

Her eyes danced along the shade-covered area, scanning for those eyes once more. But they were gone.

Nothing in the human realm had eyes like that. Kaleopei was sure of it. Only a wrent and those wouldn't be caught dead lurking around in daylight.

It felt like it was watching them.

"Kaleopei, what's wrong?"

But she could just be tired. They had been moving for a decent amount of the day. Would it be worth putting the other two on edge?

Like a hunter stalking their prey, she watched. Waited...

Nothing.

It could've been a flower reflecting in the setting suns, or simply her eyes playing tricks on her.

"Just a hare. Caught me by surprise."

Zara bought it and kept up the pace behind her. Kaleopei didn't even look. She knew Keylan would question it later. Somehow, he always knew.

But he wouldn't dare to mention it in front of Zara, he'd wait until they were alone. For that, she was grateful.

"How much longer until we should settle for the night?" Zara was the one to mention it. The sunlight was claimed by night as hours passed.

"Why? Can't keep up?" Kaleopei threw a sly smirk over her shoulder.

"I just think moving in light is advantageous compared to guessing."

"I'm not guessing a thing; I know the forest like the palm of my hand."

"Well, then, yes, I need some beauty rest."

"That was all you had to say, darling." Keylan held a smile but didn't say anything. That little shit.

"Who's in the mood for dried venison?" Keylan pulled out some salty-smelling pieces of cured meat.

"Did you just take those out of your pocket?" Zara looked wildly at him.

"Yes. It's pocket meat." That earned him a slap to the back of the head from Kaleopei, who was rolling out a bedroll.

"Don't ever refer to it as *pocket meat*. I'd like to keep my appetite, thank you very much."

"Fine. More pocket meat for me then." The twins stared at each other before breaking into a full belly laugh.

"There is something wrong with you."

"That means there is also something wrong with you, sweet sister." Kaleopei saw Zara smiling, whilst making her own bedroll on the grass.

"If you say so, Key."

"Oh, I know so."

Chapter 12

Casimir returned to his room, the sun still showing off the cloudy afternoon. He had been approached been some of his Father's council, asking questions. Questions he didn't know the answer to.

Somehow, he had ended up back in his bed, looking at the ceiling, eyes glassy with unsaid emotion.

He vaguely recalled seeing Princess Melody's things moved into the vacant room across from him. Usually reserved for when Zaratella visited.

After everything that happened today, he was expected to court the girl.

Casimir dragged his hands down his face. Turning so he could cover his face with the smooth silk of the pillows.

He recoiled. Feeling a lump underneath him.

The books.

Kelvin had shoved them into his bed before he was arrested.

They were the exact same as the day prior. Still not legible to Casimir's eyes. But they had to mean *something* to his Uncle. Why would he risk his last moments, giving them to Casimir?

Setting the battered books on the ground, he sat. Laying them out, trying to see if he could make sense of anything.

Soft footsteps echoed in the hallway. Casimir had left the door cracked. Unintentional, blinded by his own feelings.

"Prince Casimir?" The voice was soft, song-like. The Princess was barefoot but still wearing the same simple silk dress decorated with pearls and shells.

Casimir cleared his throat, trying to make his face pleasant.

"Have you settled in alright?"

"Yes, I have. I actually wanted to apologize for the atmosphere I created with the King. I was tired from the journey, and my words reflected such."

"Are you kidding? Seeing him so worked up was the highlight of my day."

It wasn't a lie.

The morning hadn't been entirely terrible. At least it had one upside.

Melody shifted her weight back and forth, cautiously taking in the sights of his room. She was also forced into this situation. It wasn't just him.

"Is he always like that?"

"Unfortunately. Can't say he's the most welcoming person."

Those ocean eyes gazed at him like she was picking him apart.

"Have I upset you?" Her voice was cautious, not wanting to pry and be her meek expression.

"Not in the slightest. I'm just adjusting."

"I can imagine my Mother was against this arrangement entirely. But I've accepted my fate. As the youngest daughter, I didn't have much of a say. I always assumed I'd be sent off to another realm. Though the Human Realm did come as a bit of a shock."

It was unsaid, but he could see the turmoil turning behind her gaza, forcing herself to hold a conversation with him.

"Well, I hope I'm not too insufferable. Would you like a tour?"

"That sounds lovely. I can't say I'm not curious."

"Then let's not delay."

***

Melody's company wasn't what he'd thought it would be. She was kind and curious. Asked plenty of questions about the architecture and some of the materials used. Genuinely aiming to learn about what little culture the humans had.

Casimir found himself smiling throughout the better part of the day. Actually enjoying his time with the girl. He wasn't high, and he was still able to get through the day. Able to push away any thoughts about the morning and night prior.

Now wasn't the time to deal with that. Not when he had so much on his plate. He was supposed to be stepping up for his father, but all he wished to do was curl up in his bed with a book and some myth.

"What's out there?" She pointed to the garden square. His mother's garden.

"My favorite part of the castle," Gently he took her hand. Pushing through the doors and into the grassy hideaway.

"It's gorgeous." He watched as she took it all in, looking at the long, overgrown bushes and plants.

"It used to be so colorful. My mother took such pride in it."

"I've heard about the Queen's condition. I'm terribly sorry."

"She doesn't see anyone nowadays; she just stays held up in her room. I only see her rarely."

"That is terrible. Is it an illness?" Casimir didn't miss the way her voice changed, gathering intel. He actually found himself smiling at the fact.

"The doctors think it's something new; they haven't seen anything like it before. She's seen many doctors from across the realm."

"I'm well versed with medicinal remedies. Perhaps Acadar has some insight? Assuming you'd, and your King would be open to outside aid?"

His Father would be furious if a non-human even dared to look after the Queen. That didn't diminish the fact that it could prove useful. Many of the Mer are versed in healing power.

"That sounds like something worth exploring. I'll bring it up to the council. However, I can't guarantee my opinion will have any sway." Silently, he recalled the last time he had been in the council chamber. With all those eyes on him, each one holding some kind of malice towards him.

"I'm glad I can offer that. She seems to mean a great deal to you."

"She does."

Casimir breathed in the scents. Looking over all the wildflowers that were overtaking the grass. It was wild and beautiful. In the corner of the garden, he made note of the wilted and dying flowers underneath a large shrub.

"What other slight views does the castle have?"

Casimir showed her everything he could. To some of the few paintings that lined the smaller dining areas, ones that were old and worn. None from the modern era. They wandered, him leading her to the library, showing the thousands of books and the corner that he deemed as the best reading nook.

Walked her through the kitchen, showing off some of his own culinary preferences. Melody went along with it all, absorbing whatever Casimir threw at her.

The two of them ended back in the hallway, where it began. The sun long set as Melody rocked on her still shoeless heels.

He'd make a note to ask about that in the future.

Their future. Because that's what was in store for him.

"I had fun, Casimir."

"Same to you, Melody."

"Mel, only people in court call me Melody. It's too formal for my liking." There was a pause, "I wasn't sure what I was expecting when I came here. I can say with certainty that it wasn't this."

"Likewise, Mel." Casimir was glowing, eyes creasing from how wide his smile was. Wordlessly, he placed a kiss on the back of her hand. The rich, deep tone was glimmering in the low candlelight.

"See you in the morning?" She took a couple of steps back. He nodded, fighting an odd feeling that welled up inside him.

"Of course."

Melody disappeared into the door behind her. He watched until the door shut. Finding himself pushing against the door just in case.

Placing a hand on his chest, he felt the beating grow faster. Casimir clutched at his tunic, sinking into his thoughts of being alone.

That was what he was. Utterly alone, no dotting Uncle who will check up on him. No friendly face when walking into those council sessions. Kelvin wouldn't be there for advice or able to offer a shoulder to lean on.

All he had was himself in that swarm of vultures who wanted to tear him to pieces.

Casimir receded back to his own room, lighting the candles. The unfamiliar books are still strewn about on the floor. He ignored them all, picking up a rather classic novel, and settled himself down. Escaping into a world that wasn't his own.

Chapter 13

They had been traveling for three days, and finally, they had some sort of end in sight. There was only so much never-ending small talk Kaleopei could handle. Keylan and Zaratella were so much alike that it actually scared her. So much so that when Skipper got brought up, Zaratella thought it was unique. Just wait until she heard how that name came to be.

Kaleopei was still on edge. Constantly checking over her shoulder, feeling something unusual. It wasn't magical. At least, she didn't think it was. Keylan hadn't said anything about the behavior, but it was obvious he wanted to. Constantly sending the girl worried glances, or quick to offer comforting gestures.

The sun was beginning to give into the oncoming night. The moon wasn't bright tonight. Good for sneaking into a heavily monitored castle. The capital skyline was just on the horizon. They had made it.

"We'll go through the sewage way, staying off the streets." Zara appeared at Kaleopei's side, Keylan only a step behind.

"Do you know the sewage way well enough to guide us?" Kaleopei raised a brow at the carver.

"I know the city well."

"What about the sewers?"

"Not entirely, but they can't be too much different, right?"

Keylan laughed, sensing his sister's growing frustration. That earned him an elbow to the ribs.

"We're going to trek through filth to *maybe* find a way to the castle."

"It's either that or we scale the wall around the castle. But that's a feat in itself, usually heavily fortified. Especially in the King's absence."

Scaling a wall seemed more efficient than wandering aimlessly in the dark, especially where Zara was concerned. She would be flying blind, unlike the twins, who had more sensitive eyes.

"How tall of a wall are we talking about?" As if Keylan knew what she was thinking, he shook his head.

"The curtain wall is easily fifty feet. They usually have sentry's atop of them as well."

"How is your climbing, darling?" Kaleopei had a wicked smile, excitement building in her veins. It had been a long while since she had scaled something so tall.

"That's a good one, Kaleopei," She laughed but looked between Keylan and me. "Keylan, please tell me she's joking."

"Wish I could. But she is absolutely convinced to climb."

"Okay, let's for only a moment. Entertainment is the idea that, by some means, we all manage to make it over. We are dealing with fully trained guards. Guards who won't hesitate to kill on sight." Zaratella was pacing, looking between them. Kaleopei noticed the way her skin seemed to glow underneath the pale moonlight.

"Did that stop you when you killed seventeen of them in Alstead?" Kaleopei went for the throat. Still uncertain as to how she accomplished that.

All Zara had said was it was luck they were sleeping. That was it. The twins saw through the lies she fabricated, but didn't call her out on it. All parties were still lightly treading as they navigated their alliance.

"I'm not worried about my safety. I can't protect you two and myself."

The group was still moving, circling the city's outskirts. Luckily, the castle was placed a good distance away from the resident sections. Meaning that the back wall was practically wide open to the landscape.

Lanterns were lit atop the wall, humanoid figures striding around. Keylan and her had never had a problem dispatching Bellheim soldiers before, this time wouldn't be different.

"I recall saying that I can handle myself. Keylan isn't a pushover, either."

Zaratella looked doubtful, glancing between the wall and the twins. Keylan was pulling out a rope from his pack. Tying two strands into a single line.

"Fine, but I'm not responsible for your untimely death should it come to that."

"Deal," Kaleopei tied one end around her waist, already sizing up the stone wall in front of her. It was indeed an intimidating height, but it was aged. Many places for footholds and even some alcoves that she could potentially grip.

She fiddled with a dagger, mapping out weak points in the stone. She could bury the daggers if she needed a quick grip. But that would be loud. Banging metal into the stone would draw attention.

She thrust the rope through the straps of her pack, ensuring it would stay if it slipped off her shoulders. Her bow was next, sliding it around her chest.

"Turn around," Keylan walked up to Kaleopei, tugging at the rope secured around her waist.

"I know how to tie a knot, Key." She whispered, keeping their voices low. Keylan acted as if he didn't even hear her, just continued checking her work. "You're an ass."

"I love you too, Kaleopei." He ruffled the top of her head, then tapped her shoulders. Giving one final tug to the rope around her waist. "Straight shot, no showing off."

"No promises," Kaleopei smiled, walking up the wall. She analyzed a basic route, seeing the places she should step and the dents that looked like they could cave. She shook out her hands, placing the lone dagger between her teeth.

Kaleopei sprung into action, stretching and grabbing. Getting higher and higher with each hold she secured.

"She's insane." She could barely make out the voice of Zaratella from below her. Their hushed voices were nothing more than a slight whisper.

Kaleopei kept scaling, contouring her limbs in whatever fashion she could to gain another foot. She climbed her way, not daring to look down and see how far up she actually was.

Her arms outstretched, reaching for another hold. Fingertips grasping at the weathered stone. She shifted her weight, and the stone pulled away as her grip tightened. Rubble fell from the wall, small chunks of the wall cascading towards the ground.

Kaleopei's face upturned in a grimace, reaching in a different direction. This time, pulling slightly on the rock, checking its stability before putting her weight on it.

The end was in sight, the lip of the upper wall almost within reach. Another couple of feet and her hand graced the top of the stone; slowly, Kaleopei pulled herself up.

A quick glance to see if any of the guards were at least thirty feet away. None of them seemed to be looking in her direction. She used this time to swing her feet over the edge, letting them hit the stone floor with a silent thud.

Taking the dagger out of her mouth, she tied the end of the rope to the hilt. From the vantage point, she could see the inside of the castle walls, seeing the large stone structure looming in the dim moonlight.

The only way to keep the rope taut would be to plunge it into the stone, but that would make noise.

Kaleopei didn't hesitate, using her body as a force to wedge it between a crack. The sound rattled out, and two guards from opposite sides of her turned to her. Seeing Kaleopei crouched down against the ledge.

"You! Halt your actions!"

Her bow was in her hands, still using her foot to secure the dagger. The two guards were closing the distance. Kaleopei nocked the bow, an arrow at the ready.

She let it fly. The iron-tipped arrow embedded itself into the neck of one of the guards. With a swift motion, she was already nocking another arrow, hearing the collapse of the guard behind her.

Kaleopei's breathing relaxed, looking down at the sight her arrow created. This man had a bow at the ready, already aimed at her.

Eyes narrowed at the incoming attack. Kaleopei jumped to her side, letting her own arrow fly as she avoided what would have been a possibly fatal blow. It landed on her thigh.

Once again, her arrow flew, lodging into the bottom of his Addams apple. Kaleopei watched as whatever words were about to come dissipated into a gurgle. Asphyxiated from the blood welling in his own punctuated throat. Collapsing to his knees, the guard clawed at the arrow that suffocated him.

Kaleopei turned on her heel, seeing his companion in the same state. Drowning in their own crimson blood.

Taking a moment, she looked down at her own leg, the arrow only imbedded a few inches into the upper part of her thigh. With a grunt, she broke the arrow right behind the arrowhead, throwing the wooden shaft to the side. Deeming it best to keep in as much blood as possible, Kaleopei ripped the end of her cloak and securely fastened it around her thigh.

"That could've gone better." She kept her head low, using the wall's lip to hide her from the other guards.

One of them was yelling, better to stay low.

Keeping her head and body low, she dragged the body over to the other. Winching as crimson blood stained the stone, holding her breath, Kaleopei pulled the arrows from the two men.

With a quick peripheral check, she wiped the blood on their exposed tunic. Then slipped them back into the quiver on her hip.

"Hello, sister. I smell blood."

"Lower your voice, Key. It's not even mine." Whirling her head around to see Keylan pulling himself over the edge. Doing her best to avoid eye contact as she lied to the male.

"And hello to your friends as well." Kaleopei slapped his chest as he motioned to the two bodies sitting next to each other.

"Where's Zara?"

"Presumably climbing," He was quick to reply. The taut rope was tugging against the lodged dagger, giving them their answer.

"You're useless," Kaleopei muttered. She peeked her head over the side. Through the darkness, she could make out the pale figure of Zaratella, slowly inching her way up.

"I'm an asset, actually." He was grabbing the dagger, backing himself up, so his back was pressed against the edge. Then he was pulling, drawing the rope closer and closer to himself.

"No, your muscles are the real asset. You just so happen to be a package deal." Kaleopei's voice was just under a whisper, soft as not to alert any of the surrounding watches.

Another look over the edge, showed Zaratella was nearing the top. Kaleopei dropped her arm, using her head to notion to it. Zara's face turned before she reached out, locking fingers. Kaleopei pulled her up over the edge and ushered for her to stay low.

"Holy gods," Zaratella was winded.

"My arms are not meant to be used like that."

Regaining her breath, she saw the two bodies. "Oh, gods."

"In my defense, they tried to shoot me first." Kaleopei quipped, hands up and in a defensive position. She ignored the pain that flared in her leg.

"Where do we go from here?" Keylan was the one to peek out into the interior of the wall. The landscape of the castle grounds spanned for at least a hundred feet before the large structure ahead of them. It was grassy plains decorated with wildflowers and carefully kept hedges.

Under different circumstances, Kaleopei would think they are gorgeous. The architecture was different from any castle she'd seen before. With a gray-colored stone and ivy growing from the cracks, the castle was huge.

"We need to get to that eastern wing," Zaratella pointed vaguely, centering the twins' vision on one of the many perturbing wings. "From there, I can get us inside without being spotted."

"So we just stand between a dozen archers and a castle. Easy, right?" Kaleopei etched the route into her mind. The trio would have to be utterly silent the entire time. Keylan clasped a hand over her shoulder, giving her a reassuring look.

"Lucky for us, we've got the better shot."

"Can't shoot more than one arrow at once." Keylan was met with her icy cold stare boring into his green eyes.

"You two are quite strange," The iron-eyed girl looked between the duo. "There are stairs inside the wall. We just need to get to a tower point. The closest is probably the east stairs. Then from there, it's basically just a straight dash to the eastern wing."

"You could have said that before." Kaleopei was already moving, using the wall as cover. A bloody arrow was already nocked into the bow, lowered just below her eye.

The three moved in unison, keeping low. Kaleopei could make out where the stairs would be.

"How many guards are usually on the stairs?"

"One above, one below, maybe?" Zara answered, gaining both of the twins' gazes. "What, I've never actually been up here. Just a wild guess."

"Do you know what's inside the towers?"

"Stairs... probably?" Zara shrugged. Definitely reassuring.

Kaleopei shook her head, seeing a guard now in their sight. He was peering out into the woods over the edge. She readied her bow, almost releasing it until Zaratella pressed her shoulder.

"I can handle this one," The twins watched curiously. The girl moved her hands. Drawing the blood from the arrow, Kaleopei held and into the air. Kaleopei gawked as the blood took the shape of an arrow's tip. Then lost track as it went flying toward the guard. The next thing she could see was a trickle of blood flowing out of the man's temple. His body was slumping forward, off the railing.

"That definitely isn't in the usual arsenal of a Carver."

"I'm special for a reason," Zara winked, continuing on as if nothing had happened.

She had the nerve to call us strange.

Blood magic: Zaratella had just used blood magic. Can humans even do that?

"Words later. Run now." Keylan was still crouching, moving as fast as his feet would carry. The girls followed suit, Kaleopei taking a moment to listen. Faintly, she could make out the sudden exhale of a person below the surface of the wall.

"At least one below." Keylan was pulling on the hatch, peering into the staircase. Nodding at his sister's words.

"Wreak havoc, sister." Without a word, Kaleopei dropped into the darkness. Emerald eyes can just make out shapes in the dim lighting.

The stairs whirled downward in a spiral motion. At the mid-level sat a man whittling a stick with the edge of his short sword.

Kaleopei didn't even let the arrow fly. Simply used her entry as a surprise to deliver a swift kick to his temple with her injured leg. The eyes of the guard rolled back before slumping to the ground. Humans were never the most perceptive of races, especially when surrounded by darkness.

"Let's go," She muttered under her breath. Keylan would hear it without issue. Without looking behind, she kept descending, careful to pick up any other signs of life. There wasn't any.

All that was between them was the castle grounds and the wing in front of them.

"Did I mention it wasn't on the ground floor?" Zara came up next to her, wincing as she saw the height of the walls.

"I thought you said you could get in without issue?"

"Well, I can. It's just we need to get to that upper window. I have the key." To further per point, she spun a ring of keys around her thumb.

"Please tell me you grabbed two ropes?" Kaleopei turned to face her brother. Sheepishly, he had a hand behind his head. "Taking that as a no."

"You didn't either!"

"I wasn't the one who held it last."

"The details aren't relevant." Kaleopei rolled her eyes at his antics. Instead, choosing to glance at the wall in front of them and the window they needed to reach. It wouldn't be impossible to scale. She'd just need a boost from Keylan.

"So we're screwed?" Zaratella cringed as the two argued.

"No, not yet, at least. I can reach the ivy if Keylan throws me." Kaleopei nodded along to her words, knowing it would be a risky maneuver. "Then I should be able to make it to the window."

"You're just going to throw her?"

"Got any other suggestions, Darling?" Kaleopei smiled at the pale-skinned girl.

"No, please, continue."

It wasn't anything the twins hadn't done before. Keylan had crouched down, lacing his fingers together. Kaleopei placed her good foot on his hands, gripping his shoulders.

"Straight shot, no showing off, Key." He laughed at her words, bouncing a few times before shooting her up.

Kaleopei was propelling up, and swung her arm to reach some of the vines that were stuck to the second story. The plants made a ripping sound. All she could do was hold on as she dropped a foot. The vines are still holding.

Using their strength to her advantage, she went up, using the Keys to flip the lock on the window. Then, there was a frill scream.

"Shit."

"You alright, Kaleopei?" One look down showed Keylan had a worried glance. Zaratella seemed to only cock her head at the sound.

"Fucking peachy." Kaleopei pushed the window in before reaching back out to cut some of the hanging vines. Hoping they would be long enough to reach the duo at the bottom. "Get up here!"

Kaleopei was unsheathing her hunting knives, readying herself for whatever lay beyond the semi-cracked door.

Chapter 14

A high-pitched scream echoed into Casimir's head. Around him were books scattered and thrown about. Translation and language dictation books are stacked on his desk.

He dropped his charcoal, moving to the door. His chin-length blonde hair was half pulled out of his face. Opening the door, he saw the sea foam eyes of Melody starring at him. Posture rigid and trembling.

"What's going on?" His voice was rasp, hoarse from the lack of sleep. Gods only know what time it was.

"People. There were people. Outside my window." Melody's voice shook with terror, her dark skin ever so slightly flushed.

The rooms they occupied were two stories off the ground level. Who could possibly be at her window?

"Are you certain?"

"Yes. Yes, I am certain. There was a face in the window." Casimir spun on his heel, reaching for the rapier placed against his armoire.

"Stay put, I'll check it out." Melody nodded, not saying anything else as he ducked out the door. The hallway was long and dimly lit, candles lined the upper portion of the wall. No other motion in the hall beside him.

He placed his ear against the wooden door, pressing to hear anything. Faintly, he could make out the murmur of voices and the slight scuffing of steps.

Weighing his options carefully, Casimir thought of alerting the guards of the intruders or simply turning around and hiding out in his chambers until morning. There were multiple sets of voices. It likely was the possibility they had come with ill intent.

Gathering all of his better judgment and tossing it to the side, Casimir twisted the handle, winching as the metal clicked.

The movement on the other end came to an abrupt halt. The door swung inwards. He had his hand placed on the rapier's hilt.

It did no such good.

A single step into the dark chamber, an arm was circled around his throat, his arm locked behind his back.

He should have listened to his judgment.

Letting out a grunt of agony, feeling the metal point pressed against the middle of his throat. Casimir winced, reaching for his sword with his other hand. Now was a good time. He had never actually brandished a sword against someone who actually wished harm upon him.

In an instance, as if the figures were predicting his moves, his other arm was pinned against the wall, this time by another, broader figure. "Please, stop. He's fine. Not a threat." A female voice, soft in nature and eerily familiar. Casimir pried his eyes open through the pain. Pale skin and black hair invaded his vision. The familiar frame pushed against the female who had pinned his arm.

"Then a liability?" The female from behind him pressed the knife further against his throat. From her actions and voice, Casimir didn't need to see her figure to know she was serious.

"Cas, it's fine, just relax. And he is, for the most part, not a liability." That was Zara's voice, but that couldn't be possible. She was supposed to be in the Elven realm with his father.

The two brown-haired advisories worked in tandem, stripping him of his rapier before letting him go. The male of the two closed the door, quickly peering into the hall and then nodding to his partner. "Zara?" His voice was so quiet he didn't even know if he wanted an answer. Judgment might have won today if Zaratella was really in front of him.

"Cas, it's me. I promise." The figure approached him, placing a calming hand on top of his palm.

"What did you do on my eighth birthday?" Only Zara would know; Casimir had to be certain. A smile widened across the girl's features.

"I stole your crown," She uttered. "Then I tossed it into the stew."

The world shattered around him, and he just collapsed in his arms. His dearest friend standing in front of him, not miles away, posted at some prison sanctioned by his father.

"Cas..." Tears welled in his eyes. "Are you alright?"

"They killed him, Zara, executed him in front of me." All the weight of reality finally crashed down on him. The pain of everything crumbled as he held Zara close. A breaking stride from the numbness he had been feeling.

"Who?"

"Kelvin." A flash of recognition crossed her features. Only the slightest nod showed she understood. Casimir was pulled tighter into the embrace. It was comforting, having Zara back in his grasp. Everything was wry, but this was a semblance of good.

"This is the crown prince of Bellheim?"

"Shut it, you brute." He could make out the voices of the duo standing a few feet from him. Their eyes awkwardly studied anything else in the room, avoiding Zara and him as they laughed among themselves.

Casimir couldn't find it in himself to care as a few tears rolled down his cheeks. Zara had brought them here. How bad could they be?

"Under what jurisdiction?" Zara maneuvered the both of them so he was sitting on the bed. Odd trinkets and oddities not from this realm scattered the room. Casimir could still make out some of the decorations Zara had contributed whenever she stayed in the castle.

"Accused of treason," Casimir recalled. Reliving the moment, the guards burst into his room, whisking Kelvin away.

"The trial found him guilty?" Casimir watched as Zaratella tried to make sense of all of his ramblings. Nonetheless, she listened, uncaring of the audience they had. He wasn't sure how he could ever repay her kindness.

"No trial; he was accused by the King."

His father had killed his own brother. What sort of twisted, sick games was his father toying with?

Silence. No words were exchanged between them. Just a silent, morbid understanding.

"We'll make him pay, Cas."

"I'm so tired, Zara." His voice was broken. All the pent-up emotion and frustration finally caught up to him. Unable to avoid them, Zara broke him down.

"I know, Cas." Zara ran a hand through his golden hair. "These people are going to help."

For the first time, he looked at the duo off to the side. Really saw them as they were pointing jokes at each other. Both had brown locks, and the females split into two. The male had a blunt cut to his shoulders, both with emerald eyes that scanned over him like a vulture.

"Apologies for my appearance. I've had a time. My name is Crowned Prince Casimir Haven of Bellheim."

"And I'm a god," The female crossed her arms over her chest, looking unsure of him.

Casimir stayed unmoving, wide-eyed. The aura radiating from the two was intense. Slowly, the girl smiled, showing a hint of her teeth.

She was joking... he hoped.

"Kaleopei. This is my brother, Keylan." The female started again, standing her ground, gesturing to the male beside her.

"We're not gods, just to clarify." Casimir felt the corners of his lips tug upwards at the male's comment.

"I most definitely saw another girl in here before. Is she a liability?"

"A girl? Of Melody. She is to be my bride."

Zara whirled around, looking at him.

"What?!"

"Decreed the day you left, I believe."

"The King actually set up a marriage for you?" She gaped.

"To the Mer Realm. Their youngest daughter."

"Cas, that's insane. You didn't stand up to him?"

"What was I supposed to do?" An emotion that seemed to punch him in the gut. Guilt or shame, he wasn't sure. "*We* don't get choices."

"Starting now, we do. *We* get a say in what our fate brings." So much hope fluttered in her eyes. Asking him to take the leap with her, it seemed. What was she dragging him into?

"What do you want me to say, Zara? Even just the thought of what you are insinuating could have us hung."

"I know." Zara took a couple of steps back, gesturing to the siblings. "We can't live like this. You know you would rather not rule like *him*. If you continue to follow him like a dog, you *will* end up like him."

"He has armies under his command."

"People *love* you, Cas. You could lead them to a brighter future. Something better than living in constant fear."

Casimir fiddled with the ring around his finger. His feet tapped repeatedly against the wooden floor. Weighing every word that Zaratella said.

Kaleopei stepped forward, her steps uneven, favoring one leg. The carefree posture from before going, "Are you aware of what goes on in Louth?"

"Louth? Isn't that in the Elven Realm? Aren't you supposed to be there, Zara? It's a prison, from what I've gathered." Casimir furrowed his brows, crossing his own arms.

Unfiltered, icy rage seemed to well into the emerald eye girl. Her glare was terrifying, and it was directed at him.

A silent conversation seemed to be happening between Zara and Keylan.

"I don't understand what is happening." Casimir glanced between Zara and Kaleopei, gauging what they all seemed to be communicating about. It was clear that it wasn't anything good.

"Cas, he's killing people. Innocent people. Some face a worse fate." Casimir knew his Father wasn't deemed a good man. "Elves, half-elves, anything with innate magic."

"Why would he do that?" None of this made sense. Nothing of what was happening made sense.

"I don't know. It's what we," Zara crouched down to his onyx eyes level with his, "are trying to figure out. He wants something that requires a lot of magic. I've seen the vaults at Louth. There extensive. Whatever he intends to do could be catastrophic."

"What are you even proposing? Kill the King, start a coup? That's insane, us and what armies? The four of us. Something tells me we'll need more than that."

"We start small scale, shutting down Louth should give us more time. Please, Cas, listen to what I'm saying."

"I am. Gods, I'm trying so hard to wrap my head around all of this."

Kaleopei stepped forward, putting her fingers to her lips, "Someone's at the door."

Casimir took a moment and realized all the weapons the two had stashed on them. Hunting knives, daggers, swords, and bows all decorated their body like one would show off jewels.

"How many?" Keylan eyed his sister. Casimir noticed her head twitch, cocking to the side.

"One, female. Unarmed, I think, her steps aren't heavy." What was she doing? That had to be Melody. No one else would be in this wing at the early hour. "It smells... fishy?"

"Melody, I left her in my room."

"Tell her you're fine. We need more time to talk." Zara motioned towards the door, voice level.

"Fine." Casimir swaggered to the door, keeping his confident stride even through the turmoil.

"Mel, everything's fine. Just some friends of mine playing a harmless joke." When he opened the door, she was rocking on her feet. Her face was etched into one of worry.

"Are they pleasant?" Slowly, her demeanor shifted, the tension in her shoulder drifting.

"Indeed, we'll be catching up for the time being. You are welcome to sleep in my chamber." Casimir smiled at her, seeing the shock unravel.

"Nonsense, allow me to meet your compatriots."

Melody shoved her way into the room, seeing the trio on the other side of the door. The Princess stopped mid-step, clenching her fists tightly. The sea-foam eyes scanned the three of them, eyes blown wide.

"This is unexpected. Care to explain why two elves and a witch stand before me?" The world just stopped.

Time slowed, and everyone just stared at each other.

Chapter 15

"Mel, what are you talking about?" The Prince was confused, frantically looking between Kaleopei, Keylan, and Zaratella.

Kaleopei kept her own perplexed emotions off her face, keeping them inside. To say she was shocked wouldn't be right. She had seen the magic Zara yielded without a conduit. She saw the blood magic wielded in front of her, but still, it was a slight shock.

Yet, she held most of the features of a human. Kaleopei recalled back to Alstead, seeing Zara's eyes flashy, a deep hue of red. A common trait among witches.

"These two are Elven. High Elf, judging by the reserves of mana. I thought Elves and Humans didn't get along?" The Princess of the Mer Realm pointed at Keylan and her. She had piercing sea-foam eyes. Kaleopei didn't miss the soft glow they gave off when looking them over. Defiantly magical in a sense.

The monarchy of the Mer Realm was mostly Siren in lineage. They each possessed unique abilities, and it seems this Princess had the gift of clairvoyance.

Kaleopei studied the Princess, taking in her dark skin and pearl-white hair that faded into a rich teal.

Maizelin spoke highly of the Mer Realm.

Biting her tongue, Kaleopei bowed her head. A sign of respect the Prince didn't earn.

"She speaks the truth," Keylan brushed his hair behind his ears. "No point sliding around the truth. Kaleopei and I bear no shame in what we are. Only taught to hide it for being caught by your men, uh, no offense."

"Alright," The Prince nodded, his eyes casting towards Zara, whose worry grew with each passing second. "Zaratella is human, without a doubt. I grew up with her. We've known each other since we were babes."

"My eyes do not lie, Casimir." Melody didn't take her gaze off Zara. A hint of uncertainty, and was undoubtedly sizing up the shorter girl, analyzing the threat she could pose.

"I wasn't certain, Cas. I never lied to you." Zara frantically fumbled over words, cheeks turning a pale shade of pink. "I had my suspicions, but obviously no way to check them. You know, I never met my mother, and my father won't utter a single word about her. I figured out I wasn't fully human when I used my magic for the first time. My father covered it up, saying I was able to harness a conduit from a young age."

"No," Casimir stepped back. Kaleopei noted the way his frame moved, readying herself if he posed any sort of danger.

"I never meant to lie to you. I just had no way of knowing the absolute truth. I've always been different, Cas."

"You're you, Zara. Not a blood-drinking, curse-casting Witch." The words hit home. The physical recoil from Zara was proof enough. Perhaps the Prince wouldn't be willing to join them in this fight. It would be simpler to slit his throat where he stood.

"They're still people," Keylan was quick to jump to Zara's defense. It was in his nature to be protective. Kaleopei had seen it many times. Part of her felt strange, knowing he jumped to the girl's defense. "Regardless of stereotypes and appearance. "

"I thought you were different from dear old daddy," Kaleopei spits out the words with more venom than she intended. Her words, however, piercing true.

"Witches don't leave the Witch Realm. We have no idea of what they are capable of." Casimir raced to defend himself. His eyes were blown wide, his hands shaking in front of him.

"I'm still your Zara. Nothing has changed."

"You deceived me."

"I did no such thing! I have *always* been there for you. I've never even been to the Witch Realm. How could I know anything about what they're like? I wasn't raised in a coven. I was by your side for most of our childhood." Zaratella's fists clenched, her body tensing with each word. The tension in the room was thick.

Kaleopei dared a glance over to Melody. The slightest smirk was set on her lips, somehow enjoying all the heated emotions coursing through the room.

"I just want to understand this all! I don't resent you at all, Zara. I'm hurt, yes. But I'm not mad at you. Gods, I could never be mad at you."

Kaleopei shuffled on her feet, unsure of if she should be stepping in. A glance and shake of the head from Keylan told her not to say anything. He was better at reading in a tense room.

"Then why are you scared? Your heart is racing, I can feel it. I've always felt it." Tears raced down her too pale face, leaving fresh streaks on her pale cheeks.

"I'm terrified of what's just been said in this room. My father could, *will*, kill us all if anything said here got out. You're life, Zara. Their lives."

"It's a risk I'm willing to take. Change won't come about from staying complacent. I want the choice to dictate my own life." Kaleopei resonated with Zara's choice. Understanding a little more as to her motive in all of this.

"You know I want the same, but this Realm would fall to ruin."

"My realm fell to ruin, yet there are still good people. I believe those people are fighting to get their homes back. Somewhere, they are grieving for what they lost. A land without its people still exists. I pray every night for it." Keylan grabbed Kaleopei's hand. Comforting his sister as he voiced his thoughts.

The Elven Realm fell in a matter of nights. One day thrived, and the next, the King, Queen, and Crown Princess were ambushed in their own home. Kaleopei remembered that day well, eight years ago. The white flags that had flown in Eviera. The humans ignored the surrender and plundered anyway, killing any who dared to exist.

"You are loved by many, Cas. So many would rally under your cause. You were the one who gained their trust, not your Father." Zara grasped the Prince's hands.

Kaleopei witnessed the spiral of emotions flooding through the Prince. This was a precarious situation they had found themselves in. The anger that should be boiling in her skin, this Prince, is a direct blood connection to the man who caused her so much agony. Yet, she somehow sympathized with him. He is able to understand the position he has been put into. For a second, he looked like Maizelin. The unrelenting pressure she was constantly in and how it showed in the Prince's face.

"What if I fail? I'd be letting down my people." The pressure could be suffocation. The twins faced it daily. Casimir mirrored the stress and burdens.

"Then we try again and again until the gods deem it our time. I will be there with you. You will not be alone." Kaleopei found herself squeezing Keylan's hand throughout Zara's speech.

Both of them had come to terms with the cards fate dealt them. The stakes were always present for them. Even just existing inside the Human Realm puts their lives on the line.

"We offer our services as well, under a few conditions." Keylan puffed himself up, flaunting his broadness. His pride will be the death of him.

"I have an inkling as to what you wish, but continue."

"When this is over, if, when you take up the throne. We'd like our Realm back, perhaps even allies." Such simple words contained so much emotion.

"If we make it out of this alive, and your people agree to it. I'd like to have a mutual relationship, one where nobody fears the other Realm. Humans and Elves."

"That's a world I hope to see," Kaleopei smiled a pure hopeful grin. A future where peace could be possible.

"I apologize for causing a disturbance. I'd assume it'd be known if they were friends of yours." Melody. Kaleopei thought back to all the stories Maizelin told them of her adventures elsewhere. The joy in her eyes when speaking of the Mer Realm and all the sights that were otherworldly. One day, Kaleopei hoped to see those sights.

But the pull at Melody's lips and the sly way she tossed her hair over her shoulder showed she may have intended the discourse.

"What do you intend to do with this information?" Kaleopei was the one to voice the unanimous voices from the room.

"Intention? I don't bear any malicious hate towards the Witch and the Elven Realm. I do, however, have issues with the Human King threatening harm to my people if I don't provide a union."

Casimir's head snapped towards the girl, "What?"

"Your King wants a child. An heir to his throne."

"That's insane. It wouldn't be human; he'd flip his shit." He was an asshole, but it wasn't without reason. There are only so many reasons the King would benefit from a child of a siren bloodline.

He'd use them. Use them just like he did the rest of his subjects.

"He wants an individual who will be an asset. You can see through somebody, correct? Like you did with us?" Kaleopei put it together. Unsure of how to approach this without causing the Prince to spiral, he seemed rather fragile at this moment. He'd have to grow a pair if we wished to become a rebel.

"That's right. You're sharp." Melody confirmed with a smile that showed off her pearly teeth, "I have refused to be any kind of weapon for him. A child isn't an act of war like kidnapping me would be. I convinced my Mother that I'd be able to handle myself here. I was under the impression by word of the tides that you weren't like your Father, Casimir."

"The Mer extended the arranged union?" Zara was catching on.

"Indeed, I will do good for my Realm. I came here of my own accord. I have no interest in telling what I saw tonight. Should you need any assistance in your endeavors, I will offer what I can. I also won't be providing an heir, no offense to you, Casimir."

"By the gods, we're all going to be hung." Casimir dragged a hand down his face. Rubbing his neck until it turned the faintest bit of red.

"There is one way to stop that," Kaleopei looked at the Prince. His heart was practically beating out of his chest. The noise was consistent. Keylan nudged her shoulder, knowing the next words that were about to spill from her lips.

"We dethrone a King. Then we get to make the rules."

***

The five of them moved rooms, moving into the Prince's chambers. Kaleopei noted the long hallway, seeing the other windows and exits.

The Prince shut the door, flipping the lock. Does he really think a lock will keep us all safe? Against Humans, perhaps.

"We can't kill him. It will cause mayhem. Chaos is not something that will do us any good." Keylan was the first to begin the inevitable conversation. Kaleopei sat herself against the wall, imagining all the ways she could kill the King.

Death was a mercy she wasn't certain he deserved.

"There are also some dead guards on the wall right now," Zara sheepishly spoke. Casimir only gave her a raised brow before the conversation continued.

For the first time, she was able to focus on the wound in her thigh. Once she unwrapped the bloodied cloak, it wasn't a pretty sight. Her pants were tight against her legs, the arrowhead buried into fabric and skin.

"Gods, I smelt blood, but I didn't think it was yours," Keylan was at her side in almost an instant. Kneeling beside her, looking over the bloodied thigh of his sister. Out of instinct, Keylan went to shroud his hands in the familiar healing magic he possessed, but Kaleopei quickly smacked his arms away.

"Don't be vain. We're in a city crawling with carvers who can sense that shit. No magic." Then Kaleopei was pulling down her pants, slipping out of the tight brown fabric that clung to her. Pale, scarred legs were revealed with each inch of fabric that was removed. The long tunic covered everything deemed indecent, as did the tan fabric of her undergarments.

A few gasps sounded from the people around her, but she paid little mind. Her sole focus was on the pain that was emitting from her thigh.

"Let me help," Keylan asked, moving to see that the arrowhead remained embedded in her skin. Without another thought, she pushed him away.

"Are you alright?" It was the soft voice of Melody who noticed the blood first.

"That's some stories you have to tell," Zaratella spoke between gritted teeth, looking upon the dozens of reminders of all Kaleopei had endured.

"Don't suppose you have any kind of alcohol handy?" Kaleopei ignored everyone whilst shoving her brother away. With hope, those emerald eyes looked at Casimir. His eyes were wide, seeing the amount of blood that was pooling at the entry wound.

Casimir walked around to his desk, littered with paper and books. On the floor were a few books that looked ancient. They had text written, but not in a language Kaleopei could read. The Prince threw a drawer open, and immediately, the room smelt of Myth.

"Light some of that up while you're at it," Kaleopei shrugged. Through clenched teeth, the wound oozed, metallic-smelling blood dripping down her thigh as she pried the arrowhead from herself. The metal clanked as it hit the marble floor.

"Maybe be a little gentler? You're mauling yourself." Melody cringed.

"Not your leg," Without missing a beat, she sent a look to the Princess before turning back to Casimir, "Booze, please."

In a crystal pitcher, a deep brine-colored liquid swirled on the inside. Evidently, it was some top-shelf liquor. Taking the crystal cork off with a loud pop, she swung a sip into her throat. Feeling the familiar tang as the whiskey hit the back of her throat.

Top shelf, indeed.

Then Kaleopei dumped the contents into the wound. It stung. Stung a lot. Yet, she made little notice of it, having done this countless times.

"Continue plan talk. I'm capable of input. You people act like you've never seen a little blood." Kaleopei rolled those green eyes, casting a smirk on everyone who had a look of disbelief on their faces besides Keylan.

"Right, can't kill the King outright," Zara nodded, looking at the group like nothing had happened. But, Kaleopei swore she saw the girl's eyes flash with concern. "However, we can rally support if we were to go public with our findings in Louth."

"Provided we find concrete evidence and a reason, I doubt there'd be many wanting to stay under his rule," Kaleopei tossed in, still tightly wrapping her torn cloak on her thigh, keeping the blood in her body to the best of her ability.

"Hope is a dangerous weapon in itself," Melody looked contemplative, her hands tapping against her own thigh. "It isn't a bad idea. Hope can be harder to kill than a sea serpent."

"We're all going to be hung," Casimir blew out a puff of smoke, passing the pipe to Kaleopei. Her eyes were shown with gratitude as she inhaled a breath of that almost sweet herb.

"That was likely Keylan, and I's fate anyway. Rather, have an actual reason besides existing." Casimir stiffened as Kaleopei spoke.

"I'm with my sister, with or without your aid. He will pay for what he's done," Keylan had a flick of rage in his eyes. It was subdued, something he'd been holding on to for a long while. Since the day she was captured.

"Any ideas where dear ole' daddy would hide sensitive documents, Cas?" The pipe had found its way back into the blonde's palm. He looked at Zaratella.

"His office, but getting in isn't easy."

"You're in charge, are you not?" Zara had a look on her face. She was scheming, and Kaleopei couldn't hide her smirk.

"Yes?"

"Then just walk right in, make something up, saying he left a schedule of rotations in her office before departing. Then just prance into there like you own the place." Zaratella looked at the Prince, watching his reactions carefully.

His head fell to the side, "Zara, you are insane."

"You love me," she laughed, sticking her tongue out.

Well, she didn't lie about having contact inside. Nor about the fact that she knew the Prince.

"In the morning, it'd be odd if I went now."

"We don't have that kind of time. Those dead bodies will be found whenever the next guard takes over." Keylan spoke slowly, like he himself was still processing everything.

"He's right, Cas. It has to be now. Make something up. You lie well. Use that to your advantage." Zaratella walked up to him, holding his hands tightly. "This is our chance to carve our own path. We can do this."

A look of doubt briefly appeared on his face, and then Casimir was shrugging his shoulders and marching for the door. Whatever silent conversation the two had seemed to be enough for him.

"We'll be here," Zara promised, not breaking gaze with the prince. Then Casimir was out the door, it shutting softly in his wake.

Kaleopei stood up for the first time, putting pressure on her leg. A small inconvenience, but it beats having taken the arrow to her chest.

"How fucked are we if we let him do this without backup?" Kaleopei took it upon herself to voice the thought lurking in her mind. Peering over to the books laid on the floor, still not able to make sense of the writing.

"Have a little faith, Cas means well. He's always been watched like a hawk, so forgive him if he's hesitant." Zaratella looks unconvinced by her own words. "He trusts me a great deal; the only reason why he's even fathoming is possibly acting out of line."

"Do you think he can do this?" Melody shifted to sit on the edge of the bed. Even the way she sat screamed royalty and confidence. Kaleopei could see why Maizelin spoke highly of the Mer Realm.

"I do. Casimir is good-hearted. The man cries while reading books. He'll make a fine King in succession to his father. That I'm sure of."

"So, should I be tailing him right now?" Kaleopei prodded, seeing the flash of contemplation once more.

"No," she decided. "His greatest skill is his charisma. A sword or anything like that will take some work."

"Then we wait," Kaleopei picked up one of the books and flipped through the contents.

It was old, that was obvious. The writing seemed familiar, but still, she couldn't make any sense of it. What were these?

"Key, does this look familiar?" Kaleopei showed a page to the male. Her eyes fluttered over the page, analyzing what he could make of it.

Gaining the intreats of the other women, they both looked over. Zaratella shrugged, and Melody shook her head.

"This looks like the tombs the Hag kept." That was it. She had seen writing like this before. A lot, actually.

"Didn't she say it was a language long forgotten? Why would Casimir have these?" Looking for an answer, Kaleopei turned to the person he seemed the closest to, Zaratella.

"Wait, go back to that page," was the only thing the carver said. "That looks similar to Kelvin's penmanship. I've seen it on many documents in that color, called the orange ink lucky."

"That still doesn't explain why it's in his possession. Wasn't that the person that he was distraught over?"

Could it have been a sentimental thing? If the death was recent, that would explain why they were scattered about. It was possibly Casimir was reminiscing.

"It was his Uncle, the King's right hand. But I've never seen this language before. It looks as if Kelvin annotated parts or took notes, maybe?"

Flipping through more and more pages, Kaleopei just saw the same script. So she picked up another book, rifling through its contents. Keylan mirrored her actions.

"This one has some common. It looks like a note. 'Dearest Nephew, I tried. I write this as I found something of note that, hey!" The iron-eyed girl snatched the book from him.

"Casimir should read it, not us." The book snapped shut in her grasp. Kaleopei sighed, reaching for the still-burning pipe on the desk.

Keylan quirked a brow, "is that the wisest thing to be doing?"

"Bite your tongue. It's been a long day." She hissed at the male, ignoring the smirk that played on his lips.

Keylan took the pipe, hitting it himself.

"Gods, is this some good Myth? Who knew royal money sponsored quality drugs." Keylan coughed, hitting his chest as he passed it back to Kaleopei.

"Thank you," She smiled, taking the moment to laugh at her brother. Melody and Zaratella both watched with amusement. "What? You want in?"

"You're an awful influence." Keylan was still trying to clear his throat.

"Take it as a celebration of new allies."

The myth got passed around, easing the tension that had been building. As well as a way to pass the time Casimir was gone.

Kaleopei noticed as Melody slipped away, her bare feet not making a sound as she made her way out the balcony door. Brow quirked, and Kaleopei shifted her posture. She was certain that the girl was more heavy-footed from when she first heard her approach.

With a huff of smoke, she passed the pipe to her brother, who was engrossed in whatever text these books were in. Kaleopei followed the girl outside, the soft breeze welcoming against her skin.

"I hear seers are rare among sirens."

"Green flames aren't something seen regularly either."

Kaleopei smirked, seeing the white-haired girl cast a knowing smirk over her shoulder. Everything seemed to fall into place presently, a slight weight being lifted off of her shoulders.

"Let's talk about what you're really up to." Kaleopei leaned over the railing, looking down into the overgrowth. This conversation would be one that would weigh on Kaleopei.

"You look a great deal like your sister."

Chapter 16

The objective is simple. Walk in, get what was needed from the office, then walk out. Easy. Casimir shook out his shoulders, taking confident strides down the halls. The boots on his feet echoed with each step he took.

"Confidence, I'm confident," he spoke softly under his breath. But it was unclear if that was his brain or the Myth clouding his senses. Convincing himself that the task ahead was a simple one.

Every step he took was a battle against himself, trying to talk him out of the madness. Zaratella could be lying. This could lead them all to an early grave. There were two Elves lounging in his quarters. Turning them in would curry favor with the King.

A shake of the head.

No.

That wouldn't solve anything; those two were victims of the war the King started eight years ago. They were children then, same as he. It likely was their family was no longer walking this land, taken too soon.

Casimir's strides grew, nodding courtly to the guard he passed.

The watch rotation was at sunrise. That was all the time they'd have to come to a decision. If those corpses were found, the castle would erupt with mayhem. Zaratella would be found guilty of treason, and a world without his best friend isn't one he'd hope to experience anytime soon.

"Prince Casimir." The door to the office was within sight. When had he gotten so close? Across the hall were two guards stationed at the door, like there always were.

"Good evening, gentlemen. It seems my Father had forgotten to leave some documents that I require in his office. I need them for some courtly business." He lied through his smiling teeth. Not a hint of wavering even graced his voice. Even managing to keep a pleasant expression instead of the shock he felt.

"We're under strict orders to not let anyone in," the guard looked to his partner, exchanging subtle glances.

The scones along the wall flickered as Casimir took another step towards the door. There wasn't a lot of time before the sun rose, and his friend would be found out.

"I understand, but as Crown Prince, I have the authority to relieve you of that order. Or would you rather have me report your lack of respect to Captain Argyle?"

"No, sir, that won't be necessary. Excuse my confusion." The guard nodded to his companion, removing themselves from in front of the double doors. The tan oak was worn and had intricate red details that wove into a bell where the door crowned. Ornate patterns were carved into wood. He just had to make it through. Get inside and see what the niceties were concealing.

"Thank you, gentlemen. Your loyalty won't go unnoticed." With swagger, he reached for the door, pulling it open.

He was met with darkness, not a single lit candle in the room. The only light came from the window behind his desk and illuminated the room in a dim glow. Everything was set in a place, not a single loose paper. Even the ink and quills were organized in neat rows.

Order and control.

The office screamed for his Father. Casimir hadn't stepped foot inside this room since he was little, then the room seemed huge. Bookcases towering over him, the desk at shoulder height. How much had the King been hiding from him then?

Casimir ran his hands along the desk, feeling the dark stained wood brush against his fingertips. A singular notebook lay on the desk closed. No title or writing on the bound leather book.

Casimir rifled through the pages, simply a ledger. Each page is filled with dozens of purchases. Ordinary things: servant wages, produce, maintenance.

But one thing stood out. The label wasn't a product or want. It was simply a name. A name Casimir knew well.

Isla.

There was an abundance of accounts, all large amounts of silver. Why would so much silver be going to the Queen? She had many medications and personal medics, but this amount of silver was too much even for all of that. It easily was a sum in the thousands, perhaps even more from just this year alone.

Casimir moved to the drawers, and the neatly organized files continued. He rifled through the contents, taking a careful look at each of the labels.

It wasn't until he reached the third drawer did something of worth jumped at him. It was an unlabeled folder in the back of the drawer.

The documents were unreadable, in a language he didn't understand. Vaguely, the script mirrored the ones his Uncle had forced upon him.

"What is this?" In between the lettering were words scrawled in common. This was taking too long. The guards might report his coming and going if he lingers anymore.

Quietly, he shoved the parchment under his coat. Pressing the fabric so it seemed seamless, there was no trace that he could be hiding anything underneath. Everything around the room seemed to be screaming at him to look through, like something else was hiding. Casimir didn't have the time.

With the same smile he wore, he exited the room. Nodding to the two as he made his leave.

****

Casimir strode back into his room, letting the facade slip off his face. An arrow whizzed by him, piercing the wall next to him.

"Gods!" Casimir shrieked, panting as he scanned the room. The siblings were at the ready, like a danger lurking within him.

"You could have shot him," Zaratella reprimanded the female. Kaleopei was her name, and everything came back to him of what had happened before his escapade.

"I swerved when I saw who it was. A shame to waste a nocked arrow." The girl shrugged, tossing her brown-brained hair over her shoulder. Kaleopei waltzed towards him, each step like a dangerous dance. "Apologies, Princeling."

She leaned in closer, pulling the arrow out of the wall. Like a serpent, she hissed, "Did you sell us out?"

"What?" Casimir stiffened under the piercing emerald eyes and accusation.

"Either you were tailed, or you tattled the first chance you got." She has been a predator ever since the word. A fire was lit in her stare, like she could make out everything he was thinking.

"Calm down, he wouldn't do that," Zara reigned the girl in, pulling her away from him. He noticed the look Kaleopei gave to his friend, noting the subtle surrender to Zaratella. Where did Zaratella find these two? That part was never really discussed during their introductions.

"How many, Kaleopei?" Her brother spoke, lifting his head from whatever he was doing. It looked like he held a book of some sort, but the cover wasn't visible.

"One. Light steps too, either someone trained in espionage or is a petite female." How did she know that? At this angle, he could see her ears, no longer shielded by her hair. He could make out scar tissue towards the tips, just like the ones that covered her legs. If he had to guess, he'd say that her arms matched, concealed by the fabric of her long-sleeved tunic and torn cloak. He noted that she was wearing pants once more, but not the same as before. They were from Zara's stash in the dresser.

"It's probably just a servant making their rounds," Casimir muttered, "I only encountered four guards in total."

"It's not a guard, no armor clanking. I don't understand how such monstrosities are practical. To wear it. Anyway, I imagine it would be rather encumbering. A single well-placed shot to any joint defeats the metal entirely." Kaleopei stalked over to Keylan, sharing her thoughts aloud. Melody sat silent, looking out the window. The dark-skinned Mer stared into his Mother's garden.

"Complain later. Should we assess the person?" The taller male flicked his sister's forehead.

"I wouldn't be complaining if I thought they were a threat. Whatever they were doing, it took them down the hall, never stopping in pace. So relax that scowl, and allow me to explain my superior opinions."

"Did you find anything," Zara was hopeful, simply ignoring the rambling behind her. Something Casimir hadn't seen in the girl in a long time.

"Nothing directly related to Louth or anything like that. A couple of odd ledgers. But I did find this," he said, taking the folder out of his coat. "It's an odd language. I can't read all of it, but it was tucked away. Figured it would have some kind of importance. There are bits of common. It looks like an equation or calculations of sorts."

"It's the same glyphs as those books you have." Zara handed him one of the leather-bound books from Kelvin. Softly giving his hand a gentle squeeze, "Read the last page. It's in common."

"Rest assured, I didn't let any of these mongrels read it." Zaratella sent him a playful wink, making light of the situation.

"Heard that." Both Kaleopei and Keylan said over their shoulders. He was able to make out another book in the male's hands as one of the four.

"You were supposed to." The conversation between the three seemed easy. No real tension laced any of their voices. It was oddly comforting.

With shaking hands, he flipped through the pages. Landing on a mostly blank page with words, he understood. Written in orange ink.

Dearest Nephew,

I tried. I write this as I found something of note that is honestly terrifying. Darren has been executing some unsettling experiments up in the Elven Realm. He wants magic. I stole these books from his office. He hasn't noticed yet, but I suspect he will soon. I won't ever give them to you unless I see no other option.

You are good; don't be like him, Prince of The New Dawn. His obsession with these studies has become corrosive and has swayed his morals greatly. It's my belief that something has taken hold of him through these studies. He's more void, irrational, and utterly ignorant of other's opinions and emotions. Whatever empathy he once had is now forgotten.

At this point, I have yet to uncover his reasoning for pursuing such complex and dangerous research, let alone in the field of magic. Darren never was the scholarly type. It's my assumption it has something to do with Isla's worsening health, but that is simply speculation.

I hope this note never makes it to you. It means I most likely failed. But I tried.

Stay safe, Kelvin.

Casimir hadn't realized the silent tears that rolled down his face, completely absorbed into the words that were left. It was Kelvin's final words. Written for him, and him alone. Nevertheless, it left him with more questions.

What information was so important to his father? Vital enough to cast everything else aside.

"Are you alright, Cas?" Zara whispered, brushing his cheek with her thumb.

"Yeah, it appears that there is some tangible proof. Kelvin wrote it here. I think what we're looking for is written inside these books. A type of study he had become engrossed with." Casimir flicked his fingers under his tired eyes, wiping away the tears. "It mentions some kind of dangerous research my father was looking into. It's not something I had been aware of. I can't recall him ever mentioning it."

"What are you leaving out?" The brown hair girl cocked her head, arms crossing over her chest, showing off the knives sheathed at her hips. The hilts were gleaming in the dim light.

An open threat.

Casimir could tell with ease that she wasn't bluffing either.

"What do you mean?" Casimir rebutted.

"Don't act like you don't know."

"I mean, I can only speculate what I'm thinking. Kelvin thought that whatever research the King is after relates to magic in some way." Casimir spoke slowly, watching the girls' reactions.

"Louth has to be where he conducts his research." Zara piped up, looking between him and Kaleopei.

"Looks like I get to see Willow again." Kaleopei flicked her brother's head, then shoved him off the desk chair.

"She's probably grown more."

Keylan walked over to Zara and him, Kaleopei shortly on his tail. The eerily threatening demeanor that loomed over her vanished in a matter of seconds. Everything about her seemed to click in his mind. She was a person to be tested. It seemed her and her brother's survival was her priority. Clearly, she wasn't afraid to resort to extreme measures to do so. Casimir could see the determination practically radiating from her.

On the other side it appeared she was still just a child. She was keen to play jokes and have fun where she could. Kaleopei also appeared to have a rather short temper when it came to things she was passionate about.

"We have a contact that, we assume, can decipher the writing." Kaleopei held up the other three books in her arms. A sickly sweet smile crossed over her face, "Ever hear of The Mystic."

The way her eyes gleaned with mischief instilled little confidence into Casimir. Gulping down whatever liquid had accumulated in his mouth.

"You're joking," Zaratella lowered her voice. These two must be lacking a brain that was a legend of old. The fable dates back centuries, the same time the gods still walked the earth.

"'Course not." She dropped the books into Casimir's arms. "Swear on Keylan's life."

"I don't think they're joking, Zara."

The elven girl might also be insane.

***

The duo is out of their minds. There was no other explanation for their behavior. Casimir found himself laughing through his tear-stained face. First the Mystic, then this.

"What, afraid we'll be bad kidnappers?" The brown-haired girl sat braiding her hair, acting as if nothing were out of line.

"I think kidnapping me would be a one-way ticket to your own execution."

"Please, you talk too much of hanging. At least give the King a *reason* to actually kill us," she shrugged. Right, their living was a miracle in itself. "Besides, we all already talked it over while you were busy breaking into the King's office. Melody will vouch for the story. It aligns with the dead ones on the wall. We'll raise a ruckus and then make our exit. Melody will play the princess in distress, crying that the love of her life was taken from his own bed late at night."

How much Myth had this girl smoked?

"She's like this normally." Keylan seemed to be reading his mind. "You get used to it."

"Are you willing to do that, Mel?"

"I am," she confirmed from where she lounged atop a few pillows on the floor. "Besides, perhaps it allows me some freedom here. I'll research what I can while I'm here, providing eyes on the inside."

"You don't have to do that," Casimir argued, trying to understand what exactly she would gain from this. He did note the slight glance she tossed to Kaleopei.

"I wish to consider it as vengeance for the show your father made in the throne room."

"We already discussed this. We're just wasting time." Kaleopei sighed.

"I just want to make sure we're all on the same page. This isn't a light decision," Casimir started, but was cut off by Kaleopei.

"Or we'll all be hung? You've said that a few times. I understand that from your position, you have a lot to lose, so make your choice, *prince*." Fire. A fire burned with each word she spoke. It seemed this meant a great deal by the way the siblings looked at each other.

Casimir realized that they had nothing left to lose. They just wanted to go home, and his father stood in their way.

Countless nights were spent under the tutelage of the man they hate, with good reason. Casimir felt for them and saw the pain they carried with them. He wanted to be a part of the reason that they could go home; he would rather not stay as an oppressor.

That's what he has been, not by choice but by the role he was thrust into.

"Let's do this then." Zara had been silent this entire time. Letting Casimir make his choice alone. She smiled at him, wrapping her arms around his neck.

"Let's make our own choices from now on, Cas, even if it is a death wish. We made that choice, and I am okay if I die because of it."

"Sweet, let's get a move on." Keylan was the first up, knocking the desk over, books and papers going flying.

"What are you doing?" Casimir hissed, rushing to pick up the dropped novel. Brushing any bits of dirt off the cover.

"Staging a struggle," Keylan shrugged, taking the blankets off the bed and throwing them on the ground all the way to the balcony door.

Zaratella sprung into action, joining the male in the destruction. The wreckage echoed throughout the room.

"I can hear footsteps, these one heavy." Kaleopei walked to the door, a dagger secured between her fingers.

"Suppose I should seem surprised." Melody was moving from her spot, moving to sit in his bed. She clutched a candleholder in her hand, a satin sheet pooled around her waist.

"Wait, we're fighting?" Casimir wasn't ready for all of this. Maybe this wasn't a good idea after all.

"Not you, Cas. Her." Zara was tugging at his shirt, handing him a pack. He shoved the books into it, following Zaratella to the balcony. Keylan was securing a rope to the railing, descending right into his Mother's garden. He would miss her dearly, even if he hadn't seen her recently.

He hoped this would be over before she drew her last breath.

Wishful thinking.

The four had been busy in his absence. Fleshing out a full-scale plan before he even agreed to it. It was a posisibility that they had planned to actually kidnap him if he didn't agree.

"Ladies first," Keylan used his hand to point to the rope. "No climbing this time, just hold on."

"Send him after me." Zara was sliding down the rope shortly after. Casimir watched as her feet hit the grassy floor. He pulled the pack over his shoulder, winching as he grabbed the rope between his palm.

"Key!" From inside, Casimir could make out the girl looking at them. The door behind her pounded. It seemed someone had taken notice of the commotion.

Then she whistled. Pulled her brother's cloak that she now bore over her head and a scarf around her mouth.

Keylan whistled back before ushering him down the line. Was now really the time to be whistling?

With all his strength, Casimir held on, feeling the rope burn on his palms. His feet hit the grass. He was still upright somehow, even though his legs felt like jelly.

He heard a high-pitched scream from above, sounding like the Acadar Princess. The debt he owed her for her role in this would be plenty. However, something ticked in the back of his mind, saying she wanted this. For whatever reason, he didn't know.

Keylan landed next to him, yanking the rope with force. It didn't budge.

"Where are we going?" Casimir urged, seeing that the rope wasn't going to come undone. Nonetheless, Keylan gave another tug. Before giving up and throwing a knife at the rope, it landed what looked like a foot away, embedding itself into the railing.

"Damn, Kaleopei makes it look easy." Keylan drew another dagger, closing an eye. Zara was quicker, taking the dagger and nicking Keylan's finger. He recoiled before extending his hand out, seeing Zara's face. "A little warning next time?"

She swiped his palm, and the crimson blood smeared across her finger. Casimir flinched, watching as she peeled the liquid off her finger and sent it towards the rope in congealed droplets. Severed by Keylan's blood. No use in denying the witch part now.

"Brooding won't do any good. We need to make it to the sewers." Zara looked at the brown-haired male, nodding her head away from the balcony.

Then, they were running through the garden. Casimir's breath hitched, his lungs gasping for air as they raced. He could see the sun beginning to rise on the horizon. It was becoming dawn.

Thrust into darkness once more, Zara led them through the castle interior, sticking to servant tunnels, remaining unseen. Casimir thought of the girl fighting above somewhere.

"Shouldn't we worry for Kaleopei?"

He had seen the way she was light on her feet and the calm aura that shrouded her at times. She could, more than likely, handle herself.

"That's my job," Keylan snarled. Another sharp corner. "She's probably having the time of her life."

"Have I mentioned there is something truly wrong with her?" Zara mused, ducking into the stairwell. Finding themselves deeper in the castle.

"Don't lie, you like her." Keylan laughed, wiggling his brow. For a split second, Casimir would bet Zara had a faint tint of red across her pale face.

"We're close." They were the only words that came from his best friend. Zara struggled to lift the sewage grate in the basement of the castle. Keylan pushed her to the side, lifting it out of place with a grunt.

"Don't brood now." Then, he dropped into the darkness below. Gods, how were they supposed to see down there?

"It's clear," Keylan called from below. How was he sure? Zara didn't waste time jumping down. A soft splash of water was all Casimir heard.

Slowly, he sat on the ledge, lowering himself slowly. Until he made the fall, his shoes squelched into the water and its contents. Casimir didn't allow himself to think about what he was stepping in.

"Kaleopei is meeting us at the cross underneath the marketplace," Zara was in front of him, judging by the voice.

"How can you see anything?"

A pause.

"Shit."

"You can't see?" Zaratella sounded confused. "It's not that dark."

"I can't see anything."

"Humans," Keylan laughed. Zara found him, grabbing his hand. "Seems your witch half came with a dark vision of the covens."

"I doubt I can see as well as you," she scoffed. He heard Zara rummage through her pack.

"Got a match?"

"I am always around a living match stick, so no, I don't have a match."

"Right," she sighed, then seemed to pause. "It's fine. I have a few left."

He heard the faint sound of the match striking. Then he could make out Zara's face in the warm light. She handed it to him, along with four others.

"Make 'em count. That's all I got. Now, we need to move with precision. I only knew certain parts of the sewer, any wrong turn, and we're running blind."

"This explains why you were so good at hide and seek when we were kids." Casimir joked, following as Zaratella led the charge through the sewers.

It reeked of filth. That was a given.

This was something he could cross off his never-done list. Striding through the sewers of Bellheim with an Elf and a Witch.

He wasn't sure how long they moved for, the only consistent thing was the long hallways. Twisting in ways he couldn't comprehend, seemed only Zara could.

"How will Kaleopei figure her pathing underground?"

"I drew up a map from the district sewer entrance she'd be taking at the Vizen Market."

"You sent her where?" Casimir reeled, not understanding his friend's motive. "She'll be skinned alive there."

"Have you ever actually been to the street? The group is entirely passive to, let's say, odd visitors. She'll fit right in." Zaratella spoke in a firm voice, authoritative. Still, the Vizen Market was rumored to be a place where criminals gather and trade information. He'd seen the hip-high stacks of reports and oddities that happened there.

If it is like Zara said, his father could aim to shut it down. Argyle, the crown guard's very best, hadn't been able to shut it down. Deemed it docile enough to the general public, just advised citizens to stay astray from the particular street.

Casimir followed the two in front of him, striking a match once the previous one had gone out. Winding paths of filth, and trash was what they trekked through, until coming across an intersection.

"This is the point."

"I'm on the last match." Casimir clutched the burning match in between his fingers. The cross-section wasn't huge, but it seemed enormous as there were paths on all sides stretching into darkness.

"We're not alone," That alone made Casimir place a hand on his rapier. Keylan had his eyes narrowed on the path ahead. "It's a Wrent, makes sense they'd be roaming here."

In the spotty lighting the match gave off, down the southern path was a creature of nightmares. The face of a rodent, was large and sat awkwardly atop the large rat-like body. It had to be taller than a castle hound, and Casimir's mouth fell open when he laid eyes upon the saliva that dripped from its needle-like teeth.

Casimir was sure today was his last day. That creature was hideous, its fur matted to its skin. He let out a shrill screech as the match's light burned low. Flickering until it went nuff.

The last thing he saw was a flash of white teeth hurtling towards them and a glint of metal from Keylan's broadsword.

Then everything went black.

Casimir was able to make out the sound of metal hitting the stone. Faint wails, he hoped we were the wrents and not his company. He bore the thin sword in one hand, thrusting it in front of him aimlessly.

Heat.

The temperature had risen in the tunnel.

Then there was light.

On top of the Wrent was Kaleopei, brandishing two large hunting knives that looked like they had been dipped in green flames. A swirl of deep emeralds shades that mixed to lighter tones is not something fire should do naturally. The head of the creature lay unmoving in the filth, severed from its spinal cord.

Bile rose in his throat. Then, it was mixed into the filth at his feet.

"I brought friends, it seems." Kaleopei shook the blades, twirling back into the sheaths at her hip. With them concealed, the light went once more.

Chapter 17

"What's his ordeal? Looks like you saw a ghost, Prince." Kaleopei dismounted the Wrent, moving to stand next to Keylan, who gave her a side embrace. Subtly checking her for any new injuries. Only finding the bloodied cloth on her thigh.

"Fine, Key. Lost 'em before I even left the castle. Aren't the brightest, surprisingly enough," she joked, still sending glances at the bent-over Prince who was losing his lunch into the sewage. "Wish I had time to peruse that market, lots of intrigue there. Some man tried to sell me Myth at an absurd price."

"Tell me you didn't buy drugs," Keylan looked at his sister. Her jaw fell open, feigning hurt. Keylan thought so poorly of her.

"Course not, Brother." Keylan quirked his brow at her antics. "I swiped it when he walked away. I'm not falling into that scandal of outrageous prices. That amount of silver could have fed Alstead for a week."

Kaleopei elbowed him in the stomach, watching as a smile spread across his lips.

"Want to be a light for Cas? Do that fancy trick with the fire." Kaleopei looked to Zaratella, who was currently rubbing the boy's shoulder. She was certain the Prince had seen finer days.

"Is that wise while we're in this space? Any grates we pass will be able to see us." Kaleopei made a gesture to the iron above them, a couple of feet away.

"I only did it with my knives to get through the Wrent's skin efficiently. I also wasn't under a grate where any passing eyes could see the light."

"Looks like you get to play tag along." Keylan was tying an edge of a rope to his belt, then handed the ending to Casimir like a parent would do to their child in a large crowd.

"Try not to drag 'em too much." Zaratella threw a smile towards the male before leading them through the sewers.

***

"We're actually going to The Mystic?" Casimir dipped his feet into the river, cleaning himself of the filth the best he could. Along the rocks sat Kaleopei, staring into the fading spring suns. Fenyah, an Elven holiday, wasn't too far away. She hoped she actually gets to spend it with her brother this year, not locked in the pit.

"Don't call the Hag that. It'll go straight to her head." Kaleopei laughed at Keylan's description.

How was Wisp doing? It had been more than a couple of months since she last saw her. Keylan was right. She had to have grown some.

"Isn't she, well, ancient?"

"Don't call her old, either. She gets all moody if you do." This time, Kaleopei chimed in, cringing at the last time some even alluded to the Hag being old.

"What *can* we say to her?" Zaratella asked, wringing out her lock of black hair into the stream. Trees lined the area, keeping their movements covered from any wandering hunters. Kaleopei hadn't let them stop until they could no longer see the capital on the horizon. The distance was what they needed. The

160

more that they could put between them and any soldiers was for the best. It was likely that the Prince being kidnapped was being spread among the guard.

"Anything else is on the table; just don't be surprised if she is in a mood. She won't physically harm you." Keylan concluded, sounding sure of himself. Kaleopei silently noted the expressive features the Prince made. Showing all the emotion on his pale face.

"Didn't she drain an entire lake to prove a point?" Casimir spoke like he was remembering a story, his face going pale.

"The Hag is a lot of things, but she won't do anything to you if you're with Key and me." Kaleopei rinsed her hunting knives in the water, flicking off bits of fur into the stream. Meticulously cleaned until the ornate handles were rid of any filth.

"Where do we find her?"

"Vesper Woods, her abode, is there."

"In the human realm?"

"There is no other Vesper woods I'm aware of." Kaleopei shrugged, sheathing her blades once more. Keylan had stripped down to his undergarments. Wading himself into the water. Kaleopei watched as he let out a breath of relief, relaxed in his element.

"Can I mend your leg now, Kaleopei?" She mulled over it for a moment. It wasn't a bad idea. Silently, she was taking off Zara's pants, and pulling her shirt overhead.

Blood still soaked her old cloak, noting that she'd have to get this one replaced. Crimson wasn't her color. At least, that's what Maizelin would say.

"Better watch out," she warned. Standing to run off the rocks, jumping into the frigid water. However, temperature had never been a problem for her.

"There's probably mud crawlers in there!" Casimir shouted from across the way.

Keylan retaliated from the splash and sent a small geyser raging towards her. Kaleopei ducked under the water's surface, nearly avoiding it.

"We'll be fine." She made out Key's voice when she resurfaced. The two swam further into the river, where they could no longer touch the bottom. Keylan pulled her under, and for a moment, Kaleopei held her breath. Until the water dispersed from around them, and her feet hit the gravel and dirt river floor.

Keylan created a bubble underneath the surface. Allowing them to have a moment of solitude, just the two of them. Kaleopei sat on the ground, watching some fish swim by them. Confused at the disturbance in their space.

"What are you thinking about?"

Keylan didn't waste time, moving to remove any stray pieces of dirt from her wound. Taking care that nothing would remain inside the cut when he closed it up. What was on her mind?

Simply put, a lot. In the last couple of days, they had found out many things. She was eager to put an end to Louth, but what comes after that? Could they actually pull off a coup? Would she and Key finally be able to return home?

"Do you think that Prince can even wield his pointy stick?" Out of everything she could have said, that's what came out of her mouth.

"His pointy stick is a rapier, and I think he might be able to stitch with it." Keylan laughed, gliding his hand along her bloodied and semi-scabbed thigh.

"You should work with him. He'll need the practice."

"What are you actually thinking about?"

"It's almost Fenyah." Another diversion of topics. Kaleopei didn't want to indulge in all that being a rebel meant. She knew the costs.

"Kaleopei," his tone dropped, no longer the playful voice he usually had.

"I want us to make it out of this. I want to go home."

She placed her forehead on his shoulder, not wanting to look at him, the male. Keylan knew she didn't like being emotive. He practically had to drag it out of her. He'd always understood her, even without words.

"We will."

"There's no guarantee."

"We will," he said with such confidence that there was never even a doubt in his mind. Keylan was always so optimistic and always reassured her. "We'll go home together."

"I miss Maize."

"I do, too."

"Why did we survive, Key? Why us?" It was a thought that plagued her mind like a sick chant. Lurking deep in her conscious, prodding any lingering bits of joy she knew.

"Because that's what the Gods decided."

"Fuck the Gods." Her voice wavered, "Why do they make choices for people they know nothing about? Maize should be here, not me. She'd know what to do."

"We make a decent enough team. I think the Gods liked it. It's what they've kept us together all this time." Kaleopei would never nock her brother's beliefs. He was free to think as he wished, but she had the most faith in herself. Knew her strengths and weaknesses and learned how to cover those shortcomings. How would some people who lived far too long ago know her better than herself?

"You ever think what we'd be if Bellheim had never slaughtered the Elven Realm?"

"I'd be a general, serving under the Queen. Have armies to command and be able to protect anybody in the realm. In my off time, I'd catch a couple of your shows at the Dream Theater, then we'd celebrate and drink our asses off. Raid Ma's liquor."

Kaleopei smiled at him. He had always been her biggest supporter. No matter what she tried to pursue, he was always the first to encourage her. Even when the hobbies were niche and often ended quickly, Keylan was the first to offer her something new.

"Do you remember that one time you tried to learn the piano for me? You were horrid,"

"I was six!" Keylan's mouth fell open, halting any healing he was doing.

"Ma would walk around with cotton in her ears just to block out the noise. Maize was livid when you insisted on playing for her."

Laughter rang out through the bubble. The only witnesses were the aquatic organisms around them. Kaleopei hadn't realized when he had finished healing her leg. Only a thin white line remained. Adding to her expansive collection of stories that painted her skin.

"In my defense, I never did have lessons, I only tried so you wouldn't sing without a pianist."

"It meant a lot, you know. Not just the piano," Kaleopei looked at Keylan, "but you being you. You have that attitude, always caring."

"Did you just outright compliment me?" Keylan laughed, the sound music in its own right. They longed for the once carefree life they had before the downfall of the Elven Realm.

"I would do no such thing," she snickered. "You are obnoxiously consistent in your dotting."

"What would you do, you know, if you had the opportunity to go back in time?"

"That's a loaded question, brother." Kaleopei let herself imagine. Imagining what her life could have been like. "I would be the best damn intellect emissary the Elven Realm had ever seen. I'd be the epitome and grace in public, but then the Queen of Darkness who lurked in the shadows. Catching others' deepest secrets, and even those of other Realms. Maybe I'd travel much, singing wherever I could. To an audience who wished to be serenaded."

"You haven't sung in a long time. Why is that?" Keylan looked like he was questioning his words. It was true. She hadn't sung how she'd liked to. Only uses it to her advantage in situations. Even then, she never got to perform, no opportunities to put on a show she was proud of. Only singing melodies of Bellheim's composure, for anything else would be considered treason.

The King was feeble like that, unable to entertain the thought of words being used to disgrace his throne. People should be able to speak as they wish and have their own opinions. But no, the King wanted to cultivate his citizens like they were a single entity. One bred and tamed to carry out his opinions. Fault and inconsistency would not be tolerated.

"Do you not wish to elaborate on that?"

"I'll sing when the King's head rolls. Perhaps I'll sing in the elven tongue when we see to his downfall."

"I miss your voice. Maizelin was right when she said Tehila had blessed you." Kaleopei didn't know what to say. It was rare that they were able to talk to one another so freely. He had been her entire world, always present and nearby if she ever needed someone to simply hold her. Thus instilling some hope for humanity, even if it was only for a singular moment.

Keylan was like a stubborn leech most of the time, constantly coddling and worrying about her. Secretly, she enjoyed it, loved that he loved her as much as she loved him.

The two of them worked best together. A force to behold. With no other choice than to lean on each other for survival.

Kaleopei wasn't sure what would have become of their bond if they hadn't been forced into exile. Her mind couldn't even comprehend what life would be like without the presence of her broad-shouldered twin. Imagining a life without him was difficult, which was why he would survive no matter the consequences. No matter what becomes of the world, she would risk everything for him.

"If, or when, we do this. We're in this shit show together. Whatever happens, I'm happy we did it side by side."

"Don't talk like the end is determined. This world we dream of will happen, and we'll return home side by side. It isn't our time for the earth to take us. There is still so much we have to accomplish."

Keylan's optimism wasn't surprising. Oddly enough, she considered herself to be a realist, able to quantify the odds of the situation rather than hope. They were polar opposites, yet they still held the common goal. "We do not stray," Kaleopei muttered in a soft, subtle voice.

"Not agin, Kaleopei."

***

The twins emerged from their small getaway. Still weightless in the water, Kaleopei gasped for a breath of fresh air as she resurfaced. She was in the two suns that were directly above her, casting a subtle bask of warmth onto her face.

"We thought you two were drowning!"

The Prince hollered, waist-deep in the water. Was he coming to check on them? How cute of him. Thinking they needed saving.

"No problems on our end, simply got into a competition on who could hold their breath longer." Kaleopei waded her way toward the river bank, finding sand and gravel she could stand on.

"Which I won," Keylan interjected. "Just so the record isn't misconstrued."

"You two were under there for minutes! Neither of you should be breathing right now!" Casimir looked frantic, like he was ready to scold them.

"We're both just overly competitive. What more can I say?" Kaleopei shrugged, making her way out of the water. Her skin began growing warm, the water that drenched her turning to steam in seconds.

"That seems unfair. Not all of us have a built-in heater. I still have sopping wet hair." Kaleopei smirked as Zaratella was still trying to wring her hair free of water.

Without a word between them, Kaleopei walked up to her. Suddenly finding her confidence falter, "Would you like some help with that, darling?"

"I'm perfectly content just squeezing by myself," Zara turned away, her body tensing.

"Just let me help you." Kaleopei placed a hand on her shoulder, still clad in nothing more than undershorts and a thin bra that covered her breasts. It's not like she had very much to show off.

"Fine, but don't burn my scalp."

"Wouldn't dream of it."

Kaleopei warmed her hands to a comfortable temperature, careful not to engulf her hands in any flames. Burnt hair was not a fragrance she was fond of. Then she was running her fingers through her soft black hair, careful to keep the flames at bay.

"This is actually kind of nice," she spoke, her shoulders relaxing as Kaleopei worked. "Not uncomfortable like I thought it would be."

Even while damp, the girl's curl pattern was still evident. Soft tresses of black hair passed easily through Kaleopei's fingers.

"We should start moving, and our goal should be to cross the Stillwater south of Alstead." Keylan was leaning over the map, plotting their next course. His voice brought her back to reality.

"No. We should stay along the Stillwater until we reach the split, then go northeast. Use the running water to muffle any movements we make."

It was logical. Kaleopei knew the river like the back of her hand. The only complications they could possibly run into are some fishermen and mud crawlers. Nothing that would prove to be a challenge.

"You would rather not stock up at Silverdale?" They had a stash there. Containing an extra quiver, some dried meats, and other smaller needs the two could have while traveling.

"I still have a few daggers, and I only lost three arrows since we left Alstead. Unless you need something from there, I think we should take the more efficient route."

Kaleopei shrugged, not taking her eyes from Zara's hair.

"I figured you'd want to grab an extra quiver."

"I can manage, brother."

"Right, then I guess we are following Kaleopei's lead." Keylan nodded, slipping back into his clothes. Casimir looked through his belongings, his face unreadable. He hasn't said very much since they fled the capital. The Prince looked lost, unsure of what he was doing.

"Casimir, you know how to use that sword of yours?" Kaleopei called out to the Prince, gaining his attention. Kaleopei had never laid eyes upon the King, but from all the accounts, she was sure that Casimir was the spitting image of his Father.

"I've been training with my tutor since I could stand," he seemed unsure of her question. It was clear that he was questioning himself and lacking confidence.

"Why don't you and Key go at it a bit? Before we have to get a move on." Kaleopei finished drying Zara's hair, the strands warm against her hands. The untamed curls from before now tamed and straighter from the heat.

Casimir sized up Keylan, looking at the broadsword compared to his rapier. It was likely he was trained in the show, but if he is prepared to handle dirty fighting that happens in the streets is another story. Keylan could make him better. Kaleopei was sure of it. Her brother knew his way with a sword. With any luck, Casimir would be able to pick up Keylan's movements.

"Alright. Do you want to do this, Keylan?" Kaleopei almost laughed at Casimir, seeking permission. This wasn't how fights began. His head would already be rolling if he were in an actual fight.

Keylan didn't answer; he simply drew his sword, brandishing it in front of him. Kaleopei narrowed her eyes, watching as the Prince placed a singular hand on his rapier, the other behind his back. The two danced in a whirlwind of brown and blonde hair. Kaleopei has seen her brother fight countless times. His movements were ingrained in her brain. He was fluid on his feet. Each strike he made struck for an opening in his opponent. His grace and strategy made him deadly. Comparing the two wasn't possible. Casimir lost the second he tucked a hand behind his back. That motion alone left his entire left side defenseless.

However, the prince wasn't completely defenseless. Kaleopei had witnessed and been a part of many fights. He was nimble, able to correct his body in a matter of seconds. Being able to adapt to Keylan's brute strength and battle prowess was a feat in itself.

When pitted against the skill her twin possessed, it was nothing.

Keylan knocked the boy to the ground, pointing Skipper towards the boy's exposed throat. Casimir threw his head back, hitting the soft grass below.

"I should have expected this outcome," he laughed. Accepting the hand, Keylan extended.

"Your footwork isn't bad. Being able to anticipate movements and correct yourself is a good skill. You'd have more chance with a short sword, I reckon. I have a feeling you're more of a watcher. Able to read others is not something anybody can master." Keylan analyzed the Prince. Checking the same boxes she had. "With that stick of yours, you won't ever get a good hit in. That's a show sword, too flexible and can't cut through shit."

"That's a compliment coming from mister sword master." Kaleopei laughed, noting the tension that Casimir held in his shoulders.

"Thanks? I guess," he uttered, managing to dust himself off. He wasn't much more than bone; for someone in a position of privilege, it didn't seem that he ate a lot. He'd have to gain more fat to put on muscle.

"My pleasure," Keylan feigned a bow, "We'll start working every sunset."

"You're going to train me?"

"Why wouldn't I?" Her brother looked confused. "You're not going to take what I give you and backstab us, right?"

"God's no, I've seen you both, mostly her, in action." He was aware of who he was acquitting himself with. "I'd not survive an encounter with the both of you."

"Keep your wits, and you'll do just fine." Keylan clasped his hand onto the prince's shoulder, frame shaking from the force. "Now, dear sister. What do you say to a demonstration for the man."

"Eager to lose, Key?"

"Your humbleness knows no limits, does it?"

"I like to think I just know my worth." Kaleopei stepped away from the black-haired girl, who seemed to be lost in her own thoughts. Already, Kaleopei was pulling a hunting knife from her discarded clothing.

"Fancy footwork isn't quite my thing. Casimir would do good to see how it can be advantageous when used."

"Very well, watch carefully, Prince." Kaleopei cracked her neck to the side, feeling the soft drum of adrenaline begins to build beneath her skin. Widening her stance before brandishing the other knife, and locking emerald eyes with Keylan.

He had a lopsided grin on his face, taking up his own stance. Kaleopei used the blades as an extension of herself, speed and agility aiding her to work her way closer. The two collided in a flurry of blows.

Anything around her disappeared as she placed her sole focus on watching for Keylan's broad swings. He paused after each wide swing, a period of time needed for recovery. That's when she struck.

Weaving into his space, ducking below Skipper to place a well-timed blow to his abdomen. The hilt of her blades did most of the damage, not truly seeking to hurt Keylan. The next few days could turn upside down if they weren't careful, they'd need to make sure to have each other's back. Which meant no fatal injuries from sparring, even if she did sometime want to nick him with the pointy side.

Their sparring ended as quickly as it started. Keylan laughing as Kaleopei pinned him to the ground. Using her heel to keep Skipper from moving in Keylan's grasp.

"Just be like, Kaleopei. Knock me on my ass and that's how you win." The prince looked as if he had seen a vilken. Eyes wide as Keylan moved to square up against him once more.

"He's delusional, right?"

"Afraid not." She found herself laughing, tilting her head up to bask in the soft wind.

Kaleopei knew she thrived in the forest, the trees providing comfort. The fauna would also be their biggest asset in moving without being traced. The longer they could maintain a constant cover, the more likely it was they wouldn't be found. She intended to keep it that way.

***

The grove the Hag took up as her own was just as Kaleopei had remembered it. Lucious plants and greenery kept the small entrance to her Cabin unknown to prying eyes and adventurers. If that didn't work, the wards assured they wouldn't find an easy way in.

Kaleopei could just faintly make out the sheer transparency of the wards. Decorated with old runes that the Hag loved.

It had been about three months since she had last stepped foot in the grove. But nonetheless, Kaleopei wouldn't let that stop her by any means. With Keylan at her side, they pushed their hands against the ward. Then she sent a pulse of her magic through it, the energy appearing as fire that climbed the shield. Keylan's showed as a jet stream of water, flying up the side in tandem with her magic. The wards recognized them, able to identify their magic.

"Well, let's go," she decided, stepping through the ward. If she were anyone else, it would have fried her. Casimir and Zaratella would have no issues so if they followed right behind the twins, which they did. A wise choice.

Chapter 18

Wandering upon a cabin, moss and luscious plants coated the exterior. Wooden panels hidden underneath, signs of rot and lichen showed the age. Kaleopei had brought them through a ward, prancing about in front of Casimir as if none of this was off-putting. The girl was practically glowing, an emotion he hadn't seen from her gracing her face.

Goosebumps lined his arms. He was terrified. The Mystic was fabled to be nothing more than a rumor lost to the ages. She was around while Gods like Paxian, Byrne, and Calsi. If the stories were true, she fought alongside Calsi and her armies during the Realm War. While Calsi was recognized in plenty for her luck and generosity, she was still a feared commander and served what would become the Elven Realm. And he was walking right towards her right hand, into the heart of her advisor. He said the twins were telling lies and had led them into a trap, but he was not convinced that was the case.

The brown-haired siblings engaged in a conversation, carelessly parading their way through the dense forest towards the unsettling abode. For the most part, it looks like Zaratella composed herself, or at least wasn't showing it through body language. Somehow, this was the most relaxed he had seen her as of late, not stressed by all the horrors that came with being a carver. She was simply a girl now living her life as she wanted. Even if that means she'd be becoming a rebel throughout the process.

Which was the same as him at this point...

Casimir wasn't sure how he had come to terms with it. He accepted that he would no longer stay silent and stand by his father while he harmed countless innocent people. A man like that should never have been placed on a throne in the first place.

Feet hit the ground running, causing Keylan to bellow out his laughter. Another thing he had yet to see much of. Kaleopei had begun sprinting, not towards the house, but towards the woods. There it is, just beyond the tree line a blur of black, it was large. Far larger than any creature he had encountered before, including the Wrent.

The girl ran towards it, no weapons drawn. Kaleopei dropped her pack off her shoulder. Her bow was next to be discarded. A large creature with three tails jumped towards her. Kaleopei did not balk. If anything, her body quickened.

Zaratella called out in worry. Her feet started moving towards the creature. Keylan grabbed her cloak, keeping her rooted, all while having a soft smile on his features. Not even in a fraction of worry or discomfort.

"She's not in any harm."

The beast pounced, pinning her to the ground. Then licked her face. Deep black fur and three tails that curled and wagged as it flopped to its side, kicking its paws in the air. When it was standing, it had to be around four feet to the apex of its broad shoulders, with a sloped back and a cat-like frame. Casimir only just recognized the creature, a beast he had only read about. A Vilken.

A creature of the night that stalked unsuspecting prey. Renowned as a story, parents used to scare their children. Seeing it in the flesh was paralyzing.

"What is she doing," Zara's eyes had blown wide at the sight of it getting pampered by Kaleopei. The large cat-like creature bounced on its paws, engaging in a type of play between it and Kaleopei.

"That's Wisp. A beast who doesn't understand the concept of personal space. He also has an incredibly coarse tongue, so tread lightly." Keylan smiled at the two currently wrestling in the grass. The Vilken pawed at the girl in a playful manner that was reminiscent of a hound. Everything about the Vilken screamed domesticated as it was prancing around Kaleopei.

"It's a Vilken." Zaratella gasped, unsure of how she should be responding.

"We did say we knew our way around Human Realm beasts, did we not? We were not lying."

"I didn't think knowing your way translated to domesticating childhood demons." Zara swatted at the boy, letting out her earlier frustration.

"You never asked," he shrugged.

"Actually, I do recall you saying you were running an extermination gig. This thing seems rather un-exterminated."

"Those are just mere details. Besides, Wisp is decent enough when he isn't trying to shove his tongue down your throat."

"Lovely." Zara bit her lip, once again now taking in the surroundings. Casimir hadn't spoken since arriving. Still unsure of what they were about to encounter.

It seemed he was the only person with that on their mind at the moment.

Kaleopei had climbed onto its back, just like one would a horse. Her movements were natural, not a trace of discomfort. Wisp then started running towards them, its large tongue hanging out the side of its mouth, bouncing with every stride.

"I will gut you like an overgrown fish if you trample the whisper weeds, you overgrown mutt." A shrill voice, feminine and hinted with tones of rasp, called out. Both his and Zara's heads whipped at the sound, seeing the women trailing towards them.

She was frail and had a wrinkly face. Her body was barely more than skin and bone, yet she stood tall, with only the slightest hunch at the base of her neck. Long black strands of hair flowed down her back, changing hue to a silvery gray towards its ends. Between her arms held a basket of various mushrooms and flower buds.

"Wisp won't, he's a good boy!" Kaleopei shouted back from atop the massive creature, a wide smile on her features.

"When you get your ass over here, you two can explain why you harbor a kidnapped Prince among you." The older woman leaned on a white cane in her other hand. It unsettlingly resembled that of a bone. Whittled and carved with intricate runes all along its surface.

Not nerve-wracking at all.

Absolutely nothing about this woman screamed unsettling besides the fact that she looked like a villain from one of his books, ready to hex them at any given moment. Her legend predates many others. She may have grown out of her villain stage.

Kaleopei and the Vilken approached them, seemingly not concerned with the appearance of this figure. Kaleopei simply swung her leg over the side of the vilken, sliding down its back until her feet hit the gravel with a soft thud.

"Nice to see you too, Old Hag." Kaleopei nodded her head at the figure, a surprising gesture from the girl.

"Don't go getting soft on me, Girl." The woman smiled softly, showing her aged teeth that filled her mouth.

Again, not unsettling.

"Wouldn't dream of it." Then she was moving, drawing her hunting dagger. With swift movements that resembled a dance more than fighting, she pushed forward. Readying herself to strike at the woman. With no warning, Kaleopei's smile had faded, that calculated calm he'd seen before returning.

Casimir, in the past hour, learned she had far more depth than the killing calm she adapted to.

It was swift when the two made contact, the conflict ending with Kaleopei's arm bent behind her back. The knife inches away from the nape of her neck.

It was then he saw the older woman's movements. They were the same stalking and grace-like movements Kaleopei had.

"You still have a few years before you can slit my throat, Girl."

"Don't suppose you have any of that lavender tea going?" The two were talking like nothing had ever happened. Zara's face showed the tiniest bit of shock, reflecting what they both were feeling.

"I began brewing it the moment you slipped through the words. Come along, children, I wish to hear your tale."

"You're The Mystic?" Zaratella questioned, looking more closely at the girl.

"One of many names time has bestowed upon me. Just call me Hag. It's more personable, in my opinion."

Just like that, Casimir was dragged along into the cabin of an ancient creature forgotten by time.

"And leave the beast outside this time, Girl. Last time, he left a catastrophe in his wake."

"You ruin all my fun."

***

The Mystic's cabin emanated a soothing ambiance, wrapped in the subtle fragrances of potent herbs and mystical incense. As Casimir stepped inside, the air seemed to hum with an enchanting energy. The cabin, though modest in size, held an otherworldly charm that transcended anything he had ever seen before. This was a scene that I could only fathom under the influence of Myth.

For the record, he was not.

"Make yourselves comfortable. Kaleopei, why don't you start talking." Upon closer inspection, he could see the oddities she had littered in the space. Shelves that loomed over the space, not leaving an inch of wall space, were covered in jars and what he only assumed were ancient relics.

"Do you still have those old books, the ones you kept in the sanctum?" The Mystic offered Kaleopei a cup made of clay, steam emitting from the contents.

"I have numerous old books, girl. You need to be more specific."

"Casimir, show the Hag." He was caught off guard by his name being spoken. Casimir hadn't dared to utter a word in the presence of this entity.

Could they trust her? From the stories he's heard, the Mystic only cares for her own interests and doesn't delve into other affairs. Then, everything he knew was approved by his father, who didn't seem keen on history.

"I don't bite, Prince." She spoke like she understood his turmoil. Reading minds didn't seem to be an unrealistic trait of hers. She could read body language the way he does.

"Of course," he forced a smile, slinging the bag over his chest. One by one, he took out the books, only handing one over to her. Her nimble fingers graced the worn leather, her neck craning to look at him. "Call me Imogen," she hissed, laying her eyes on the pages. "Or Hag, if you prefer, makes no difference to me."

"Language ring any bells?" Keylan asked, grabbing another cup from the counter covered in herbs and vials. The whole one-room cabin had such a complexity of smells, varying from fungi to decay and even the most aromatic flowers.

"This isn't something mortals come across every day. This predates even my existence, well, some of it. Lucky for you, I enjoy linguistics."

"Can you read it or not?" Kaleopei nodded her head. It seemed the girl's patience was running thin.

"I can," she ran her long fingernails over the pages. Casimir carefully examined every face she made, trying to dictate what she was reading. "Do you know what you have given me, Prince?"

"I can't say that I do, Imogen." Playing nice and being respectful seemed like the right way to approach this. Casimir didn't have a gauge on her personality yet. Her actions didn't seem deceitful in any way. The twins surely had a great deal of trust in her.

"People will have killed for this." He listened intently, watching as she wove through the space. Pacing as she read the contents. "You finally going to tell me what you experienced, girl? Or is your tongue still numb?"

"Don't speak to her like that. You don't understand." Keylan was quick to stand up. This perked Casimir's ears, hearing the prodding tone of the Mystic.

"Relax, boy. The choice is ultimately hers, but I suspect this little rebellion you're trying to spark didn't come from nowhere." What was Imogen alluding to? Was there something he wasn't aware of?

"The King is collecting elemental magic from Elves that they capture. They dry them out like husks, then leave them to rot."

"You couldn't have spoken this months ago?"

"I could've. I didn't want to believe it. I wanted to forget. I've decided I will no longer let my people suffer in silence."

"You are just like your sister, girl."

"Don't speak her name."

"Why shouldn't I? Resentful?"

Casimir was sure he and Zaratella were overstepping and hearing something they weren't supposed to. For a moment, Kaleopei looked like she might snap. One more word could bring her to the brink. Her emerald eyes glowed in the dim lighting, Imogen only looking until a smile crept onto her features.

"Do not be angry at me, girl. I am not controlling your fate."

"What does that book say?"

"Patience. Back to Louth, what were they using to drain magic?"

"I'm not entirely sure; it was a crystal. Utilized by Carver's, they were able to take magic from a person. We were in complete darkness. Even with my sight, I could only make out the others around me and the faint glow of the crystal overhead."

"Well, that certainly complicates things. These books are blueprints. That's the best way to describe them. Aetherite, was the crystal deep purple in color? Semi-translucent?"

"Yes."

"If they were to continue on with their work and take more magic. I would only assume their goal is to create a weapon."

"You're not serious?" Casimir interjected. Confused about how his father could do such a thing. The Realm was already in a great position of power, feared by most of the Realms. Could he want to conquer more? Was his next target the Mer Realm?

"Afraid, it's written right here. There are additives to the text throughout this tomb. All writings and ideas to best utilize this technology."

No. She was mistaken. Kelvin wrote those. He knew that hideous orange ink anywhere.

"Seems somebody apart from myself is able to translate such old text. I was under the impression it was a dead language. Only spoken and written by those like me. Immortal beings that roamed the continents before your other folk came along."

"So you're saying Bellheim had access to this, able to decipher it?" Zaratella spoke for the first time, her voice entirely too soft for Casimir's liking. She seemed fragile, coming to terms with all they were learning. He couldn't blame her. He himself was unsure of how he was supposed to feel.

Anger? Sadness? Disappointment?

"It seems that's the truth. What other tombs do you possess?"

Casimir didn't say anything; he simply placed the other three books on the small table. Dejected and confused. When did this start? Was this always his father's goal?

"Why don't you go take a minute to converse? I'll get myself acquainted with these." Imogen sat herself down, taking her time as she opened the second book. How were they supposed to just continue on after that knowledge? This changed everything. They were now on a time crunch. Who knows how far they are into this project? If a weapon like that was possible, it would be genocide in his father's hands.

Kaleopei was the first out the door, fists clenched as she burst out the door. Zaratella was next, placing a hand on his shoulder as she briskly exited. Keylan didn't make a single move, like he was rooted to where he stood.

Casimir could understand the fog clouding Keylan's eyes. He felt it as well. Everything was becoming all too real; what they were doing was real.

How do you just carry on after learning something so horrible? The only conclusion he came to was to leave the cabin and light up a pipe.

Chapter 19

The air in the Hag's cabin hung heavy with the weight of unspoken truths, and Keylan found himself restlessly pacing amidst the ancient runes etched into the wooden floor. Imogen, with her black and silver hair cascading like a river of moonlight, watched him with an understanding gaze. The soft glow of crystals cast a muted illumination, emphasizing the gravity of the conversation that loomed.

"Imogen, I don't understand why you were so indifferent when you asked Kaleopei about Louth and those siphon crystals. She's been through hell, and you act like it's just another tale for her to tell." Keylan wasn't sure how to channel all of what he'd learned in the past hours. His sister and companions were outside, yet here he was. Trying to get some answers from the Hag, whose indifference, struck a nerve within Keylan.

"Boy, the echoes of Louth reverberate throughout the realms. No one was certain of what went on there. She was the sole survivor. The existence of the Aetherite Siphons is a wound in the weave of magic, and your sister, resilient as she is, bears those scars. I am simply curious as to what abnormalities we're taking place."

The Hag saw her as an experiment. How does that make her any different from what the Humans are doing? Keylan shot a glance toward the shelves where the notebooks from Casimir lay, the covers decorated with symbols hinting at the secrets within.

"She is not a being to study. Those tombs speak of experiments, of elves drained of their essence, of their entire being! Louth was no mere getaway for her. It's a nightmare etched in Kaleopei's soul, a carved stain. There won't be a day that goes by that she isn't constantly reminded."

"Keylan, your pain is palpable," The Hag placed the tomb she had down. Taking a moment to look at him, "and I sense the turmoil within you. But you must understand, I've lived a very long life. My path often requires detachment, a balance between compassion and the necessity of knowing."

Keylan clenched his fists, feeling the geyser of emotions swirling within. The mention of detachment only fueled his frustration. Could it be that simple to simply stop caring for someone?

"Detachment? Kaleopei was held captive, her magic drained, and you speak of detachment? How can you be so indifferent to her suffering? She is still dealing with the aftermath that place caused."

Imogen approached Keylan with measured steps, her eyes reflecting both ancient wisdom and a hint of empathy. He mirrored her steps, moving backward to keep his distance from her approach.

"Boy, your sister's resilience is an ode to her strength. My debt with life means I must navigate the currents of emotion and knowledge. Occasionally, the river of understanding runs deeper than the surface suggests."

His voice came out strained, grinding his teeth as he spoke, "I just want to protect her. I want to understand how those Aetherite Siphons that you speak of work so no one else has to endure what she went through. So Kaleopei can put this event behind her permanently."

"I understand your frustration and your desire to shield those you love. The Aetherite Siphons are ancient artifacts born of dark ambitions. We will decipher their secrets, and your sister's strength will guide us to that solution." Keylan stopped moving, allowing her to rest a hand on his shoulder.

"She's confided in me some of the terrors she witnessed there."

"Then let's not waste time. Go clear your head, and we'll continue."

Keylan, though still tense, felt a glimmer of reassurance in Imogen's words. The Mystic's cabin, usually a haven of ancient wisdom, became a sanctuary where the vulnerabilities of both mentor and student intertwined. In the delicate dance between frustration and understanding, the threads of fate began to weave a path forward.

Keylan knew he needed to swing at something and allow himself a moment to disregard the deep swell of anger and frustration he was currently feeling.

Imogen's words didn't sit well with him. He knew he couldn't risk storming away. She was an asset they needed.

***

The small training ground, nestled within the heart of the grove, echoed with the clash of metal as Keylan, fueled by an undercurrent of pent-up frustration, swung his broadsword, Skipper, through the air. The metal collided with the bark of a tree, and the Hag would scold him later. Or perhaps she understood.

Either way, he kept swinging.

Sweat dripped down his forehead. He swung again. He hadn't said a word to any of the eyes that seemed taken aback by his demeanor. It wasn't often

187

he got like this, especially in company. Kaleopei, recognizing her brother's turmoil, stepped forward, her twin hunting knives glinting in the flickering sunlight filtering through the leaves.

"Not now, Kaleopei." He didn't even turn his head at her. Simply kept the entirety of his focus ahead. Keylan didn't typically show his temper, but it rivaled that of Kaleopei's. Their arguments could flatten cities if they let them escalate.

"I think now is the perfect time," she countered. The gleam of her blades danced like fire in the sunlight.

"Don't make this harder than it has to be," Keylan knew what she was after. She could read him like a book. At this moment, that infuriated him. Kaleopei could complain all she wanted about his worrying, but she was the same. For the Hag to completely see her as a source of knowledge made his anger swell more.

"Harder? I thought you thrived off a challenge, little brother?"

Kaleopei's taunt struck a chord, and without a word, Keylan lunged forward. Their blades clashed, a symphony of metal ringing through the training ground. The ground was slightly damp from the early morning rainfall they trekked through. The air sizzled with tension as the siblings engaged in a dance of violence, each move an extension of their body. Each strike is being parried by the other.

"No games, Kaleopei."

In response, Kaleopei tapped into her magic. The twin knives became an extension of her elemental prowess. Trails of emerald flame licked at the edges of sharpened metal, adding an unpredictable element to her attacks. Keylan, feeling the heat, channeled his own affinity, creating a barrier that sizzled as it met the fiery onslaught.

"Don't hold back on me, Key."

Keylan unleashed a torrent of water, surging toward Kaleopei with a force that sent her skidding backward. The water wrapped around her like a controlled tempest, but she met it with a defiant grin.

Kaleopei was consoling him in her own unique way. He knew this deep down. Although that wouldn't stop him from making sure she was safe, he knew she could handle anything he threw at her. Kaleopei always had.

"A little bit of water, really? That's not enough to slow me."

As the water and fire clashed, the siblings found themselves in a back-and-forth display of elemental warfare. Keylan, determined to release his aggression, swung Skipper with a newfound ferocity. Kaleopei, agile and quick, danced through the melee, her knives creating streaks of fire that cut through the air with ease.

A surge of magic coursed through Keylan as he summoned a small wall of water, deflecting Kaleopei's fiery onslaught. The leaves in the training ground swirled in response, caught in the dance of elements. Yet, Kaleopei, undeterred, twirled around the water, her knives slicing through the air. Every step she took was a nod to her agility.

"That's the brother I know."

With a burst of determination, Keylan unleashed a combination of water and used her flames to his advantage, creating a mist that shrouded the training ground. In the haze, the siblings circled each other, their instincts, and magic intertwining in a choreography of combat.

The clash of blades and elemental forces echoed through the grove, a testament to the intertwined destinies of the twins. In the dance of steel and magic, Keylan found a temporary release for the aggression that simmered beneath the surface, a release granted by the rhythmic clash of blades against the reality of their shared history.

As the mist began to dissipate, Keylan and Kaleopei found themselves standing in the aftermath of their sparring session. Both were breathless, their faces flushed with exertion, yet there was a shared glint of amusement in their eyes.

The ground itself was a mix of mud and singed grass. Keylan knew the dirt would be stained for a long while. Eventually, it'd recover.

"I forgot your talents with those," Keylan huffed out, motioning towards the twin blades. "Your eyes are usually down the neck of an arrow."

"And you swing that broadsword like you're trying to impress the whole forest, Key."

The tension that had fueled their clash transformed into contagious laughter that bubbled up from deep within. Keylan sheathed Skipper, and Kaleopei twirled her twin knives before returning them to their sheaths. Keylan didn't know what he'd do without his sister. She was his constant light. A constant reminder of what's good in the cruel world they live in.

"You're not humble either," He laughed at her face of betrayal.

"Careful, I can draw my blades quicker than you can swing that sword."

Their banter continued a lighthearted exchange that brought a sense of normalcy to the world they inhabited. Amidst the laughter and teasing, the weight of their responsibilities momentarily lifted, leaving behind the comforting warmth of shared laughter and the unbreakable bond between the twins.

If only this could last a lifetime.

Chapter 20

Casimir and Zara stood at the edge of the training ground, silent spectators to the elemental spectacle unfolding before them. The air still crackled with the residual energy of the siblings' clash, and as they exchanged laughter and banter, a mixture of surprise and awe flickered across Casimir and Zara's faces.

Casimir wasn't entirely sure what he just witnessed, but he knew the Keylan he looked at now was entirely different from the rage-filled man who had stomped out of the cabin.

"How long have they been at it?" Casimir froze at the voice. It wasn't Zara's, no, it was The Mystics. Imogen's. He didn't know what his opinion was and needed to observe the being more before coming to any sort of conclusion.

"Since he's been out here," Zara answered. "Said she was going to calm him down, then they started butting heads."

"Indeed they did. Neither of them slacked in their training. Both held back."

"You're saying they can be more dangerous?" They were slinging powerful magic against each other. He didn't want to know what destruction they could bring. They would bring in the near future.

"I taught them to utilize their talents efficiently." Off playing with a large ball composed of moss was Wisper, acting like the grove wasn't just full of magic. Casimir had never felt a concentrated magical presence, and it prickled his skin.

"They mentioned you were a mentor of sorts. You taught them to fight like that?" Zara was asking all the questions. He still wasn't sure what to make of this.

"Not fight, to protect. I did my duties well." The Mystic snapped her neck at Zara. She was insulted by the accusation. "Senseless violence won't bring about change."

Casimir and Zara exchanged a knowing glance, silently acknowledging the complexity and beauty of elven magic. Casimir was able to better understand the twins, seeing behind their thick walls. It was a brief glimpse into a world where the elements and emotions intertwined, and in that moment of shared understanding, they found themselves awed by the powerful forces at play within this emerging rebellion.

Casimir knew he wanted to be a rebel.

The twins' laughter echoed a harmonious melody that sparked resilience and hope within him.

"Collect the brutes and join me in the Sanctum. They'll know where it is." She walked at a brisk pace, faster than it looked like she was able to.

"Do you think they're done?" Casimir joked towards Zaratella. Not wanting to think of what Imogen might've found in those books.

"I doubt those two will ever be done." She laughed back. He had no doubt that she was right. Zaratella continued towards the twins, a hand on her hip as she walked.

***

The cabin was bathed in the soft glow of crystals as Imogen, flanked by the twins Casimir and Zaratella, unfurled a parchment filled with ancient symbols and verses. The air seemed to hum with anticipation as she began to unravel the mysteries contained within the tomes from Casimir's possession, along with relics from her own collection.

The Sanctum couldn't be described. It was something only Casimir had ever read about. Much like the upstairs, there wasn't a single surface besides the table they surrounded that wasn't covered with books and jars that he was sure outdated him.

"These writings, from a time before the gods became gods, speak of Aetherite. Its power, wielded with both reverence and fear, has left a gap in our history."

The group leaned in, their eyes fixated on the symbols that danced across the parchment. They had already known that, but he didn't dare object to her phrasing.

"The Aetherite Siphons, crafted with immortal skill and ancient runes, were not merely devices of extraction. They were once used to channel the essence of the elements into weapons – instruments of both creation and destruction."

Casimir's eyes widened, realizing the gravity of the revelation. He never received a formal education pertaining to the Elven Realm, but he knew each person was affiliated with an element. Are Elves direct descendants of the immortals?

"Weapons got fueled by the elements themselves? That's... unimaginable." Zaratella looked at all the scores and books Imogen had laid out. Scanning each with a new perspective.

"It's some bullshit. Magic shouldn't be used like that, there's a balance it requires high concentrates are unstable." Kaleopei scoffed.

"Indeed. The Aetherite, harnessed from organic material and imbued with elemental essence, could be forged into blades that bore the very essence of nature. These weapons, called "Elemental Blades," were wielded by legendary beings in times when gods walked among mortals. There are a few relics in temples across all the realms of these blades, but if I recall, they are void of any magic. It requires a siphon to give them the destructive power. Now they are just mere blades made of a durable crystal."

Kaleopei exchanged a glance with Keylan, the weight of which they carried becoming more apparent. His father could have turned Kaleopei into one of those very weapons.

"Why would immortal beings need a weapon of mass destruction? Weren't they magically innate already, why require more?

"Allow me to finish, girl. Aetherite, in its raw form, was used in ancient rituals to enhance the natural affinity of elemental magic. It was a time when the bond between themselves and nature was revered and celebrated. I'd imagine it was a precaution for advisories along with part of their belief system in their minds."

Keylan, who had been observing silently, spoke up.

"So, the Aetherite wasn't always a tool of manipulation. Was it once a conduit for harmony with nature? Was it used as a symbol of worship?"

"Precisely," Imogen's grin widened. A silent praise of recognition towards Keylan. "It was only in the shadows of time that dark ambitions twisted its purpose. As for worship, some did. We called her The Mother of Many. It was believed that these crystals were a symbol of her presence. The ability to store elemental magic was revolutionary. It was thought to be a gift directly from the Mother."

Casimir, still absorbing the revelations, asked a crucial question, "How were the Elemental Blades forged, and what was their true purpose?"

He didn't mention the intention of her words. Casimir was aware she was old, but to be alive during the Peace War seemed unfathomable. Imogen took her time, mulling over her words.

"The forging involved a sacred process, a communion between skilled artisans, powerful enchanters, and the very essence of the elements. As for their purpose, the Elemental Blades were often created to combat ancient threats, entities that threatened the balance of the realms. What lurks on the continents now is only a mere fraction of the beasts that roamed the land before your time."

Casimir noticed the tone dropping. She cut her sentence before another could start. Was she keeping something?

The gravity of the knowledge weighed on the room as the group absorbed the implications of the revelations. The Aetherite, once a force of harmony, had become entangled in a web of manipulation and dark ambitions. As they navigated the threads of history, the group realized the intricacies of their quest to thwart Bellheim's designs and protect the delicate balance between elves and the elemental forces that shaped their existence.

"Why is this Aetherite unknown to the world now? Something of this stature would stand against time." Kaleopei leaned her elbows on the table, crouching, so her eyes scanned the surface.

"During the peace war, some decided this information isn't something that should be common knowledge. What you call the Deep Realm used to be full of life, just like any other. Ask yourself why the Realm's history isn't known?"

"You're saying it was covered up?" Keylan added to his sister's early question.

"A war was sure to take the attention of many. Only a few still continued worship during those sixty-two years. I was young when the war first started. It's only a fragment left in my recollection."

Casimir had thought about the woman earlier, but he was near positive now.

"You're one of the Immortals?"

"Yes and no. That's a complicated question, young one. At a time, I say I was."

"You didn't want to live forever?" Casimir unraveled Imogen's layers inch by inch. Understanding more and more as she spoke in that raspy voice.

"I did what I had to in order to protect someone I cared about." This was the most emotional he had seen from her yet. She was defending her actions. "I can't die. Immortals could be killed. It was just that age didn't claim them."

Kaleopei and Keylan listened intently. It was clear that they didn't know the depth of the Mystic. Her skin was sickly, bones showing from beneath. Imogen grew many plants, most of which he was able to identify as poisonous.

"You've tried, haven't you?"

Imogen looked at him, really studying all he was saying. It was clear she was exhausted, tired of being what she was. In some twisted way, he understood. Having to endure being something that he didn't even wish for in the first place.

From across the table, Kaleopei shot him a venomous glare. A warning to stop prying. He wouldn't gain answers by staying complacent.

"I've experienced a lot. None of which is of relevance to this conversation," her voice was low, with a twinge of a quiver upon her lips.

"You know about Aetherite?" Zara's question cut through the tension.

"I know many things."

"You've never mentioned any of this before," Keylan crossed his arms over his broad chest, showing the confusion on his face.

"When would it have been relevant, boy? I haven't had the inkling that Aetherite was being used once more, most definitely not by Humans."

"How destructive can these weapons be?" Kaleopei laced her fingers together, elbows resting on the surface. Casimir had come to recognize the emotion on her face as contemplating. She was deep in thought.

"Anywhere from an inconvenience to a cataclysmic event. There are many factors to be considered, especially when taking the amount of magic a single blade holds."

"What else? You're leaving something out." Kaleopei was calm. Far too calm for the information being tossed around.

"Well, these other tombs described are written by an independent researcher. They studied, let's say, other means of using the aetherite siphons." Casimir didn't like where this was going. "Condensed magic can be volatile, entirely unpredictable when wielded by those without innate reserves. This device depicted can condense it into one blast."

"You're saying they have a way to utilize elemental magic into a single beam?"

Casimir's face went pale. Seeing the twins go at it with only their magic had seemed destructive. A device that could channel that into a single target would be devastating. He wasn't well versed in the arcane, but he knew that so much magic would cause a disturbance and potentially erupt.

"It's what I'm insinuating."

Everyone fell silent, and a sudden blanket of defeat fell over the group. The only one who seemed unfazed was Kaleopei, whose gaze could make someone shiver from its intensity.

The dim lighting in Imogen's underground sanctum flickered, tinging in hue to a soft emerald green. It was only for a brief moment, the flames returning to the orange and red mix.

"Casimir," his name coming from Kaleopei was suddenly startling him. "Is there anyplace you know of that the King might be able to store such a thing? I am almost certain that I would have felt the magic if it was housed in Louth. He has to be keeping it somewhere."

"Possibly, I mean, he owns many properties throughout the entire Realm." Casimir racked his brain. The siphon must have some kind of range. "He owns land in Lispin. It's close to the border."

"And directly south of Louth, it's almost a straight shot." Kaleopei grabbed a map from her pack, unrolling it over the ancient tombs and scrolls. "Hag, do you know if these siphons can have more than one output? Like, can it split, or are we only dealing with one?"

The Mystic's silence spoke more than any words could.

"This is not my expertise. I've never witnessed an elemental blade or a siphon. I've only seen depleted crystals. All of my further knowledge is based on assumption only."

"What would happen if the siphon was destroyed?" Kaleopei pushed.

"I'm uncertain of what would become of the device or devices."

It was a silent symphony of intellect and focus that caught Casimir's attention. Casimir couldn't help but marvel at the way her mind danced with the complexities of the written word. He saw the subtle movements of her lips, the occasional furrow of her brow, and the confident nods as she connected pieces and drew on the map. In that quiet moment, a realization dawned on Casimir. Kaleopei's intelligence wasn't merely a surface brilliance; it ran deep, a reservoir of insight and understanding. He recognized the familiar patterns of analytical thought, the nuanced approach to problem-solving that mirrored his own.

The silence in the cabin spoke volumes. Casimir, usually adept at reading people, found himself captivated by the enigma that was Kaleopei's mind. There were no words exchanged, but a silent understanding unfolded between them as she locked eyes with him.

There would be time for him to organize his emotions. At this moment, he had to help and aid her in this twisted game of figuring out his father. He so desperately wanted to end the torture happening to Elves. Casimir knew he could never understand what Kaleopei went through. He'd gathered that she'd been abused and held against her will. But from what he's heard, it's a miracle she stood in front of him.

"I broke a siphon." Kaleopei's voice wasn't timid. She held herself high. "When I was in the pit, I broke it. They aren't destructible. From the fact that we are all standing here and not in a crater, it's probably safe to assume that disengaging a siphon from its output isn't dangerous. The device more than likely seizes to gain any more magic."

Heads whipped towards her. Casimir's mind wandered, thinking of what could be done, "How easy is it to create a siphon?"

"Magic manipulators can channel preexisting sources of magic through the crystal. So long as they have the Aetherite, they can make a siphon."

"We should assume they have a few reserves in case something goes sideways," he took up a spot next to Kaleopei. Looking at the lines and notes she had jotted down.

"I agree."

Casimir, since they burst into the castle, he felt real hope. The four of them could figure this out and keep people safe from his father.

Chapter 21

Kaleopei's brain worked on overdrive. In her mind, she categorized and tried to make sense of all the intel she had gained in a short amount of time. With an unknown time crunch, time couldn't be wasted.

"We have to split up. There's no way around it, one group to Louth and the others to Lispin." Kaleopei decided, seeing most of the eyes in the room on her. She bit her lip, not wanting to give away any of the anxiety currently coursing through her. Instead, she poured her focus into a logical standpoint.

"I can't go to Lispin. To Bellheim, my not reporting to Louth is considered treason. I sent false information to the King. If any of this is known, I will be arrested on the spot, if not killed." Kaleopei nodded to Zara's argument. Doing her best to remain unshaken, even if her heart was pounding uncontrollably.

"You're not going to Louth," Keylan's eyes snapped to Kaleopei's, his voice stern.

"Like hell, I'm not. I know the layout quite well." She countered, meeting her brother's heated gaze with a fury of her own. A clash of fire and water, in this instance, did not mix. Both heated gazes are unrelenting when challenged by the other.

"Me and Zara go to Louth, you and Casimir venture to Lispin. It's still a viable option."

"Absolutely not, Key. Have you lost sense of your logic? Don't let your emotions cloud your judgment. You know I'm right."

"I'm not going to stand here and let you go back there. You didn't see what you were like when I got you back. You were broken, Kaleopei." Neither of them broke their gaze. Keylan raised his voice, pointing his finger at her. "You've come so far. I won't allow you to fall back. Vengeance be dammed. I can't lose you again."

"I determine what I can and can't do. As much as it might wound your pride, you have no actual sway over my decision." She was shaken, but her voice remained level. She refused to let her conviction slip.

Kaleopei knew what she had to do.

"It's self-destructive, Kaleopei." She would rather not hear his words. She could handle herself just fine. She had done so already. Part of her hated that Zaratella and Casimir had to witness this, knowing that her demeanor was shaken.

Kaleopei didn't want them to see her as weak. Let alone, before they split their separate ways.

"I know what awaits me if I get caught. That won't happen. Not again." Her lip trembled as her hands balled into clenched fists. The quill in her hand snapped as her knuckles turned white.

"I'll watch over her." The voice came from her left, Zara sending a wink in her direction.

"I don't need a sitter. I'm perfectly capable of handling myself while maintaining my graceful poise." Her tone put an end to the debate. Allowing her companions a moment to settle back down, her own body relaxing once more.

"It's rather simple, then. Zara and Kaleopei locate the siphons in Louth. Leaving Keylan and myself to expose Lispin. I'm not an expert on the area, but I've visited many times with Zara." Kaleopei was grateful Casimir took the verdict from her mouth. She could tell they thought alike, similar ways of strategizing.

"Hag, I got a request," she puzzled towards the elder currently flicking through pages of a tomb. The slightest hum was the only indication that she heard. "If all goes unwell, get Princess Melody of the Mer Realm out of Bellheim. Frankly, I don't give a shit how you do so, but see to it that it's done."

Heads once again spun towards her, with the most shock being from Casimir and Zara. With her head held high, she simply ignored their gazes.

"That I can promise, girl."

"You won't join our rebellion?" Zara smiled like a cat on the prowl.

"I don't indulge myself in mortal affairs."

"You won't for them?" Casimir interjected, pointing between the twins.

"Do not try to force your morals upon me. I have no such interests anymore. No matter the outcome, I will outlive it."

"Regardless of what the Hag won't and will do. We need to get our approach agreed upon." Kaleopei took the attention once more. "We'll head to Alstead and stock up on anything we might need there. Then split Louth group going north, and Lispin west. Then, we spark a rebellion, possibly overthrowing a king. Make some head rolls while we're at it."

"We shouldn't go public with this revelation?" Keylan questioned.

"It wouldn't do anything. Humans have been taught to hate elves for the past eight years. Even if I were to personally endorse these endeavors, it would be scandalized as you manipulated me. Unfortunately, I know how my father plays."

"Cas, you know what this can lead to, right? If Darren is in Louth, and we cross paths..." Zara trailed off, looking down at her hands. It was a real possibility, a likely one, too.

"Try to detain him if you can." Kaleopei carefully watched as he swallowed, searching for any hint of empathy. "Use force if need be. I would rather him rot away than be granted the mercy of a swift death."

A silent agreement settled in the room. For all she wanted to strike him through the heart with an arrow, she also could entertain the idea of him living in misery for the remainder of his days. Either way, should he cross paths with her, Kaleopei won't hesitate to raise hell.

"Team Lispin, your goal is to drain this device of any magic. The last resort is breaking it entirely. We don't know how the store magic will react. Figure out a way to drain it." Kaleopei looked between the two men. She had hoped they could do it, so long as they focused. Keylan could keep Casimir safe from most threats. If her inkling about Casimir is true, he should be able to find a way to stop the canon.

"Even if we capture the King, swaying his disciples won't be an easy task," Zara admitted.

"It will be if we make him admit guilt." She could and would. Her anger was a weapon, and in his presence, how she'd keep control was something to be seen.

"How will we communicate our findings?" Zara asked.

"We trust in the others," Casimir began. "The distance between Louth and Lispin isn't much. I'd guess only two or three hours apart on foot."

"He's right," Keylan spoke, running his hands through his hair. "But we should still set a place to regroup."

The Hag was picking through one of the shelves. Kaleopei knew her ears pricked into their conversation, listening intently. She turned to face the table once more, placing two small pearl-like beads on the table.

"Use the grove. Simply break these, and you'll return here."

"There's only two?"

"So long as the two of you remain in contact, it will bring both parties."

"It's settled then. We shouldn't waste any more time. Anything else can be flushed out along the way to Alstead." Kaleopei stood up, rolling the map and tucking it into her pack. It ushered everyone to gate her their things, packing up to be on the move once more.

"Imogen, do you mind keeping the tombs here? I don't see why they should be placed anywhere else." Kaleopei noted the conversation happening between the Hag and Casimir. The sun should be setting shortly. Moving during the night would be best.

"No one will have access to them here, Prince."

"I appreciate that."

Kaleopei wasn't sure what would be coming next, what they would endure. She didn't have very much to lose, but Casimir and Zaratella did. Both could have had normal lives, away from the conflict they brought to their doorstep.

From the confidence and fury behind Zara's eyes, Kaleopei figured that she would have done something rebellious sooner or later. Their crossing paths only accelerated that chance.

"Your gratitude isn't needed, Prince of the new dawn."

Casimir, on the other hand, didn't know. She thought Zara might've swayed him with enough persistence. Kaleopei held no anger towards the Prince. He was only a tool his father wanted to use down the line.

"I'm raiding your wardrobe." Kaleopei pushed herself from the table, walking out of the sanctum and then up the ladder back into the cabin.

"Don't touch the silks!" Imogen called out from the basement, her voice raspy even with the volume.

Kaleopei didn't answer, simply moved to the trunk by her bed, separated by a wooden divider. Even the divider had shelves and plants that cascaded down its entirety. She shuffled through the clothes, finding a few articles that would suit her needs. A hooded cloak is woven in dark green fabric with intricate hems. Perfectly attuned to her preferred style.

She also found two other cloaks, throwing them over her shoulder. A rustle from the other side of the cabin told her the others had emerged.

"Take these." She tossed both gray-colored coats toward Zara and Casimir. "Don't need you being recognized."

"I've never worn one of these before. It's usually forbidden for royalty to cloak themselves," Kaleopei noted the tone Casimir had as he fasted it around his neck. Keylan elbowed the boy in reassurance.

"Suits you, gives the ladies an element of mystery." He wiggled his shoulders, his own cloak flowing along with the movement.

"Don't let him fool you. Key's only encounters with women have been maternal or me." Kaleopei laughed as Keylan swatted her shoulder. Even with the banter, she could make out the worry that clouded his eyes. Still distraught from their earlier argument.

No matter how much it pained her to see him so withdrawn. Kaleopei had no other choice than to stand on her convictions.

If not for the sake of the elven realm, then for him. Regardless of what it might cost her. In every lifetime, she would give everything.

***

The journey to Alstead unfolded like before. With each step, everyone learned more and more about their companions. The air carried the scent of familiarity as the group approached the dwelling where Ellis had taken the twins in so long ago.

The village, nestled amidst rolling hills and shaded by ancient trees, cradled a sense of timelessness. Cobblestone pathways wound through clusters of quaint cottages, and the air hummed with a peace Kaleopei always loved.

Breathing the air in filled her with a sense of familiarity. A place she had called home.

As Casimir, Kaleopei, Keylan, and Zaratella traversed the familiar paths, the anticipation of reunion ignited the atmosphere. Kaleopei noticed Casimir, who had only glimpsed Alstead in passing from what he said, marveled at its understated beauty. It was a quiet, quaint charm.

"Alstead isn't what I thought it'd be. It's different from the grandeur of the most Human Cities, but there's a warmth here. It's rather welcoming." Casimir hummed.

"This place became our refuge when everything crumbled. Ellis was our anchor." Keylan recalled fondly, tossing a smile towards Kaleopei.

"Alstead had a lot of Elven influence eight years ago. It was the first place the King started searching for Elven refugees," Kaleopei didn't know why she felt the need to indulge this information. It would only make the Prince feel guilty, but she felt like it needed to be said. It needed to be remembered. "Ellis hid us in her floorboards while her husband was dragged from their home. Berix was a kind soul. I can only hope his end was swift."

With the mood sullen, they approached the heart of Alstead, reaching Ellis' abode, a cottage that seemed to embrace the essence of home. Or as close to home as Kaleopei has had in a long while.

The structure, adorned with climbing vines and surrounded by a riot of blooming flowers, stood as a testament to the resilience of life even in the wake of change. As they approached the door, memories of the first time Zaratella met the twins flooded her mind.

"It feels like a lifetime ago when I first came here. Hard to believe it's only been twelve days." In those twelve days, so much has changed. Kaleopei knew it would continue to change.

Kaleopei, her heart aflutter with anticipation, pushed on the door. Moments later, Ellis, a figure whose kindness had left an indelible mark on the twins' journey, peeked around the corner, her face wide with a grin.

"Well, look who's back. You brought the company this time." The reunion sparked a cascade of emotions as the twins embraced Ellis. The lines etched by time on Ellis' face mirrored the trials and triumphs that had shaped their shared history. "I've missed you two. And you, Zaratella, it's good to see you again. Glad these two haven't worn you down."

"It's a pleasure to be back." There was something so domestic about the scene. A sight that felt so foreign, yet Kaleopei couldn't help but long for it, for the simplicity it brought.

"Well, don't let me keep you, come in. Come in. You? I don't believe we've met." Ellis turned to Casimir, pulling him in for an impromptu hug. Kaleopei stepped into the cottage. Alstead, with its rolling hills and familiar faces, became a haven where the past intertwined with the present. The reunion wouldn't be echoed with laughter and adventure-filled stories this time around. No, this would be far different.

"My name is Casimir. It's delightful to meet you." Kaleopei resisted the urge to burst into a fit of laughter. Seeing this formal version of the Prince was something she hadn't seen commonly. Traveling, he had seen Casimir and Zaratella throwing insults like sailors would, much like her and Keylan.

"The pleasure is all mine, darling." Ellis ushered us all inside, accompanying us to the table. Many of the bowls filled with ingredients were laid out. Ellis had been baking, and Kaleopei knew that meant she'd been stressed. Says sweets make her feel at ease. "It's good you came through when you did. This place has been crawling with soldiers as of late. The most recent batch left in the early morning. What have you two done?"

"Light murder and a whole lot of treason. Possibly kidnapping?" Kaleopei smiled, occupying herself with kneading a ball of dough on the counter. Something simple that occupied her body.

"All warranted, I assume?"

"We won't stay long, we just need supplies." Kaleopei tossed back at the older woman, her face showing signs of her age. Reminding her that Ellis was human.

"She's right. We don't intend to bring you any trouble." Casimir threw in. Taking a seat on one of the chairs.

"I assume they kidnapped you, Crowned Prince."

"I went willingly, ma'am."

"I'm sure you did." Kaleopei watched as Ellis studied Casimir. Sizing him up the same way she did to Zaratella. "That's neither here nor there. You four should spend the night. The fire festival is being put on tonight."

"Time has flown by recently. I completely forgot." Keylan joined Kaleopei in the baking prep, with Ellis tending to the fire.

"We're on a timer. We don't have the time to spare." Kaleopei looked at her brother. Quirking a brow at his enthusiasm. *Fenyah* meant a lot to both of them. It's a miracle that they have lived to see another. In the human tongue, it was called the Fire Festival, and a lot less tradition was involved in this Realm.

"Should we have a night of celebration before we turn the world upside down?" Keylan nudged her shoulder, earning an eye roll from his sister. Kaleopei looked towards Casimir, and Zara, asking to back her up.

"I think it sounds like a lovely idea. All we've done recently is stress. One night won't kill us." Casimir nodded along to Zara's words. Kaleopei sent a glare towards the girl, whose face was illuminated by the fire.

Traitor.

But she didn't deny the fact that Zara would look divine, basking in the warm glow of a raging fire. The warm drinks that were served were divine. Kaleopei could practically taste the spiked cider rushing down her throat.

"It's settled then. You four will remain here for the night. You can depart on whatever it is on your agenda in the morning after we celebrate." Ellis was determined to see this through. Kaleopei couldn't find a reason to complain. Dressing up and dancing all around a fire was her ideal night. She'd have to rummage her closet to find something suitable to wear. Hoping whatever she owned would still fit her frame.

"Whatever you wish, Ellis."

"Damn right, it is." The laughter that rang through the room was comforting. A sense of normalcy after all they had been through. All they had learned. "The festival starts at sunset. I hear we have a traveling band in town who intends to play."

"Sounds lovely." Kaleopei smiled, brushing the flour off her hands. She needed a nice warm bath before the festivities began.

Chapter 22

"What makes them so bold? How do they keep moving forward after everything?" Casimir's head hung low. His blue eyes seemed murkier than the lake they were gathered around. Just on the outskirts of Alstead, a large bonfire emitted warmth after the sun went away. Far off, he could make out the dancing of the twins, smiles spread across their faces as they jumped and frolicked in tune with the traveling band.

It wasn't something he was accustomed to. Sure, they celebrated the Fire Festival in the capital, but it's done in a proper manner. A royal ball hosted by the King, which, no doubt, has been canceled this year. Others only celebrated in their homes, not daring enough to risk the possible accusation of insubordination.

His father would somehow call the beautiful scene this treason.

"They hide it well. Those two will always put the needs of the other over themselves." The older woman leaned onto her cane, gazing into the raging fire that was being kept in the dark of night. "It's also the beginning of *Fenyah,* an older Elven Holiday, much like our Fire Festival. It also happens to be their day of birth. While Elves do live longer, they seem to have a deeper appreciation for life than we do, child."

"I don't think I could ever catch up to them. They keep rising to whatever challenges they face and coming out of it." The crowned princes' eyes never left as more people joined in on the beautiful dancing that seemed to be going on. They were teaching the humans what they were doing, and they followed along, thinking it was some kind of odd dance the two had made up in the spur of the moment. Zara fit in nicely, like she wasn't trained to rip every ounce of magic from those his father deemed lesser. Dressed in an ornate lavender dress, Ellis had put together for her. She and Kaleopei made a nice pair. Casimir could see the way they snuck glances at each other. Both were completely enamored by the other, but still too unsure to do anything about it.

"They don't come out unscathed. They bore more scars than anyone could ever imagine. Those two would die for each other and the world they dream about. It's a scary thing for me, never knowing if they'll return, but it's what keeps them going. They won't let the other die for them, so they keep fighting tooth and nail. Have been that way since I hid them in my floorboards almost nine years ago."

"Why'd you save them? Pardon my brashness. Kaleopei had explained some of their story before we arrived. If someone found out, you would've been executed. My father would have seen to it personally." Ellis wasn't sure what the boy's position was, but she knew a lost soul when she saw one.

"Because they had the same look in their eyes as you do now. You will also grow into something you could only ever dream about. You all are doing good for Kaleopei. It's clear she's blossoming."

His blue eyes locked with emerald ones, and across the fire was Keylan. A smile broad on his face as he laughed at something his sister said into his ear. Then he was moving closer, extending out a hand towards Casimir.

"I'm not as young as I look," Ellis seemed to notice and used the back of her cane to push the prince forward. "Have fun tonight. There will be tomorrow to brood, Prince of the New Dawn."

Casimir only quirked a brow at the repeating words he kept seeming to hear. With no time to react to them, Keylan whisked him into the commotion. The warmth of the blazing fire sent a pleasant glow inside of him.

He could dwell on it later. Letting loose seemed warranted.

***

"Loosen up a little bit. You look stiff." Keylan laughed at him, music coursing through the air. A mix of folk and drums, intense and powerful. Like fire. Casimir's extent of dancing was only done in galas, and he'd count each step he made.

"I'm trying," he countered. Moving between his feet in an erratic manner. Nothing about this was organized. Keylan told him to just move as he felt.

Elves are often thought of as proper and the epitome of grace. This kind of dancing seemed to go against everything he was ever taught. It was graceful in its own way. The way Kaleopei glided on her feet was akin to the way she prowled during a fight. Skidded and jumped around to the beat. It was an unusual grace, different but still graceful.

Across the fire, he made out Zara and Kaleopei engaged in a mesmerizing dance. Seems Zara was able to pick up on it far quicker than him. Keylan was showing a human girl how to stomp her feet to the beat. A carelessness he hadn't seen from either of the twins. It made him feel like he had missed out on a whole other culture, one stereotyped and manipulated by the Human education he received. Experiencing something he had only ever read about.

215

Casimir was offered a drink and accepted it. Everyone was sloshed, all drinking and partying to their hearts' content. It made sense for Alstead to go all out, with the knowledge that it had Elven influence.

The music fell into a slightly calmer tone. He caught Zaratella talking to one of the drummers. Without the drumming, it was all upbeat, with no undertone backing the other instruments.

"Attention all! I was told we have a little songbird in our midst!" With Zaratella standing by the drummers' side, she pointed at Kaleopei. Whose face was flushed in the warm lighting the fire gave off. "Why don't you come on up here!"

Keylan whistled from his spot, laughing as Kaleopei strode forward. Staring down at Zara as she brushed past her.

"What's your name, dear?"

"Kaleopei," She laughed, taking the microphone from his hands. She swayed slightly, clearly having had a few drinks. "It's almost my birthday and my brother's! Keylan, where are you?"

Said twin raised his hand, a few yelling their congratulations at both of them. "Alright, but who wants a song from Elva's very own singer?" The mass of people roared with cheer. Casimir watched as she whispered a few words to the musicians.

"Alright now, I don't usually sing such hymns, but I figured tonight feels like a good night." Kaleopei worked the crowd, them roaring with positive feedback. The girl was beaming with a smile, searching over the crowd that began to form. "Who are we to deny the songbird of what she wants?" The band handed over the crowd to her, smiling in suspense.

"Why is that for me?" Kaleopei crouched down, taking a flower from a human child. Gracefully sticking it behind her ear, the orange color a stark contrast to her brown curls and emerald eyes. "Ain't that kind of you."

Casimir couldn't hear the rest of the exchange that happened between the two. Only able to watch with amusement. Kaleopei nodded to the band, straightening herself out.

The music changed, a more raw sound coming from them all. Harmonizing in the lower notes. Then Kaleopei's voice filled the emptiness the music was missing.

In the heart of the embers, where shadows slowly dance,

A flame is kindled in a fiery trance.

Born from the whispers of ancient desire,

I sing the tale of the untamed fire.

It was like a spell had come over the crowd. All eyes were fixated on Kaleopei, wearing an emerald green dress that puffed at her waist. The top was snug against her skin, showing off her figure. Her arms extenuating the words she sang.

Oh, the dance of flames, a wild ballet,

A symphony of warmth that lights our way.

From flickering whispers to a roaring pyre,

I sing the ballad of the untamed fire.

A chorus, each word sung with emotion as Kaleopei moved back and forth. A mix of belts and tones weaved into a song. He hadn't known she sang. She wasn't a very talkative person when it came to aspects of herself. Zaratella somehow knew she had coaxed her into singing in front of the crowd. Each note is a testament to her talent.

A Phoenix rose from ashes and heat,

In the dance of embers, secrets are seen.

The crackle of timbers, a primal choir,

I sing the anthem of the untamed fire.

It wasn't a sanctioned song by the King. This could also be considered treason under the law. No one here seemed to notice, all entranced by her voice. Casimir found himself mesmerized by her words, each barring her emotions.

With every flicker, a story unfolds,

In the heart of the blaze, where passion molds.

A dance with danger, a seductive liar,

I sing the saga of the untamed fire.

He could feel the music building, matching her tone. Casimir wondered what she told the musicians. It certainly wasn't any well-known composure. It was nearing its end, the final dip in the music.

In the darkest corners, where shadows conspire,

The flame's embrace, a relentless heat.

A beacon of hope, an element untamed,

I sing the hymn of the flourishing fire.

The band played the last note, allowing her final line to be sung without any backing. Casimir felt himself lost in her trance. Melody might be the siren, but Kaleopei's voice was moving without magic.

Casimir then realized, under the moonlight, basked in flame. Kaleopei was a force of nature, able to put on a facade to help others. Never has he seen her put herself first in any situation, every time volunteering to be put into a dangerous and complicated situation,

It wasn't confirmed. Casimir could be completely off the mark. But he decided she faced a lot of turmoil, constantly in a state of guilt. Guilt that she is alive. Kaleopei and Keylan become a lot clearer during the night. The sheer passion and ideals they have pushed forward by their guilt and need to protect.

His father had caused that. All the pain that the twins felt was brought on by the King. A tyrant who wanted nothing more than to put them down. Through it all, they pushed against the world that tried to drown them.

Chapter 23

Kaleopei allowed the flames to move her body, swaying in the red, flickering light of the bonfire. Fenyah was never about grace or order. It was as volatile as fire. Unpredictable and utterly beautiful. Just like the Witch that stood far too close to her, both faces flushed with alcohol. It was almost reminiscent of the first time they met inside Elva's tavern, where Kaleopei was spying on the capital carver, which she found coated in blood.

How far they had come from that moment was beyond her.

Zara copied her dancing, throwing her arms around and stomping her feet to the beat of the drums. Kaleopei's heart was beating loudly, a thrilling event that she had always taken pride in. It was like Fenyah was made specifically for her. Every moment fueled her own flame, feeling the magic lick beneath her skin.

The night danced with vibrant hues as flames leaped to the rhythm of the night. Kaleopei, swaying slightly under the influence of the festival's spirits, found herself surrounded by her companions – Keylan, Zaratella, and Casimir. The air was alive with laughter, music, and the collective heartbeat of a moment suspended in time.

The atmosphere echoed with their shared toast as the group clinked their cups, the warmth of the festival's glow illuminating their faces. Kaleopei felt like she was on fire, every part of her alive with the flames.

"Someone's feeling the Fenyah spirit a bit too much." The lick of Elven coming from Zara went straight to her stomach. Made her not second guess the pair of red eyes that seemed to be glaring at her from the center of the fire.

"Keylan, my dearest brother, can I please have your cup? Mine has run dry," To further her point, she tipped her glass upside down, showing the lack of contents. And the ever-doting brother of hers handed over his half-full glass.

As they moved through the festival's lively crowd, they encountered mesmerizing dancers who followed their earlier dance lessons and musicians whose melodies seemed to weave tales of courage and defiance. Kaleopei basked in it all, truly surrounded by her element.

She let herself bask in it. Feel everything around her, from the soil to the slight breeze the night brought.

"You sure you're up for this, sister? You're practically floating over there."

"I'm just savoring the warmth of Fenyah, brother. Tomorrow, it's a different kind of fire we face." Kaleopei found herself laughing at her own words, "No joke intended."

"Enjoying the festival spirits, Kaleopei?" She found herself studying the Prince. His eyes were shallow but still seemed to study her, observant and clever. Kaleopei had a feeling he would make a good King. One the Human Realm needed. No longer was she concerned that they would be replacing one tyrant with another. Casimir was nothing like his father.

"We deserve a night of joy before, well, whatever the hell we are jumping into, don't we?"

The group found a spot near a roaring bonfire, its flames casting an enchanting glow. The Fenyah Festival embodied a celebration of life, unity, and the enduring spirit of rebellion.

"To unlikely alliances and the strength forged in the crucible of adversity." She thrust her cup into the air, some liquid spilling onto her arm.

Their cups met in a shared acknowledgment of the trials that bound them. As the night unfolded, the Fenyah flames mirrored the intensity of their resolve.

The revelry continued, the group immersed in the festival's spirited embrace. Amidst the swirl of colors, laughter, and flickering flames, Kaleopei and her companions seized the final moments of freedom, the echoes of Fenyah becoming a symphony that Kaleopei hoped would resonate in their hearts long after the festival's embers dimmed.

As the night wore on, Kaleopei, tipsy but alive with the spirit of rebellion, found solace in the warmth of friendship and the shared fire that burned within each of them. Tomorrow awaited promising challenges and the forging of destinies in the crucible of Louth's shadows.

But that was tomorrow. Kaleopei supposed it was fate that they would descend to that wicked place on her day of birth. Tonight, she would take in all her friends had to offer.

"Zara, look what a kid made! It's perfect for Fenyah," A wide smile was present on Kaleopei's face. Showing the crown made of flowers colored like the spring.

"You want to put a flower crown on me?"

"Absolutely! It'll make you look even more enchanting than you already do."

They shared a quiet moment as Kaleopei carefully placed the flower crown on Zaratella's head, the colorful blossoms contrasting beautifully with her dark hair.

"How do I look?" Zara did a small twirl, the ends of her dress spiraling out.

"Like the queen of the Fenyah Festival. No one else could compare."

As they wandered through the festival, Zaratella couldn't resist pulling Kaleopei toward a lively group of dancers.

"Care to dance the night away?"

"Lead the way, darling."

"Keep calling me that. I like the way it sounds coming from you." Zaratella grabbed her hand, not responding as she pulled them towards the bonfire.

Hand in hand, they twirled and danced among the revelers, the flickering flames and joyful atmosphere creating a cocoon of shared moments that whispered promises of joy and laughter.

Later, as they sat by the bonfire, Zaratella leaned against Kaleopei's shoulder, and they watched the embers dance in silent companionship, knowing that the Fenyah Festival had woven another chapter into the tapestry of their journey together, until Kaleopei found herself drifting off, staring into the deep burgundy flames that called her name.

***

"I feel like I got into a fight with a skinwalker and lost." Kaleopei held the side of her head, pushing herself to walk in a straight line towards the table.

"She lives!" Keylan roared, laughing as she sank into a chair.

"Don't be so loud, you oaf." Kaleopei reached for his steaming cup, taking the tea away from him. A moan left her mouth as she drank the herbal tea, savoring the hints of lavender.

"I never expected you to get so messed up," The prince was settled into a chair, nursing his own cup beneath his fingers. "It was enlightening."

"Please, you haven't seen anything. Just wait until I get some myth added to the equation. I'm fun to be around." Kaleopei looked over at Zara, whose face was hidden as she was hunched over the table. "Seems I wasn't the only one to wake up in a mood."

"She isn't the friendliest person to be around after drinking." Casimir laughed, placing a hand on his friend's back in a gesture of comfort. His point was proven when Zara slapped his arm away and leaned further into her arm. "Cas, I will put you six feet under if you raise your voice anymore."

"Well, at least you get to accompany each other instead of hearing your own complaints." Keylan took the cup back, finishing off the warm tea.

It was early in the morning, the early summer sun only barely rising in the distance. Kaleopei probably still had far too much liquid in her, still coursing her body.

"We should start moving soon," she spoke, standing to pour her own cup of heavenly tea. The tea was warm against her throat. "The longer we wait, the more they get away with."

"Just give me a minute." It was a sight to see Zaratella so miserable in the morning. Her eyes lidded with the signs of a hangover. Her face was still slightly flushed with alcohol.

She looked breathtaking, but Kaleopei made an effort to keep that part to herself.

"Do you need to restock anything you were missing?" Keylan being worried made sense. Always concerned for Kaleopei's wellbeing.

"We did it together yesterday. I have enough." Kaleopei could see the thought behind his emerald eyes, a moment away from saying this wasn't a good plan. It was the only plan that had a sliver of working. Kaleopei knew it well, regardless of whether her brother thought the same or not.

"Well, I, for one, am thrilled to spend my last possible day with Keylan." Casimir slapped a hand onto Key's shoulder. With a slight gruff laugh, she realized he was trying to lighten the mood.

Kaleopei wasn't sure what to think of the blonde. Initially, he was easily spooked and void of any confidence. Even in the few weeks they'd spent together, she had seen him grow. No longer was the extremely timid Prince who was locked away in his palace. By no means was he a fearless warrior. His skills with a sword were anything but impressive, but they would suffice. His charisma and charm when talking were what would get him far. Words often pierced deeper than any arrow.

"You children don't think you're leaving without me seeing you one last time?" The voice was light, a hint of exhaustion. Ellis stumbled her way down the stairs, using her cane to keep herself steady. Her age was beginning to have effects on her. A reminder that humans only had a fraction of her lifespan.

"Of course not," Keylan was up and aiding her. His face grinned as she embraced him. It was bittersweet, nothing like their usual goodbyes.

The stakes were much higher than simply going on an adventure like they had done in the past. Even Ellis understood what they were doing. The sheer look of discomfort on her face showed Kaleopei that this was real.

"Come on, Kaleopei," her voice waivers the smell of salty tears pricking in the room. Kaleopei didn't waste any time, leaping from her position to throw her arms around Keylan and Ellis.

Shuffling in the corner of the room were Zara and Casimir, each unsure of where to look.

"You two will always be children in my eyes, but it is clear as day when I look to see the young men and woman you have become." Her tears were no longer subtle, rolling down her cheeks in clusters. She nuzzled her head deeper into the embrace, trying to get as close as possible.

"Thank you for everything, Ellis. I know we weren't the easiest to raise." Kaleopei recalled many memories of this house and the surrounding area. All the fights she and Keylan got into, too, the way Ellis's face lit up whenever they came home. All of it was priceless, and Kaleopei could never fully thank the woman for her kindness.

"Come on, you two, you may as well be my children as well," Ellis called out over to Zara and Casimir, both awkwardly joining the hug. With a large smile, Ellis pulled them closer, their heads colliding in the process. "I haven't known you as long, but you are equally beautiful and amazing. What you are all doing isn't for the faint of heart. Promise me you'll come home?"

"We promise," Keylan was the one to confirm it. A deep pit settled in the depths of Kaleopei's stomach. She didn't make promises she couldn't keep.

Her emerald eyes softened as she took in Ellis, laying herself bare with emotion, and Kaleopei couldn't find the strength in her to make such an oath.

As if sensing Kaleopei wouldn't say anything, she pulled her closers. The sweet scent of lavender was still fresh in her hair.

"Good, when you return, we'll celebrate your birth for real. In good Elven tradition."

"I look forward to it."

Keylan said. Once again, being the voice of the two. Silently, Kaleopei nodded, seeing Ellis glance over at her. She placed a kiss on her forehead, saying a faint Elven prayer into the space.

Then they were splitting. The girls going north, and the boys to the west.

"Kaleopei," Keylan's voice was stern, "promise me you won't stray."

"I won't. I know what I am supposed to do." Kaleopei was pulled into yet another embrace, Keylan's broad shoulders encasing her. A comfort she wasn't sure she would ever have again. So she savored it, took in the woodsy smell he was encased in, and noticed the healthy weight he had put on in the past few months.

"I know you don't like my prayers. But let the Gods be with you, both of you." On their side, Zaratella and Casimir were saying their own goodbyes. A shroud of uneasiness filled the space.

Once the goodbyes were said, they were off. Kaleopei didn't even spare a glance behind as they pushed ahead towards the border.

Chapter 24

The journey to Louth stretched before Kaleopei and Zaratella like an uncertain path, fraught with shadows and hidden dangers. The air hung heavy with unspoken truths, and Kaleopei grappled with the weight of a decision that could alter the course of their lives.

"Zara, when this is all over. What do you see yourself doing?"

Kaleopei watched the black-haired girl, her hair pulled into a messy bun. Her beauty was something Kaleopei had come to terms with. Zara rivaled the soft glow of the moon.

"That's a deep question you're dishing out, but honestly?" Zara began. "I want to see the other Realms, maybe visit the Witch Realm to see what it's like."

Kaleopei listened intently, taking in the simple moments before the chaos that was at their doorstep. Between her fingers, she fiddled with the small blue crystal, weighing her options carefully.

"That sounds lovely."

"What do you want to do?"

With a heavy feeling in her chest, Kaleopei turned to the forest. It was serene. She always loved the woodlands of the Elven Realm, and each tree was a home to many creatures. The environment aided each other in whatever way it could.

"I want to live."

"What are you doing now?"

"Surviving." The word left Kaleopei's lips before she could ponder on it. It was the truth. All this time, she hadn't truly lived life how she wanted. Every decision she made reflected the need to help her people. There were few things Kaleopei did for herself, not selfish enough to take time away from getting her home back.

"We could learn together," Zara put herself next to Kaleopei. Silently, the girl grabbed Kaleopei's hand, intertwining their fingers with the softest touch. Her body began to grow tense. It was all too much. "We could go anywhere we wanted."

Zaratella could go anywhere she wanted. Kaleopei would be rooted in the Elven Realm if she even saw the aftermath. Rebuilding and coming to terms with what was lost. Convincing her people that it was safe to return, giving them the life they deserved.

Unsure of how to voice these thoughts, only a conformation left her mouth, "Yeah."

"I'm not leaving you alone in this, Kaleopei. We face it together. Isn't that what the blood rite ensured?"

Not exactly. It prevented Zara from lying to her. Never was there an agreement it would extend to both parties when the rite was done, an oversight Kaleopei was grateful for.

Kaleopei, torn between protecting Zara and the inevitability of the peril that awaited them, reached a crossroads where words seemed insufficient. Kaleopei couldn't lay down everything on her mind with the time they had left, so she kept them to herself.

As they walked through the dense forest on the outskirts of Louth, the air thickened with tension between the girls. Kaleopei, feeling the gravity of the moment, halted their steps. Her choice had already been made. Before they even left the Hag's cabin, Kaleopei knew what needed to be done for this to be successful. Knew the choice she had to make.

"Zara, there's something I need to do before we go further." Kaleopei had never heard her voice so soft, so unsure. Internally, she was freaking out, unsure of how Zaratella would react. During her time on this soil, Kaleopei learned to deal with insults and crude outbursts from others, but never from the ones she cared about. Keylan and her had their fair share of arguments, but in the end, they never meant the crude words they had uttered.

Zaratella, sensing the shift in the atmosphere, observed Kaleopei with a mixture of concern and unspoken frustration. In a vulnerable moment, Kaleopei's hand felt Zara's, giving it a light squeeze. Her hand was soft and present in hers, a reminder that this was real. The quiet forest became a haven for emotions unsaid.

There was a spark between them.

"Zara, I need you to understand. This might be the last time..."

Before she could finish, Zaratella gently silenced her with a tender kiss. It was a shared promise, an unspoken acknowledgment from the Carver. Kaleopei returned it with a different promise: she would make sure Zara was protected regardless of the outcome.

The kiss was everything Kaleopei had ever imagined. Gentle, soft with a slight hint of urgency between the two. Zara's face was flushed as she pulled back, taking Kaleopei's other hand. With their hands intertwined, Kaleopei wanted this to be the future.

"We'll face whatever comes our way together."

Kaleopei wished that was true. Together, had a nice ring to it. A time where she wouldn't shoulder the entire burden. In this lifetime, it wasn't possible. In another, it could be a pleasant comfort.

The forest, the only soul bearing witness to the intimacy of that moment, seemed to hold its breath as the two connected. As they continued their journey toward Louth, Kaleopei's heart carried the imprint of that stolen kiss, a bittersweet reminder of the sacrifices and the unwavering connection that bound them to this fate, even in the face of an uncertain destiny that laid before her.

Kaleopei had made her choice. Zaratella would never set foot inside of Louth. She'd give her life before that came to be.

Louth was on the horizon. Kaleopei knew it well. The trees wilted like the place had sucked the life out of them. Likely, that was the cause. Any residual magic was sucked from them, leaving the trees to decay at an exponential rate. The place screamed of distress and darkness, the landscape reflecting it well.

This was it. Kaleopei knew what had to be done.

Her hands shook, one still interlaced with Zara's, who refused to let go. Kaleopei could imagine a life with her, both of them relieved of the stress they currently bore. Able to live a life where they could enjoy the finer things and, most of all, each other.

"Kaleopei, are you alright? You're shaking."

"I'm so sorry." Zara's eyes were etched with worry. Kaleopei held the crystal between her fingers, keeping it out of the other's view.

"Don't be. Your fear is justified. It was a traumatic thing you endured, even if I don't know the full extent-"

Kaleopei closed the distance between them, interlocking their lips in a fiery dance, not able to get enough of the pale girl, shocked before her. Zara reciprocated the intensity, dropping her hand to place her arms around Kaleopei's neck, pulling them closer together. Kaleopei savored every moment of the kiss, having a taste, knowing she'd never experience it again. She was content with it, glad she had the chance now. Able to experience it even for a few seconds.

She tasted of something familiar, a feeling Kaleopei couldn't quite place.

Slowly, Kaleopei pulled her head back, resting her forehead against Zara's. Kaleopei wanted this to last an eternity. But it wasn't on the table for her. She had a task to complete.

"There is no sense in both of us dying here."

Kaleopei crushed the crystal in her palm, bringing her hand up to Zara's face.

"What do you mean?" Kaleopei flinched as she saw Zara recoil from her touch. But the dust had already been placed. Zaratella began to glow the faintest color of blue, like the morning sky, coming from the darkness of the setting moon.

"I'm sorry. I'm so, so sorry."

Realization dawned upon Zara's face, an emotion Kaleopei knew she had caused. Zara was hurt, her eyes hardening as she reached out for Kaleopei. With shaking hands and a heavy heart, Kaleopei mustered the best smile she could. Tears cascaded down Zara's pale face.

"Kaleopei, think this through! Don't be brash!"

Kaleopei stepped back, not allowing any contact between the two. Couldn't risk accidentally going along with Zaratella back to the Hag. "*Please*! I'm begging you, stop!" Broken. Shattered, that's the one way Kaleopei could describe the voice screaming at her.

Kaleopei imprinted her image to memory, tears and all.

Then she was gone.

The stillness in the air suffocated Kaleopei. Silence for the first time since they departed from Alstead. Her path was clear from this point. All Kaleopei had to do was clear out Louth. Wipe its doings from the Realms once and for all.

Then it would be over.

Kaleopei wouldn't have to survive much longer after that.

Only then would she be done.

Silently, tears fell from her cheeks. Kaleopei brushed the back of her hand against her face. Took a deep breath. Then walked towards the unknown.

***

In the dimly lit confines of Louth, Kaleopei moved with the shadows, navigating the labyrinthine passages of the old elven temple that Bellheim repurposed. The air hung heavy with the scent of metal and damp stone, a stark contrast to the freedom of the groves and forest she had once known. Not even the stark white interior of Fenrah's temple remained. The once intricate details carved into the walls seemed dull in the lack of light. Fenrah would hate this, being the god of light and flame. It went against everything people praised her for. Kaleopei could only imagine the goddess rolling in her grave. Kaleopei had thought about how she would enact her revenge many times. How'd she become the King's worst nightmare? A being not to be trifled with. But none of that mattered at the moment.

The prison camp echoed with the silent cries of captive elves, their spirits dampened by the oppressive atmosphere. The very same one that she had been forced to endure. The shadows seemed to cling to the walls, the remains of those who were depleted in the pit.

She'd save them, set them free, before anything else. She owed them that much, at least.

Kaleopei rushed down the stone halls, using the darkness to cloak her movement. Like a predator, she stalked closer and closer to the cells. She counted four guards, all armed and stationed. With practiced ease, she was knocking an arrow.

Letting it fly was her spark of action. The first piercing into the side of a guard's neck, his gargled speech inhibited by the blood clogging his throat. Akin to a dance, her feet moved swiftly against the stone, dragging her twin blades out from their sheath in a smooth motion.

"Stop what you're doing!" A pitiful attempt to try to subdue her.

He was the next to fall, unable to even draw his weapon. A laceration she inflicted straight to his jugular, there would be no mercy here today. Kaleopei would make them pay for the pain they caused, and the anger coursing through her only made her blow bloodier.

She let her knives fly. Like a streak of metallic lightning, they aimed true, stopping the men in their pointless pursuit. Then there was silence. Only her breath echoed in the hall, falling in even intervals.

From the bodies she took their ring of keys, then she was striding for one of the two iron doors. It took a few trials to find the right key. But then she pushed the door open. The tiny room housed nine people, all huddled in one corner. Leaning on one another for a flicker of warmth. Kaleopei was releasing an aura of her magic the moment she laid eyes upon their shaking frames, warmth filling the room.

The walls were plated in lead, and the only commodity they had was a lead pot. Everything was covered in lead, subduing any hope of the elf's half of using magic to save them. All the hooded eyes were on her. Seeing them all, so void of life made her want to scream into the abyss. Her skin shivered in a fit of rage, fire flicking off her skin.

"You guys are safe," she began, moving to remove their cuffs one by one. "My name is Kaleopei Azgaeda Florence. I know your position. I've been here before. But you mustn't give in. Rely on each other to get out of here."

Each set of eyes was trained on her, all confused as she set them free. There wasn't a lot of hope behind their expressions.

"A Florence?" A male asked, looking up from where he was crouched. Kaleopei only nodded, offering a smile.

"We're exhausted."

"I understand, but you must push through it. Know that once you're out of this room, you battle until it is over. Stay hidden until you can return home." Kaleopei begged of them. They had to make it out alive. All she was doing couldn't be for nothing. Even if only a few were saved during her endeavors, it meant she had done something. All of this wouldn't be in vain.

Kaleopei spotted what looked like the most capable male, who still had some muscle definition on his frame. Handing the door and manacle keys to him. "Across the hall is another room identical to this one. Get them out. I will cover you for as long as possible."

"Thank you, malady." The male dipped his head, accepting the keys, as he ushered some others to their feet. Kaleopei dropped her pack onto the floor.

"Don't thank me, I'd do it again. Everything you need to survive a few days is in there. Do try your best to make it last. I gathered as much as I could carry."

"Your efforts won't go unappreciated." Another woman with blonde hair bowed her head. A gesture of gratitude and respect. Kaleopei had given them a reason to hope. That was all the thanks she needed. So long as they escaped, that would be enough.

"I will buy you as much time as possible. Use it wisely." Kaleopei was out the door, seeing a group of new guards who had come to check on the noise. They inspected the bodies that were sprawled in the hall, a sick painting that encapsulated the violence the humans loved so much.

Kaleopei gathered a vortex of magic beneath her skin, building it quickly before the guards noticed her presence. A wall of emerald flames engulfed them, burning in the wake as their screams dissipated. She kept the wall up, blocking off any other guards from proceeding down this hall.

The potent and grim stench of flesh burning filled the space. Though not once did she falter. No, she stood her ground well.

Concentrating hard on her magic, Kaleopei went the other way, carving a path in her wake for the others to follow. Once she could see the end, Kaleopei branched off. Letting her wall fall, she crept down a barren hall. Each step echoed her footfall.

As she approached a secured chamber, one she didn't recall from before, Kaleopei caught sight of an Aetherite crystal, a foreboding presence that seemed to pulse with contained energy. Her senses heightened, and she realized that their previous guess about its location was false – it wasn't in Lispin but here, within the very heart of Louth. Just as she predicted it would be.

"It's here. The Aetherite Canon is here."

Chapter 25

Lispin was awake in the dull and warm afternoon, people working, merchants haggling, and kids running the streets. It was a much tamer vibe when compared to the capital, whose people seemed to be constantly on edge. Casimir knew it was because of Lord Eldridge, Zaratella's father. He was a decent man, always wanting and providing the best for his city.

His father owned a warehouse in the production district. Lispin was known for its metal-making. Mostly ornate swords and weapons and intricate armor pieces. All costly, of course, the price was in the craft. Casimir's old rapier was crafted by none other than Alec Brevatto, a well-known blacksmith whose work reaches other Realms.

"Have you been here before?" Casimir found himself asking the brooding Keylan. His demeanor turned sour the moment he left Alstead, separating from Kaleopei and Zara. The emotion was warranted. Those two were prancing straight into a wasp's nest while they searched a city.

"A handful of times, Kaleopei likes the arrowheads a merchant makes here."

"They'll be fine. Those two together scare the shit out of me. I'm sure men will recoil in their presence."

"Is Zara trustworthy? You two seem rather close?"

"You've seen it too, huh?" Casimir tugged on his hood, keeping his face obstructed from any prying eyes.

"I think the only people who haven't are Kaleopei and Zara." Those two weren't subtle, not in the slightest. Constant casting longing gazed when the other wasn't looking. It was like a scene from his novels every time he saw it. Somehow, those girls haven't realized the other is in love.

"Zara doesn't give her kindness easily. She is a stubbornly determined woman. She's an instigator, always looking to cause chaos in her regimented routine," he reminisced. Ever since, she showed up in the wake of the moon, flanked by the twins. She smiled more. Happier. "She would shatter the world for the people she loves. Those two together would be formidable. I don't know whether I'd be excited for them or terrified of them."

"Kaleopei has a tendency not to allow herself happiness. She's never outright mentioned she liked girls, but I've had the suspicion since we were young. Subtle isn't a word in her vocabulary."

"Zara was going to be my bride, an arrangement made between Lord Eldridge and my Father. That was before she got forced into Carver training. They decided the marriage would happen when I came of age. When Zara became a carver, my father wouldn't entertain the idea of her being my wife." Casimir laughed at the memory playing in his head. "One day, she kissed me out of the blue. When Zara pulled away, she started gagging, going on about how 'boys are icky.' It was honestly kind of traumatic for me. I thought she meant I was a bad kisser, but I eventually connected the dots."

"I just want her to be happy. I fear the day she no longer needs me." Casimir saw the despair hidden deep in the male's eyes.

"She will always need you. You two have a bond unlike any other. As the Gods kept you together for a reason, surely anybody you've met will tell you the same."

"When she becomes Queen, she will need me even less."

What?

Casimir stopped dead mid-step, casting a glance at the male. He'd known brown hair and green eyes were common in the royal elf line. But not once did he ever suspect the two to be a part of it. There was only one elven princess, and she was killed eight years ago.

"Come again."

"When Kaleopei takes the throne, and I am a part of her court, overseeing the armies, she won't need me around. She's older, if only by a few minutes. It's quite possible I will be away often." It was the way Keylan shrugged off the comment and continued his stride that made Casimir realize the man wasn't lying. Casimir knew that Keylan had accepted what was being said, coming to terms with what a rebellion meant for the elven twins he had come to know.

"You understand what you're saying, right?"

"You're not the only prince committing crimes these days," Keylan had the audacity to wink at him. Not once did the apparent Elven Prince even stumble in his footing, continuing each stride with his chin held high. It was as if he were talking about the weather.

"You are, and Kaleopei are... royalty?"

Suddenly, nothing seemed to make sense. Lord Eldridge wouldn't consciously put the people of Lispin in danger. Why would he agree to house a weapon of mass destruction in his city limits?

"Was that not clear? Yes, we are, but neither of us really wanted that. Our sister, Maizelin, was to be the heir who took the throne." Casimir wasn't sure how low his mouth hung, coming to grasp everything Keylan was saying.

"Why keep that a secret from us?"

"Did we? Both of us have said we wish to help our people get our homes back. I'm positive we've mentioned Maize before." They both have been devoted and passionate about what they are trying to accomplish. "Also, just dropping that we are the heirs to a throne your father wants dead wouldn't be the most logical. We're careful about who knows. There isn't many."

For some odd reason, Casimir found solace in knowing someone else held a title like his. The envy in his chest at Keylan's outlook made him conflicted. Casimir would take up a throne after this, and he'd have a good relationship with the Queen of Eviera. It was comforting knowing he'd have friends to count on in the aftermath, the same they could rely on him.

Provided they all live to see the aftermath. Casimir still wasn't sure how the two would deal with the Aetherite canon. Can a mineral like that even be destroyed by conventional means? He supposed Keylan wasn't necessarily conventional and might have an idea.

"How come you weren't coronated officially?" Elven twins didn't happen often. Even Casimir knew that. He's sure he'd have known about the two being heirs, regardless of when they were born.

"When we were born, there were… issues? I guess you could say." Casimir could sense the hesitancy prodding at Keylan's tone. "Kaleopei was born with the Emerald flame, which hasn't happened in generations. She is touched by the flame goddess herself, which means she has a lot of magical reserve, and it is frequently unpredictable. We were supposed to be publicly announced when we hit our first decade. Our parents brought us to the Hag for tutoring. She was able to control the outbursts Kaleopei had, and they still happen but not frequently, and then every couple days we'd go there after we turned three."

"That's… I can't even imagine."

"It's what he had to do, to keep our people safe. I was always capable of curving her temper, so they kept us together."

Casimir couldn't help but find a sense of camaraderie with Keylan, realizing that titles and lineage were but one layer of a person's story. He also realized he agreed to send the future queen of the Elven Realm into Louth. Did Zara know? Or even suspect who the twins really were?

"Well, I'm glad you're here. We'll navigate this together, title or not. But I will be calling you Prince, like you and sister do me."

"I could say the same thing to you, Prince." Keylan laughed. "Kaleopei will chop your manhood off without a second thought. She's got a temper, like I mentioned. While my sister isn't humble in the slightest, she isn't fond of the whole title thing."

Keylan's gaze met Casimir's, and in that exchange, a silent understanding formed, binding them in the shared complexities of their intertwined destinies of a mere throne. For a moment, Casimir let his thoughts wander. Could they have been friends if his father had never conquered the Elven Realm? Maybe even a diplomatic relationship where he and Keylan may have made an alliance in some off chance of life.

"I don't doubt that," Casimir let out a breath. Praying that Zara and Kaleopei would remain safe, they undoubtedly had reached Louth by now.

As the warehouse approached his vision, Casimir squinted. He didn't recall the sign being hung above the large sliding door. It was used as storage. They're no reason to have a sign, especially one hung on display.

"The King owns a fabric industry?" Keylan snorted.

"I don't believe he does."

"Something tells me he's not hiding a population-wiping weapon among all that cloth."

"Let's just go in, say we were sent by the king to check inventory." Casimir thought on his feet, not letting his confusion get the better of him. Still, none of it seemed to make any sense.

"I'll," he placed a hand in front of Casimir, "go in. You are a Prince thought to be missing. Just stick to the shadows."

"That's practically my middle name. Casimir Shadow-Stalker Haven."

"Say your name a little louder, why don't you."

Keylan stalked forward, disappearing from his vision as he passed the door. With an intent stare, Casimir stayed put. Arms crossed over his chest, fixing his hood every time someone seemed to be looking too closely at him. It had been a while since his last visit to Lispin, but it was still beautiful.

Stone paths are disturbed by small weeds and near-blooming flowers. Simply architecture that overcame the test of time. Lispin was one of the first founded Human cities after the Peace war. Fabled that Calsi once walked these very streets, gracing the wounded survivors with a charm of her luck. With many resources put into the constantly evolving medical techniques, all the Queen's nurses have hailed from Lispin.

Though, Casimir wouldn't think twice about what Keylan's magic could accomplish. He had seen it in action only a few subtle times, offering to help Kaleopei every time she so much gained a scratch. He recalled the time during their travel that she had come back from the river with Keylan with only the faintest of scars, showing an arrow had once penetrated her thigh. The possibilities seemed endless if Keylan were to offer his services inside of a clinic.

The sun moved in the sky, now hanging high in the sky from its once-rising position. Keylan had been inside for an oddly long time. Surely, he would have sent some kind of signal if he was in trouble? Casimir wasn't sure if the male would.

Another handful of minutes passed, and Casimir's brow furrowed in worry. It wasn't until he noticed Keylan emerging from the sliding door with a scowl on his face. The rigid and tense posture is a contrast to his earlier stature.

"What'd you find?"

"Your father sold this place just days after Kaleopei escaped Louth." Keylan's voice was low, grabbing Casimir's wrist and pulling him into an alley. "I suspect the canon *was* here."

"You're saying it's not?" Casimir thought of what that meant. He was filled in on how Kaleopei destroyed a siphon months ago, how she escaped that place by a miracle. To Casimir, it sounded like her escape was all in her skill and less up to fate. It was possible that the siphon could no longer carry magic a distance... that meant.

"I'm saying my sister understood the situation more than I did. Now I understand why she wanted to go to Louth so badly."

"You think she knew the Aetherite canon had been moved?" The words fell out of Casimir's mouth. But he already knew the answer to that question. He had already suspected that they were following a null lead.

"Kaleopei is dangerously insightful. Not once did she say where she thought the canon was. She only admitted it wasn't in Louth when she was there. That doesn't mean it couldn't be there now."

"She willingly sent herself towards a weapon that could be a bomb?" Casimir knew she was insane, but this only confirmed it.

"Kaleopei *is* a ticking bomb."

Chapter 26

The gravity of the situation weighed on Kaleopei as she noticed guards patrolling the area, their armor glinting in the low candlelight. Determination fueled her every step as she devised a plan to stop the impending catastrophe this device could cause. She still had to destroy the siphon in the pit. The two connected in a way she didn't fully comprehend. Now was not the time for learning.

The guards cast vigilant eyes on their surroundings. Kaleopei, recognizing the urgency, moved swiftly, trying to remain a shadow in the darkness.

In a daring bout of confidence, she left the chamber. The new goal was to go for the Aetherite Siphon, a device intricately connected to the Canon. How? She was unsure, but The Hag wasn't lying about the web that connected the two.

If I can break the Siphon, I can sever its connection to the Canon. Buy myself some time to figure out how to drain it.

Kaleopei stalked the halls, light on her feet as she noted the red stains on the stone below. She had caused a portion of those, spilling the soldiers' blood months ago. The layout hadn't changed. She remembered it in bits, her rage blinding her escape partly. The pit, however, was not something one could just forget. She would remember it for as long as she remained on this soil, however long it may be.

It was the epitome of death.

Quickened steps propelled her through the halls, her feet silent as they hit the stone floors. Kaleopei could feel the light thrumming the siphon gave off, growing closer. The power increased as the halls turned vaguely familiar.

She wasn't alone. The path ahead was guarded.

The still air crackled with tension as Kaleopei faced the line of Bellheim soldiers blocking her path to the pit. Determination etched into every line of her face, she stood tall, a solitary figure against those who opposed her. Calloused hands tightened around the hilt of her knives, a silent vow echoing in her heart.

This wouldn't be where it ended.

As the first soldier lunged forward, Kaleopei's reflexes kicked into overdrive. With fluid grace, she sidestepped the attack, the clash of steel ringing out like a battle cry against the silence of the stone that encased them. With each strike, she wove a dance of defiance and determination, her movements a testament to the indomitable spirit that fueled her resolve.

The soldiers pressed forward, their numbers seeming to multiply with every passing moment. Yet, Kaleopei refused to yield, her focus unwavering as she met their onslaught with unwavering ferocity. With every swing of her blades, she carved a path through the chaos, a lone beacon of resistance against the tide of opposition.

Walls echoed with the sounds of battle, the clash of steel and the roar of defiance mingling with the rustle of leaves overhead. With every passing moment, Kaleopei's determination burned brighter, a relentless fire that fueled her every movement.

Emerald flames licked the tip of her blades, herself becoming a whirlwind of violence and fire. Mercy wasn't a virtue she could spare.

As the final soldier fell, defeated by the sheer force of Kaleopei's will, she stood amidst the aftermath of the conflict, her breath ragged but her spirit unbroken. With a steely resolve, she turned her gaze toward the Aetherite Siphon; the promise of its power thrummed in her head. Dangerously close to the crystal she had once bested.

She found not only the strength to endure but the courage to rise, a solitary warrior against the darkness, determined to claim victory at any cost. She'd already come this far.

Her fingers worked deftly, scanning the siphon. Another door across the chamber creaked open, letting in trace amounts of torchlight. More guards began to flood her vision. To them, she was an intruder to be dealt with. They moved in her direction, their weapons drawn. So she resorted to what she did best.

With one hand, she withdrew one of the hunting knives, heating the metal in her hands. Kaleopei flipped the knife in her palm, striking with all her might. She jammed the hilt of the knife into the crystal. It cracked, but it required more force.

"Intruder! Lock this place down!" Kaleopei's heart raced, her focus unwavering on the task at hand. She knew she had little time before the guards closed in.

Again and again, she wailed on the crystal. Chunks of the deep purple material scatter with each hit. Bludgeoning the crystal until she felt a large portion drop into the pit below. Reminiscent of how it fell months ago.

Fire trickled onto her body, green flames dancing as they put a barrier between her and the oncoming guards. With the crystal down, all she had to do was deactivate the canon.

After sending Zaratella back to the grove, Kaleopei knew she wouldn't be coming out of this intact. In the days prior, Kaleopei knew she would protect the ex-carver the same she would her brother. Kaleopei would gladly give her life for either of them, and maybe even Casimir.

Kaleopei wouldn't leave the job unfinished. It would end here and now. The future of many rested on her completion. Kaleopei was far from done.

With a surge of determination, Kaleopei ran through the green flames, face to face with a guard. She didn't hesitate, sinking the knives into the gap the armor missed under his armpit. The blade buried deep, a splatter of blood hitting the floor as Kaleopei removed the blade, adding to the mess on the floor.

Then she was moving. With the siphon gone, there was still one more object she had to deal with.

Kaleopei resisted the urge to let out a scream as an arrow struck her shoulder. It stung, which only meant one thing.

Lead.

All the weapons carried by soldiers were plated in lead. To make it deadly to a magic wielded. They precisely knew who they were dealing with. With a strained grunt, she pulled the arrow out. The lead would have dampened her magic. She couldn't have that now.

Kaleopei sidestepped another arrow, now able to focus on the fight in front of her. Her hand became engulfed in a fiery flame. Without a second to question herself, Kaleopei pressed the bundle of warmth straight to the wound. Cauterizing it along with some scraps of her clothing.

In the heat of conflict, Kaleopei wasn't sure what she would do to the canon. There has to be a threshold of magic it can hold, pouring as magic as she could into it would be risky. Uncertain that the amount of magic she had would be sufficient. The canon could activate automatically anyway, wiping the entirety of the Elven, and possibly Human, realm to nothing but an ash-filled crater. Destruction that would not discriminate.

So, she ran. Ran like the lives of others deadened on her.

Which it did.

Upon returning to the canon, she made a split-second decision. The only way to prevent the devastation was to transfer the Aetherite's contained magic into herself and then release it from her own body. It could effortlessly kill her. Overcharging a body with magic often comes with high consequences. Even the most experienced users can make a simple error and tear themselves apart from within. Spellspent wasn't a condition Kaleopei had ever actually dealt with before, the consequences being grave.

But, if only for a second, she could control the outburst, it would save many. It would save her brother and her friends. Save those who she loved.

You don't fret in the eye of danger; you deal it back with your teeth barred.

Maize's words echoed in her head, coaching her as she made the difficult decision.

It was a gamble Kaleopei was willing to make.

"Halt! What are you doing here?"

Ignoring the guards' commands, Kaleopei took a deep breath, her eyes fixed on the Aetherite Canon. In a desperate act, her hands connected to the deep purple crystal weapon, channeling the abundance of elemental magic within the device into herself. Nobody could ever prepare themselves when feeling the raw power surge through her veins, threading to tear her apart from the inside out. Unfamiliar, foreign, it felt wrong. A mass of magic sourced from different people surely made a recipe for unknown chaos.

None of it belonged to her.

Not all magic is compatible with others, and she could feel all the discourse fighting it in her bones as she took more and more. With each bit of magic that flooded into her, Kaleopei felt a rush akin to adrenaline-filled. An unexplainable surge, strong and forceful, a pulse that itched for release.

"It's her, I remember those eyes." Kaleopei was delighted to find she left an impression on those who survived their last encounter. Most who saw her fire didn't live to tell the tale. She made the unfortunate mistake of keeping some alive in her last encounter in Louth.

They would not experience the same mistakes she had made before.

Like a beating arcane heart, the magic pulsed inside of her. Kaleopei had never experienced such a vehement state of the arcane. Elemental forces pushing and pulling, unwilling to coexist inside of her. It wasn't something she had felt since before she could control her flames. Tan olive skin began to burn as the magic rose to the surface.

It was too much. Too many sources of magic itching to take control.

The energy had an agenda of its own. Each fragment is fighting to outdo the others Kaleopei inherited. Intense and uncomfortable, Kaleopei writhed against it, her hands igniting against the crystal weapon. Iridescent lines that resembled veins spread up her arms, stemming from the connection point.

"You mustn't fall."

The light grew brighter with every passing second. Magic building far beyond anything she had ever felt before.

Kaleopei needed to get rid of it. For a second, she swore she saw red eyes gleaming back at her from the center of the crystal.

As the guards closed in, she centered her vision on them. Trying to reign in the storm that was inside of her. Kaleopei had never been one to feel the heat, but currently, she was sweating, burning with a lack of control. She gave into the feelings and released the magic in a brilliant burst, shattering the Aetherite Canon in the wake.

The shockwave of the outburst rippled throughout the chamber, and in the chaos that ensued, Kaleopei's vision blurred as the released energy coursed out of her. A chaotic surge fanning into the areas around her. The walls of this chamber were blown out, giving her a better view of the guards that surrounded her. Kaleopei hoped the others had gotten far from here with the time she was able to buy them.

"Seal the area! Seal it now!" The guards who remained standing fell into disorder. A panic settles into the air.

"What part?"

With the canon broken, a wave of relief flicked inside Kaleopei. Still, this wasn't over.

"There's little left to seal."

Kaleopei found herself breathless, the expenditure of magic leaving her feeling drained, a profound weariness settling in her limbs, threatening her rigid stance. Despite the temporary surge of triumph, the realization of the toll on her own reserves became apparent.

Magic still coursed through her, an echo of the immense energy she had just manipulated. It lingered like a tempest within, her own magic refusing to settle among the influx of others. It was as if the Aetherite's essence had imprinted itself onto her very core, an indelible mark that resonated with her regular flow of magic.

"Seal it now!"

Kaleopei couldn't concentrate on their voices anymore.

Physically, she was experiencing an odd tingling sensation akin to the aftermath of a storm when the air was charged with latent electricity. Her breaths were labored, and there was a sense of a profound burden, as if she carried the weight of the unleashed magic within her very soul.

Kaleopei still felt its presence.

She stood amidst the echoes of her magical feat. Kaleopei found herself at the crossroads of triumph and vulnerability, where the currents of ancient enchantments still surged within, an untamed force awaiting its sorceress's next command.

As the guards scrambled to contain the aftermath of that display, Kaleopei slumped to the ground, drained yet resolute. The Aetherite's destructive potential had been thwarted, but at a cost – the toll on her body and the uncertain consequences of wielding such formidable magic lingered.

Another surge of unkept magic left her exhausted body like waves crashing against the tide. The guards were blown back, and most stayed down, unmoving.

Kaleopei basked in the destruction, falling to her side as her muscles gave out. Exhaustion weighed heavily on Kaleopei as she lay on the cold stone floor, her body drained of magic. Every muscle ached, and an unfathomable weariness settled deep beneath her skin. The lack of magical energy made her feel hollow, like a vessel emptied of its essence.

Was this how her people felt when being drained? Reaching a depletion state often had varying levels of side effects, the most severe being death. A factor Kaleopei seemed to face at every turn these days.

Was this what being Spellspent felt like?

The chamber echoed with the approaching footsteps of guards, their armor clinking as they closed in on the fallen elf. Even in this state, the sound of their presence resonated in her ears. Kaleopei's eyes, once vibrant with determination, now held a wearied glint as she struggled to rise to her knees.

"Look at this one. She's drained herself, not the same sight we saw seconds ago."

Kaleopei would go down swinging. Wouldn't allow herself to be bested. She would fight until the bitter end when the soil called her name.

"Thought you could challenge Bellheim? Foolish elf."

As the guards closed in, Kaleopei found herself surrounded, her body unable to respond to the threat efficiently. All Kaleopei could manage was to sluggishly swing towards the men who were closing the distance. She let out an animalistic scream, those around her going up in a green cascade of fire. Kaleopei staggered to the left, evading a blow from those who closed in. In mere moments, they had her restrained, binding her wrists with lead cuffs that nullified any latent magic. Corpses scattered around her, all burnt to a crisp from her final lash of magic.

Kaleopei had nothing left inside of her, the lead of the cuffs now dampening any reserves she had left.

"Bring her to the King. He's sure to have heard the commotion. He'll decide her fate."

The guard's voice carried a stern authority as they led Kaleopei through the corridors of Louth. The once-familiar temple she had visited with her mother now felt like a cage closing in around her, and Kaleopei's thoughts raced with the uncertainty of what awaited her before the Human King of Bellheim.

Kaleopei couldn't do much with the paralyzing feel of her muscles. Each one disobeyed her order to fight. "I'd do it again if it meant saving my people."

As they reached another corridor, Kaleopei's eyes locked onto the figure seated upon an ornate chair, hunched over at a desk. King Darren Haven, his eyes ablaze with a furious intensity, glared at her.

"You dare defy me, elf? What have you done?"

Kaleopei, weakened but not broken, met the King's gaze with unwavering defiance. At that moment, she caught a glimpse of the tangled threads of fate that had led them to this moment – a complex dance of power, sacrifice, and consequences that would shape the unfolding events of their intertwined fates. Kaleopei wanted to make sure he burned with her.

As Kaleopei tried to will her magic forward, she felt bile rise to her throat. Then, it was splattered on the ground, all over the King's feet. She figured it was karma collecting its debt in odd ways.

"Bring her to an escort cart. I don't even want to look at her again until I reach the capital. There, she will receive her sentence."

It was then that Kaleopei decided she would drag him down, down to the depths of hell that was awaiting their arrival. Either by her own violence or an act in the name of her legacy, she wasn't sure. But one thing remained certain: she would be no easy prisoner. She was prepared to make these guards' lives a living hell.

Chapter 27

"We should go back to the Grove. We've spent too much time here. It's likely they have already left Louth." "Or something happened." Casimir saw Keylan take the orb out of his pocket. Remembering Imogen's words, Casimir placed his hand on Keylan's shoulder.

The world was enveloped in a soft glow as Keylan crushed the crystal between his hands.

It was an odd feeling, a weightlessness and surrounded by white. The sensation didn't last long. Soon, he felt his feet collide with the ground once more. A creak of floorboards beneath his feet and an overwhelming smell of incense and herbs flooded his nostrils.

Casimir's sight was returned, seeing the familiar sight of the inside of Imogen's cabin. But something was wrong. Casimir could feel it in his very being. Shelves were overturned, and various liquids and trinkets were scattered on the ground.

"Shit," Keylan broke into a run, throwing himself towards that ladder to the basement. It was clear he heard something, but Casimir's ears couldn't pick up on anything. With trembling legs, Casimir rushed to keep up with the lost Prince.

Keylan threw the hatch open, sliding down the ladder in a swift motion. Casimir followed closely behind, unsure of what was happening. He could now hear the ruckus that stirred beneath.

"And you just listened to her!" It was Zara's voice. Casimir knew that well. Something pricked at the girl's booming voice, the ending cracking with emotion.

"I promised the girl I wouldn't interfere. I will abide by that."

"What's going on?" Keylan was quick to speak up. Casimir saw the state Zara was in, eyes puffy, her hands were bleeding a black colored blood. She was distressed as she sat on the floor, looking up at Imogen much like a wounded child would.

"Kaleopei went into Louth alone. This bitch knew the entire time, and still, let us go! Kaleopei forced me back here."

The betrayal was clear on Zara's face, hurt by the elven girl. Zaratella was usually a calm and logical person. Bringing her to this disarray was terrifying in its own right. If Casimir was to be honest, this didn't surprise him. That girl was reckless and utterly insane. A stunt like this seemed tame to some of her previous actions. Wanting to go in alone was surely up her alley. Silently, he was kicking himself for not putting the pieces together earlier.

"You knew?" Keylan's voice was broken, staring at Imogen. Casimir watched as his fists were balled and trembling.

"She asked me not to inform you. Kaleopei is a stubborn girl. I'm sure you, of all people, are aware of her persuasions."

Casimir was sure Keylan was seeing red. Every bit of his posture went rigid.

"You willingly deceived us so she could go in alone?"

"I did no such thing. The girl is a force in her own right. Any foul play and deception was brought on by her. She is wise beyond many I've encountered. Kaleopei understood the risks of the situation and sought to minimize the consequences.”

“She will die there!” Keylan was shouting, an anger Casimir hadn’t witnessed before. His voice boomed and echoed across the space, his teeth barred aggressively.

“Your sister made her choice. I advised her otherwise, offering anything I could. The situation you find yourselves in is perilous. Kaleopei knew what would happen if the Aetherite canon was destroyed. It would detonate, a wave of destruction that wouldn’t discriminate. She sought to save you all. From how we are all still talking, I can only assume her words were true.”

“You let her die!” Casimir had never heard Zara’s voice so broken. Her hands bled as she punched at the ground repeatedly. He wasn’t sure if he should comfort the girl or not. Tears stained her face. Every part of her was trembling in grief.

“The king will be dead. I move at night for the capital. His head will be mine.” Casimir saw the intensity that gleamed in the other Prince’s eyes. This was the authority Kaleopei had carried across various instances. It wasn’t a determined voice. It was the voice of a King.

“Don’t be brash, boy, wait a day. I have already informed some allies of mine, and they will fight with you. They are on their way now.” Casimir wasn’t sure what to think at the moment. “Your sister lives. I can still feel her, as you should be able to, too. As can, she. You are intelligent as well; don’t let the anger make your decisions.”

Imogen looked between Zara and Keylan, then lifted her hand. A healing scar was shown across the back of her hand, lined across her knuckles.

"When did you make the rite with her?" Keylan was shocked by the reveal. It appeared Casimir was missing a pivotal point in this exchange. He recalled seeing something similar lined on the palm of Zara's hand.

"The blood rite responds to magic. It would have dissipated if she was no longer breathing. As to when it was during your last visit. I promised I wouldn't interfere directly, so I shan't."

The blood rite sounded like something Casimir didn't want to mess with. To know all the others in the room had made him slightly on edge. Was it dark magic of sorts?

"You're saying Kaleopei had planned all of this?" Casimir was slowly coming to terms with what had transpired. The sheer deceptive manner of the elf girl he had been spending so much time with as of late. He stood by his earlier thoughts: Kaleopei is a storm not to be messed with.

"That girl is wildly stupid, but she does not do so without wisdom. Being wise comes from experience, not age, as so many believe. Kaleopei has an advantage over others she faces because of her wisdom combined with intelligence."

"But it doesn't make sense. How did she even know what was going to happen?" Zara's voice was still raw. She had been screaming. Casimir could only fathom the emotions she felt.

"She was led in this direction by a seer if I'm not mistaken. The girl wouldn't say who. As far as I knew, none have existed in decades. But that isn't a claim Kaleopei would make without reason. I didn't pry any further than that. She asked me to distance myself from the commotion, avoiding any sort of prying eyes as my reputation tends to precede me."

"That's impossible, Kaleopei knows no seer." Keylan was quick to call out.

Casimir took it in for a moment, recalling the interaction of when he first met the twins when the Princess burst into the room shortly after.

"It's Mel. That's who she knew."

"This is more information than Kaleopei disclosed." Casimir wasn't sure if he should say any more on the matter. The information was something even Kaleopei hadn't given to Imogen. He wouldn't distrust her judgment.

"But that is neither here nor there. Kaleopei figured she would be brought to Bellheim for a public execution. I told her I wouldn't interfere directly, that's why I'm telling you what I am. Along with the reinforcements that will be here shortly. Not once did she forbid me from interfering indirectly. Kaleopei is intelligent, but she'd need to be more when making a deal with me."

"I apologize for my anger. Her safety isn't something I take lightly." Keylan nodded his head at Imogen. A notion to show his sorrow, but it did little to quell his anger.

"Nonsense boy, unfortunately, I care too much for the girl to leave her stranded like she wanted. She reminds me too much of Calsi. Your anger shows your dedication. You should teach Kaleopei how to do that."

Then, all they had to do was lie in wait for aid. Stock up on what Imogen could offer and plan to storm the capital.

Chapter 28

Everything was dark, not a lick of light in the cold dungeons she was kept in. Kaleopei lost track of how long she had been sitting in the barren cell, stomach roaring with unquenched hunger. She couldn't remember the last time she had felt cold. Her teeth were chattering, and her hands were shaking. The only really she could see anything was thanks to her Elven bloodline, the dark vision aiding her to see the bars and walls, along with a bucket in the corner of the room.

Every muscle in her fragile body ached with exhaustion. The only sleep she had gotten was the few hours after she depleted her magic, exhaustion forcing her to pass out.

The cold, damp cell beneath the Bellheim palace cast a gloom over Kaleopei as she sat in solitude, shackled by the weight of chains and the uncertainty of her fate. In the hushed silence, the echoing footsteps of a visitor reached her ears. Soft and quickened as they walked down the hall.

A grace a guard wouldn't bother with.

"Kaleopei, is that you? Are you down here?"

The door to her hallway creaked open, and Melody, the princess with a gift of foresight, entered with a small loaf of bread tucked under her arm. The flickering torchlight painted shadows on the damp stone walls as Melody approached, her expression a mix of curiosity and concern.

"I heard about the events in Louth, the description of the girl they brought in. Figured you had to be down here somewhere, Quite the destruction you caused."

Kaleopei struggled to find her voice. It was cracking with her recent silence. "It was like you saw. The weapon you saw was in Louth. I managed to keep the others away from it. They are safe."

Melody sat on the other side of the bars, offering the bread as a gesture of solidarity in their predicament. Kaleopei accepted the small gift, pecking at the bread. Feeling the starch go down her throat was a relief.

"Are you content with that choice?" Kaleopei thought about the question and all that it entailed. Kaleopei knew there was only one answer.

"I'd do it in every timeline without a thought. It's better if I'm a martyr, than our entire efforts be in vain. Bellheim will be in for a treat when they realize who they made an enemy of."

There was a slight silence that hung between them. A wave of relief washed over Kaleopei, knowing she would be the only casualty of her friends and brother. They would get to live. That's all she needed to know as she headed for a certain death.

"Can you do me a favor, Melody?" her voice was uncertain, "Tell Zaratella I'm sorry. Tell her I should have kept my emotions to myself and not involved her."

"Something tells me that she'll disagree, but I will nonetheless. Is there anything I can do to offer you solace?"

Kaleopei shook her head. Melody had already given so much for her. Far more than most had ever dared.

"Just make sure they're okay. I don't want Keylan to see the wake of my death. It'll wound him greatly, but he has to go on. He doesn't understand his own value sometimes, always caught up in making sure I'm alright. I do hope this will take some of that burden. I know I can be a lot."

Melody didn't speak, simply taking in all that Kaleopei had to say. Listening to all of her worries being laid on the ground, barren for the other Princess to see. The bread, a simple offering in the shadows of captivity, became a communion of struggles. Melody, a reluctant witness to the unfolding events, sought to ease the thoughts of Kaleopei.

"The visions I had... they showed me unrest, rebellion, and a clash of fate. But I can't see your future any longer. It's like a haze when I focus on it. I'm not certain it will lead to your death."

It was like that escaped arrow she dodged to her chest plunged deeper than the scar on her thigh. Confirmed that she would die, marked her, but she wouldn't let it be for nothing.

"Visions can be elusive and left for interpretation by the viewer. They show fragments, not always the whole truth. I don't think it means the end. Perhaps a beginning of a new era that even I can't see." Melody observed Kaleopei's weary demeanor and the weight of imprisonment and tried to ease what she was feeling. It was a gesture she was thankful, even if the words were sweet, that she attempted to quell the looming fear. "I can't offer you any closure on what is to come, but I do promise I will see it out."

"I know I'm not making it out of this. That was never the intention. But I will go down fighting. That much is certain."

"You are very much like your sister, Kaleopei Florence. I won't let your acts go unheard." The princess spoke intently, her eyes reflecting a mix of empathy and realization.

"Maybe someone will write a song about me one day." Kaleopei nodded, appreciating the depth of Melody's understanding. In that cold cell, a connection, unexpected yet profound, began to form. "Tell me about how you met Maize."

"She is much alike you and your brother. That girl was a wild one. My mother quite liked her. As did my eldest sibling, I didn't get the chance to speak with her one-on-one. Anytime she spoke in the presence of an audience, she commanded such authority. I thought it was her I saw in my visions. Your time may be over, but your story is not. I will see to it myself."

As the torchlight flickered on the walls behind the princess, Melody's words resonated in the confined space, leaving an enigmatic echo that stirred both uncertainty and a glimmer of resilience in the heart of Kaleopei.

"Thank you for trusting me enough that night," Kaleopei recalled the night they met and how she had cornered the girl on the balcony, asking questions. Melody wasn't innocent in this game, either. She, too, had many queries.

"My sister spoke highly of the Mer Realm. It'd be a bad omen to not acknowledge her opinion. You'd make a great advisor, should that be what you pursue."

Melody glanced around the cell, smiling faintly before turning back to Kaleopei.

"Perhaps this is the beginning of the end instead of something new. That much remains in the hands of fate. For the record, I am truly sorry it was you I saw. I've seen you many times. When I first met Maizelin, I thought she was you. Thought she was the girl who'd bring hope. But it appeared I was wrong. My visions are a blessing and a burden."

"You don't control fate. It's something nobody can avoid. Having your guidance was beyond more than I could ask for, it kept Keylan safe. That is far more than I could ever bargain for."

"You don't believe in Gods, right?"

"I think they were people who existed at one point in time. People who scorched their legacies into the very soil we still walk on. I don't think they have any say in what happens now. Or perhaps they are watching events unfold, laughing at the game they are playing. If that is the case," Kaleopei raised her middle finger towards the ceiling, "I do hope they see this."

Melody stifled a laugh, understanding being known between the two. Unlikely allies in this tide of the unknown they were coasting towards. Kaleopei wasn't sure how this rebellion would have gone without the aid of Melody, making some things clear for the girl in the beginning.

"You are brave beyond compare, Kaleopei Florence. Your spirit will live on."

"Thank you, Melody. Make sure you let Casimir down gently when you dump his ass. Poor male can only take so much in a short amount of time."

Melody cracked a smile, leaving another half of the bread in Kaleopei's hands.

"You mean I can't bring my *actual* fiancé to him? I think it would be a sight to see his pretty little head spin."

"That is something I would have loved to witness."

"It will be so catastrophic even the Deep will hear of it. Word travels fast. I'm sure wherever you end up, you'll know how embarrassed the Prince of the New Dawn was."

"New Dawn? Wasn't that what Calsi referred to us after the realm war? You aren't the first to refer to him as such."

"An older prophecy was said that one with blonde hair like Calsi would step forward and bring about a change. It's old and dated, but I like to think another seer saw it true. And he fits the description perfectly."

The cell, once a symbol of captivity, became an unexpected safe haven where the threads of fate converged, revealing a deeper connection between the elven rebel and the princess with the gift of a seer. United in a bout of fate, who together might bring down a King.

Melody turned before stepping out of the hall.

"If the definition of a god is one who leaves behind a legacy, then you, Kaleopei Florence, might find yourself being worshipped in the near future."

"Tell my worshippers I really liked Myth. That should be their offerings."

"I'll pass the memoir along, so long, Kaleopei."

Kaleopei waited for the chamber door to shut. The torchlights diminished in her wake. Once again confined to just her thoughts. Unlike before, they were subdued. She found herself laughing.

"Keylan will be pissed if I become a god and he doesn't."

Chapter 29

Keylan was far too aware of his surroundings, every crack the fire made, every noise his sleeping allies made. His sense was heightened and has been ever since he learned that Kaleopei was, in fact, taken to the Capital. Ellis had written, saying a prisoner cart was hauling towards the capital.

That was two days ago. Kaleopei should be arriving at Bellheim within the day. Keylan and his group were still lagging by a day. They'd have to make a quick pace throughout the day to reach her in time. He was glad he took the Hag's advice, waiting for the allies she had called on. Their numbers are increasing by a dozen.

A dozen skilled elven warriors, all willing to rally together and fight for their princess. Keylan didn't have the words to express his gratitude. He had damn neared cried when the group showed up, all clad in battle attire that would put the Bellheim guards to shame.

Each lick of light the flame gave was a constant reminder of what he'd lost. This was the longest they'd been apart since Kaleopei's last time in Louth, and that was agonizing. Knowing she was in the heart of Bellheim made his skin crawl. He was sure he could itch his skin raw, and that feeling would still be there.

In the absence of Kaleopei, Keylan found himself ensnared by a suffocating darkness that seemed to echo the shadows of their shared past. The once-vibrant spirit that fueled his every step now waned, replaced by a heavy cloud of melancholy that clung to him like a relentless specter.

"Keylan, you can't stay awake all night." Casimir's voice was soft. He had been comforting Zara all night, who thought this whole situation was her fault.

It wasn't. It was his.

Kaleopei always thought steps ahead, always knowing what her goal would be. He was naive for thinking she had her best interests in mind. She would throw herself in any sort of situation if it meant she was the only one getting hurt. Keylan had seen it time and time again.

"I can't shake this feeling, Casimir. It's like a part of me is missing." All of this was wrong. The only person who'd heard of his anxiousness had been his sister, and she was suffering in conditions only the Gods knew about.

"She's strong unlike any other, Keylan. We'll find a way to get her back."

The words offered little solace as Keylan's mind became a battleground of memories and unspoken fears. The weight of responsibility, now amplified by the absence of his sister, bore down on him with an unforgiving force. Keylan's laughter, once a resounding melody, was replaced by a haunting silence that seemed to resonate with the echoes of a world fractured by the loss of Kaleopei.

"She's put herself through so much, unable to see the light that she is. I want her to be happy. She doesn't deserve any of this."

"And you do?" Yes.

He deserved it tenfold for what she had already been through.

"For how much I let her down, I do," Keylan confirmed, not a trace of doubt.

"Have you considered that she feels the same? Constantly making efforts to make sure you're safe. You two play a dangerous game, living like that."

"It's all we've known."

In the quiet moments, he found himself revisiting memories of their shared laughter, the warmth of their bond, and the unspoken understanding that had always been their compass. The absence of Kaleopei, once his partner in both joy and adversity, left a void that seemed insurmountable. They had done everything together.

"What do you admire about her? I only ask that in instances, reminding her could make you feel closer. Like a reminder of what you're fighting for."

Keylan furrowed his brows, casting his lidded eyes in the direction of the blonde Prince.

"That's not going to work, I admire everything. She's my sister. How could I not?" Keylan took a chance, glancing at those sleeping around him.

"Specifics, Keylan."

The Elven male thought on it for a moment, basking in the fire that was his sister. She was a person he could always look up to, always rely on.

"Kaleopei has the courage to confront any challenge, able to make a joke while doing so. Her laughter is contagious. It's not sweet and subtle. It's a loud hackle, one truly unique to her. Kaleopei is the most ungraceful person to ever exist. Trips over her skirts when she wears them and stumbles into strangers when she's lost in her thoughts. But, when she is in the midst of battle or wearing a personality that isn't her own, she flourishes."

"She'll still be all that when we get to her. From the stories I've heard, Kaleopei can handle herself well. Always the first to volunteer for something dangerous, regardless of the risks. Not even my father could break her spirits."

Keylan wanted nothing than to believe Casimir's kind words, but, the tendrils of despair had wound themselves around Keylan's heart, suffocating the light within. Without her to see the results of what they accomplished, was it even worth it?

The weight of guilt and self-blame hung heavy in the air as Keylan spiraled deeper into the abyss of his own despair, a tempest that threatened to consume him whole. The journey to save Kaleopei became not only an external quest but an internal battle against the encroaching shadows that sought to extinguish the very essence of himself.

"Try and get some sleep. You'll be no good to her running off fumes."

Casimir clasped his hand over Keylan's shoulder, giving it a firm squeeze. Casimir then turned to his side, laying on whatever patch of grass felt the softest.

"Promise me something, from one prince to another?" Keylan's mind raced a thought that had been playing on his mind for a while. Casimir only made a low hum, showing he was listening. "If all goes wry, get everyone out. I'll buy time. If Kaleopei and I don't make it out, *she* has to."

The silence between them was deafening. Keylan knew Casimir had heard him, currently processing what he was saying. The Prince didn't even look at him, his frame falling in even breaths.

"It won't come to that," he was so confident in that answer. It gave Keylan a flicker of hope, but in the lack of Kaleopei's presence, his optimism wasn't shown. Usually upbeat and cheery personality, he was replaced by this husk of a male.

"Promise me if it does."

Casimir's head drifted to the side, looking over at the sleeping woman currently cuddling with Wisp. The sight made Keylan's heartache as he saw the chocolate brown hair rustling from beside the beast.

"I swear it, but that won't be the outcome."

"Thank you. For everything, Casimir. I was weary at the start, your presence unsettling. You've proven you're nothing like the man that raised you."

"You have been the closest thing to a brother I will ever know," Casimir smiled, turning to face Keylan, whose gaze never left the flames.

"Same for me."

Casimir turned his back to him once more, somehow finding sleep in this chaos they had found themselves in.

Leaving Keylan to his own thoughts as he gazed into the burning red flames the fire produced, wishing there was a flicker of green. Silently, he prayed to Calsi, Fenrah, Paxian, and Byrne like they were the only thing that could help them. Tomorrow, they were marching into the heart of the enemy, the place where the throne and king resided.

Keylan prayed they weren't ready for the barrage they would inflict. A public display that the King is replaceable isn't the end-all for the Human Realm. Most of all proves there is still some hope for humans to live in harmony with the other Realms. The rate the current King was setting proved he wanted all to fear him. There would never be peace. Always an unsettling wait for the moment when another war breaks out.

Nobody wished for a world like that, constantly in fear. Keylan hoped the Humans would see that and would rally behind their cause.

At the end of it all, he was just a brother who longed to gain his sister back. Suppose the world fell to pieces in the process; who would always choose her? Without her, he wasn't even sure what he would do.

Regardless of the outcome, all that mattered was returning to a life with his sister beside him; however that may be.

Chapter 30

Kaleopei was dragged, her hands and feet shackled with lead cuffs. Her magic was dampened and drained from what she accomplished at Louth. The throne room was enormous, every detail a testament to the King's power. To instill fear in his enemies and those who would ever dare cross him.

All Kaleopei could bring herself to feel was rage.

"Well, what do we have here, bird of Louth? Spread your wings enough, then decide to fly right on back?" Even his voice made her want to gag, but she thought back to her conversation with Melody. The reason she was going through all of this, the outcome was worth more than her suffering. The King was the embodiment of men pulling power over others. It made her stomach churn. "Heard you put on quite the show. Demolished all the hard work my associates had accomplished."

Kaleopei bit her tongue. She knew her execution would be public. He was that kind of person. Knew everything she wanted to say to him would have to wait until her neck was encased by rope, strung before a crowd of listeners. This cold throne room, with only a few presents, wasn't the place.

Kaleopei thought about death more than she should as of late. The place you go after the soil takes you was something she didn't want to know, but still, something pricked her brain. Why would she would fear death? Recalling the moments when she told Keylan she was scared of dying. Telling Zaratella that she wanted to live. In those instances, Kaleopei wasn't lying. She was selfish for even thinking that her life mattered more than generations to come. Her death would be the end of an era, a retribution to be carried out by those who come after her.

That was the fate she was bound to.

Dying seemed oddly comforting, knowing it was her fate, the rest in capable hands. Her death would be a turning point. Knowing she'd only have to suffer a few more hours in this cruel Realm. These past few days, being transported here by the psycho king, showed it was a merciful way to go, as selfish as it was.

Kaleopei didn't know what was worse. Dying for a cause that was forced upon her or facing death with no terror. Part of her thought she was tricking herself and kept repeating death didn't scare her until it rang true. A way to thwart any distractions from the path she was forced to walk.

"What? Vilken, got your tongue? You're not going to grace us with your words. You've made me angry. Your little stunt was costly. It will take ages to build up what you destroyed. You got greedy, coming back for more."

He was lounged on the red throne, an ode to all those he had killed during his reign. The sheer number of dead was uncertain. She doubted he even knew the number of people he sent to their deaths. The countless slaughtered for his own gain.

"Oh, I understand now. You must have been young eight years ago, or is it almost nine? You lack an education. You probably can't even speak. None of my soldiers ever recounted you talking. That makes sense now, Elf. Or does your kind simply not age? How old are you?" The way he belittled her seemed almost comedic, showing his ignorance knew no bounds.

Her long tresses of hair, unbound and messy, fell around her face all the way to her stomach. Kaleopei wouldn't allow him to look her in the eye. It wouldn't give him the satisfaction of seeing her falter. Since arriving, she had refused to even look at the man, afraid she'd see too much resemblance to the Prince she had grown fond of.

A swift kick to the back of her knees made her tremble. The pain was intense on her worn-out bones, but she refused to kneel. They'd have to cut her legs off before she gave in. Another strike, her body hissed. Kaleopei did not falter, only barred her teeth in defiance.

"I do not bow to the likes of you," she seethed through gritted teeth. Looking through her hair at the King, still not allowing him clear sight to her eyes. Even the throne was raised above whoever was below him, asserting his lack of domineering over those who were literally beneath him.

"So she can speak! And you will bow." The pleasure in his voice made her arms raise with goosebumps. "Do you care to tell me why you escaped and then returned of your own volition? To what? Try to save a couple of people. Here's the bottom-line, sweetheart: you are nothing compared to me and my Kingdom. Nothing. You came crawling back to me of your own choice. No one made you do that. And look where it landed you."

Kaleopei hated the thought of praying to a god, but she hoped that Renlys had his way with the tyrant before her. Picked his meat clean off those bones. Maybe even the proclaimed Gods could agree that this man deserved no eternal rest after his death, which Kaleopei hoped would be painfully slow.

Kaleopei bit her tongue, tasing the crimson in her mouth. In no world would she give this man any satisfaction in making her speak. Instead, she'd save her words and wait until they would have the most impact. She straightened her back and held her head up high, still refusing to look at the man.

"Still staying silent, sweetheart? At least you're a pretty thing, without the ears, that is. Maybe my men can have their way with you?" Kaleopei knew she'd cut off their favorite parts before they could even approach her. Even with the cuffs, exhaustion, and magic, depletion is only a mere inconvenience against the feminine rage coursing through her. "But I want a spectacle out of you, something to show others like you, your kind won't be tolerated. You'll wish you had died in the pit like the rest of your pitiful kind."

If that's how the King thought of her, Kaleopei could only imagine what he thought of himself. He conquered a nation, slaughtered children, burned cities, and nearly destroyed an entire future of a Realm. She was a child whose wrongs out weighed the King's in some twisted fate. It took all she could to keep her laughter to herself, not willing to risk her vow of silence.

She could only imagine how his blue eyes would control with rage at the mere thought. A lesser being like her, laughing at him. No less in front of so many of those he controlled. Knowing the outcome would be pleasurable, so she'd wait.

Kaleopei's body shook, not in fear. No, the rage swelling inside of her rivaled the mightiest of catastrophic storms. Kaleopei was basking in pride that she was his greatest opponent. How'd she flipped his world upside down? The man who killed her family led armies, and controlled thousands of citizens was outdone by a barley adolescent teenager.

Kaleopei had no regrets. Everything she has done has been to better the lives of others and for Keylan to survive. She only wished she could have said goodbye to Keylan, her other half. And Zaratella, who she hadn't known for a long while but left an impact. Somehow, the onyx-eyed girl had imprinted herself into her life, a connection that would have lasted a lifetime if fate permitted. Kaleopei told herself in another life. It might have been tangible. But not this one. Imagining herself having a life with the witch was peaceful, something she hadn't even known she craved for. I wasn't sure when that feeling had taken hold, but it didn't matter now.

"Cancel any executions for the day. Fit them in with the lot tomorrow. Take her to the square. She shall be flogged. Whipped thirty-seven times, one for each of my men she killed." The King demanded, "then she will be hung for the entire capital to see. Make them watch what happens when you don't obey the rules."

Kaleopei didn't resist as the tugging against her shackles yanked her in another direction. She was flanked by four guards who pushed her along. Metallic blood still soaked the inside of her mouth, swishing it in her mouth before spitting it onto the white flooring. Staining the pure, extravagant white quartz with the rich crimson of her blood. Kaleopei looked over her shoulder, locking eyes with the King as she licked the front of her teeth, barring her bloodied canine for him to see.

One thing was for certain: she wouldn't go quietly.

Chapter 31

"What I'm saying is I'll be with the group who intercepts the actual execution. I will not stand by as she is hurting in the square." Zara's voice echoed in the sewers of Bellheim. All moved into their positions when Keylan proposed she'd be with the second wave of aid if things were to go wrong.

Keylan wasn't sure why he wanted her far from the conflict. Only that it would wound Kaleopei if Zara were to get hurt because of her. Mixed within, a twinge of jealousy he felt. Emotions of his own seemed so trivial when thinking about what was at stake.

His twin. Sister.

"I'm not saying you stay complacent. You are cunning. Use that to your advantage." Keylan tried to voice his thoughts in a manner that sounded convincing, but he tumbled with impatience. Each second they spent waiting was a second they lost to get Kaleopei out of there.

"We're not arguing about this. What's done is done. I'm not being forced away again. I *will* be with you in the square." Then Zaratella was leading the charge. Their group followed her as she led them through the confusing tunnels underneath the capital. A twisted maze that kept them from the looming presence above.

Zara was an asset. Keylan understood that well. He Knew her knowledge of the underside of the city was unmatched, knowing when grates would leak light, possibly giving away their position. Casimir was with the other team, following a different route to the square with another portion of their numbers. He would be fine, so long as he listens to the women left in charge. Keylan still wasn't sure what he thought of her. Too many mixed emotions ran rampant inside of him to have a clear understanding of what had transpired over the eight years. Deciding it's better to split, both groups couldn't be compromised, not with all the commotion about the mandatory execution being hosted at noon.

Keylan's impatience was clear to every single person who traveled in toe. Some even made the extra effort to stay clear of his path. The way his skin seemed to itch and his constant sweating only added to it. Step after step, he was closer to Kaleopei. Closer to the man who caused all their heartache and pain.

He wouldn't let himself break now. He was deep in these treacherous waters. Refusing to show a weakness that could keep him from his sister any longer. Keylan could only imagine the way she was hurting, the torture they might have put her through. The thought made his fist ball, turning white. Keylan was fueled by anger. Knowing if he laid eyes on the King, his head would be the one hanging from a rope for Bellheim to see. Delivered on a tray of lies and deceit, decorated by crimson and Darren Haven's head as the centerpiece. What a display that would be.

Keylan's anger wasn't only his. It belonged to every person the King of Bellheim had wronged and betrayed. All the elves that had fallen victim to his wrath. They all fueled him, gathered inside like the waves preparing for high tide. Laying in a silent wait would strike when the forces are put into play.

The King should, would, fear him and the fury he will bring.

Chapter 32

She didn't know how long the early summer sun had been beating down on her bare back. They had cut the tunic she wore, exposing bare skin. The warmth didn't bother her. It brought her comfort like a warm embrace. Every fiber of her being ached, her body still not recovered from her display at Louth.

Kaleopei's eyes were shut, listening to her breathing. Concentrating on anything that wasn't painful. She could hear the crowd gathering; it seemed executions were an ordeal in the capital, and Kaleopei had a front-row view.

With a bout of confidence, she pried her eyes open. Looking out, she saw many faces all gathered to watch her death. Was it even their choice? Or had it been a mandatory event?

A throne was set a few feet away from her, seemed she warranted the King to see to her death personally. Unlike the throne room, the man wasn't lounging. The King smiled. Standing and gesturing out to the audience who threw him praise.

"Good afternoon to my friends here in the capital. I hope you didn't miss me too much in my absence, but I come bearing gifts!" The King walked up to his throne, addressing the crowd. "This elven girl slaughtered my men. Possibly your loved ones and family. In cold blood, she murdered thirty-seven of the royal guard without any remorse."

A mix of reactions from the crowd, some shocked, others sullen. However, the consistency was their hatred towards her. Kaleopei didn't know why they followed the King with such loyalty; perhaps it was fear, or he held things they loved in a constant state of jeopardy. Always ready to take what is theirs right from their devoted hands. They practically worshipped the ground he walked on for fear they would end up in her position.

"Some shitty men that fell to a girl," she mumbled. All focus shifted to her, with wide eyes at her bout of speech. "I'd consider upping the qualifications when hiring your guard. Too many fell before I got serious."

"It seems she wishes to entertain us with her tongue. I think she would be prettier without it, but then we couldn't hear her screams properly. That, my loyal friends, is part of the fun." The first strike came as a shock, stinging her back where the whip struck the small of her back. Biting her lip, forcing herself not to make a sound, she took the lashing. He would receive no such satisfaction from her. The reactions were what he took pride in. His ability to hurt others by simply willing it so.

Kaleopei couldn't even see her abuser, only able to look out into the crowd of people who stared up at her. Gods, she prayed her capture hadn't reached Keylan. He didn't deserve to witness the cruelty of the humans, the pain that lurked around every corner as this man reigned. Keylan would only hear of it in the aftermath of her plan, never having to witness it himself.

"He is manipulating and abusing you all!" She screamed out, another two hits lashing at each shoulder. Kaleopei felt the blood run down her back, the smell fresh in her nostrils as the pain flared in her back.

She barred her teeth, piercing her lip with the force behind the bite. Hot, vicious liquid trickled down her chin.

"Me? I give my people everything they could ever ask for." He laughed. Laughed in the faces of his citizens as another lash was bestowed upon her. Mocking them in every way possible. "They are safe, have homes, food, happiness. Anything a person could want can be obtained in this here Kingdom."

"I had a home too, but that was a long time ago until you decided I was unworthy," her voice came out strained, the King's temper growing shorter as he commanded more strikes. One after another. Unrelenting. "How long until you deem your own people a waste of space? How long until they're unworthy of your existence."

Kaleopei needed the crowd to sympathize with her. Even the slightest bit would sell her performance. Rebellion was a finicky thing. Just takes one person to start a spark, then others will follow. Then, more in the wake of those sparks, fanning out until a raging fire burned in their hearts. She was the match that'd ignite the fire to come. Kaleopei's words were the force bestowed upon a match to make that spark.

"I do think you talk quite a lot. It'd be appreciated if you'd only writhe in pain from here on out."

After another couple of strikes, her lip was bleeding more with each strike, containing herself. It was excruciating. She could feel the cuts along her back, agitated with every new one another stung. Kaleopei could only imagine the horror of her back. The whip smacked against the cobbled stone. It was ringing in her ears like a sick mantra.

"To kill me is to declare war on the Elven Realm."

"What Realm girl? I own that land!" He had thrown his hands out, his far too heavy velvet cape extenuating his movements to make them seem grander. To Kaleopei, it only made it appear as compensation for a craving for validation.

Kaleopei lost track of how many times the whip had lacerated her skin. The only thing on her mind was how this was the end. Once she made her declaration, she could be done. Finally, be done.

"There are more like me, lying in wait to take our home back. Refugees scattered through the other Realms, willing to aid us as you slaughtered thousands," she smiled. Grinned through the pain and each strike that continued during her speech. Watching as the crowd watched in intrigue and horror, still a mix, but Kaleopei was making progress. "It isn't I who should be chained in your square. You have much more than I do to atone for. You alone have orchestrated far more crimes than I have. The only reason you still stand on this soil is because you are a loose canon. Much like the weapon you harbored."

"She thinks she's entitled! Girl, let them come. I'll deal with them just like before. You are nothing here! Spewing lies from your lips, you'd say anything to get out of your position."

Somehow, in all of this mess, he saw her as the entitled one.

"That's the difference. I would give *everything* to my people. You'd give *everyone* to better yourself. I am a Queen. My people look up to me in a time of sorrow. Rise to the challenge when threatened. My death will only cause them to stir. You are not the kind of King who can command empathy. People would spit on your rotting corpse as it hung from this here wood." Kaleopei spoke with authority. It was who she was. No lies echoed from her mouth. "My people would worship this site, deliver offerings. Really grieve my loss, not thrive in my downfall."

"Lies! I killed the entire Florence bloodline when my armies marched on Eviera!"

"My name is Kaleopei Azgaeda Florence, rightful heir to the Garden Throne. Princess of Light, bearer of the emerald flame and descendant of Fenrah. Tell all of my return because the bloodline does not end with me today." Six consecutive strikes to her back, willing her to silence. Kaleopei would not give in. She did not fear at this moment.

Almost done.

She was far past thirty-seven lashes at this point, not counting, but aware of the pain that encased her. Darren could kill her any second. She had to make them count.

Kaleopei was a fire in every aspect, stubborn against the wind of change, resilient against any dousing she could receive. The Emerald flame was a trait few inherited in the Florence bloodline. They are said to be blessed by the fire god herself and touched by the goddess of luck. Kaleopei never thought of herself as blessed. When she was born, her flames engulfed the doctor, who birthed her with green flames.

Never once had she been lucky.

Everything she got was earned through the blood and tears she shed to make them possible. It wasn't luck that got her here. That much was clear.

The King and Queen decided it'd be better to keep her and Keylan away from the public eye until Kaleopei learned to harness and control the fire within.

It was the reason few knew of her existence. Kaleopei was never supposed to rule; that was Maizelin's title, but after her death, the responsibility was hers to bear. Just like it will be Keylan's title by the end of the day. Sooner, if she was lucky, but it's been established that she's not.

"Silence! I won't tolerate another word." The King lashed out, his words aiming to strike like a whip, but they didn't even land close. "This is the ramblings of a scared little girl facing her death."

"You maimed my blood, slaughtering them in the dead of night. There was no honor in that. You commanded the death of children and innocent bystanders. Endangered the entire continent because of your morbid fascination in harnessing *elven* magic." Kaleopei felt the anger building up. She felt no pain as lash after lash mangled her back. Through her vision, all she could see was red-hot rage simmering for a release.

"I said not another word!"

"I do not answer to you." Kaleopei's chest ached as she summoned her magic, pushing through the lead containing her. Flames trickled her body, small sparks of green light emitting from her. "Nor do I take demands from pathetic Kings."

"Stop the lashings. Kill her where she stands!" Kaleopei tried to call to her reserve of magic. Calling for the flame to grow brighter. Every plea, a deaf chant, didn't notice when her executioner came to her front, bearing a gleaming blade that dazzled in the sunlight. Or when a whistle came from the crowd.

Please, please, please.

This was the end.

"Lovkin Valera Kaleopei Azgaeda, Florence ez Eviera."

Eyes forced shut, willing her fire to ignite. She heard the indictment from the crowd. A single person had seen her as a Queen. Wishing for the heat to come to her palms, to defend herself to the bitter end. They didn't. All she had was a small puddle of her usual ocean of power. The releasing of the magic the Aetherite Canon consumed had taken a great deal of her magic with it. She hadn't had time or rest to regain it. Kaleopei was running on empty. The fumes of her talents lingered.

Faintly, she heard a scream that wasn't hers. Then, she was looking around, becoming aware of her surroundings once more. Two folks from the sea of people were repeating the welcoming of a new Queen.

"Lovkin Valera Kaleopei Azgaeda Florence ez Eviera."

The crowd was in panic, looking to their neighbors for a sign of what to do. During the commotion and rising unease, Kaleopei felt the pulse of magic, but not from herself.

Then, there were hands on her wrists. Unhooking her from the post she was shackled to, Kaleopei dropped to her knees, taking in a deep breath as she noticed the executioner had dropped his blade. Before she could note anything else, black hair engulfed her vision, and kneeling in front of her was a familiar set of onyx eyes.

Was this death?

Had Renlys dragged her into some kind of hell.

"Hey, hey, you're okay. You're fine." The voice belonged to Zaratella, who was currently massaging her shackle-free wrists, blood pouring down her forearms. Kaleopei squeezed the hands back, taking a moment to hear the battle roar of a large creature who stalked in the square. In the center of the square were Keylan, Wisp, and Casimir, all keeping the guards at bay.

"... How?" It was the only thing that left her lips, unable to understand how they learned of her location so quickly.

"Turns out Imogen knows a few people." It was then Kaleopei saw the others, all with pointed ears, bearing weapons and magic alike, some even using a combination of the two. Telling citizens to stand back and guards to stay where they stood. By the king stood a figure, tall in stature, muscles corded in her arms, with braided brown hair sitting atop her head like a crown and a familiar scar across her collarbone. Kaleopei didn't even notice the tears dripping down her face, pooling into the hands of the Carver before her.

Kaleopei could have been dead for all she knew, for standing in front of her was a ghost of the past. The muscled figure of Maize holding a dagger to the King's throat was not something Kaleopei ever thought possible. She had to be dead.

"Never thought I'd see the day when my baby sister claimed she was Queen. If I recall correctly, you said you hated the thought of being royalty. Declaring yourself as Queen is a step up from princess, as I'm sure you are aware." Even the woman's voice was as comforting as she remembered, laced with playfulness only her dreams remember.

"Maize?"

"You've done well, Kali. Leave the rest to us. You've earned it." Kaleopei tried to push herself to her feet, but her knees buckled. All the pain came flooding into her, and then Keylan and Casimir stepped up to her. Keylan's hands were already making quick work on her back. It was an immediate relief to the constant, near-unbearable stinging. If they survive this, the healing process will be tortious.

Maybe not dead? She certainly felt alive. Far too alive with the amount of pain she was dealing with.

"I'm going to kill him," Keylan spoke to himself, but she knew he meant it. Each word laced with venom and anger, she knew he had been subduing so he could aid her instead.

"Glad to see you're alive, almost had me worried for a second." Even Casimir was smiling, only lingering around her for a second before moving towards his father. Who was now kneeling in front of Maize?

A sight she had never given Bellheim's King the pleasure of seeing. Here, he knelt, shaking with terror, as two elves moved to secure his wrists behind his back.

"You cower before me in front of all your people. Even my sister didn't balk at you, and I understand why now."

"You're supposed to be dead."

"You can't kill a storm."

"You're a monster!" The King shouted, finally seeing his son walking towards him. "Boy, you must help me. I am your father. I gave you everything!"

Casimir swiped the crown from the King's head, placing it on his own blonde head. With confidence, Kaleopei had only witnessed in small snippets. Fiddling as it sat awkwardly on his head, clearly not a mold he was made to fit. That could be changed, just as leadership is.

"From this day on, I will be coronated as King of the Human Realm and allied to the Elven Realm indefinitely. Along with peace with the Mer realm, today Darren Haven is to be stripped of his title and arrested for treason, backed by a list of other felonies he shall atone for." Casimir's voice was shaky but held an undertone of authority and confidence. A side Kaleopei had only seen briefly. It's difficult to believe they had only met mere weeks ago.

Where was Melody in all of this? The King, or rather, the Ex-King, didn't find any traces of their rendezvous in the cell. Was Darren so blatant to kill a princess of a powerful Realm who has the seas at their disposal? Kaleopei didn't think it was true. Melody had that man wrapped around her finger somehow.

Zara held her hands through the entirety of Keylan's healing. A silent comforting as the world unfolded around her. Kaleopei wasn't sure what she was feeling. She was just ready to die. How does one just come back from that?

Kaleopei wasn't sure. All she knew was that the relief was overwhelming. Her world turned black as she fell into comforting, gentle arms that soothed her into a lull of needed sleep.

Chapter 33

Casimir's entire world had been flipped upside down in a matter of a few hours. Darren Haven was locked up in the castle dungeons, constant surveillance on him done by one of the gracious Elves who were lingering around the capital for the time being. Casimir was stuck trying to figure out how to run a Realm, and all the inner workings of it all in a quickened pace.

Spoiler: it was far more than he could ever imagine. Many were willing to step up during this trying time. Zaratella, his friend, was currently seeing the end to any Carver schools that ran under the old King's discretion within the city limits. She refused to leave Kaleopei's vicinity until she woke up.

It had been six days since the incident in the square. Keylan, like Zara, refused to leave until his sister was well. He owed a great deal to the trio. Far more than his life, yet they said the same to him. Still Keylan aided in assigning guards and creating posts where they needed.

Melody, surprisingly was the most supporting of all, her being the one he turned to when addressing a more political move. Creating a court, addressing the Lords and Ladies of the Realm in a pleasant manner laced with words to weed out the ones who still had loyalty to Darren.

She was there throughout it all, often accompanying him when giving speeches throughout the capital. Shortly, he'd be setting out to visit as many cities and towns with the Human Realm as possible. To see more of the damage the previous monarch had done and what measures he could take to undo them.

Maizelin Florence was somehow nearly identical to her younger sister. The two sharing features and traits he could of sword those two were twins, and not the two he'd come to know so well. Maizelin was even more menacing and commanding than Kaleopei, her voice a beacon of authority across many who already followed her.

He was under the pretense that no person could get more intimidating than Kaleopei. Here, he was proven infinitely wrong.

The rebels they had come across, now just regular citizens under his latest decree, were all elves who escaped eight years ago. All of varying ages and backgrounds rallied under her cause, and they laid in wait in the Realm of Many across the east sea. Harboring their numbers into its own force, apparently, they were over four hundred strong. It was a feat Casimir was unsure was true; it was so insane, but Maizelin was a Florence, just like the two he'd come to look up to.

One thing was true: those siblings are utterly in-fucking-sane. Nothing about them should be plausible, yet they all were currently residing within his city's walls. Casimir was grateful that the middle one was still in a deep slumber, something about the side effects of magic depletion; otherwise, he didn't want to know the chaos the three of them could cause. Two in one room was surely enough for his entire lifetime.

"Um, Lord Casimir?"

"Cadence, just call me Casimir. Everything is already too formal." The blue-eyed man threw a gaze over his shoulder. Looking at the girl in the doorway who was holding an armful of papers and files piled up to her chin.

"Right, Casimir. Where do you want these?"

"A top of the numerous other piles that seem to plague my entire existence, reading was an escape. Now it's a chore."

He loosed his tunic, done with any public outings he'd set out to do today. Finally able to relax within the massive workload he had in front of him. Suppose you could count filing documents as relaxing.

But! He could do so without any eyes watching his every movement.

"Right," Cadence added to the pile of never-ending words, tripping over the hem of her dress as she did so. Chocolate eyes wide for a brief moment before she caught her footing, face turning red. "Sorry! If I messed anything up."

"Nonsense, only doing me a favor." He laughed, striding towards her, subtly checking to make sure nothing was actually wrong with the girl. Flickers of insecurity flashed across her face like she was a child who was about to be scolded.

"I can help! That's if you want it. I don't actually know what I can do, but I can try." Tripping on her dress wasn't the only thing it seemed, fumbling over her words. He did nothing but smile at the girl who stepped up to bear some of the bureaucratic responsibilities when transitioning from prince to ruler.

"Can you forge my child-like signature?"

"I think I could after a few tries."

"Then, by all means, make yourself comfortable and don't sign anything that seems too absurd. Most of it is just bullshit anyway."

She nodded her head, moving to occupy a chair that was across from him. Grabbing her own pile, she watched him sign his sloppy signature into the parchment, moving it off to the side.

"I'll do my best," she said.

"You'll do fine." Casimir spared a glance, seeing her entranced in perfecting the signature. It was nice to have company during this while all his friends were scattered, helping in other ways that kept them away.

"Have they said when the girl is to wake up?" Cadence's voice was airy in the confined space like a burst of wind lifted when she spoke, even if the subject was macabre.

"No one speaks of it in depth, like it's some sort of taboo thing to even be uttered. Keylan referred to her state as Spellspent." He recalled remembering the turmoil in Keylan's eyes as he carried his unconscious sister into the castle walls. Kaleopei was scalding hot. The buckets of ice-cold water they doused the girl in were enough to give a normal human hypothermia.

It was obvious she was not such. He could recall the amount of steam that water had turned into.

"I'm not the most knowledgeable with magic or anything. Is that a problem?"

"I did some research of my own the first night. It's when a person has exuded a quintile amount of their magic in a small time frame. Their body requires magic to sustain itself. Losing so much can lead to many complications. The worst was death, which Kaleopei has faced far too many times to succumb to it now. Keylan says it all depends on when she's recharged enough to wake."

"So, it's a waiting game?"

"An entirely nerve-wracking one." Casimir fiddled with a ring on his finger, spinning it as a way to distract himself from the worry he felt. He had bile rise to his throat when he thought back to the lacerations and wounds Kaleopei had received. The mangled cuts and scars over came any amount of skin on her back. It was raw and bloody.

Gruesome was a light way to put it. Never before had he ever seen such mangled flesh. Death seemed like a mercy. Alas, Kaleopei was too stubborn.

It was a possibility that she hadn't lied when they first met. No mortal should be able to come back from what she endured.

"The Princess is something else entirely. I don't think I'd be able to handle a lashing like that."

"Kaleopei has endured far mare than any person can fathom. I fear I don't even know the majority."

"I think she does it out of love." Love? That was one word to categorize her recklessness. "Not wanting any harm to come to those she cares about. I wouldn't mind her as a Queen. She's brave and driven. Perhaps you should take notes... Not that you're bad or anything! I just was speaking freely. I know I probably shouldn't, as you are a King, but you being a Prince never seemed to stop my rambling."

Casimir listened to every word Cadence spoke, finding humor in the innocent voice. It was calming, serene to the life he had been living. Being around her was like reading lines on a page, a tone Casimir was unsure how to describe.

"Maybe you should be my Royal Advisor. Tell me how to be a good King."

"No, no, no, I wasn't insinuating anything in that manner. I personally think you'll make a wonderful King, not that there's very much competition in the Human Realm."

"I understand you," he placed a hand atop hers. Locking gazes with chocolate-colored eyes. "You don't have to explain yourself."

"I won't, sorry."

"Don't apologize for speaking your mind. I want people to be able to come to me when speaking their minds." It was the truth. Any person in the Human Realm should be able to express themselves without fear of his actions.

"I have no doubt you'll do exactly that, your highness." She repeated the phrase like it was engraved on her tongue, a trait no doubt drilled into her head by his father.

"Casimir, not fancy titles." He reminded.

"Right, Casimir."

Falling into. A comfortable silence was heavenly to him. He was able to just zone in on the work at hand without the added stress of talking in proper sentences or making sure his head was held high as he annunciated every word. The ideals drilled into his head by the few he trusted.

Nothing good can ever last when an elven guard by the name of Verick comes rushing to the door. Fists heavy against the wooden door, Casimir was sure it would come off its hinges. It didn't... barely.

"King Cash, I have word from Prince Keylan," Cash? "He says his sister stirs."

Casimir stood from his seat, leaving all his outer layers on the chair as he rummaged for something in his drawer. Blue eyes fixated on the intricate wooden object and a small jar next to it.

"It's Casimir, not Cash." The man looked taken back.

"Sorry, sir, Keylan said you preferred it. I don't question what he says." The loyalty created within their knit was already tight. He'd seen how they had gotten along. Spent evenings interacting and all of the elves getting to know each other... except for Kaleopei.

"Sure, it works. Close enough," he couldn't find a reason to be worried about the small details. Kaleopei was worth more than some dumb nickname.

***

He pocketed the jar and object, not bothering to put on all the fancy attire Melody insisted that he needed to wear to be taken seriously. Why couldn't he be a fun King? Uptight wasn't his style in the slightest. Preferred to dress down any time of day.

His hair was tousled as he rushed through the halls of the castle. They were far too clean. All white and pristine, he'd find someone to paint them. The castle wasn't complete without art colors depicting a tale of old or one of new.

There was a commotion in the wing he sanctioned for the siblings. All had separate rooms, but none ever seemed to sleep apart. An instinctual need to protect the sleeping Kaleopei.

The door was open, and he could hear chatter from the inside. Making out familiar voices, some laughing, others more in a scolding tone. Nonetheless, it brought a smile to his features, brightening his wide features. The tone, as of late, had been rather melancholy, so any change was enlightening.

He peaked his head inside, knowing his presence was already aware to most in the room. Keylan and Maizelin were sat on the far side of the bed, closest to the window. While Zara and Melody were posted on the other side, all interlocked in fretting for the half-awake Kaleopei.

"I swear to god, I will burn all of you if you don't let me wake in peace," she mumbled, her hands rubbing at her eyes as if she were trying to clear them. Then her gaze shot to him, realization coming to her face, accompanied by a smirk. "You have three seconds to get it out, or else I burn your shiny new Realm. That is correct, right? Or did I just get publicly lashed for nothing?"

Apparently, she had already reached the joking stage of trauma. Skipping everything else and just coping through humor, somehow, it was fitting. Only she could crack jokes quicker than those could comprehend.

Casimir considered himself a smart person and was not in the business of denying the girl what she asked for. From his pockets, he fished out the pipe, already packed and ready to light.

"I love you. You are the best ever," He couldn't tell if she was talking to him or the Myth. It didn't matter, she was talking.

"I am going to overlook the King giving drugs to a wounded Princess and pretend I never say anything." Melody laughed, but he could see the redness around her eyes and how the sea foam seemed almost glassy. That told him enough.

"Is that really a wise idea, sister?" Keylan was trying to take the pipe out of her grasp. Anyone who knew him would see how gentle the man was being when compared to their usual antics.

Casimir couldn't help if the corner of lips upturned.

"Bite me, bitch." Kaleopei chomped her teeth at his hand, the quick motion making a snapping sound. It was a side he was learning of Kaleopei, seeing it progress as they were together. The subtle way she jokes, her lack of personal space when comfortable, and the silliness she has in certain moments. Most when she was just getting up or was being taunted by Keylan.

Kaleopei raised the pipe to her lips, lifting her lips to create a seal. Bandages were tightly laced up to her neck, all secured and some stained from the original white they once were. Keylan had spent countless hours working on her back, mending whatever he could. Saying it was like trying to glue shards of glass back into one piece. That would take a miracle.

Casimir dared a glance at Zara, who's head was resting at the end of the board. Face close to Wisp, who was passed out on Kaleopei's legs, subtly purring, tails swaying silently in his slumber. Her iron eyes were glazed in a tired haze. Casimir didn't miss the look of admiration and relief in the girl's gaze as she looked at Kaleopei. Between Zaratella and Keylan, Casimir wasn't sure who worried more. The girl he grew up with would never willingly stay awake around the clock watching someone sleep. It came as a surprise when Zara began taking meals in Kaleopei's room, often spending many hours with the twins.

"You better not be about to light that with magic. We just got you back from a Spellspent." Maizelin scolded the girl who brought her hand to where one would put a match.

"That basically means I got a full charge, right?" She smirked.

"You were on the brink of death. The soil was practically staking its claim!" Keylan countered. It was a sight. All of Florence's siblings engaged in an argument over medicinal drugs over the possibility of death.

Fitting.

"Death is a mercy when compared to listening to you two yap in my ears." Kaleopei rolled her eyes, but everyone knew she didn't mean it. Or perhaps she did. That was simply her nature.

Then she actually went in for a hit, bringing her hand to the pipe, but instead of a flame flickering, the grounded herb was blown into Keylan's face.

Nobody moved.

Nobody blinked.

"Just to be sure, the window isn't open, right?" Melody was the first to speak. Then, it was Zara who looked on with curiosity.

"Your reactions make me believe you couldn't do that before."

Kaleopei looked at the black-haired girl, head now propped up on one of her arms. A look of intrigue across her features, studying what had just happened.

"So I didn't just get really high on one hit and imagined that?" Kaleopei blankly looked at Keylan, the herb dusting across his face. He moved to clear it, the small particles still lingering on his skin.

"Nope," Keylan spit out a breath of air, specks of Myth floating into the air as he did. "Most definitely did not."

"And I didn't die, and this isn't what my version of what the hell looks like?"

"Still breathing, Kali." Maizelin slapped her shoulder. Only Mel looked like nothing had just occurred. Simply placed a gentle hand on Kaleopei's leg with the faintest touch.

"Good, then would you all wish to inform me of what I've missed? Later, we can discuss the whole magic thing that just happened, but even I need time to process it all."

Chapter 34

"So Casimir became a king," Kaleopei began looking between all the figures in the room. Her head bursting with all the information that had just been spouted. "Nullifying the marriage between the Mer and Human Realm."

A nod from the blonde King and white-haired Princess told her she was computing all the ongoing.

"Zara, you're going around shutting down any of the Carver operations? Melody has been acting like a pimp for Casimir's public appearances." That earned a chuckle from her brother, who looked at her as if she were the only thing he could see. "Keylan is currently assigning and maintaining Human armies? And Maize, well, honestly, I don't know how the fuck you are sitting there and just smiling. We were under the impression you were dead."

The mentioned sister cocked her head to the side, a distant look in her gaze. Guilt, if Kaleopei wasn't mistaken. A look of stress and anxiety she had seen many times during her childhood.

She hated that look.

"I didn't know you were alive, either. It wasn't until Imogen told me such that I knew. You two were in the castle that day. I was not." Maizelin began telling her story. "I was out of Eviera with an emissary at the time. He stashed me on a boat with a few water wielders, and soon enough, I was in the Realm of Many. Convinced that whoever didn't make it out fell victim to the Human armies. Or apparently were taken and used to make a weapon, one you seemed to have dealt with?”

Maizelin was nearly twenty years older than the twins. Their parents had a hard time conceiving her and thus opted to wait a few decades before having more. Maizelin was still considered young to most elves, still in her age of new adulthood.

She had suffered no different from them. Across the seas on another continent entirely, she had been plagued with the same thoughts as us. She is only able to imagine the swift death of her loved ones to subdue her grief. Except she was alone. Had no twin to rely on in times of unease.

Kaleopei wanted to know how she did it. Did the Hag know this whole time? Why hadn’t she said something about their sister being alive?

Too many questions. Not nearly enough, Myth. Maizelin survived completely on her own, gaining a following even under those conditions. All of the Elven Realm knew of her existence, being the crowned princess of the Elven Realm. She was the epitome of hope when Talia and Farrow hadn’t had an heir during their forty-year marriage and their mother’s sixth decade on the Garden Throne. A child of miracles.

“And you, my dear sister. You are now my queen. My Valera.”

“I, by law, am *technically* a Queen of the Elven Realm.” That was the hardest thing to comprehend. Her announcement in the square meant she was indicted into a position of power by Elven tradition. A tradition she wasn’t too fond of right now.

"I'm unsure how much you actually heard, too busy not dying or whatever, but you had dozens of people chanting in Elven tongue. All ringing the words of coronation and acceptance."

"But aren't you Queen?"

"Yes and no, I was never accepted on this continent. By tradition and right, you are Queen to this soil." Was that actually what Kaleopei wanted? To be an idol to many people, looked up to by so many in their time of need?

Would Kaleopei even be able to handle that? Maize was the obvious touch, taught and learned how to lead since she was born.

"Can't I just, I don't know. Give the title to you. I'd be a terrible Valera?" It had been years since she uttered the word. Usually opting to say the equivalent in common. It was strange, foreign against her tongue.

"You can't just give the title away. We can have a ceremony when we rebuild Eviera. Until then, you have to reap what you spoke, sister. Many have already accepted you as their Valera, grateful for all you have done. There was word sent to the Realm of Many, and dozens of Elf made the trek back home. There was also a group who showed up at the place yesterday, saying they wished to thank you for saving them in Louth."

All of this was too tough to swallow. Kaleopei actually accomplished what she set out to do, and those in the holding cells had escaped her wrath. Kaleopei dethroned a king whose rule seemed endless. Somehow, in the end, keeping her life in the process. Just when she had come to terms with dying.

"Now that we've told you all that, why don't you explain that little stunt you pulled with Imogen." It was Zara's words that caught her off guard. Kaleopei couldn't quite read what was happening behind those iron eyes. Unsure of where they currently stood. Kaleopei had caused her heartache in their last moments together, and she had no idea how to deal with the aftermath of that. In the forest that surrounded Louth, many things were left unspoken.

The witch had still shown up in the end. Kaleopei still felt the girl's trembling hands encasing her own.

"Melody refused to say anything until you were able to participate in that conversation."

"The Hag and I made a deal," Kaleopei trod lightly, unsure of how much Melody wanted to revel to them about herself. Did they know she was a seer? Or has she still kept that hidden? "Simple as that. She knew what I wanted, and I offered her a bit of truth I knew. Tidbits of information that she couldn't turn down."

"Which was?" Casimir was the one who seemed most puzzled by all of this, actually trying to understand Kaleopei's perspective. His brain was working overtime with the combined stress of what Kaleopei had done and royal duties. Nothing had to be easy for him. He was a newly crowned King, grappling with all that entailed.

"Not my secret to share." A secret she wasn't sure anybody should know. One that could alter the course of the world as they know it. A world they had just worked hard to save. This secret wasn't one everybody should know. "I also had some help from Melody. I recognized her for what she was almost immediately."

"I do admit to aiding her, coming to Bellheim out of a morbid sight I had. One that involved her. Actively, my goal was to find her. It was only luck that brought us together so soon after my initial visit." Melody's voice was calm, even under the heavy scrutiny Keylan's emerald eyes gave her. They had to know she was a seer. Or was it inferred, given the context?

"You had been plotting your capture since we met?" Casimir asked, searching her emerald eyes for an answer her words did not convey. It wasn't entirely the truth. Kaleopei had tried to entertain other possible ideas. One that lessened the risks she had to bear, but in the end, it was the easiest to simply be a martyr.

More importantly, nobody else was put in line with danger. "I do apologize for my distance during the first few days of knowing you all. But I can't seem to separate my heart from you all, somehow making an impact." Kaleopei recalled the facade she had worn, like a second skin that showed itself to those around her. Never truly letting them all see who she was for fear of getting too close. Still, she had many moments when that mask slipped. "My self-control, while wildly perfected, isn't set in stone. I couldn't risk swaying in my decisiveness. I don't apologize for my actions. Furthermore, I did what I had to do, and I'd do it again."

"I'll forgive you if you promise not to do something so reckless again," Casimir nodded at the girl. "You aren't as terrible as I once thought." "You have yourself a deal, golden boy, but I do promise I am every bit as insufferable as you imagine." Kaleopei threw in a wink at the end of her sentence, a hint of a smirk playing onto her lips. "That part wasn't an act."

It wasn't Casimir's forgiveness she was after. With a lack of that aforementioned self-control, Kaleopei let her gaze linger on Zaratella, who hadn't spoken very much. More keen on listening. Her mind was occupied with whatever currently racked her brain. It wasn't likely that she would forgive as easily. Kaleopei expected that outcome. The witch had proved she held a grudge.

If she were to be honest, Kaleopei would rather have a violent rejection than the subtle disappointment she was currently receiving.

Kaleopei knew Zara well enough that she wouldn't say anything until there weren't any other ears. A space for the two of them would have to wait. After all, it had been almost a week since everything happened. Kaleopei had no idea what emotions could have been festering during that span of time, too possessed by her own recovery.

Painful. That was one word she used to describe it. Taking another hit off the pipe, this time her flames coming to life. Nothing a miss. Deep within her flame, she felt something stirring. Not entirely hers, like an unfamiliar force was currently dancing along with her fire. An intricate set of movements swirling around inside of her.

Kaleopei didn't want to know what that meant. While foreign, she didn't hate the feeling. It sparked a bout of curiosity, a mix of ideas appearing in her head.

The chaos she could cause if her hypothesis was correct.

A limitless amount of fun.

The herb relieved her of some of the lingering pain that lit in her back each time she moved slightly against the sheets under her. Keylan had said he couldn't count how many open lacerations were cut into her skin. Little trace that a whip had been the weapon that afflicted the mangled flesh.

"I have some matters to attend to," Melody excused herself from the room. Offering a small grin as a goodbye.

"I got a meeting with my scouts. We're preparing to head across the border in a few days." Maizelin also stood up, looking just as Kaleopei remembered, even down to the scar across her collarbone that just peeked out of her tunic. However, the most noticeable was the blunt cut of hair that fell just above her shoulders. Not the long, wavy strands of hair that she can recall from before. But this suited her, gave her a more subtle intimidation with the bluntness. "Rest up, Kali."

Then, there were the four of them left in the room. The group that sought to create a change. A change that came to be true, but there was still much to be done in the wake of everything. Not everybody will be happy with the outcome. It was all expected. People often don't take the concept of change well, let alone the actual outcome of it. They can learn to accept it in due time. It was the least they could do for a tide a calm.

A time of peace. Where nobody feared what tomorrow would bring, able to enjoy their lives, Kaleopei felt an indefinite sense of pride at their accomplishments.

"Well, nobody died. I count that as a success." Kaleopei attempted to lighten the mood, exhaling another breath of smoke.

"You had us worried sick. Keylan spent hours trying to save you." Casimir took up where Melody had been sitting, placing a hand on Zara's back.

Her hair was sprawled out underneath her arm. Even utterly exhausted, she was stunning. Kaleopei could only imagine what she looked like when waking up, which sent a spark of excitement down her spine.

Zara was still angry with her. Kaleopei had to keep reminding herself, even if the two kisses they shared replayed in her memory.

"All of you got out mostly unscathed, right?" Allowing her mind to drift from the previous thoughts, she assessed each one of them, searching for any injuries in the group. Finding nothing but the normal amount of bruising and signs of exhaustion present.

They were physically fine, but she figured it would take Keylan at least a year to recover from her antics. Kaleopei would do it again without a thought if it meant the same outcome.

"You understand you could have died, right?" Keylan was giving her the 'I'm mad at you, but I love you' look. Those emerald eyes glared at her with rare intensity. Reminding her of their father, and his pitifully unconvincing scolding gazes.

"We've been over this already. I know what I did. I almost died. But didn't!"

"Then why did you do it?" Zara. The girl pushed herself off the bed, those iron eyes more lifeless than she had seen prior. A pang of guilt rang through Kaleopei, deciding she'd do anything to see her laugh again.

"Figured it was the best decision. I had the most logical success rate going into Louth and harnessing the canon."

"So, you did know? We could have done it together!" Zara wasn't yelling, but her voice rose enough for Kaleopei to hear the pain behind her voice. "I was terrified. You didn't give me a choice! I couldn't do anything to help."

"I knew what I was doing." Kaleopei wasn't sure what she should say. Zara's anger was warranted, but it left Kaleopei with a heavy burden on her shoulders. With all of that on Kaleopei's mind, she still wasn't sorry. Wouldn't be.

"Imogen said you didn't expect to make it out," Casimir added to the conversation. Seeing Zaratella shaking with whatever thoughts and emotions that currently coursed through her. "You made the rite, or whatever, with her so she wouldn't interfere."

"What do you want me to say?" This felt like a wrongful scolding, nothing ended up badly. The outcome, all things considered, could have been drastically worse. "I couldn't risk your lives. The danger in Louth was too unpredictable, too dangerous. If something went wrong, I needed to be the only one at risk. No sense in two of us dying when it could have been one."

"You can't just make these decisions on your own, Kaleopei. We're a team, remember? You said we would be honest to each other the first night we met."

Kaleopei did remember. That fateful night in Alstead altered their future when she met the pretty Carver, who seemed so bored in the middle of a lively tavern. Only to discover that she had killed over a dozen trained soldiers in their slumber.

"I remember, Zaratella. The burden only needed to fall on one. I couldn't let the danger touch you, any of you."

Casimir's expression softened, his eyes reflecting a blend of understanding and frustration. At least one person could sympathize with her reasoning.

"I know what you are saying, and I'm not sure that I could have willed myself to the same conviction you did should I have been in your position. I don't condone what you did, but I do believe you had the intention of protecting us, the only way you know. Risking everything."

It was sad when Casimir put it in such a morbid way. All Kaleopei had ever known was she could handle herself in an altercation. The upbringing she had molded her into a weapon of stubborn courage and delusional bravery. Kaleopei wouldn't be sitting in this room if she had been raised any other way. She had fought with blood and sweat until she passed out. Never once breaking in front of the enemy, it would have been a fitting end for her.

Kaleopei accepted her fate at that moment. No shred of power trickled in her veins after her stunt. She had waited for the executioner to string her up. Anticipated that her last breath would fall before her neck snapped and the soil claimed her.

She was ready to die. She might have even prayed to whatever gods listened that her death would be a swift one.

"You risked everything," Keylan pleaded, "What if you hadn't made it back? What would I have done without you? The only consistent thing in my life has been you and me."

"You'd learn how to live, you'd adapt. I felt comfortable leaving you with our friends. They would have comforted you. You'd have lived, Key."

Kaleopei's gaze lingered on Keylan, a mixture of gratitude and only a little regret in her eyes. She was sure that he wouldn't have been alone. Yes, Keylan's grieving was inevitable, but he'd see that he couldn't be saddened for eternity.

"I could *never* get over that. You have to understand that." That is a sweet thought. Knowing that she meant so much to him.

"You would. Eventually, I'd become just a figment of your past, just like we did with Maize. We never forgot about her, but we were able to come to terms with her death. We had no other choice, so we moved on." They were proven wrong recently, however, the fact still remained. "You'd have been okay, been alive. I'd live with that, was okay with that."

"You *promised* not to stray again." The words struck a chord with her. Kaleopei held her word and promised a sense of pridefulness. A mantra she has followed, not lying to those she loves.

"I know. Our souls have always been close. Even death wouldn't change that." Kaleopei squeezed her brother's hand. A reminder of her presence. She wasn't dead and wasn't going anywhere for now. "I'd haunt your ass, that much is sure. So no lies have spewed from my lips."

The soil would have to try a lot harder if it wanted to contain all her glory. Sensing their conversation was trickling off, the Prince shifted in his seat. Subtly passing over the pipe to Kaleopei.

"What happened inside? How are you alive?" Casimir puzzled. Quickly throwing his arms up, shaking his head in disbelief. "Not that I don't think you could handle yourself. It's just we heard about the damage Louth undertook."

"I put the canon inside of me."

A second passed. All just blinking with a sudden curiosity.

"Kaleopei, what does that mean?" Keylan voiced the seemingly unanimous thoughts they had.

"Y'know consumed all the magic from inside of it into me. I practically became a siphon, if that's how you want to look at it." She shrugged. Not wanting to dwell on what that meant.

Everything inside of Louth happened so fast that Kaleopei hadn't really thought too hard about what she did. Just knew that she couldn't risk breaking it.

"But how?" Casimir posed all the questions, ascertaining information in the way he knew best. Endless amount of questions. By the Gods, he had a plethora of them.

"I don't know, put my hands on it. Then, thought about the magic moving from one object into the next." Kaleopei looked down at her hands, noticing the lightning-like veins that still graced her hands. Faint but still present, the pattern was trickling up to her forearm before ending abruptly at her elbow.

"That's how most Carvers harness a conduit, use it as an extension of themselves. It creates a reserve for them." Zaratella was still mad but partook in the discussion. "Carvers who harness more powerful conduits can experience similar markings."

"I don't know any of that. I'm not exactly adept in arcane." Casimir blinked between the two women, unsure of all that was happening. How was it that Humans had survived so long without magic was a mystery.

"You read, Cas."

"Stories! Only a little of what I read is actually informative." The Prince. No. The King shrugged.

"So I made the Aetherite Canon my bitch?" Kaleopei summed up what Zara was saying. Using it as one would be a conduit that made a little sense.

Does the Aetherite still have more power in those shards? Or had she completely removed the magic from the crystal?

"You used it like a Carver; instead of projecting the magic outwards, you took it in." It was like Kaleopei was back in a lecture, hearing Zara's tone turn more informative. Expanding more on what Kaleopei had accomplished.

"Well, I figured I'd have more luck dispelling it with some kind of control if it came from me."

"None of this is making me feel better, but did it work?" The air in the room was odd. Tension still floated about, the mood shifted, though. To one similar to what it had been like when they traveled as a group. The small talk instead of the events at Louth.

It was oddly soothing to Kaleopei. Not the scolding and berating she was getting before. Instead, it felt like she was telling a story, no stakes prodded at her words. Simply telling her friends what had transpired.

"I'm sitting here, aren't I?" Kaleopei laughed. "But I was able to release the magic in waves rather than one massive blast. So, I'm taking that as it worked."

"You understand how utterly insane that is? You could have torn yourself apart."

"Keylan, you're beating a dead horse. Get it through your insanely thick skull, and understand that I'm alive." As if to further her point, Kaleopei gestured to herself. The bruised and beaten body of herself twinged in pain, her back rubbing against the sheets. "But yes, I did feel like I was about to implode on myself. An odd sensation, not very pleasant."

"I know you're here, and I will be thanking the Gods for as long as I remain."

"Do whatever makes you happy, brother." Keylan stood, brushing off imaginary dirt from his tunic. Her brow quirked, watching as Casimir and Keylan exchanged a subtle glance, emerald and blue clashing.

They were conversing through glances! Kaleopei felt her heart flutter at their closeness. Who'd have thought that their ragtag group of abolitionists would become friends?

"I will insult your recklessness more later. I have to deal with the consequences of overthrowing a King and placing this dimwit in charge. Armies can't command themselves, but I guess that's just the Human in them." Keylan tossed a laugh at Casimir, rolling his eyes. Kaleopei's eyes went wide, concerned at what had come over her brother. He was willingly leaving her side after a near-death experience.

The last time she left Louth, it took him a whole month before he would even sleep in a separate room. The silent conversation he had with Zaratella left a sour taste in her mouth. She wouldn't be alone.

Were these two setting them up right now?

It felt like a trap.

She took back anything she said about being friends. Keylan and Casimir had become partners in crime.

Keylan was heading for the door, not even glancing back. Casimir was soon to follow, tapping Kaleopei's shoulder.

"Keep the Myth, and try not to kill each other. The sooner you two figure yourselves out, the sooner we can all get back to leading Realms." She hated that he was right. Kaleopei and Zara couldn't go forward with the strained way things were now. It was bound to get brought up sooner or later.

Kaleopei wished it was later.

***

The air crackled with tension as Kaleopei and Zaratella faced each other. Kaleopei knew her anger was palpable. Frustration and unresolved emotions hung in the space between them, creating an undeniable magnetic pull that Kaleopei wished wasn't there.

Zara sat up, eyes now level with her own. Kaleopei wanted to push away, but the wall behind her didn't appear very flexible. She was stuck between a wall and the unnerving gaze of Zaratella.

A swirl of onyx-flecked eyes bore directly into her, unable to discern their nature. What was Zaratella going to say? Kaleopei knew she was angry; she had seen the emotion littered on her face moments ago. Now, there was nothing.

Without a word, Zara closed the distance, her lips crashing against Kaleopei's in a fierce kiss.

Kaleopei wasn't about to reciprocate, despite the undiscussed anger. That could come later.

The kiss was a clash of conflicting emotions, a turbulent storm of anger and desire. Zara's lips moved forcefully, seeking dominance. Kaleopei pushed back, refusing to yield. Each moment felt like a challenge, a declaration of power and vulnerability entwined.

Kaleopei responded with equal intensity, her fingers hesitantly gripping Zara's shoulders as if trying to anchor herself. The taste of anger lingered against Zara's rose-red lips, mingling with a hint of desperation. It was a collision of fire and ice, a tumultuous dance fueled by a tempest of emotions they had yet to discuss.

Talking about feelings was the last thing on Kaleopei's mind.

As the kiss deepened, their anger transformed into a different kind of heat, a passionate inferno. A heated moment of catharsis expressed the unspoken turmoil that had simmered beneath the surface of Zara's skin.

Yet, even in the midst of their fiery exchange, there lingered a thread of something deeper—an acknowledgment that their connection surpassed mere anger. It was a complex interplay of emotions, a storm of passion that defied easy categorization.

When they finally pulled away, breathless and entangled in the aftermath of their connection, the room seemed to be still. The unresolved tension still lingered, but now it hung in the air with a different weight.

"I hate you," Zara's weight collapsed into Kaleopei's chest, refusing to let go. Without thinking her actions through, Kaleopei ran her fingers through the black tresses. Placing a kiss on the girl's forehead.

"Really? That little stunt says otherwise." Kaleopei pulled the girl onto the bed, now sitting practically in her lap. Not that she minded.

Kaleopei didn't ponder a moment longer on their predicament. The only goal was to comfort the witch in any way she could. Willing to give everything for her to smile.

Kaleopei was better with actions than words, anyway. At first, she didn't know what to say. This felt natural, able to convey her guilt and emotions through touch. The only time Kaleopei was good with words was when she played a part. She wouldn't do that in front of those she cared about if she could help it. Not anymore, for she had nothing else to keep secret.

She was who she was. No longer was she the forgotten princess, hidden beneath old floorboards. She was Kaleopei Azgaeda Florence, queen of the Elven Realm.

The room echoed with heavy, frantic breaths. Silence lingered for a heartbeat, each staring into the other's eyes.

As the realization of what had transpired settled between them, a moment of vulnerability emerged. Zaratella lifted her head, gaze softening, the intensity of anger replaced by a glimmer of something more complex. Kaleopei, too, found herself caught in the gravity of the unspoken, a torrent of conflicting emotions that neither could fully articulate through words.

Zara reached out, her fingers tracing the line of Kaleopei's jaw. It was a gesture that spoke volumes, a silent acknowledgment that their connection went beyond the storm of anger. Somehow, Kaleopei knew they would be okay. The tension in the room shifted, evolving into an intricate dance of intimacy and unspoken understanding.

"I'm still mad at you," Zara brushed her thumb against Kaleopei's bottom lip. "I'm just so relieved that you're alive."

Kaleopei, still grappling with the remnants of the emotional maelstrom, met Zara's gaze with a mix of defiance and vulnerability. It was a silent challenge and an invitation all at once. In that charged moment, they stood on the precipice of something undefined, their connection redefined by the turbulence of their emotions.

"I'd do it again. You have to know that I'm not sorry for anything I did." It was the truth.

"I know you would, and I don't understand why that makes you so amazing." Kaleopei wanted to laugh at Zara's confession. Finding the irony in their situation.

"Darling, I am anything but perfect." Kaleopei did laugh. "But I do feel troubled by how we left things. I'm not going to apologize, but I do wish to make it up to you."

Zaratella's answer was lips brushing against Kaleopei's in a softer, more tender kiss. It carried the weight of Kaleopei's unspoken apologies and the fragility of emotions laid bare. The room seemed to breathe with them, the stiff air being the only witness to their vulnerable intimacy.

As they parted once more, a new understanding lingered in the air. The unresolved emotions still simmered, but now there was a shared acknowledgment that their connection, however odd, was a force that couldn't be easily extinguished. The room held the echoes of their passionate collision, a testament to the complexities woven into the fabric of their intertwined destinies.

They would be okay.

"Come with me," Kaleopei whispered, carefully not to break the atmosphere. "To the Elven Realm."

Even if it took time, they would overcome this.

"I thought you'd never ask." Zara bit her tongue, the corner of her lip upturning. "But what if I wished to remain here?"

"Then I'd respect that." Would she actually? The short answer is no. "But I taunt you any second I could. Wishing that you'd come home with me."

Home. Together.

That thought alone made Kaleopei's heart soar.

"How daunting that would be for me. Wishing I could have you." Zara smiled, playing with the ends of Kaleopei's tangled hair. Kaleopei pulled her closer, resting her heavy head on Zara's shoulder.

"So, what is your answer, darling?"

"I'd follow you to the deep and back." Wisp stirred in his peaceful slumber, tails wagging through whatever dreams seemed to have overcome the beast. Zara moved, so their eyes met once more, "but this doesn't mean you're off the hook. You still have some atonement to do."

"I haven't forgotten." Kaleopei feared she had just signed up for an abundance of trouble. Intertwining their lives seemed like a recipe for disaster.

Kaleopei couldn't wait.

The brown-haired elf pulled Zara closer so they were both lying down. Placing a firm kiss on the girls' forehead as they entangled themselves. "This is me making it up to you. Stay with me?"

"My, don't you know it's unfitting of a queen to bed a woman before wedlock?" Zara brushed her dark locks off her shoulder, exposing her pale collarbones. The heat was something Kaleopei was well acquainted with, but the warmth that spread to her cheeks was new.

"Nothing like that." Kaleopei quickly found herself deflecting the blush. Stumbling over her words wasn't something that happened often. The onyx-eyed beauty just had that effect on her. "Can we just sleep?"

"Whatever you want, firefly."

Chapter 35

In the serene quiet of the Bellheim stables, Keylan and Maize sat amidst scattered belongings, the task of packing a mere distraction from the unspoken weight of their shared history. Moonlight filtered through the canopy overhead, casting a gentle glow on their faces as they navigated the delicate threads of simply existing.

"It's hard to believe we're finally going back to Eviera, isn't it?"

Maizelin nodded to his words, her gaze distant as he folded a garment with practiced hands. The revelation of Maize's survival had woven an intricate wave of emotions that Keylan had a hard time fully articulating. Since Kaleopei had woken, all he thought about was Maize. She was alive.

"I never thought I'd see this day, Keylan. It's like waking up from a centuries-long dream." Even her voice instilled a sense of comfort. He had looked up to Maize a great deal and often spent time sparring and learning from her. "We have a chance to rebuild, to heal. And it's all thanks to you and Kaleopei."

A bittersweet smile touched Keylan's lips. The mention of Kaleopei evoked a myriad of emotions, a complex dance of gratitude and longing. Anger could be set aside if it meant she was alive and stood by his side. Kaleopei hadn't strayed.

"Kaleopei has become my anchor, hasn't she? She's going to be Queen for a while, and it's strange to think about it."

Maize observed her younger brother. Keylan noted her eyes filled with a mix of affection and understanding. Keylan still felt as if he was seeing a living ghost, a shell of a person he once knew. It was the same Maize he remembered, but she had grown. Just like he had, Keylan would have to learn her all over again.

"She's a remarkable leader, Keylan. The elves need someone like her to guide them through this healing process. From what I've heard, she's the reason your little rugrat group made it this far."

If only it were that simple. Kaleopei had lied and didn't fully trust them with important parts of her plan. While that might not have been his sister's intentions, it's certainly how it came across. That's where most of his anger resided. The thought of Kaleopei not trusting him made his stomach upset.

Keylan sighed, his fingers idly tracing patterns on the fabric before him. Counting the amount of crates they had to bring home.

Home. Keylan felt a ping of pride at the word. They hadn't had one of those in a while.

"It's just... I never imagined her as a queen. She's always been this fierce, independent force. Now, she's taking on the responsibility of a realm. Even if it isn't permeant, and you'll take up the Garden Throne. I think we both know that Kaleopei won't take the responsibilities lightly. She'll consume herself with it." Keylan struggled to choose his words. Worried. "She'll apply herself fully. I'm concerned she's already burnt out from the weight on her shoulders. I don't want this to make it worse."

"Sometimes, destiny chooses the most unexpected champions. Kaleopei has a strength that resonates with people, even if she isn't the most charismatic Florence sibling. She's still exactly what Eviera needs right now."

Their conversation paused as Keylan carefully packed a trinket that had survived the chaos of their journey. Zara had carried it with them since the events at Fenyah. A simple wildflower crown. He could feel Maize's eyes as they studied him, sensing the unspoken thoughts swirling beneath the surface.

"What's on your mind, little brother?" Everything.

Maizelin always knew when something was wrong, just like Kaleopei.

"I just hope Kaleopei finds moments of peace in all of this. She's been through so much, and she deserves some happiness. She and Zara have been practically inseparable since they made up. I want them to be happy."

Maize placed a hand on Keylan's shoulder, a simple gesture of reassurance.

"She's not alone, Keylan. We're a family, and we'll face whatever comes our way together. From what I've gathered, the King and Zaratella have become part of ours. We take care of our own. Kaleopei being queen won't change that."

As they continued packing, the moonlight cast a gentle glow on the siblings, their shared past intertwining with the promise of a hopeful future. The journey ahead would be challenging, but with their newfound unity, the elves of Eviera had a chance at restoration and renewal. That chance alone made Keylan's heart soar.

"She doesn't want to be Queen." Keylan knew his sister well. She hadn't admitted such a thing, but he knew. Kaleopei never wanted the title, comfortable living her life from the shadows.

"It won't be forever, Key. Just until the chaos has settled."

"Kaleopei does strive with the unknown." He wanted to laugh at the irony. His sister was the embodiment of chaos. Having her as a queen would undoubtedly be eventful.

"I think it's a fire thing. She is much like our mother. When she resigns, Kaleopei will be free to do whatever she pleases. She's earned that much. Her life will be hers, as is yours."

"What about you?" Maize didn't answer right away. Instead occupying herself with the weapons of steel she was placing into crates.

"It's always been my fate, brother. Never yours. You have also earned your freedom. Whatever you want to do, you shall accomplish." Maizelin smiled at him. "Now enough with all this dreary conversation, tell me about what I've missed. Like, when did you gain so much muscle? I remember you as a scrawny little thing."

"A lot changes when you're forced to survive."

As Keylan kept up a simple conversation with Maize, the weight of returning to Eviera settled into the recesses of his heart. The journey home, once a distant dream, now unfolded before him like an untold chapter.

Mixed emotions swirled within him – a blend of anticipation, apprehension, and a flicker of hope. Eviera, once a fractured city, was on the cusp of rebirth, and the prospect of rebuilding stirred a quiet sense of duty within Keylan. He couldn't shake the memories of the Elven Realm's fall, the haunting echoes of Bellheim's invasion still lingering. Yet, as he folded his past into the fabric of his journey, there was a burgeoning determination, a silent promise to reclaim the land that had been their home. With his sisters by his side, it didn't seem so daunting. He'd give everything to aid them. The journey ahead felt like a convergence of destinies, an opportunity to mend the wounds of a realm and rediscover the essence of Elvenkind.

Keylan couldn't help the bittersweet feeling that bubbled within him. He'd be saying goodbye to all the people he'd met here. Not forever. But he's grown attached to Casimir and even Melody.

With the adventure they have had, their relationship is set. They won't be too far, and he plans on visiting often.

***

"Keylan!" Kaleopei shouted through gritted teeth from across the clearing. Bow brandished between her arms, an arrow nocked.

Sweat dripped down his brow, wincing at her tone. Kaleopei was standing, moving with little notice of her prior injuries. Sight trained down the neck of the arrow at her twin.

"I asked you to spare," she continued, "not be a target for aim practice. Which you apparently are terrible at. I'd have killed you at least six times by now."

Sunlight filtered through the leaves, casting a mosaic of shadows on the ground. Keylan and Kaleopei faced each other. Kaleopei was still recovering from the lashes inflicted by the former King, yet she stood with resilience etched across her features. Keylan, though concerned, recognized the silent determination in her eyes.

It was clear Kaleopei was serious. Wanting to cross blades. Was she even ready for that?

As if to answer his question, Kaleopei began twisting her torso. Bending either way and stretching her arms overhead.

"Good enough?"

With a begrudging nod, they began their sparring dance. Keylan moved with the grace of the tide, his every motion fluid and unpredictable. Watching Kaleopei's every move for any sign of pain.

Keylan would only be in for a scolding if he held back. Still, he worried for her health. Not wanting Kaleopei to take on too much before fully recovering.

It had been a week since she had graced the land of the living once more. Every day, she asked to spar. Keylan kept finding reasons to push it off, saying she had to rest more. It was safe to say his twin wasn't having any of it. Constantly finding ways to exert herself across the castle.

Today was Kaleopei's last straw. She had practically cornered him during breakfast. Demanding that he would spar with her at noon. So here they are.

Kaleopei, despite the lingering pain he could see in her emerald eyes, met his advances with a fiery tenacity. The clash of steel on steel echoed through the training grounds, a rhythmic cadence mirroring the resilience within their elven spirits.

To their sidelines were Zara and Melody. Both found this overly amusing as Kaleopei berated him for not trying hard enough. He'd hold back no longer. Growing tired, Kaleopei threw. Every insult she could put at him.

Man up, you brute. Melody can wield a sword better. I've fought harder mud crabs.

That last one kind of hurt.

Even with her injuries, Kaleopei demonstrated a tactical brilliance that surprised even Keylan. Her movements, harmonious blends of strategic finesse and instinctive reactions, hinted at a depth of experience honed through trials.

Each step forward was a declaration of strength, a defiance against the physical scars marring her back.

She was a Queen. Showing the qualities she usually kept hidden from any prying eyes.

As the sparring intensified, Keylan's concern morphed into admiration for Kaleopei's unwavering determination. The dance of blades echoed the unspoken connection between them, her hunting knives clashing against Skipper. Each strike caused a loud clash of metal to echo across the space.

Those going about their day stopped to witness the exchange. Concerned that one of them would meet their end. Keylan paid them no mind, engrossed with the unrivaled Queen that bestowed blow after blow.

Their movements didn't slow, blades moving in a flurry of calculated strikes and swift dodges. However, Keylan's surprise deepened as he observed Kaleopei's movements transcending the bounds of conventional elven combat. Her attacks carried an otherworldly grace, and, to his amazement, she began to incorporate her flame magic into her techniques.

He'd seen this many times, but it still couldn't prepare him for her next course of action.

Kaleopei sent a gust of air as she crossed the daggers in front of her. Keylan stumbled for a moment, realizing what his sister had just done just like she had a week ago.

Gods above.

Somehow, she tapped into the unknown magic that now coursed through her veins. A flicker of flames danced along the blade of her sword, and a gust of wind followed her swift footwork. The very elements seemed to heed her call and were an extension of her movements.

As Keylan parried her strikes, he felt the heat of controlled fire and the cool rush of manipulated air, a mesmerizing display of newfound prowess. Even with the confusion, he felt a spark of pride.

The corners of his mouth twitched upwards. Keylan's eyes widened, a mix of astonishment and realization settling in. "Kaleopei, you've been tampering with the Aetherite's magic?"

"You catch on quickly, little brother." She grinned, a blend of mischief and triumph in her gaze. It appeared she had been up to more than she let on. Getting into trouble while Keylan was avoiding her.

"Was this why you wanted to spar so badly?"

Their blows evolved into a symphony of elements, with Kaleopei seamlessly transitioning between fire, air, and the natural grace of elven combat. Each strike became a manifestation of the untamed magic she now commanded. Keylan, once her training partner, now found himself facing a sorceress who had unlocked a dimension of power previously unseen by any before.

"Does it matter? I got you here, did I not?" Kaleopei's smug tone didn't go unnoticed. Through all that transpired, he only found it in him to laugh.

It was unheard of for Elf's to have more than one affinity.

Kaleopei always was the anomaly.

As the dance of blades flourished, Keylan marveled at Kaleopei's adaptability. The scars on her back whispered tales of suffering, but in this moment, she wielded the echoes of that pain as a source of strength.

Made it bend to her.

Made it her own.

The elements responded to her will, a testament to all she's accomplished. Keylan couldn't be prouder of the woman he called his sister. Taking anything the Gods threw at her and brandishing it tenfold.

In the midst of their sparring, an understanding unfolded – the transformative nature of adversity and the boundless potential hidden within an elven spirit. The training grounds and the two women watching bore witness to the melding of fire, air, and steel, a harmonious convergence that spoke of newfound abilities and an unyielding commitment to face whatever challenges lay ahead.

Kaleopei would excel on the throne, even if she hadn't originally wanted the power. And he'd be there every step of the way, standing by her side.

Chapter 36

In the throne room of the Bellheim castle, the group of five all stood with their heads held high. Kaleopei hated this room. It was still all too white and pristine for her liking, but Casimir had begun to make changes. She found herself excited about when she would visit next. Planning on holding him to the promise of art decorating the walls of the Human castle.

There was a looming feeling hanging above them all. The air carried a poignant sense of departure. Kaleopei wasn't sure she was quite ready to say farewell.

The trio—Kaleopei, Zaratella, and Keylan—stood amidst the red carpet and pillars of quartz, their expressions a blend of determination and farewell. Behind them stood a small party that had wished to show their gratitude. At their helm was Maizelin. Kaleopei gripped the wood of her bow, finding comfort in its familiarity.

Casimir and Melody, allies forged in the crucible of shared battles, stood with them on the ground. Gone was the throne that loomed above others.

"This is goodbye, right?" Kaleopei was the one to break the silence, uncomfortable with the tension. Unsure if cracking a joke would be wise, she opened for the obvious.

"Take care, all of you. Eviera awaits, and I believe you'll shape its destiny." Casimir lightly laughed at her urgency. But still nodded along to Melody's words.

"No, this isn't goodbye. We'll see each other soon. Besides, you can't keep my best friend from me forever." Casimir's gaze, once cloaked in shadows of doubt, now held a glimmer of confidence. Gone was the fragile prince who was unsure of what he was doing, now a reigning Melody, with her seer's insight, shared a nod of encouragement.

"I think I could live a few years without seeing your face." Zara laughed, pulling the King into a sweet embrace. The longing that flickered across the former carver's face showed that her words were nothing but lies.

"The threads of fate weave a complex story. You three will surely find a way to tell it differently." Melody tossed a glance at Kaleopei, tossing her locked hair over her shoulder.

She would be staying in Bellheim. Helping Casimir in any way she could for the time being. They all know he needed it, even though he himself admitted to not being ready to be left alone.

They would only be a letter away. Still, it seemed far.

Kaleopei wanted to laugh as Keylan gripped Casimir's forearm in a warrior's salute, a silent acknowledgment of their titles. Even if Casimir's look of pain said otherwise. Zaratella exchanged a meaningful glance with Melody, recognizing the unspoken connection forged between them.

"You can't expect to get rid of me that easily, Cas. I'll still be around to cause trouble whenever I see fit." Zara rested her head on Kaleopei's shoulder, interlocking their fingers. Squeezing lightly, Kaleopei did her best to offer comfort.

"You two are somehow disgustingly good for each other." Kaleopei, the alleged leader of the trip, stepped forward. Casimir extended a hand, and she clasped it with a firm grip, scanning those ocean eyes as he smiled at her. "You hurt her again. I'll be the most annoying thorn you've ever met."

Kaleopei reached up, fixing the crooked crown on his head. Blonde hair tangled throughout the metal. "Chin up, threats don't suit you very well."

He swatted her hands away, pushing the crown to an even more crooked position. Kaleopei didn't stifle her laugh as she turned to Melody, giving her a soft hug.

"Make sure he doesn't look too terrible, Mel."

Casimir rolled his eyes, ignoring her antics. "Lead Eviera with the strength I've witnessed in you, Kaleopei. I believe in the future you'll carve. However long you reign."

Kaleopei's eyes held a mixture of gratitude and determination. Maizelin already ushered their forces towards Eviera, leading the charge across the border. Their departure marked the beginning of a new chapter—one they hoped would mend the fractured realm.

"I'll mess it up somehow. Thank you for standing with us, even in the shadows."

Casimir interrupted her words with an embrace. All his lingering words came across in the gesture. He took the proximity to pull the band from one of her braids.

"Now we're even." Casimir pulled back, admiring his mischief. Tresses of semi-curled hair fell down her left side, the other still thankfully plaited to her head.

"Touché, crybaby. Or do you prefer vomit, boy?"

"That was one time!"

Kaleopei pulled back to hear the tail end of a conversation between Mel and Zara. "Your insights have been invaluable, Melody. We'll carry them with us as we face what lies ahead."

Kaleopei observed Melody's gaze, a mixture of compassion and foresight. "May the currents of magic guide you, Zara. Trust in the unseen threads that bind us all."

Keylan moved, standing beside Casimir, and shared a brief but meaningful nod. Their camaraderie had been forged in the crucible of adversity, and each unspoken gesture carried the weight of their adventure.

"Casimir, thanks for everything. When the time is right, we'll reunite and share tales of victory."

Casimir's gaze was steady, his voice carrying a note of quiet confidence. "The journey may be challenging, but I believe in the strength of your bond. Eviera's fate rests in capable hands. Just be sure not to set the place ablaze."

Kaleopei, the leader burdened with the weight of a realm's expectations, took a moment to absorb the significance of the departure. She turned to Casimir with a determined glint in her eyes.

"Casimir, your support has meant more than words can convey. Eviera will rise from the ashes, as you should ensure a better future for Bellheim."

Casimir's response was a nod filled with trust. "I plan on doing so. For you, Eviera's destiny is entwined with yours. I have no doubt we'll have a long-lasting relationship between Realms."

As they began to depart, the air resonated with the silent understanding that their paths, though diverging for now, would intersect again. The echoes of shared battles lingered in the room, promising a future where they would reconvene to share the triumphs and challenges faced in the name of change.

The beginning of a time of peace.

"Take care, Prince of the New Dawn."

Chapter 37

The sun dipped below the horizon, casting a warm, golden glow over the rejuvenated realm of Eviera. Time had woven its intricate story into the very soil, healing the scars inflicted by Bellheim's invasion so many years ago. In the heart of the Elven Realm, where once stood remnants of destruction, now bloomed vibrant life.

Kaleopei, whose title now was Queen of Eviera, stood on the balcony of the newly reconstructed palace. The gentle breeze carried the whispers of a realm reborn, and her gaze extended beyond the treetops to where the horizon met the sky in a subtle gradient of oranges and reds. The resilience of the elves, combined with the unity forged through trials, had breathed life back into their sacred land.

The palace courtyard below sang with rambunctious activity, a testament to the bustling life that had returned to Eviera. Elven craftsmen, musicians, and scholars moved about, their shared purpose transcending the memories of hardship that once lingered in the air.

It was everything the twins had ever dreamed about. The sheer revelation that it was a reality still baffled Kaleopei, even as she led these people to where they were. Kaleopei would be lying if she said it was only her. She had a revolutionary support system that others couldn't even fathom. With her partner Zara still at her side.

It had been two years since they returned to Eviera, building it anew. Kaleopei wasn't sure how she felt about all the change that had come, the time that had passed. Yes, she was overjoyed with the time of peace, yet part of her longed for the thrill of an adventure.

She still held the throne. Maize constantly said the time wasn't right.

Nothing was ever right, according to Maizelin.

Kaleopei wanted nothing more than to travel the realms with Zara by her side. Seeing the many sites other Realms had to offer. Going on a boat had always peaked their intreats, taking them off this continent.

Though, Kaleopei wouldn't walk away from all that has transpired over the two years. The progress that had been made. The last time she had exchanged letters with Casimir, Melody was no longer aiding his every decision. Instead, he had founded his own footing in the world of ruling, making the Human realm a better place one day at a time.

Sitting somewhere on her desk, filled with endless papers that needed signing. Encased in an intricate sea foam envelope, sealed with the royal Mer sigil, was an invitation to visit the oceanic realm. The two set to entertain an on-paper relationship of peace for the Mer and Elven realms.

But, as did most things these days, it had to be put aside.

As night descended, the stars glittered overhead the flourishing city, reflecting the shimmering magic that now flowed freely through Eviera. A safe space for Elves once more. Kaleopei's heart fluttered with unspoken pride at what they had accomplished. The scars of the past would become stories told to the younger generation, a reminder of the resilience and courage undertaken by an unlikely group who sought after their homeland.

A new dawn began—a chapter where the elves of Eviera, guided by their Queen, forged a destiny that celebrated restoration, unity, and the enduring spirit that defined their existence. And so, beneath the cosmic tapestry of stars, the tale of Eviera unfolded, promising a future where the echoes of past struggles were transformed into the melody of a reborn realm.

In the two years, Eviera thrived under Kaleopei's new and compassionate rule. The elven city, once marred by the shadows of conflict, now sparkled like a gem beneath the watchful canopy of ancient trees. Kaleopei couldn't take all the glory. Those who surrounded her made it possible. The bonds forged during their perilous journey remained unbroken, becoming the foundation of a realm where a sense of unity prevailed.

Keylan, the ever-vigilant guardian, not only trained warriors but also led efforts to cultivate sustainable practices that harmonized with the land. The once war-scarred landscapes now bloomed with vibrant flora, a testament to his commitment to balance and preservation. Kaleopei never would have guessed he was so intrigued by agriculture. It wasn't that she hadn't picked up her own new hobbies. Peace seemed to allow them both to explore their interests.

As seasons cycled through the years, festivals and celebrations adorned Eviera, each marking a milestone in their collective journey. They have always found time during Fenyah to celebrate themselves, a time when it was just the teenagers who wanted to enjoy the finer things.

Mostly myth. Casimir and her found an understanding of the herb. Oftentimes, it would lead to who could smoke more Myth. If it was a tie, they'd add booze into the equation.

In a quiet moment, beneath the canopy of the sacred trees, Kaleopei reflected on their shared triumphs. The palace balcony, once witness to the scars of conflict, now framed a place of serenity for her. The elven people, once scattered and broken, had not only rebuilt their realm but had pained a mural of enduring strength and hope.

The echoes of their tale resonated beyond the borders of Eviera, becoming a legend that inspired neighboring realms to seek unity in the face of adversity.

Though, things ran deeper than Kaleopei let on to her people. She herself was still healing from all she had endured physically. Kaleopei was fine. With Zara's help, slowly, Kaleopei was able to gather her bearings with living. Not just surviving. Kaleopei would always thrive off of adrenaline and adventure, but she had learned to just enjoy the simplicity peace brought.

Not to mention the rift and dangers growing in the Deep Realm. A place Maize has become obsessed with as of late. Everything the elven princess does somehow relates to learning the Deep Realm like it had consumed her entire being.

In front of others, Kaleopei put on a spectacle, able to take the act of whatever was needed for her people. A practiced motion she'd been doing for years, the facade of composed dignity. Behind the imaginary curtains of stunning dresses and sweet speeches, everything was far from fine.

Maize has been missing for almost four weeks longer than she had predicted. No words or letters have been exchanged within the month. It was unlike her sister to up and disappear, especially without a word. Yes, like Kaleopei, she was an utterly unpredictable loose canon. But she always kept them updated, even if the information was usually unwarranted and pertained only to some mushroom she had eaten.

Kaleopei's entire body slumped into her desk chair, head leaning against the backrest. Not to mention, the entirety of her people didn't know the truth about her magic, unsure of the chaos wielding multiple affinities would cause. A call was made by Keylan, but it was understandable.

Elves only had one affinity.

That's how it had always been.

It's what her people would continue thinking. So, the balance that had been carefully fabricated would remain intact. Still, Kaleopei couldn't help herself to ponder what Maize was getting up to. It was a gut feeling that settled in the deepest pit of her stomach.

Whatever was happening wouldn't be good.

Chapter 38

Blood pumped through his pale skin, filling him as he ran down the freshly painted halls. Not halting his movements for anybody who got in Casimir's path.

He had one objective. And one objective alone.

Get to his Mother.

The presence of the ring on his finger was what drove his every stride. Isla Haven had been in a deep sleep for years, which explained why he hadn't been permitted to enter her chambers when he was still a prince.

Casimir knew she was ill. Cursed with a sickness, no healers had ever even seen before. Since his reign began, he'd tried endless amounts of medicine and remedies. Hired the most experienced practitioners he could find.

Not once did the sickly pale women even stir. Just lay there like a corpse. The only thing that showed signs of life was the even rise and fall of her chest.

"King Casimir, I must remind you not to get your hopes up." The most recent healer he hired scrambled to keep pace. An individual was recommended by Keylan a few months back. "I am still unsure as to her condition. What I was telling you was to keep you informed."

Casimir couldn't find his voice and simply slowed his steps as the door came into view. The doctor threw himself in front of it, his arms blocking the entrance.

"You said she stirred? That must be a sign of some sort."

"Like I tried saying, she is still unresponsive! If you had just listened to what I was trying to say, you'd understand more clearly. Isla isn't responding to any stimulation we've tried." The elven male breathed hard, trying to regain his composure. "What you might see inside might be crude. I'd advise you to take this into consideration before making any decisions."

"She's my mother. I think I can handle it. It can't be anything worse than I've already seen." Casimir took a step forward, winning the fight as he dismissively waved his hand.

"You can't say I didn't try." The doctor stepped out of the way, his shoulders slumping.

It was clear the man was distraught and unsure of how to handle the situation. Casimir knew he was concerned and almost seemed frightened. None of that mattered.

"I appreciate your concern, Rilwen." Casimir made the call to smile kindly. Then opened the door.

It was frigid. A cool stream of air escaped the room, causing goosebumps to decorate his exposed arms. It only took him one look until bile priced at the back of his throat.

He turned away, slamming the door behind him. Casimir's hand covered his mouth, halting the gags that wanted to escape.

"Sir, I tried to warn-"

"You're dismissed." Casimir surprised himself when the words came past his lips, and nothing else followed. Every part of his body wanted to get far away. Wanted to get his hands on some Myth before the image could plague him more.

It was too late.

The image of Isla, his mother, lying fragile in a large silk bed. She was covered in blisters, her hands resting over her chest. That wasn't what haunted him. Not her odd posture or the markings that were adjourned on her skin.

It was the red eyes.

They were open, staring into the ceiling. Glowing a faint crimson color that was far too reminiscent of blood.

Casimir managed to make it until he was alone to empty the contents of his stomach out of a window. Heaving as the image corrupted his thoughts.

What the fuck?

Chapter 39

"Imogen wrote." Speak of the devil. Keylan strode into her office, dressed in his commander attire. Swells of pride filled the girl, knowing her brother was finally where he wanted to be. Not to mention he did a damn good job too.

"Anything I actually want to know? Or is the Hag just playing her mind games again." Kaleopei brushed off his arrival, looking boredom through a stack of papers. She didn't miss the urgency that pricked at his tone.

"We might want to get Zara in here." Keylan had his serious face on, staring his sister down.

Kaleopei wasn't one to complain about the black-haired woman joining their company.

It only took a few minutes before she waltzed in, dressed in a simple lavender sundress. That fell to her knees in all its pleated glory. Zara was a spectacle.

And she was mine. Kaleopei still balked at the vision that was Zaratella.

"You called for me, Firefly?"

"Yes, darling," they exchanged a kiss, "the Hag sent a letter. Keylan said you should be here."

Her nose scrunched, looking between the twins.

"Was it something important?"

Considering the male was still keeping his composure, Kaleopei was unsure of the letter's content. Usually, she was able to read her brother with practiced ease, but this was different. The only emotion she could recognize was the flicker of anger that swirled behind his eyes and the rigid tenseness that encased him. Anger, Keylan was angry.

"Maize has gone to the Deep Realm."

He was joking, right? That wasn't even possible. All passage into the Deep Realm is overseen by the Fairy Realm. No soul has even stepped foot into the wasteland territory for hundreds of years.

"That isn't something to joke about, Keylan." Zara's hands were placed firmly on Kaleopei's tense shoulders, giving a slight squeeze.

It only took her a mere glance to see her brother wasn't playing and joke. His emerald eyes gave off an almost haunted glint.

Maize had indeed gone to the deep realm. Kaleopei figured Maizelin's research delved deeper than she let on. Maize was smarter than go waltzing into the Deep.

Wasn't she?

Truth be told, Kaleopei wasn't entirely sure as to her sister's character. The older sister she remembered had been fearless and passionate. Maizelin's motives could have swayed entirely since then.

"What did the Hag say?" Kaleopei cracked her neck to the side, leaning into her palms.

"She's terrified. Wouldn't write a damn thing other than her concern."

"Please, that's not a word in her vocabulary. Not funny, Keylan." Kaleopei knew Zaratella was observant, but she wasn't dumb. She saw Keylan's expression just like she had. There wasn't an inch of playfulness etched into the man's features. It still didn't stop the witch from hoping.

"The Hag is on her way. Said she wanted to discuss something by mouth. Wasn't willing to risk anything being intercepted in her letters."

"She wouldn't directly say Maize was in the Deep. Are you positive you interpreted as intended?" Kaleopei grasped for any sort of naivety she could muster. Unwilling to accept what her brother was implying.

"I am certain."

Kaleopei knew he was right. He never sought to lie to her. Keylan placed the rolled parchment onto her desk.

"What is it she wants to learn of the Deep Realm?" Kaleopei glanced up at the onyx-eyed beauty standing behind her.

"Your guess is as good as mine. Maize hasn't really elaborated on what she wanted to ascertain. The Deep Realm is nothing more than a graveyard."

Keylan moved to sink into one of the plush chairs that were gifted to Kaleopei a few months ago. The male's posture was rigid, his head leaning against the back of the seat.

"My sisters have a tendency to become very involved in their devices. Kaleopei is practically a copy of Maize in terms of stubbornness and drive."

"That doesn't bode very well." Zara's melodic laugh echoed through the room.

"I'm sitting right here, you know." Kaleopei rolled her eyes.

"When can we expect to greet Imogen?" Zara moved to sit herself on the desk, crossing her legs. Reminiscent of how they found her that day in the inn.

"Any hour, I'd assume? Her letter arrived not too long ago. Kaleopei her writings were rushed. It wasn't like her."

"Can I see it?" Keylan leaned forward, unfolding the wrinkled edges of the parchment onto the desk. The broken seal was a swirl of purple and black wax. It screamed of the Hag in every way. Her lettering was intricate and severely dated, just like Kaleopei had known it to be.

Kaleopei realized the discrepancies almost immediately. The smeared ink and strikethroughs on certain words. It was manic.

"Do we prepare for the worst?" Keylan looked like he was ready to drop everything and depart. The family was everything to him. Kaleopei knew that well.

"Discreetly. We make no abrasive decisions until The Hag tells us more." Kaleopei hated the words that came from her mouth. Feeling foreign as she spoke.

"Sister, do not use your pretty words on me. I know you don't mean that. What is it you wish to do, not the Queen."

"Key, if I spoke what I wanted, we wouldn't have a city right now."

Zara placed a hand over Kaleopei's balled fist. Kaleopei felt flicks of magic itching to be released, flames wanting to devour.

"Your words will not leave this chamber."

Her nails tapped against the wooden desk, glancing between the two. Trust wasn't the issue. No, Kaleopei trusted these two with more than her life. Never once had she complained about being on the throne, knowing it had to be done. If she were to speak of her thoughts, then her selfishness would be known. No longer a mere thought in the back of her mind.

It had been two years of biting her tongue.

"I want to go charge into the Deep Realm and drag her dumbass back." Kaleopei began, "But I also know that we aren't teenagers with nothing to lose anymore. I have an entire Realm that looks to me for a reason."

Two years of silence were thrown into the fire.

"You being mindful of others is new."

"You're an ass, Key." Kaleopei knew she was overthinking their reactions. Neither of the two judged her, but it was on principle. Selfishness was a weakness she wasn't proud of.

"That's the sister I know and love."

Not a single person could have prepared her for the amount of responsibility that came along with being Queen. Two years ago, it was just the thought of returning home and seeing the people that kept her going. Kaleopei could have been reckless and hot-headed then, but it felt like she had everything to lose now. She wasn't a quitter; she would remain Queen until Maize took over or she drew her last breath.

"Is there any actual information regarding the Deep Realm? Isn't most of it kept in the Fairy Realm?" Zara had her thinking face on. Nose scrunched as she dragged a chair to the edge of the desk. Gracefully placing herself down and crossing her legs.

Who gave her permission to look like a goddess? Kaleopei knew she'd worship this one endlessly.

"Allegedly, it was where the Realm war took place centuries ago. When the gods all decided to go at each other throats, thus leaving the land void and decayed of anything living, practically sucking the magic out of everything." His words snapped her out of her lustful thoughts. Reminding them what they were discussing.

Right. Worshiping Zaratella would come later, preferably when they were alone.

"What Keylan is trying to say is, it's a glorified god graveyard."

"And Maize is interested in that?" Was she really? Or could it have been something that lay beyond that?

"Let's call it a morbid curiosity. She always was a history buff. It doesn't explain why she'd drop everything to venture into the Deep. Maize isn't naïve. She understands risk." Kaleopei was spewing her thoughts. Knowing the other two would soak up everything she was saying, adding their own opinions into the mix.

"So whatever she's after is worth the risk. Well, in Maize's opinion, anyway." Keylan mindlessly passed a thread of water between his palms.

"It's fabled that there are still relics that survived the aftermath of the war. Would that be something your sister is interested in?" Relics were an interesting thought. Maizelin had liked collecting oddities, displaying them as her own collection.

"Not likely. Maize wouldn't be willing to risk everything over a relic." Keylan replied.

"Correct, boy."

Kaleopei had her flame brandished in mere seconds, ready to set the intruder ablaze. Emerald eyes met the Hag's, recognizing their glint. With a shrug,

Kaleopei extinguished herself. Noting that, the two others reluctantly lowered their own guards.

"A little warning would have been nice," Kaleopei sank back into her chair. Sending a glare towards the old woman, who only smiled through her untamed bangs.

"It isn't the relic she seeks." She rolled her eyes at the Hag's ignorance. Not a care as she came to stand next to Keylan. The Hag's composure didn't match the distress of the letter. Almost the exact opposite.

"You know what Maizelin is after?" Zaratella placed a comforting hand on Kaleopei's shoulder, voicing what they all thought.

"I might."

"So, she is in the Deep Realm?" Keylan asked.

"Was my message not direct enough? I thought I taught you better." Her long nails scraped against the wood, leaning forward to make eye contact with Keylan.

"Then why don't you explain exactly how Maize got into the Deep on her lonesome?" Kaleopei snapped her fingers, not liking how the Hag seemed to be ignoring her.

"Can't even spare a hello for dear old Imogen?"

"Like how you kindly greeted us with your presence?" Kaleopei snarled at the Mystic. Something about her nonchalant attitude seemed to aggravate every bone in the Queen's body. Setting Kaleopei's temper ablaze. A fault she had grown to accept.

Anger was a deadly weapon when wielded consciously.

A weapon Kaleopei learned to harness.

"Seems you are still the same spitfire I remember." Imogen paused, taking a second to do a once-over on Kaleopei. "The crown suits you, girl."

The Hag was spinning in circles, not answering a question they asked. Dancing and weaving her way around each word. It all seemed to be practiced.

Wordlessly, Kaleopei took the silver band off her head, placing it atop the mess that had accumulated over the past months. The metal was molded to be that of ivy and mountain flowers. Intricate fastens held it all together, with small emeralds of green that contrasted against the pure silver.

"Wish I could say the same about your avoidance." The soft look on the Hag's face was replaced by a smirk. The lead eyes bred down onto her.

"Then start asking the right questions." The questions shouldn't matter.

"Well, aren't you a ray of sunshine today, Imogen?" Zara's melodic voice filled the silence. Noticing Kaleopei's sudden quizzical silence, and jumped to occupy the space.

"You're still parading around with these two? I thought you were smarter than that."

"Your humor will never cease to amaze me. No wonder Kaleopei's is so dry." The aforementioned Queen didn't even register what they were saying. Too caught up in the Mystics's words.

"You can't answer me, can you?" Kaleopei leaned back into her chair, crossing her arms over her chest. Not liking the outcome she had made in her mind. The bodice of her dress suddenly felt constricting.

"Now you're using that cultivated mind of yours." Still not an answer.

"What do you mean she can't?" Keylan was still a step behind. Looking between the Hag and her, trying to ascertain what was happening.

In slow motion, Kaleopei lifted her palm, two thin white scars now intertwining with the small lighting marks that adorned her arms. In tangent, the Hag lifted her own. The same one Kaleopei had made the rite with.

Keylan understood.

Apparently, Kaleopei wasn't the only Florence who excelled in making blood rites.

"Imogen, I am very calmly going to ask you what drugs you were on when you thought it was a good idea to make the rite with Maize. Not even considering that the deal made revolved around the Deep, a place where we are forbidden from even setting foot into." Kaleopei chose her words very carefully. A calculated spew that wouldn't end with her losing her cool. "Then you are going to respond with the exact strand of Myth you were on. And if you can obtain some for me, then perhaps I won't pray for your damnation."

"I'd watch your tone with me, girl." The Hag straightened herself upright, raising a brow in challenge. "Don't forget I know you inside and out. I taught you everything you know but not everything I know."

"Maize would only make the rite if she was desperate. Kaleopei, use that brain and figure out why she would be desperate." Keylan was angry, too. It wasn't just her. In this instance, he chose to be the bigger person, pleading for them to fizzle out whatever argument was brewing before it could begin.

"Listen to your brother, girl." Kaleopei just had to keep her anger tamed. She hadn't had to do that as of late. The Hag wasn't making it easy.

"We have everything we have ever dreamed about. The Elven Realm is back on its feet. Eviera is practically anew, albeit with changes. We have alliances with Mer and Human Realm. What more could she want?" The world she and Keylan had dared to dream about was becoming a reality. Kaleopei had been willing to sacrifice everything, and yet she was still here.

"Has Maizelin ever said what it is she desires in life?" Zara's words practically slapped her across the face. Had they ever even asked?

"She's not mentioned anything else she wanted?" Keylan words came out of his mouth slowly, as if coming to a similar realization.

Maize had lived an entire life without them. Had a group she trusted and fought to one day reclaim Eviera. Then everything flipped when her two dead siblings, who weren't actually dead, decided to jump-start her whole plan tenfold.

"When did you make the rite with Maize?" A sunken pit began forming in her stomach.

"Try again." Right. It wasn't clear how decisive the particular rite between them was. The details that had been agreed upon before mixing blood. Kaleopei had to deliberately try to find the loophole between an immortal Hag and her older sister. It'd be easier to light a single blade of grass on fire.

"Was I the first of my siblings to strike a bargain?"

"No." Kaleopei had figured the Hag had a connection to Maize long before the twins learned of her survival. The extent, however, seemed to be far longer than Kaleopei had expected.

"Are we skipping over the fact that she didn't bother informing us that Maizelin lived?" Keylan broke Kaleopei's train of thought. It was a conversation that had yet to be made. Unfortunately, now wasn't the time.

"What is Maizelin after in the Deep?" It wasn't an answerable question, that much she Kaleopei knew. She just needed some sense of direction. What should she be asking?

"Not what, girl. Who?" Using magic Kaleopei doesn't dare try to comprehend, Imogen conjured a leather bound book. Placing it on the desk with a light thud. Kaleopei didn't like that she recognized the cover, what she now knew to be read as Aetherite.

Pages began flipping, showing off the scrawl that was etched into the parchment. Coming to life as the Hag flicked her fingers. The glyphs from before were altered, and now in clear common were pages upon pages of writing.

"You're saying Aetherite is somehow connected to this all?"

"It appears my magic seemed to have malfunctioned. It hasn't done that in a long time." Imogen winked in her own oddly charming manner. Before Kaleopei could grab onto the book, Imogen snatched it. "This can not fall into the wrong hands. Burn it when you are done."

"That's not concerning at all," Zara made an attempt to laugh. The sound is like a song to Kaleopei's ears. "What's next? You going to try and sacrifice us all?"

"Careful what you say. It just might become true."

"Again, not concerned in the least."

"I wish you luck. I fear your sister may be unwell." A chill ran down her spine, not liking the Hag's overall tone. It was far too calm for what they were discussing. Everything about the situation made her want to set something on fire.

Instead, she stood herself up, casting a small smile on Zara before throwing her hands up. "I need Myth before I read this."

"I'll start. You do what you need to do." Keylan took her spot, already beginning to delve into the numerous pages.

"I love you, Key." She meant it.

"You better." He winked.

"If you have any questions you think I can answer, please let me know." "Because you've been such a great help so far?" Kaleopei couldn't find it in her to stifle the laugh that erupted from her lips. Zara's quick tongue was rare in mixed company, but it still made her smile.

"Maybe I misjudged you, Zaratella." Imogen had a flicker of a smirk on her features. Wrinkled skin only extenuating the look that'd cause others to fear the Mystic.

"Let's go, Hag." Kaleopei gripped the back of her long cloak, pulling the women towards the exit.

"Tell me, girl. What strands does royal money buy?"

"The same shit I used to swipe off the street." Kaleopei wasn't one to really care about her image. However, she had a funny feeling that a queen buying Myth would reflect poorly on the reputation Keylan fought to maintain.

"Consider me intrigued."

Chapter 40

"Those two getting high after all that doesn't concern you?" Zara had sat across from Keylan. Taking her own section of the reading. He snorted, "It'd do them some good. Both are practically simmering. Some recreational Myth should help."

"Recreation isn't a word in Kaleopei's vocabulary." Zara had come a long way since they first met in the moonlight of Alstead. No longer was the standoffish girl who kept secrets. She was proud of who she was and helped Kaleopei in ways Keylan couldn't even fathom.

Zaratella had a way of connecting to his sister. Always seeming to understand what she needs, just like he had. Never once had Keylan been jealous of their relationship. Kaleopei had found an equal with whom to share part of the burden of being queen. With every obstacle and challenge, the two took it with a smile on their faces.

Keylan only felt pride. Seeing the black-haired witch as his family.

Keylan's eyes trained on the pages of words. Wishing some kind of magic could just insert the information directly into his head. It undeniably would save a drastic amount of time.

"I would rather not bring it up before, but Cas wrote me." Zara didn't stop her work; she simply kept her voice level.

"Detailing his most latest read, I presume?"

Zara looked up as if studying him intently. Her gaze pierced the moment.

"No, he actually requested our presence in the Human Realm." Her voice hadn't changed, the same softly sweet tone she usually used. It didn't have to. Keylan could practically see the bite clouding her face.

"This pertains to me how?" Keylan's brows furrowed, giving his whole attention to the girl.

"He all but demanded I return."

"That's not like him."

"I'm aware, which is why it concerns me. My plan was to mention it over dinner, but it seems life has other ideas." She was serious. Casimir had really wanted her back in the Human Realm.

"Did something happen?"

"Apparently, Isla's condition has become," her words trailed off. Leaving Keylan to assume she was pondering her wording. "Concerning?"

"You seem unsure."

"I'm almost certain Casimir didn't write the letter." It wasn't usual for a king to leave writing correspondence to those in their court. Keylan knew Casimir wasn't like that, especially when pertaining to his friends. He'd take the time to make sure it was personalized. Just like Kaleopei did to those she cares about.

"Perhaps he's distraught?"

"Even that wouldn't stop him from writing me directly."

"What do you wish to do?" Keylan asked the question. Unsure of what he was supposed to do in this situation.

"I'm going to travel south. I just need a tiny favor from you." She had a grin on her face. Nothing good could come from this.

"It doesn't have to do with my sister, does it?"

"And they say you're the dumb one!" She exclaimed. "Kaleopei will want to tag along. It is clear, especially from today's events, that she is needed here. I will do my part to learn about the Deep during my travels. All I need is you to convince her to stay."

"You want me to deceive her?"

"Like she hasn't done worse."

"And it took me a long while to fully forgive those actions," Keylan spoke slowly. "Besides, shouldn't you be worried as to what she'll think?"

"I'm doing this because I care. Kaleopei, whether she likes it or not, can't be in multiple places at once, even if she tries to be. So, I'm taking her decision out of her control. She wants to be here, not dealing with whatever Cas got himself into." Zaratella was adamant, her decision not wavering.

"So you intend to do exactly what she did two years ago?"

"It's not the same, Keylan."

"You're lying to yourself. It's exactly the same. Taking away her choice. Isn't that what pissed you off so much about being a carver?"

"I'm not running off with the intent of dying. There is a big difference."

"My answer is no."

"Keylan, you can't be serious!"

"But I am. I have no intent to lie to my sister." Keylan nodded. Going back to his reading. "You may do as you wish, but do try just telling her."

"Kaleopei's stubborn! You know that better than anyone. She'll do it anyway." Zara's voice rose in the slightest way possible. She showed signs of frustration as she hit the desk with her fist.

"Isn't that what makes us love her?" Keylan smiled. Of course, he knew his sister best. Tell her the rules, and she'll go and change the game.

"I hate that you're right."

"Good. I'm glad you came to your sensible self." Keylan nodded. "Besides, we both know that if you left, she'd be only a step behind you."

Zara sank further into her chair, her arms crossed firmly over her chest. "I know."

"So, you only sought my council to confirm what you already knew?"

"Don't start talking like the Hag."

"Don't you mean Imogen? I swear you're the only one who calls her that."

"Is it not her name?"

"I'm poking fun, Zaratella."

"Don't Zaratella me. I know damn well what my partner is like. I just wanted to take some of the burden from her." Zara relaxed into her hand, aimlessly drawing circles with her finger.

"You've already done so much just by being present. Kaleopei respects you unlike any other."

"She respects you."

"No, she tolerates me. To her, I will forever be her nagging little brother." He knew Kaleopei loved him unconditionally. She relies on him to an extent, always willing to discuss sensitive matters.

"Could you really imagine Kaleopei leading armies?"

"Yes, and that alone is terrifying." Keylan laughed at Zara's question. Knowing that his twin would be an effective commander, leading with compassion and an absolute iron fist. "Which is why I'm in charge."

"Because she respects you."

"Can we talk about my twin later? I'd rather make some headway with these tombs before she comes back."

"Always the pleaser, Key."

"What can I say? I strive for the best."

Chapter 41

Kaleopei's head was pounding with thought. Everything that had transpired in the last few hours seemed to be too much, which is how she found herself high as the sky with the Hag lounging across her bed.

She had broken into her special stash of Myth. The one she kept for special occasions or rock bottom. Rock bottom was the reason this time. Imogen had her back against Kaleopei's silk sheets, puffing out a long drag of smoke. This stash was from some poor fool who tried to sell it to her in the Vizen market. Money wasn't the issue. She simply swiped it on principle. Silently, she took a mental note to track the human down on her next visit to Bellheim.

"Life would be so much easier if I had just died."

"Careful, if those two hear you, they just might question your psyche." Kaleopei couldn't help but laugh.

"Like they don't do that on the daily. Keylan once asked me if I was suicidal."

"Are you not?" The Hag sat upright, passing the pipe.

It still hummed with warmth.

"I'm still not the happiest with you. Making a deal with Maize isn't wise."

"I can't help but recall that we did the same."

"Whatever."

Kaleopei's head snapped up. Looking towards the door of her and Zara's room. A person was barreling down the hall. No. It was two people.

She had her eyes trained on the entryway, flames igniting at the tips of her fingers. The green flame is ready to fly at the drop of a pin.

"Relax, they're not a threat." The Hag snuffed out her flames, taking strides towards the door. Swinging it open, two figures came tumbling in.

"Kaleopei!" Keylan was the first to talk, his face etched with panic.

"Can this wait? Still getting high?"

"Firefly, you have to pay attention here." Zara's voice piqued her interest. Her face was a mirror of Keylan's as she grasped onto Kaleopei's hands.

"Alright, alright. I'm listening."

"Kaleopei."

"Yes, Zara. I'm listening."

"Spit it out, you two. We haven't got all day." Kaleopei only spared a second to send a glare at the Hag. I'm not entirely a fan of the tone she was taking.

"They're trying to resurrect dead people in the Deep Realm."

Kaleopei found herself laughing at Keylan's words. Unsure of what joke they were playing. Apparently, having the time to orchestrate some kind of prank during their time alone.

"Okay, I'll bite. Who are they bringing back to life?"

"We're serious. The tombs depict a ritual that is used for necromancy purposes."

"Why would Maize have any intreats in such?" The way the two were serious slowly made Kaleopei realize they weren't playing a joke. They were dead serious. No pun intended.

"Gods. Kaleopei. Darren Haven had intended to bring back the gods."

"Repeat that?"

"Calsi. Irilla. Fenrah. Renlys. Any, maybe even all of them. He wasn't trying to make a weapon with the magic he harnessed at Louth. He needed enough to fuel God's resurrection. There will be no Gods to save us if they start another war."

"This isn't one of your tricks to make me pray to some deity, Key?"

"If Byrne and Renlys are to walk among the living once more, I fear it'll be the end of life."

One quick glance at Imogen and Kaleopei knew it was true. A solemn nod was all it took for her world to come crashing done once again.

"Do we know how far they got?"

"No, but it said they had promising signs."

"Why would Daren know a language of old?" Keylan was scowling. Not liking the insinuation by the tombs.

"Looks like we're going to visit, Casimir." Kaleopei shrugged, not wanting to dwell on the information any longer. It was too fresh.

Keylan and Zara both spared a glance at one another. Having a silent conversation among them. She didn't make a comment. Clearly, there was something else amiss. It didn't matter.

Gods are being revived.

***

Acknowledgments

I don't know where to start or really what to say here. It's more than likely going to be insufferable, and you might cringe while reading this. With that warning, prepare for more cheese than a calzone, and read at your own risk. So, I'll start off by apologizing for my sleep schedule, as you suffered the most throughout this entire process. I'm sorry for the inconsistency and disturbance caused by my tendency to do my best brainstorming in the dark hours of the night.

First off, I'd like to thank all of the people who worked on Fate: Intertwined! You are all marvelous people, and it is quite incredible that you put up with me and my silly little fantasy story. Seriously, none of this would have been possible without them.

A big warm hug goes out to my parents for devoting themselves to me and my siblings. For always letting me follow my passions no matter how outlandish they were. For sitting through the endless amount of recitals and competitions without complaining. Believe it or not, I don't think I would have ever written a novel without dancing, as it was my first expression of storytelling. So, thank you for giving me that opportunity and teaching me to always be myself.

Secondly, I'd like to thank Quarantine for introducing me to Dungeons & Dragons. Without creating my own homebrew worlds, crafting a fantasy world would have seemed impossible. It allowed me to be creative with friends where everything seemed limitless. Whether it was lore-breaking character developments or crazy characters who would have us laughing for hours at my party, I would have never made it this far without your presence and constant support.

Fin and Alyxa, my platonic soulmates. The peanut butter and jelly to my bread. There are no words I can use to describe how much you two mean to me; regardless of how much time we spend apart, I know you will always be there for me, and the gesture extends to you, too. Thank you for being weird with me and being unapologetically ourselves for as long as we've been friends. Also, I'm pretty sure I can shake ass the best, but to each their own.

Lastly, for the readers who took a chance on my writing, this would have sucked if only my family read it. So, for your support, I wish you endless amounts of support and love. No matter if you found this book on a whim or came from one of my social media, you are safe in this environment. You are loved.

Obviously, I can't thank every single person in my life, for I fear it'll be longer than the story you just read. That will be left for my next adventure in the whimsical world of writing.

About The Author

Hailey Monette is an emerging author who was raised in New England. She spends a lot of time reading, a trait she inherited from her mother. She lives with three dogs, two large shepherds, Salem and Mystic, along with a stubborn but loveable corgi whose name is Dexter Hamilton. Hailey finds solace in nature and likes to surround herself with it constantly, often taking hikes with one of the shepherds (usually Mystic, which she calls Sticky).

Hailey has had a love for anything and everything fantasy related. From video games like The Witcher and Skyrim all the way to playing tabletop games like Dungeons and Dragons in her free time. She grew up with names like *Harry Potter, Magic Tree House,* and *Percy Jackson,* all fueled her passion to become an author.